People Stories

Inside the Outside

Conversations Overheard
in the Middle of the Night
on the Wrong Side of Town

Austin, Texas

Copyright © 2006 by Wizard Academy Press. All rights reserved.

Printed in United States.

Permission to reproduce or transmit in any form or by any means, electronic or mechanical, including photocopying and recording, or by an information storage and retrieval system, must be obtained by writing to the publisher at the address below:
Wizard Academy Press
16221 Crystal Hills Dr
Austin, TX 78737
512.295.5700 voice, 512.295.5701 fax
www.WizardAcademyPress.com

Ordering Information
To order additional copies, contact your local bookstore, visit www.WizardAcademyPress.com, or call 1.800.425.4769
Quantity discounts are available.

ISBN: 1932226508 Softcover

Library of Congress Cataloging-in-Publication Data

Williams, Roy H.
   People stories: inside the outside; conversations overheard in the middle of the night on the wrong side of town /Roy H. Williams.
       p.   cm.
   ISBN 1932226508

                                                           2006923135

Credits
   Editor: Roy H. Williams
   Cover design/ text design/production: Sean Taylor

First printing: April 2006

Table of Contents

Preface vii
Inside the Outside viii
1. Richard Solay 11
2. Lena L. West 14
3. Ken Hughes 17
4. Scott Fraser 18
5. Stewart Redwine 21
6. Kevin Sullivan 23
7. Rob Clark 26
8. Galen Sonntag 28
9. Tom Smith 31
10. Judy Davis 34
11. Tom Wanek 36
12. Mike Sales 38
13. Rick Copper 39
14. Col Kenna 41
15. Woody Grubb 43
16. David Favor 45
17. Bill Wayland 46
18. Sean McNally 48
19. Michelle Stearns 50
20. Alexander Vickers 52
21. Shane Speal 54
22. Christian Clapton 56
23. Nancy Smith 58
24. Andrew Francis 60
25. Tim Kirk 62
26. Catherine Astalos 69
27. Daniel Granger 71
28. Bart O'Shea 74
29. Cathy Mosier 77
30. Joanna Hannigan 79
31. Mary Lou Davis 81
32. Ken Wentz 82
33. Michael Jones 84
34. Carlin Comm 85
35. Hundley Batts 87
36. Brian Schmitt 88
37. Daryl Eldridge 90
38. Rhonda Mills 91
39. Marta Rode 94
40. Melanie Scherencel Bockmann 96

41. Al Rider 100
42. Matt Hunt 102
43. Tony Armstrong 104
44. Jason Foux 106
45. K.C. Fleming 108
46. Don Saathoff 112
47. Brent Nightingale 114
48. Bertwin Lord 117
49. Marty Murray 119
50. Danielle Delgado 121
51. Bob Emmert 123
52. Larry Muller 125
53. Jeff Dunn 126
54. Eric Peterson 128
55. Mark Mackesy 130
56. Jack Ancona 132
57. Evan T Williams 133
58. Glennan Wrinkle 135
59. Robin J. Elliott 137
60. Jonathon Durbin 138
61. Josh Withell 140
62. Larry Beaverson 141
63. Jim Rubart 143
64. Lew Hofmann 145
65. Melvin Laskin 146
66. Tracy See 147
67. Patrick Rice 148
68. Luis Alejandro López 150
69. Robert M. Pratt 154
70. Kristy Iris 156
71. J.D. Cave 159
72. Delia McCallister 164
73. Wayne Lincourt 165
74. Phillip Mahan 168
75. Michelle Butler Hallett 169
76. Michael Staires 172
77. Curt Dieckelt 177
78. Anne Sallee Miles 178
79. Todd C. Roth 182
80. Jeff Burns 185
81. Blaine Parker 187
82. Jeff Lukesh 190
83. Don Morelock 191
84. Anna Huthmaker 192
85. Mike Kenyon 194

86. Gregg Stutts ... 198
87. Jesse Zellmer ... 201
88. Jack McAdory ... 204
89. Dave Baxter ... 205
90. Terri Pauser Wolf ... 206
91. Mark Fox ... 208
92. Antonio Guerrero ... 212
93. Ken Wieczorek ... 215
94. Mirta Calderon ... 218
95. Bryan Nielsen ... 220
96. Bill Reilly ... 222
97. Bill Oehler ... 223
98. Aaron Atkinson ... 225
99. Mike Lawson ... 228
100. Jay Larkin ... 232
101. Susan MacLean ... 233
102. Christopher Jaquess ... 235
103. Andrea Blachly ... 238
104. Chris Ramey ... 239
105. Cory Crawford ... 240
106. Daniel Fryar ... 241
107. Duane Marcy ... 244
108. Robert Wickman ... 246
109. Danna Vitt Rooks ... 253
110. Debbie Platt ... 254
111. Stephen Hernandez ... 256
112. Helen Harb ... 257
113. Cynthia Williamson ... 259
114. Bill Alford ... 261
115. Mark Clark ... 263
116. Shawn Smith ... 264
117. Bobby McGee ... 266
118. Steve Rae ... 269
119. Lane Dixon ... 272
120. Charles Moger ... 273
121. Jurie Pieterse ... 275
122. Daniel Joehnk ... 278
123. Wendy McNally ... 280
124. Steve Bleile ... 282
125. R.J. Laino ... 285
126. Donna Snapp ... 290
127. Jay White ... 293
128. Kim Dunn ... 295
129. David Cahn ... 297
130. Michael Urkoski ... 298

131. Michael Lofranco······299
132. Kay Larrick······303
133. Chris Hoffman······305
134. Erin O'Hare······308
135. Zeke Cox······310
136. Gair Maxwell······312
137. Lynn Burkholder······313
138. Steve Wunderink······315
139. Steve Lindt······317
140. Lori LaShawn Brown······318
141. John Davis······322
142. Michael K. Schmidt······323
143. Greg De Rue······327

About Wizard Academy······330

Preface

Humans are peculiar creatures. We are capable of much, yet do little. Doubt, insecurity, fear and ambition blind our wide-open eyes to the rainbow colors of meaningful life.

We hibernate, deep in the bellies of our comfort zones.

Recklessly, I threw down this gauntlet to 32,000 readers of my Monday Morning Memo. One hundred and forty-three of them picked it up.

They awakened, did the deed, and wrote about it for an audience of one.

What they wrote was never meant to be a book. It was correspondence. Full of misspellings and bad grammar and half composed sentences, their emails rang with lofty faith and hummed with low despair. They itched with curiosity and bled with pity. A few of them just had a good time.

Their unedited emails are contained in the pages that follow. Not a word has been changed.

Prepare to meet a whole other America.

Roy H. Williams
April 22, 2006

This is the Monday Morning Memo that started it all:
January 9, 2006

Inside the Outside

It hit me. *"I've become an eavesdropper, listening to the conversations of strangers."*

It's 5:00AM and I'm sitting at the bar of an all-night café on the wrong side of town eating a three-dollar breakfast, listening to the smelly, funny stories of downtrodden people who know each other well. Their sparkling banter gives me a glimpse into problems I'll never touch, victories I'll never celebrate, a life I'll never have. These are they who will never have internet access, a credit card or cable TV.

But they seem happy.

I've come here to learn what it means to be an outsider in America.

People tell me they want to write. I respond, "You can't find a pencil?" In truth, few want to write. Most want only to have written. People tell me they want to travel, have adventures, meet interesting people and learn about different cultures. They want to expand their world. I'm betting you can guess my answer to that one... "If you will expand your world, you must crawl on your hands and knees, get on your belly and squirm under the fence that surrounds your insulated life."

For most people, travel means being pampered by accommodating servants in exotic places. But interesting people, strange cultures and high adventure don't await you on the other side of the world. They await you on the other side of town.

Are you willing to get on your belly and crawl under that fence? Will you invest an hour to enlarge your world? If you will actually do it, not just think about it, but really do it, and write to me about it, I will send you a special gift of initiation. These are the rules:

1. You must arrive and be seated in a 24-hour eating establishment between 1:30AM and 5:30AM in a part of town where you rarely go. Or perhaps a truckstop beyond town's edge. The further outside your comfort zone, the better.

2. If a man, you must go alone. If a woman and concerned for your safety, you can take one other person with you. But make sure your friend understands the goal isn't to chat with each other, but to glimpse a whole other world that exists side-by-side with the one you know.

3. While you're eating and listening and absorbing this strange new reality, think of what these people need most and how you might help them get it. While you're at it, you might also think a little about what they have that you don't. There is a rich sense of community among the outcast.

4. Write the details of your excursion within 24 hours of your meal and email them to Corrine@WizardAcademy.com Be sure to provide a mailing address where we can send your special Gift of Initiation. I don't yet know what it will be.

Want to hear something that will shock you? I'm fairly confident that fewer than 12 readers from among my 31,000 subscribers will actually do what I've just described, and more than half of these will be Canadian. We Americans are unlikely to discomfort ourselves except for purposes of recreation.

How accurate are my predictions? A few weeks ago when I offered to send readers a free copy of my favorite book, I accurately predicted for the shipping department – within seven – the precise number of people who would respond to that offer. (Yes, that number was deep into the hundreds.)

Will you join this strange new fraternity? Your gift of initiation awaits.

Roy H. Williams

PS – In a nationwide phone survey of 1,279 adults, respondents were much more likely to claim that an experiential purchase made them happier than a material one – 57 percent versus 34 percent – even after accounting for differences in price. (Experiential spending is concert tickets, etc. And in my opinion, early morning meals eaten among interesting strangers…)

"People travel to faraway places to watch,
in fascination, the kind of people
they ignore at home."
– Dagobert D. Runes, (1902-1982)

Richard Solay

1

Sent: Tuesday, January 10, 2006 6:38 AM
To: Corrine@wizardacademy.com
Subject: DISCOMFORT AT 4AM ON 8TH AVE.

So, I decided to take the challenge of going somewhere in my town that made me uncomfortable and have breakfast at 4AM. I'd better tell you that I live in mid-town Manhattan. It takes a lot to make me uncomfortable.

My first thought was Harlem. But, no. Harlem was now becoming chic and there were trendy little coffee shops serving latés and stuff. So, that won't do.

Brooklyn was long gone.

And Queens? Well, that was more like Mumbai, Sanaa or Peshwar and I never felt uncomfortable when I was actually in those places.

I'd be more uncomfortable in the Long Island suburbs with soccer moms discussing lawn fertilizer and SUV's. But, then I'd have to rent a car and I wasn't about to shell out more than coffee and a bacon, egg and cheese on a roll. I mean, this wasn't a paid assignment. It was an experiment, and someone else's at that. So let's keep it real.

The Fulton Fish Market had moved to the Bronx. Scratch that.

The Meatpacking District was now crawling with revelers all night long.

Even the Lower East Side was awash with new boutiques and trendy restaurants.

Years ago I used to love going for a 3AM breakfast at the coffee shop that used to be on the corner of Carnegie Hall. There'd be musicians. And actors/actresses. And hookers. And transvestites. And artists. And drunks. And tourists. The tourists were dangerous. They'd stare at you trying to figure out if you were someone they should know. They usually never caught on that the trannies were guys and not good looking women. But that's long gone and I'm rarely awake to have breakfast at 3AM any more.

Where? Where? Where? Where? And then it came to me. There was a 24hr. McDonalds about 3 blocks from my apartment. I'd never been in there in the morning. The idea of their strange breakfast combinations I find weird. I want two eggs scrambled soft, with bacon, home fries, wholewheat toast and coffee. Not some flying saucer of eggthing on a mini pancake. I want my bacon crisp. I want butter melting on the toast.

I want strong coffee with free refills. And, I love the free little orange juice the waitress or counterman usually brings without you asking for it.

I think the people in the McDonald's at 4AM may not be the usual crowd that's in there during the day. Maybe I'll feel uncomfortable. I mean this is pretty far outside of my comfort zone. It's worth a try. I hope the Wizard's "special gift of initiation" is worth getting up at 3AM for. My wife thinks I'm nuts.

Where the hell did they dredge these people from. They must lurk deep in dark alleys during daylight. Or perhaps they share the sewer system with those mysterious alligators that are supposed to be down there. Or maybe they're my neighbors.

An older woman wearing everything she owns that won't fit into her rolling shopping cart, which is overflowing with all of her other stuff. An indeterminately aged, long bearded guy I've seen in the neighborhood every now and then, lying on the sidewalk during the day. A group of five, somewhat threatening looking, black kids wearing do-rags, over-sized clothes and their pants around their knees. Well, I don't think they can run too fast in those outfits. At least I hope not. There's a mother with 2 scraggly, snotty kids kicking their legs back and forth. Two middle aged Asian guys. I don't think they're Chinese. The only discomfort I feel is pity for these people who seem to have nowhere else to go. At least that's the picture I have in my mind about them.

The lights are too bright. Especially for this time in the morning. A big, uniformed security guy sitting in a chair in the corner. That helps. Three young girls behind the counter. One white. One Latina. One black. She looks like she eats a few too many Big Macs. Strange. No one is looking at me when I walk up to the counter to look at the menu boards. I guess in my old, torn jeans, boots, hooded sweatshirt and 30 year old jacket, my wife keeps trying to throw out, I blend in. Somewhat. But the clothes are clean. I'm very aware that my beard and what hair I have are neatly trimmed. My face isn't weathered or badly creased. I feel that I sort of glow in the dark. Even in this bright light. But no one seems to give a damn about me. No stares that I can detect. Everyone's too busy within their own cocoon to notice me.

Egg McMuffin? I've heard of that. One of those weird little pancake and egg sandwiches — a bacon, egg and cheese McGriddle? Hell. This was an experiment. Let's experiment.

Unwrapping the strange little sandwich on my tray, I was the most nervous I'd been this morning. I was sure everyone in the place was staring at me to check my reaction to this thing.

Now, in all of my travels, I've eaten some very strange food.

Sometimes a little trepidation crept in to stare over my shoulder. But, I usually rationalized that the guy next to me was eating sheep's brains and he doesn't look like he's preparing to commit suicide, so it must be OK. I kept muttering under my breath "millions sold" "millions sold" "millions sold." Now, people probably were sneaking peeks at me. I took a sip of my coffee to see if it was hot enough to drop in my lap so I could sue.

It was black. Reasonably hot. And almost coffee. At least my definition of coffee. The only thing I could probably sue for was that it wasn't strong enough. I kept it near at hand in case I had to disguise the taste of this McGriddle thing that was now glaring at me from the unwrapped paper on the tray.

I ate it. Every last bite. No crumbs. Was I uncomfortable. No. At least not yet. Who knows what the shock of eating my first McGridle sandwich will do to my innards in a few hours, but now I didn't give a damn. The thought of a second crossed my mind. And then reality set in. I was supposed to be doing research.

Wait. Let me go back and re read the challenge.

"…think of what these people need most and how (I) might help them get it." My first wise-ass thought was Alka-Seltzer. Then I climbed down from my remote, observation tower and thought again. Jobs. Places to live. Healthy food. Medical care. Safety. Love. Hell, that sounded like what everyone needs. The group of kids pushing each other and laughing too loud still annoyed me. And still scared me.

What I got out of this was frustration. I had been all nicely and comfortably wrapped up in my own life and my own concerns. Business. Family. Etc. Every now and then I'd donate money to a cause that touched me. But this. This was a burrowing worm that the Wizard put beneath my skin that wouldn't go away. There's never enough time to spend on things like this. It's easier to ignore them and maybe they'll go away.

What do they have that I don't? Sure it'd be easy to give a bull-shit answer, but something was different. Yeah. We could all do with less. We could get by without all the stuff we accumulate. But I don't feel that I have all the answers right now. It's going to take some thought and some discussion.

This is not the conclusion that I planned to write. But it's a lot closer to my inner thoughts without the sarcasm filter in gear.

OK! You're the Wizard. What's the answer?

2　Lena L. West

Sent: Wednesday, January 11, 2006 3:27 AM
To: Corrine@WizardAcademy.com
Subject: Wizard of Ads: I Crawled Under the Fence...to the Bronx

Ok, so, I got Roy's email while I was on holiday so, this was good timing.

I live in Westchester County in New York - one of the most affluent counties in the nation. We are however, next to the Bronx - one of the poorest boroughs in NYC.

I remember this one time, I was supposed to take business course that was being offered in the Bronx. I didn't know the exact location and it sounded close enough to the Westchester border to be safe so, I went. I got there and didn't get out of the car. Needless to say I never took the course and I lost my deposit money in the process.

Monday morning was not usual. I went back. Solita. Most of my friends are too chatty.

Don't get me wrong, there are "good" sections of the Bronx where hard-working people live but, oh, there are other parts of the Bronx (the South Bronx, White Plains Road area, and Hunts Point to name a few) that I wouldn't be caught dead in during the daytime - let alone the wee hours of the morning.

I remembered that there was this "dive" - as my parents would say. It wasn't really a diner...more like an all night "lunch" counter with two booths on the opposite wall from the counter. Kinda like the restaurant that Michael Jackson saunters through in the Beat It video. Just as greasy. I wasn't sure that it would be open...I had resolved to find someplace - anyplace - if it wasn't.

Because I work from home and joyfully rarely leave home, as I left Monday morning, I remember thinking, "My neighbors must be wondering where in the heck I'm going at this hour." The truth is, no one noticed or cared. How self-important of me.

I set out to look grimey and I did. My ponytail was scruffy. My sweats had a hole in one knee and I purposely removed my deceased Aunt Dottie's 18K gold and diamond band that I have been wearing religiously since my mother gave it to me a few months after her death in April 2005. (It's funny how we humans get attached to things in hopes to feel a long-gone person's presence.)

I didn't take the fancy SUV, took the Saturn that needed a wash and had a small ding in the front bumper. "Who wants to carjack a Saturn?" I reasoned. I only carried my ID, my cell phone and $10 in cash. I carried cash not because I wanted to be safe but because, admittedly, I didn't trust "those people" with my debit card - if one could even be used there. Turns out, it couldn't anyway but, I have to admit that wasn't the reason I didn't bring it. I bought my ID - not because I couldn't legally drive without it - but so they could "identify my body" if anything happened. Funny, leaving Westchester and going to the South Bronx, I already put myself in a body bag. Morbid at best. Self-important (again) at the least.

I get in the car and head down the Deegan (the local highway that connects most of the boroughs with Westchester County and points North). I was nervous a bit. I sped. Thankfully, no cops.

All the spots were taken in front of Body Bag Dive so, rather than park out of eye-shot of the place, I sat in the car and waited for a spot to open. And, there I sat for well over 20 minutes looking at the glowing 'D' on the gear shift. It would take one second longer than I needed to pull off, if I had to put the car in drive.

I park, get out, set the alarm and walk exactly 7 steps to the door (I counted because I wanted to be able to run it with my eyes closed (where is this paranoia coming from????). I open it and everyone just stares. I oddly started to think about the Sesame Street song, "One of these things is not like the other, one of these things is not the same..."

I asked if I could sit and was told that I could take my pick. I thought I was being inconspicuous by picking a table near the door - where I could see my car - and kept my coat on.

I was the only woman in the place. Unbeknownst to anyone in Body Bag Dive, I also speak fluent Spanish.

The chisme about me started immediately, if not sooner.
"Who is she?"
"Where does she come from alone at this hour?"
"She's probably the immigration."
"I hope she has money to pay."

In my effort to "look like them", I ended up looking homeless. I was asked to pay in advance or leave. I paid but was p*ssed at the insinuation. "Do you know who I am? Do you know where I live? And, you want me to give you $4.23 in advance? Take the whole ten!" My rants percolated in my skull. P*ssed wasn't the word. But, I paid.

I reminded myself of what I was there to do so, I settled into my experience. I remember thinking, "Gosh, this is hard with no books and no journal." No distractions. I had to 'show up' or miss the experience.

15

Once the bonchinche subsided, more people came in. I sat and listened.

Many people were having trouble with bills. An illegal lottery man came in twice before taking numbers from some patrons. They really thought I was a cop! In the plate glass reflection, I saw the look of false hope as they recalled dreams and looked in a tattered book about which numbers corresponded to which dreams.

A man double-parked a delivery truck outside (great, I couldn't escape if I needed to!) and mentioned (in Spanish) that he had to pay big bucks for his daughter's quinceanero. They laughed about it but, you could tell that he was proud to be able to throw such a big party for her. Quinceaneros are a big deal, this I know. It's equivalent to a Sweet Sixteen party on speed.

A old-ish woman came in carrying tripled plastic bags in each hand and told of her monther being in the hospital. She was on her way to the church for prayers. She said at this time the world is still and God could hear her better. I passed the church on the way in and it was a good 8-10 blocks away. Do I need to mention that it's Winter in New York? For the first time, I felt sad.

These were hard-working people. Sure, some people had illegal lifestyles - the bookie. But, what would I do if I came to this country with no money and no skills? Who am I to judge?

I left the rest of the $10 on the table as a tip. The eggs were good and the toast was crisp but not burned. And, Cafe Bustelo is the best coffee there is - period.

Don't ask me how I got home. It was like I was on autopilot. I was really absorbed in my thoughts.

Why would I think "those people" would even be interested in killing me or ripping me off?

Who am I?

They have lives to live. Work to do. Sick relatives to tend to.

HUMAN concerns.

Ken Hughes

3

Sent: Tuesday, January 10, 2006 1:55 PM
To: Corrine@WizardAcademy.com
Subject: late night eavesdropping

    I chose my late night excursion not so much outside of town but in a completely different atmosphere from my own. It was a late night 24 hr "Time out" deli/gas station. The time was 2:30am in Knoxville Tn on the wrong side of the tracks. I tried to dress in a very casual fashion as not to discomfort the "natives" or interrupt their usual banter. I stayed as incognito as possible and just took in the atmosphere. It seemed that everyone new each other by nickname or just used "honey" or "brother" affectionately. These people seemed to have their own late night club. I had finally found the "Friends in low places" Garth Brooks was talking about.

    Thinking of what these people needed was obvious at first 1) bath 2) 1st shift Job. I tried to reach beyond that and come up with what they really needed. What does and outcast need? It hit me: they need someone to relate too, to belong, to know you are not so different than them. Now How can I help them attain this? I can help everyday by going out of my way to just to say hello to and unlikely friend. The only thing they have that I don't is a automatic understanding of each others lifestyle, almost to wear they don't have to speak to communicate with one another. The other thing I noticed is that during conversation something that appeared like to be and argument was mearly passion in most instances. In closure, the experience was definitely a paradigm shift and I did learn a bit about their lexicon, but besides that we are all just people..

4 Scott Fraser

Sent: Monday, January 09, 2006 8:44 AM
To: Corrine@WizardAcademy.com
Subject: Response to today's MMM

More Coffee?

"Well, I'm not staying here," I said, "I hate this place. The air is bad and I like to spend as little time in places like this as possible."

My Sister nodded. "We don't have much choice, we took the rental car back and there's nowhere close to go."

"The rental's not done yet, we still have the remainder of the morning so I'm going to call, get it back and we are going to get the hell out of here, and that is that!"

We had just been informed that the Mid-West was, once again, being pounded by a blinding snowstorm and the planes we going to be delayed. Delayed; imagine, I thought. During a normal flight we were already going to spend an inordinate amount of time in uncomfortable seats, overcrowded areas, among space invaders.

The rental car company was locally owned so one quick phone call and we were off tracing the very steps that landed us there so very early that morning.

"Where do you want to go," I asked Jane?

"I'm hungry," she murmured, "do you want to get something to eat; or what?"

"Sure, where will we go?"

"I feel like something more than coffee, let's get something a little more substantial."

I dabble in business, real estate among many other things in my life. I am always curious what makes people decide to hold out when they could get out.

Is it that the money offered was not good enough?

Are they in love with their business so much that they just wouldn't sell it no matter what? Are they makin' scads of money or, did the developer have enough land to do what they wanted to do and this place did not get the offer?

Whatever the scenario, this place stood out like a hammered thumb. The buildings all around it were new; I mean brand, spankin' new. And then there was this place.

I don't know what hit me first, the prehistoric design or the color that came from a cornucopia of crushed, deceased flowers, minced, liquified and applied sparingly.

Trucks; tow trucks, four by fours, one semi and a couple of tandems and us in our singer sewing machine.

The sign said "wait to be seated".

So, we waited.

After about five minutes we realized that they didn't really mean it.

When we were finally noticed, the waitress slash hostess asked us where we wanted to sit.

I wanted to blurt out in a boisterous voice, "where's Mary's section?"

That's really what she was asking. Whose section do you want to sit in?

We had naively waited at the sign so why did she ask us where we wanted to sit? Habit I guess.

"Over there" I said.

Just instinct for me I guess.

Cowboy movies; I don't remember much from the days of two channels and a fuzzy third but there was a part in one movie that has always stood out in my mind. The cowboys were being chased after innocently stirring the natives (yeah, right!) and they were followed into a cavernous cul-de-sac. Realizing their fate, the General Custard of the group said fatefully, "boys, we've showed them our backs, now let's show them our faces."

As I sat in the corner of the "spoon", I watched all the "goings on".

"Nothin' much went on tonight. A few breakdowns and a fender bender," he said.

"Oh yeah?," the waitress said, "more coffee?," she offered.

A police car drove up and by, came back, parked and the two Officers climbed out. Albeit brief, they stopped at the sign. They sat in the corner too. Maybe they saw the same movie, I thought satirically.

On the way to the other corner seat the Officers paused briefly. A hand movement, from one and then the other. Were they going for their radios or possibly their Smith & Wesson's.

A warm nod and a wink from the Tow Truck Driver caused them to lower their hands in a slow, relaxed manner. Just a subtle hello. They went and sat down.

Teammates, I thought. Real life teammates.

Working in a team, everyone has to know their role. In the crunch, with a great team, there are no values assessed. There is no "I" in team. What counts is the result; not the individual glory. Great teammates know that. Great Coaches foster that.

The night shift. It's a really tough shift. Quiet, can turn to chaos in a matter of a radio call.

Adrenaline is a natural drug. It can propel the average man to attain many heights never even dreamed of. It is the body's natural caffeine.

The jaws of life, neck braces, cauterizing pads, gauze, tow hooks and fire hoses. These are things that fuel adrenaline. Once you've felt it you want it more. Things happen, you're on the ball; at the top of your game. You have to be. They happen at lightening speed so if you're not on your game, the very top of your game, it could mean, well, someone's, maybe, everyone's life.

Tonight though, "Nothin' much went on tonight. A few breakdowns and a fender bender."

"More coffee?"

A rhetorical question I thought.

Stewart Redwine

Sent: Wednesday, January 11, 2006 7:55 PM
To: Corrine@WizardAcademy.com
Subject: Meeting the Challenge for Inside the Outside

Dear Mr. Williams:

This morning I arrived at Norms in Whittier, CA at 4:50 AM. Norms is a 24 hour diner and for me suites the prerequisites of your challenge.

While I was sitting there asked myself, what do these people need?

In order to keep a cover that would surely keep others away I read the Bible.

In my life I have discovered that reading the Bible in a public place is a sure way to keep others at bay.

Regardless, I sat and listened as the patrons and workers discussed their families and their jobs. This came as no surprise.

I have also discovered that 95% of the time people talk about one of three things; others, themselves, or their work. This morning at the diner was no exception. I listened as the hostess told a seventy year old man how the person she buys her plants from asks her, "Which plant do you want to kill this week." You see, she can't seem to take care of plants very well, but as she said, she loves having them around. Imagine a message custom tailored to people like her from the local florist, "Have trouble killing plants? We're okay with that. All we want to know is, which plant would you like to kill this week?"

 Or something along that order.

Since the Norms I was at is in Southern California it came as no surprise that the people here, at a least a large portion of them, need things in Spanish. The chef's and and the two hostesses/waitresses were all Spanish speakers, in fact bi-lingual.

That fact answers the other question you put to me, what do they have that I don't? The ability to speak two languages.

Well, enough of me going on here. It is doubtful you, Mr. Williams, will read this.

I met your challenge and learned that people in this country, just like everyone all over the world, care deeply about their families, loved ones, and the work of their hands. This has not changed for millenia. I pray that the few problems I heard via evsdropping today will be met by the Lord Jesus' mighty love and His Father's saving arm.

I met your challenge, so in order to complete this simple bargain I ask you to meet mine, Please visit my companies web-site below, purchase a DVD, review it and personally call or email me with your response, I would like to know how you can help.

Kevin Sullivan

6

Sent: Monday, January 23, 2006 2:00 AM
To: 'Corrine Taylor'
Subject: Diner Challenge/Encounter

4:50am King's Diner 1390 Mission
No Breakfast. The counter guy stuttered that I couldn't get the pancake special until 6am.

When I walked in I saw a group of animated homeless sharing a joint out behind the dumpster. They were loud and laughing.

In the corner booth, elderly overweight couple, she's asleep, he's reading the paper.

Other corner, sport's fan glued to an SI. His hunched shoulders haven't moved since I pulled up in the car.

Opposite me, elderly gent, lots of hair, wrinkled lines on his forehead, big ears, cratered nose with a slight frown, Danish and coffee.

A guy wallows in, says hi to the corner duo, and orders a grilled cheese in a specific manner. Bread buttered on both sides, cheese and tomato between, and golden brown, don't burn it. Large coffee.

Wrinkled nose gets the Examiner.

I just noticed that we're sitting evenly distributed about the tables. It's as if were maintaining a wide berth, minimum safe distance.

Just like guys in a stadium bathroom.

Mistake, the lady is a man. Or a lady with an incredibly cavernous voice.

SI has been read, now Sports Guy burps loud.

Place is fucking quiet. A brief comment about a headline yields no interest.

Sports Guy just put his sunglasses on, @5am in the dark.

It's like we all want to be around people, just not talk to each other.

Ooh an opening...

A full hour just evaporated. I've met Darnell. Raiders jacket w/ a candy hat. Darnell works at a xian homeless shelter. Security and cleanup. We started talking about the severance package of a local school superintendent. He didn't get a xmas bonus, and if he quits, he won't get any money. Rich people, according to Darnell, couldn't do without, like he has. He spoke about receiving a bag of groceries as a bonus, was insulted and confronted his supervisor about what she earned. She got a bonus.

Darnell then said rich people who sell secrets ain't really rich. If they know to "flip a house, they'd own the whole country." Darnell also believe Katrina was a real estate swindle. "It's not like rich people suddenly got a heart, and want to help us.,"

I asked him about self-help books, gurus, etc. "Can someone learn what they need from a book or a seminar?"

"You can't learn from a book, only experience. Street people have experience. Can't fool them because of all they've gone thru. We know both ends. Just like the people at the shelter, gov't types wouldn't take a pay cut to help us out."

His subjects changed fast, it was hard to keep up. He back to his supervisor. She seems nervous around him. He wants to know why? She told him that he might know too much. Her feelings are strong for him, but she can't see him privately.

Darnell decides to go to her church, the organization that runs the shelter. He BARTS and buses over. "Damn thing takes forever. I had to leave at 8am to make it at 11am."

He sees her outside with another lady. When he walks up, they go inside without greeting him. He sits down and notices that his Sup and the other lady are not sitting together and are avoiding looking at each other.

Darnell is angry when is he tells this. He also, doesn't look me in the eye often. He faces me only when I look away. Why?

The Pastor/preacher, announcing he's changing his sermon b/c of what's happening in the City. (2 yrs. Mayor newsome allowed the city attorney to issue marriage licenses to same sex couples) Therefore, this story is 2 years old, at least. His recall makes it seem like it happened last Sunday.

Ah ha, Darnell's got it. His shelter supervisor won't get with him because she's a lesbian? If Darnell finds out, he might tell the Pastor, (whom he knows) and she'll lose her job.

I remember asking him when did the mayor give out licenses. "Just last year. He did it for the election he was running in."

Darnell continues to talk about this supervisor, her feelings, her distance, the other woman, etc. Hard to follow, disjointed. Plus, with out him facing me, I couldn't read his lips, so I missed details.

"When the light goes on, and the cockroaches scatter, always one stays behind." Darnell wouldn't stay in the present, despite all coercion. Back to the church story. When the pastor finished an anti-gay marriage sermon, the offering was called, and the 2 ladies met a 3rd and whispered together quietly. The 2 original ladies slipped out the back.

The new, 3rd Lady, took her seat. Darnell knew her as a church council woman. (how did he know this?)

Outside at the coffee and pastry tables, the 3rd lady meets Darnell. To Darnell, she's trying to determine if the first 2 ladies are lesbians. (Darnell never uses the "l" word, he says "you know, their secret" or "you could just tell." I asked him "Are they Lesbians?" "They have to be, because women don't act like that around each other." "Like what?" "you know, all nervous and secretive, hush hush, like I don't know what's going on.")

Darnell "to this day" knows "but hasn't told anyone, cause they'll kick me out. That's what they do."

Darnell was fit, stock, a bit heavy, but his big shoulder's gave him a fullback form. Beard was grayed. Eyes, the white almost pink. Darting. Soft hands when we shook. Pinky ring on the right. Tennis shoes, white, clean. Didn't so much smile, but lift a side of his mouth. As we spoke, he eventually turned to face me, but limited eye contact.

"She's got feelings for me. Not hate or anger. So all that's left is love. But she's got to work it out, cause I don't get played, you know. I've got to protect what I've got."

As I get up to leave, Darnell asks me to let him finish his story. Wow. He follows me outside to my car.

I think Darnell hasn't talked to anyone new in months, maybe years. He's lonely, just like me and you. He would've sat in King's and talked to me all day. If I had the guts, I'd stayed and listened, but my own drama called.

I read an article recently about some local Buddhist's monks who spent 3 days living on the streets of the City. One commented, "I now know what it's like to be ignored. To not exist." I wish I could have heard him say the words, because I couldn't tell if the statement was positive or negative.

Clearly, Darnell didn't want me to leave.

Rob Clark

Sent: Wednesday, January 11, 2006 6:37 AM
To: Corrine@WizardAcademy.com
Subject: Inside Out

Good Morning,

I took up the "challenge" this morning.

I took notes of what I experienced or thought for the hour and will go through my notes to give you my thoughts. I arrived at 5:00 am and was able to eat for $2.89. I went to the far west side, which is considered the bad side of town. We have a river that splits the city and we live on the far east side, a new development that is on the edge of the city, a desirable area.

The first person I meet working is Ryan who has a large tattoo on his forearm and a bad hair dye job. It did not seem that he wanted to be there, in fact, the 3 staff members did not look happy to be there. When a new customer came in, the customer would wait at the counter while the staff would clean off a counter or start a new pot of coffee. The customers did not seem to mind that it took 30 seconds to be said hello to, but that would have bothered me.

Most of the customers looked similar. Ball caps that were dirty, work boots, and blue jeans. My assumption is that not many would have showered this morning. There was little conversation this morning. Could not feel a sense of community. No one looks healthy. People seemed rushed, they were not truckers but people heading to work. Many coming in for coffee to go. Why do they stop for coffee instead of making some at home?

What do I have that these people would not own? I would guess they do not own an ipod or know what an apple Imac G5 is used for. I assume they do not go to starbucks every other day or likely buy clothes at the Gap. But then again, those things do not mean much. I can not tell if they have a wonderful 2 year old son at home like I do or if they have a wonderful spouse that loves them very much. So I leave this question at that.

Likewise, I would not be able to guess what they have that I do not. I have everything that I could want. The things I do not want are things that are for things that I want more such as a mortgage. I do not want a mortgage, but I do want to own a home more.

What do these people need? The need to smile more and laugh.

They are spending their life doing what they are doing right now. Is this how they want to spend their life? They need the same things I need, they need to feel loved, feel important and have value. How can I make these people smile and laugh? How can I make them feel that they are important? I am not quite sure, but I would love to make them laugh and smile.

People here act like they do not want a relationship or even a conversation. They only want their food or coffee and to be left alone, but do they? If they do want to be left alone, why? We like to have our own experiences, but do not want to bring others along with us. Would not it be better to bring others along with us for our adventure? Include them in our lives and let them know that people do care for one another and we should stop running around so much to experience events instead of experiencing people.

I also wonder what the staff think of me. I am obviously out of place sitting here, done with my food for 30 minutes, and just watching them.

It was well worth the $3 and waking up a little earlier this morning. I am an American and a Canadian. I grew up in the Land of Lincoln and moved to Canada 5 years ago with my wife who grew up here. Now have dual citizenship.

8 Galen Sonntag

Sent: Monday, January 16, 2006 11:07 AM
To: Corrine@WizardAcademy.com
Subject: My Excursion

This doesn't quite fit the rules as defined, but then sticking to the rules all the time only get's you what's already known.

My family and I were at my son's hockey tournament, about 45 minutes away from our home town. We were in a small town called Viscount, Saskatchewan, with a population of a few hundred. It's not a well to do town, nor a run down place. There were no new homes, and the newest building in town looked to be at least 30 years old. I would guess most of the employment in town is either based on the potash mines nearby or the surrounding farms.

We left home at 6:30 am to make it to the rink in time for the 8:00 am game time, with mostly empty wallets, after all, there's a cash machine on every corner in our home town of Saskatoon (yes, I saw Roy Williams at the Centennial Auditorium last time he was in town). Two games later and with lunch time approaching before our next game, I set out with my 6 year old daughter for a quick run to the bank to pull out some money to buy my three kids some lunch. There are no traffic lights, and I only remember 3 stop signs in the 5 minute drive I took to find an automated teller. I returned to the rink without cash. The bank in town, closed of course on the weekend, did not have an automated teller, nor does the only restaurant in town, or the gas station (also closed). It was the time I spent in the restaurant, my last attempt to find a cash machine, that I remember most.

The restaurant is in a building at least 60 years old, with one side operated as a Chinese restaurant and the other side as a more traditional north American style restaurant. If you want a hamburger, turn right when you enter. If you want won ton soup, turn left. There are about 8 to 10 tables on each side. All but one of the tables on the Chinese side were filled. The other side, empty. "Odd", is what I thought. I also didn't recognize anyone at the tables. After spending half a day in the same hockey rink with 5 other teams, you see everyone face to face at least 3 times as you wander around between games. None of these faces were familiar, and there were only two vehicles parked out front, one was mine. The rest must have walked was my conclusion. The next closest town is 15 minutes away by highway, not walking distance in January in Saskatchewan. That makes them all locals, a theory that was proven true in a few minutes.

We strolled up to the counter at the back of the restaurant to ask if there was a cash machine. The quick answer that there was not in the restaurant, but the bar at the hotel has one. It doesn't open until 2:00 though. I checked my watch, 12:15. I checked my wallet, $10. Not enough for a meal of rink burgers back at the arena and my son's team played again at 2:00. I explained my dilemma to the waitress and she left, returning quickly with a Chinese man of about 60-65 years old. He said, "this is my restaurant, if you have no money, then bring your family and you eat free." I explained that, "I have money, I just can't get it out of the bank." I asked if I could put through charge on my credit card for some cash, but they don't have a credit card machine, the restaurant was strictly cash, exactly the thing I didn't have. After a brief discussion with the man, he offered to make my family a lunch, which I could take to the rink, at no charge. I accepted his generous offer and my daughter and I sat down on the empty side of the restaurant to wait. Very shortly, the waitress appeared and asked why we were sitting by ourselves. I had no answer, so she moved us the only empty table on the Chinese side. My daughter drew pictures on a napkin while I listened to the conversation of the locals. I'm now convinced that every winter Sunday is the same conversations, with the same topics, and the same local experts with the same opinions. Weather was everyone's topic, "how warm it has been for January", and no one can remember that last time it was above zero in January or when we had so little snow, except, for, "back in '75, or '83, or some other year, you know, the year that the Schultz kid burnt down the barn". Politics was also one the agenda, we have a National election coming in a few weeks, and everyone was against the current government (I think against all political parties in general), and, "wouldn't we all be better off if someone from here ran the country, like the Williams kid. He went and moved off to Calgary now where he's an engineer with an oil company. That kid has a good head on his shoulders and still comes back every holiday with his wife and children to help his dad harvest and every holiday." The other popular topic was hockey, NHL, the recent World Junior Championship (won by Canada), the Western Hockey League, and of course the local Viscount Vipers at every age level. Regardless of the league or the team, everyone agreed that there was a player that used to play in Viscount that was as good as any player that ever played.

I listened to their stories, and there was a clear theme, a different theme than I hear in Saskatoon most of the time. The theme was not technology or money, the two things I was in searching for. The common thread was simply people. Everyone seemed to be happy, without the need for technology or for talking about who has what or how much. It was, "remember when…", and "that kid named…", and, "the best I ever saw", and "when we all…". Happiness, in Viscount Saskatchewan, is not about technology or money, it's simply about people.

Anyway, the bagged lunch arrived, I took it to the rink and fed my surprised family with some of the tastiest Chinese food ever. We played 2 more games of hockey and went home, after a close loss in the 'A' side final. Before we left, we stopped at the bar, used the cash machine, and tried to pay for our lunch, which he wouldn't accept, even though I now clearly had the money. I asked why he didn't want the money. He said, "you needed food but had no money. I had food and I don't need money, I have all these customers." So I asked, "Why do all of your customers sat on the Chinese side of the restaurant?" The answer was so simple, it should have been obvious. He said, "I am Chinese. I make better Chinese food."

Simple rules: People matter.   Quality matters.

Tom Smith

9

Sent: Monday, January 16, 2006 9:45 AM
To: corrine@wizardacademy.com
Subject: late night / early morning observations

January 16, 2006
Wizard of Ads Assignment

This morning I found myself driving around Los Angeles – specifically near Los Angeles International Airport. One would think there would be an all night diner somewhere nearby... but I had no luck finding one. Like many, many things here in LA-LA Land... it makes no sense.

Just when I was about to throw in the towel I noticed a ton of cars in the parking lot of the well lit Hollywood Park and Casino, the time was just after 5AM. I decided to pull in and check on the crowd... surely characters would be found in the place.

I didn't hear much when I was there, and my interaction with people was minimal... but I didn't need much time to have more than enough to write about. I walked in through a side entrance, as I approached the stench of stale cigarette smoke wafted in the air.

Once in the building I found myself in the poker room. Actually, I'd been there twice before... but never @ 5AM. Not overly surprised, I saw a few tables relatively filled with players - maybe fifty to a hundred players on up to ten tables. Looking for a coffee bar, or somewhere that I could overhear conversations I continued through the room.

To the left tucked into what looked like a broom closet was a makeshift bar... completely stocked with booze and a bartender sitting in a chair nodding off. I wondered when he served his last drink... or maybe he was just opening for the day? Either way he was hardly awake.

The place was quiet overall. Not much happening at all. The gift store was open... "Spend a Buck" it was called – clever name. Two security guards walked in front of me... but not together, they were single file. The one in front was short, youthful looking and walked with a definite swagger. He looked like he could bench press a full size pickup truck and had a sleeve of tattoos on his right arm. There was zero chance of mistaking that his guy savored the power bestowed upon him... which, when I noticed he had a firearm strapped to his hip, was a bit disconcerting. The security guard walking behind the guy I was going to stay clear of seemed like he was from Africa or the Dominican Republic. He spoke in broken English when I asked him where a restaurant where I could order a cup of coffee was. He pointed and spoke of a woman in a red shirt. I was confused. He helpfully instructed me to follow him and he'd take me there. I followed.

Moments later we arrived at the opposite side of the building where gamblers were playing various table games. Caribbean Stud Poker, one of my favorites – even though the odds of winning are terrible – is one game I noticed and recognized. The other tables where short and players sat in regular sized chairs, whereas at Caribbean Stud they had to sit on stools to accommodate the higher tables.

"Trips, Trips, Trips, Trips," a Caribbean Stud player mumbled to himself over and over as the dealer revealed other players hands. 5AM and these folks are focused.

Throughout my brief stay hardly a soul noticed I was there... accept my security guard escort. He wanted to make sure I got my coffee and breakfast. , he again told me to see the woman in the red shirt sitting at a table apparently on break and talking to a man in a blue shirt... who was also apparently on break.

Realizing that the guard was directing me to servers I feared there was likely no diner at Ye' Ole Hollywood Casino, rather the place was designed for gamblers to play – not sit relax and enjoy breakfast. Indeed one could sit at a table, gamble and order food and drink to their table... but nothing was to come between the player and the play – sadly.

I began to venture back the way I came when I noticed a large window with electronics inside. Upon further inspection I saw that there inside was where the casino has the big poker games that get broadcast on television... good thing we're beaming this lifestyle directly into the homes of America and the world. How else would future gamers learn of such a way of life?

Heading back to the poker room I saw an area with tables and chairs and another woman in a red shirt not far away. Putting two and two together I asked the woman if she could bring me a cup of coffee and pointed to the location where I'd be sitting... she said it would be a few minutes.

I sat, opened my folder, pulled out a pen and jotted down some observations; there was a woman with a bowling-type shirt on. "Massage Therapist" was embroidered on the back of her shirt. She was working on a player who was sitting at a poker table. The sat backwards in his chair and had an extra cushion which looked as though he brought it from home... apparently he planned on being there awhile. When I left the area later the massage therapist was long gone but the guy still sat backwards in his chair with the extra cushion. He hardly moved except to pick up and toss his cards – dedicated.

Sitting and observing I read the signs hanging from the ceiling. "Jackets in January," hung from everywhere. They were running a promotion. 30 hours of play earns gamblers a free Hollywood Casino Jacket!

Glancing around a bit more I saw more employees in red, blue and yellow shirts. I know the red shirts indicated waiters and waitresses... not sure about the others... blue might have been dealers.

The place was mostly men though there were a few women. Every ethnicity was represented... and attire too. There were guys in velour jogging suits and guys with jeans and colored shirts... casual suits... even a fellow with a shirt, slacks, sweater, jacket and fedora. Nobody except the security guard looked to be in very good shape.

There was a player sitting and playing with a cigarette dangling from his mouth the entire time... though it wasn't lit because there's no smoking indoors in LA. Another thing that makes no sense... only because they sell cigarettes everywhere in LA!

My security guard escort suddenly reappeared and asked if I'd been helped. I told him I had and thanked him... he seemed pleased with my answer, smiled and strolled on.

Realizing I had more than enough material to write about I began packing up my belongings, cell phone, keys, newspaper and folder w/ note pad. A couple of younger guys came and sat nearby making me think twice about leaving (as they surely could have provided material)... a red shirted waiter came by to take their breakfast order... but they wanted dinner. Must have been a long night.

Upon exiting, after being their just fifteen or twenty minutes, I looked harder at the cars in the parking lot. I had to wonder a little harder when I saw a BMW X5 and a newer looking Porsche... I guess some of the gamblers are doing okay. Or maybe they just drive fancy cars... after all we are in LA-LA Land.

10 Judy Davis

Sent: Wednesday, January 18, 2006 4:31 AM
To: Corrine@WizardAcademy.com
Subject: "Where's the Soup!??"

I arrived at this drab cafe just about 1:30 a.m. on a 'dark and rainy night' to absolutely no customers. Just Thelma, graveyard waitress, behind the counter filling the salt and pepper shakers, wiping down the place and she greeted me like an old friend.... big, warm smile. Scott, the cook, was way down at the end of the bar talking to the old dishwasher, Gabe; they were just chillin' out - nothin' to do, no one to cook for or wash for, just shooting the s___.

On such a late, slow and miserable week night they were curious why I came in - so I told them - rather asked them -- I was there to write about them, what they needed most.

Thelma, without hesitation said "A raise! I've been here well over a year and I'm still must making $6.75 an hour - California minimum wage - and I deserve it!" Then she leaned down and quietly whispered to me, "and I stopped drinkin' two years ago... so that's good."

Scott and Gabe, hangin' back a bit, after thinking about it awhile and wondering if I was for real, said the same thing; "A raise." Scott's recovered stolen car (at Christmas time - yikes!) still needed over $700 in repairs to get it back in shape - and Gabe just plain ole wanted a raise - he was kind of shy and began vacuuming.

After bringing the best apple pie ala mode and coffee she could rustle up, Thelma seemed to like me, her job and her life and I could see her contentment in taking care of this cafe. As she looked around for more things to tidy up, she added, "What this cafe needs is some decorating - it's so drab and boring. It needs some flowers on the tables and outside, or maybe a new paint job - or something." You could tell she really cared and took pride of 'ownership' in the place. "Also, a new vacuum for Gabe. That thing must be 50 years old he's using right now," she yelled over the racket. "And on these cold winter nights people ask for brown sugar and raisins with their oatmeal - which they recently took away. No one wants oatmeal without brown sugar!" A long list of disappointments crossed her mind as her eyes fell to the ground yet you could see she wasn't a complainer and really enjoyed serving.

"Above all, though," she added with a lot of spark, ".... we need soup!   Would you believe it? We HAVE soup but we can't serve it after 10 p.m. and everyone coming in really late at night, when it's so cold out there - well, they want hot soup --- and I just feel so bad - here it is right behind me, and I can't serve it! Is that insane?!"

They all thought I was there doing a report from the cafe chain corporate office and Thelma quietly asked me if I visited alot of _____'s throughout California and then it hit me - they think I'm telling the big bosses what they want - ouch.   So I quickly told them, 'sorry, no..... this writing is actually for some big marketing guru in Texas who has challenged his 31,000 readers last week to go out and do this - and he said he predicts maybe 7 people will do it."   More curious now than disappointed in this news I told them a little more and we all talked on and on like old friends.

I ended up giving Thelma a great lead to a simple part-time job in town she'd be great at and I could tell we all really enjoyed meeting each other - and I left knowing 3 new friends.

How can I help them get what they most need? Certainly I can write letters of accomodation to Bessie, their manager, encouraging raises for them all. Yup, I could do that, but what we have all done for each other is increase friendship to each other - and that's priceless. That's how they helped me. Late at night now, when I can't sleep and I want some hot coffee, warm smiles and good company, I'll just get in my car and go see my new friends.   As much as I kept putting this little task off all week, even up to having to push myself out the door tonight - in this miserable cold rain - I can honestly say, this was a gas!

Thanks Roy!

11 Tom Wanek

Sent: Thursday, January 12, 2006 9:11 PM
To: Corrine@WizardAcademy.com
Subject: Inside the Outside: Cafe Communities

Café Communities

Shortly after 4AM this morning, I found myself a little more alone in life, driving my mother to the bus stop to catch the shuttle to the airport.

She's moving back to the Cleveland area to join my dad, and to care for her elderly parents. This decision leaves me solely in charge of the family business, which I now have to run with just my wife while caring for our two young daughters.

Knowing that this circumstance will take an incredible toll on my family, my mom tells me she loves and admires me, and I watch her shed a waterfall of tears as she boards the bus and drives off.

Feeling blue yet wide-awake, I decide to take Roy's advice to enlarge my world. So, I head downtown to find a late-night eatery to experience the world "outside".

Upon arriving at my chosen eatery, and only a few steps from my car, a homeless guy approaches me seemingly out of nowhere.

Fresh blood.

"Hey, gotta a smoke?" Fortunately for the both of us, I don't. So, I politely respond and continue onward.

Anxiously, I walk up to the Horseshoe Café, a modest, antique 24-hour eatery in downtown Bellingham. Yep, open as advertised.

Entering, I'm shocked by the activity at this early hour. No, it's not jam-packed, but moderately busy. Naively, I expected to be the only person on the planet interested in getting a bite to eat in this little diner, in this remote part of the world, at this time of day.

Clearly a fish out of water, I sit at the end of the bar, joining a few of the more talkative patrons trying not to stand out.

The conversations are as colorful as the characters telling them, language unclean, laughter overflowing. I listen to stories of lost opportunities, family life, financial strife, perseverance and a little known theory about why people are the size they are.

According to one of the stranger characters, if you eat "tall foods" as a child you'll grow up to be tall. Conversely, if you eat "short foods", you'll stay short as evidenced by the fact that a friend of his loves corn on the cob and stands at 6' 9", while he himself is short, fat and loves potatoes.

The story draws a ton of laughter, and a few puzzled faces.

Shortly after hearing this thrilling scientific discovery, the players quickly exit like exhausted partygoers on New Year's Eve. So, I finish my breakfast and head home.

Driving, I try to think about all the ways I could help these people or how they can help me. However, my mind always wanders back to how this interaction alone may have been beneficial to each other, almost therapeutically. It was sort of like a cleansing of the soul

You see, I'm not much different from these folks at all. Although they all seem to live simple lives lacking common luxuries such as cell phones and computers, their problems appear to be rooted in the same ground as everyone else's. We all have crosses to bear, unique stories to tell, wacky theories, opportunities lost or gained.

Hurricane Katrina displaced a friend of mine. I, myself, have family, work and financial struggles mentioned earlier. Our stories, I imagine, would fit in nicely with the folks at the Horseshoe.

However, there was one slight, yet unmistakable quality that this gathering at the Horseshoe Café offered that I sorely lack in my life. That is simply, a sense of community.

The Café Community isn't at all like your typical community or organization. You know, the kind that shares the obvious characteristics or interests such as work, neighborhood, hobby or education. No, the Café Community is an impromptu community that is more basic than any other, existing to share life's struggles, achievements, passions and laughs all without judgment. There's no membership fees, no structured topics, no initiation. Breathing is all that's required.

The desire to belong to a community is sought after by all walks of life. Wealthy individuals are no exception. To find it, look no further than the countless number of chat groups and discussion forums available on the Internet.

I imagine that there are hundreds of thousands of cafés spread across the United States hosting these Café Communities, providing people with an outlet to share life's experiences. I believe that sharing these experiences, the good and the bad, gives you coping techniques. Which, like a veteran boxer, helps you to roll with the punches.

I'm also confident that Café Community members still have days where life steals away a smile or two, but I bet when you visit any one of these cafés, you'll always find an open venue to express life, without judgment, making you feel a whole lot better.

So, will I ever visit the Horseshoe Café again?

Someday, I hope.

12   Mike Sales

Sent: Wednesday, January 18, 2006 9:15 AM
To: Corrine@WizardAcademy.com
Subject: it wasn't exactly a meal

    I had an occasion to go into a check cashing place. If they were honest in their marketing, the slogan would read, "serving all ghetto financial needs, for those who have no options, at the highest possible prices!" I had waited until the last minute to pay my electric bill.
    There were plenty of people in line, representing a cross-section of the clientele: The man who worked for a service company, in his dirty uniform (probably in for the same thing I was), there was the man who was not allowed to cash his check, the many folks making "loan" payments (more like shark payments), and then there was the chatter.
    I didn't have time to go to a restaurant. I am building a business. I didn't have time to put a deposit in the bank before my electric bill was due! I still work a full-time job, as well. I appreciated the idea of what you were saying with your assignment, but I wasn't really getting it, until I heard her speak: "I don't never turn nobody down to help out, 'cause I don't never want no one to turn my daughter down."
    I have absolutely no idea what made the woman say that, because it jarred me out of the light daze I was trying to sustain until I could leave the building. She wasn't with anyone. I think she might have assisted someone else in line. All I know is that it made me think of what you had said. It was magical to hear a person with so few options, exhibit so much faith. She was really saying, "I know what it's like to be down, and now my daughter does too. I can't shield her from the harshness of my reality, but maybe if we all do our part when we can, things will be easier for her. I'm going to take the first step toward that". Amazing!

Rick Copper

13

Sent: Tuesday, January 17, 2006 6:22 AM
To: Corrine@WizardAcademy.com
Subject: truck stop excursion

I sat at the counter of Arrowhead - a 24-hour restaurant in a T/A truck stop center off of I-90 near Hampshire, Illinois (it's not as old as New Hampshire and certainly not as old as Hampshire, so I think it should be called New New Hampshire, but I digress) in the midst of the smoking section. It's 4:10am.

I'm not a smoker. But I think if I was a trucker I could become one. Being a trucker is not a life for the low-spirited. It's lonely, tiring and really deserves more credence than generally given. Those refrigerators at your local Home Depot don't get there by chance. Neither does your milk, your meat or your Mazdas.

The truckers are doing some talking between watching a movie with Oliver Platt as a down-and-out wrestler with David Arquette and I believe Rose McGowan. Not talking about much. Just talking - The NFL playoffs (what happened to the Bears Defense and what's wrong with Peyton Manning?); coffee quality; where they were headed; why men don't take their hats off when they walk inside anymore (I subtly took mine off about 10 minutes later as my 2 eggs-over-easy, French toast, hash browns and sausage patty "Long Haul" breakfast hit the countertop); child discipline (female truckers - thank God. They were really going on about that one. Apparently sparing the rod was not one of their recommendations - flying skillets seem to be very popular). No politics. No hot stock tips. No worrying about Brittney Spears and her failing marriage.

They don't care. They plug along day-by-day, earning their living. I sat there thinking about people who screw them on a daily basis that they don't even know how they're getting screwed. Natural Gas traders. The FDA. John Ashcroft (no more digressions - sorry).

Perhaps it's best not to know? I don't think so. Is this something I can give to them? Probably not. What I can give them is their due, their respect and their dignity. As one who professes to be a writer, I believe it is not my job to tell people how miserable their lives are when they truly aren't. People who don't have - or see the need for - Tivo, a DVD-RW, Satellite Radio, a Psychotherapist and perhaps even cable TV are not necessarily living the live of "Oliver."

They have what a lot of white collars lack - an honest soul and no fear of fear itself. Most of us know at least one person who "has everything" but really nothing at all without the soul they so sorely lack.

And regarding fear? I guess the line "when you've got nothing, you've got nothing to lose" (thanks Kris Kristofferson) diminishes any thought of fear they hear about from the nightly news.

One more thing - I'll bet I'm the only person whose male order taker (I'd say waiter, but it doesn't really fit here) was named Raven. I really dug that.

Col Kenna

14

Sent: Thursday, January 19, 2006 3:26 AM
To: Corrine@WizardAcademy.com
Subject: .....the other side of town

    There are not that many places in and around Townsville that are open the hours suggested in the Memo that would attract people sober enough to tune into!!! - but here goes.
    At 2:00 am I am at an all night service station (you might call it a truck stop). Besides the staff on duty, there are only 4 other people in the place - all are men and all are seated singly at tables apart from each other. They all appear to be truck drivers. Two look like they have had their "meal" and are now engrossed in the words of a newspaper or magazine with empty plates, cutlery, cups and small silver tea-pots on the table in front of them. The other two are getting ready to order something (they walked in at about the same time as me).
    This is where I notice the first difference between me and the "truck-drivers" - whilst I was scanning the menu for the healthiest items I could, they both seemed to order their meals verbatim and their orders were almost identical, but they too sat apart.
    While I was waiting for my order, I had a look outside and saw that the four trucks that were parked in the waiting bays were all different makes - this revelation immediately blew my theory that maybe Mack truck drivers' all ordered the same type of meals while Volvo drivers ordered something else. This could also have meant that this particular truck-stop only had one decent meal on the menu and all the drivers knew it.
    The only real chance to listen in to any conversation was when the waitress delivered the meals to the waiting drivers. The conversation with both drivers was similar and went something like- "Headin' down or comin' back up"
    "Nah, comin' back and can't wait to get home"
    "Hows the road"
    "Bloody roo's everywhere - I thought the rain would keep them away, but they are all over the road"
    "Much traffic"
    "Yeah - bloody Victorians everywhere as well"
    "We had 2 cop cars in here before"
    "Which way they headed"

"South" 'Good" both conversations continued that way - and was picked up and left off with the delivery of food and the retrieval of empty plates etc.

As each of the drivers left the diner, they each said goodbye to the remaining drivers seated, as well as the staff who had served them.

To me it appeared that they are like sole business men who have chosen their occupation because they like the solitude of the road and that even spills over to their meal breaks. Maybe they struggle with face to face conversation, but could thrive under the anonymousness of their 'handle' on the CB radio, or as the karaoke country-road-king in the security of their mobile cabin.

How many decision do they make on their journey. Do they use the hours of solitude to any advantage, or does the sheer concentration required to pilot an 18 ton vehicle safely along the highways of Australia take all their energy and focus. Do they drive so they don't have to think of anything else. To them, is the time on the road, time away from everything (absenteeism from life) or is it time at work.

As they all have employment, it is difficult to know what they need other than the road in front of them, but as I was driving home, I did ponder the question "Are they happiest driving away from their home life with the truck fully loaded heading to a new destination, or when they are driving back with an empty truck, but knowing exactly what they are driving back to, at home?".

I'd dearly like to go on at least one big road trip with one of them.

Woody Grubb

15

Sent: Tuesday, January 17, 2006 7:25 PM
To: corrine@wizardacademy.com
Subject: edited copy of all night diner

The Rapture must have occurred and God forgot to tell me. At least, that's what the scene indicated as I walked through the front door of Earl's Home Cookin. The top of almost every table in the joint had dirty plates, silverware, and crumpled napkins, and there was not a person in sight. I surveyed the scene and took a couple more hesitant steps. Through a window in the back another room came into focus that had both customers and a waitress. But why did I have to exit the main dining room to get to a screened-in porch room in the back in order to get served? It became clear when the waitress came to take my order and put an ashtray on the table: this is Earl's answer to California's no smoking laws. Just add a screened-in room in the back, where everyone can freeze their butts off, but maintain the right to smoke.

Eating alone in the main dining room didn't seem to offer the experience the Wizard was seeking for me. It's a shame no one told me the non-smoking crowd leaves at 2, but I sucked it up and ordered a Spanish omelet, or as the locals call it, "grease on eggs, grease on beans, and grease on potatoes." Maybe I'm being too critical. After all, the café did serve wine. Proof was in the box of wine above the cook, on the shelf next to a can of beans. The food really didn't have much too offer, but the eclectic mix of patrons more than made up for it.

The dominant voice in the room came from a thin, tattooed and pierced young woman who started the adventure by discussing back chub, the fat that hangs over the back of tight-fitting, low-slung pants. She bemoaned her recent addition of back chub and bemoaned a post pregnancy future that would cause it to become totally disgusting. But not as disgusting as the most disgusting photos on the Internet. According to our loud, profane, but articulate lass, that honor goes to a picture that, at first glance, appears to be some very attractive cleavage, but as the camera moves away, the cleavage evolves into some really nasty looking back chub on an obese woman. It was truly refreshing to hear a female answer a question I have posed more than once, "Do women actually look in mirrors to see what they look like from behind?"

Her companions, a purple-haired female sidekick and a young submissive male, infrequently contributed to the conversation, but it mattered little. She never ran out of interesting topics and opinions, all told with graphic detail without any deleted expletives. For example," the French aren't really rude, they just hate us." She based this on personal observation during here travels in France. She said that Americans walk into a store and immediately take care of whatever business they came for, rudely eliminating the casual, pre-purchase social, verbal interactions that are integral to the European shopping experience. She may have a point. More importantly, it was her conversation about traveling in Europe that led to a conversation on the other side of the room between the waitress and a college student I came to know as Andre.

The waitress told Andre she had always wanted to go to France, with the primary purpose of touring the Louvre. Shortly thereafter, she came to refill my coffee cup. I mentioned bicycling through Europe and a fascination with the art museums and historic sites in Florence and encouraged her to set a goal of traveling to see the Louvre. Specifically, I told her to "write the goal down, because a goal that isn't written down is just wishful thinking." She went back over to Andre and told him she was thinking seriously about going to Europe and if he might be interested. All of us need more responses like Andre offered. He simply asked, "Where and when?" Never mind the how.

Paying the bill provided an opportunity to help her with her first step toward France. I gave her the first $5 toward her trip. It's not that much and it came with strings. She has to put the goal in writing today. I'm going to come back in 90 days to check on her progress.

As I drove away I thought, "That's great. You know what to do, you can tell others what they need to do, but you continue to sit on the sidelines." I've been sitting on the sidelines ever since my ex-partner blew up our promotional marketing and publication* business with cocaine and I had a heart attack in the process.

I'm going to go home and write some gutsy goals down. I've had a Nike moment; just do it. I'm also going to find someone to hold me accountable, just like I'm going to hold the waitress accountable for her goal.

The all night café was Earl's Home Cookin, "open 24 hours a day since 1970," located on Tustin Avenue in Orange, California. The adventure took place from 3:57 a.m. to 5:05 a.m., January 17.* The publication we were involved with was Young Money, a financial literacy magazine and web site for young adults, for which Roy Williams graciously contributed an original article on succeeding in the ad game.

David Favor

16

Sent: Tuesday, January 10, 2006 6:32 PM
To: Corrine@WizardAcademy.com
Subject: Marketing Doctorate via Dumpster Diving with the Homeless

I read the latest "Inside the Outside" article suggesting going to the wrong side of town... and trying on a different life for size.

Years ago I did this experiment in an odd way and gained... some unusual insight.

This followed on the heals of drug related experiences where small groups of people, with journals in hand, would consume high octane chemicals and observe self, life and others.

A significant amount of the time we noticed sharing what I'd normally term hallucinations. We came to term anything only one person sees as a probable hallucination. Things seen by more than one person, especially a group, was... well...something else.

Along these lines when I was living in Houston a few years later, I'd occasionally take to the streets and travel the homeless circuit. Tattered clothes. Nothing in my pockets.

Here's what I learned.

After a while of immersing myself in the homeless collective consciousness I was able to see/hear/feel the same type of odd experiences they were having. Even to the point of hearing the voice "Turban Man" (homeless guy who lived in the park near my house, who always wore a turban) heard and would chase down the street screaming and shaking his fist... as the voice receded.

How does this apply to marketing. What I do in all the gatherings I host is to create a very specific... collective consciousness... throughout the group. People are invited from specific, synergistic, subcultures. Music. Topics of conversation. Food. All aspects of the gathering support a specific vibe.

This vibe tends to "self edit" the room, where only those people who resonate return... usually with a friend or two in tow. :-)

So my hats off to "Turban Man" for teaching me well and greatly increasing my daily income.

And after a person is comfortable having a meal in an out of the way cafe in the early morning hours, definitely graduate to dumpster diving with the homeless for the double-espresso version of altered consciousness and master-level marketing education.

Enjoy your best day ever!

17 Bill Wayland

Sent: Tuesday, January 10, 2006 7:51 AM
To: Corrine@WizardAcademy.com
Subject: Been there-Done that

There was the night all those years ago we decided to drive to Portland Maine for a cup of coffee. We left Dorchester about midnight and it must have been about 3am when we drove into Portland (no Interstate then). Portland was asleep but we found one all night diner, had our coffee and drove home into the dawn. We were men.

Of course my mother was none too pleased. If I'd called to say we were going, we wouldn't have. It wasn't about defiance. It was about adventure. And, Bill Gorman did the driving. A man of few words, Bill was a bit older and somehow mother trusted him. Go figure.

Bill wound up a lifer in the Marine Corps and somehow through a snafu in the paperwork, he never did basic training. Believe it. They sent him to the Air Marines and last I heard of him he was in Japan. Lost track of him. I hope he's alive.

Things got better for me over the years and one night I did my eaves dropping in the dining room of the Ritz Carlton Hotel in Atlanta-Buckhead. They put me down within easy listening to a man who looked like a plantation owner, complete with big white hat by his side, and an attractive looking lady maybe half his age. I ordered a drink and dinner and hoped for a conversation leading to mortal sin upstairs (She looked Irish).

Turns out she was a lawyer sent from New York to accompany the big man to an IRS hearing next day. They rehearsed his performance and when she asked him one question he went on some about this and that. She listened, put down her fork and said, "Mister (forget his name) I assure you if you tell them that you will do several years in the slammer". I almost gave myself away but covered it with a cough. Wonder where the big man is today. Wonder where she is. She was great looking.

Where am I? I'm either retired at 70 years of age...or job hunting. Last Thursday I parted company with "Clear Channel". Its a business now and I've been in it all these years for the laughs. They're worth so much why can't you bank them?

But I've got stories. Did I ever tell you about the day I met Tip O'Neil? We get off the same airplane at LaGuardia. I introduced myself and wound up riding into the city with him. He loved Reagan. They traded jokes all the time. Tip just thought he'd forgotten where he came from. But Ronnie's era was to come. As I climbed out at my hotel, O'Neil told me to be careful I took the right bag because he had the goods on Nixon in his luggage.

But thats another story.

Oh, and Tip told a great story about the time he gave a speech in Austin Texas...and the limo they sent broke down. Nobody knew how to fix it til a guy from Somerville, O'Neil's home town, drove by. A little tinkering under the hood and they were under way. Nothing against Texans.

All the best.

18 Sean McNally

Sent: Tuesday, January 17, 2006 9:20 PM
To: corrine@wizardacademy.com
Subject: Roy's memo challenge

I found myself faced with a few distinct disadvantages as I accepted this eavesdropping challenge. One of which, the fact that I am considerably hearing impaired (a pleasant way to say "deaf as a post") I was already painfully aware of. The other, the fact that I live no less than a one hour drive from anywhere that I would even remotely consider "the other side of the tracks", had somehow escaped me for the better part of the past eight years. Doing the best I can with what I've got has become a way of life for me, so I determined that this situation would prove no different. I dragged myself out of bed at 4:30 am and proceeded to make my way down to the only 24-hour eatery of which I am aware: the Waffle House, crouching down in the shadow of the bustling Interstate. Business was sparse at 5 am in this tiny haven of breakfast foods, it's ceiling painted a shade of yellow, which is not naturally occurring in any reality I have known. The Jackson 5 roared from the jukebox, removing what little auditory function that might have remained and forcing me into the compensatory swap of senses, which over the years has become second nature; hearing for sight.

Visual eavesdropping requires far more subtlety than that which is required for a simple case of intentional accidental overhearing, especially when you're observing Mike, the giant of a concrete worker with the shaved head and pierced ears who wears his hearts tattooed on his hand, as he converses with the slender older gentleman sporting the silver ducktail haircut and the checkered shirt, sans name tag. "See ya' in the a.m," his farewell address.

An even greater level might be required while discovering peripherally that cops eat something other than donuts. To be fair, the patches on their sleeves identified them as corrections officers from a few hours South, so maybe the same stereotype doesn't apply. And as if that weren't enough, the white one was taller than the colored one.

And then it happened. I became acutely aware of the patron sitting with the beautiful woman who appeared to be his wife. (I make this assumption based on the following evidence. They held hands and his boot caressed hers under the table. A couple of times he leaned over kissing her lightly. That, and they both wore wedding rings.) Now, I can't be sure but I think that I may have sensed what can only be described as a nearly imperceptible ripple of previously unrealized racism, as the polite, articulate, young black man positioned on the opposite side of the counter greeted him with a steaming cup of coffee and a truly genuine "how you doin'?" on this morning after the federal celebration of the birth Dr. Martin Luther King Jr. His surprise seemed to change to consternation and it was almost as if he, who probably makes as much money in one day than the man serving him makes in a week was trying to reconcile a disparity between their comparative levels of current career satisfaction. Michael Jackson's recitation of alphabet and numeral gave way to a high volume hip-hop hullabaloo as bacon sizzled and danced on the grill. "Helps me get the work done," was his reasoned response.

Guilt and confusion collided as the patron gulped down the remnants of his caffeine-laden liquid breakfast, slipping a ten dollar tip under the edge of the empty cup unsure if was an impulsively exaggerated show of appreciation for nine dollars and seventy-four cents worth of services rendered or for a priceless glimpse into a shocking and challenging new reality.

But enough about me.

19 Michelle Stearns

Sent: Thursday, January 19, 2006 5:07 PM
To: corrine@wizardacademy.com
Subject: Late entry into Initiation Challenge

"Initiation" challenge

Details of your experience
I live in Regina, Saskatchewan Canada. We don't have an all-night breakfast place other than the Husky House out on the highway. And it's clean, well-lit and host to truckdrivers coming in to shower have meals and leave. Usually they sit by themselves and read novels.

I write this because the challenge to "get out a comfort zone" was issued Monday, January 9/05 and Tuesday, January 10 at 4:45 p.m. I went and served supper at Regina's one "soup kitchen." It was my first time there. It's two blocks from the downtown office where I work.

The time of day was doesn't fit within your challenge parameters. it wasn't between 1:30AM and 5:30AM, it was between 4:45 p.m and 5:30 p.m. (although I ended up staying later to vacuum the floors). I'm also past the challenge deadline.

I'm sending this story in anyway, because I feel led to do so and because I just am.

It's the smell that hit me first. It was a mix of the cabbage from the soup and the smell of unwashed and damp. And then there was the ringing of cell phones. How could homeless people have cell phones? But it's Regina, Saskatchewan CANADA – we don't have homeless people here, do we?

And then I reminded myself to get out of my mind, and get present. To just listen. I heard. I heard anger and judgement. My fragile ego heard loudest the judgements about myself.

"What are you here for? To pay for some sin? To feel better about yourself?" A man whisper-hissed into my ear when I took a moment to be still and scout the room to see if anyone needed a coffee refill.

I turned to face him and said: "No." That's not why I came. I wasn't going to lie, and I wasn't going to offer anymore information. He looked shocked. Then he softened. Then his eyes twinkled and then he told me a joke: "Do homeless people get knock-knock jokes?" I said: "I don't know." He said: "Of course they don't. They don't have doors."

Later another man walked up and said: "I hate you." When I told him I didn't know what to do with that. He said: "...you be nice to me and I'll love you."

Your challenge to us looking to step out: "think of what these people need most and how you might help them get it. While you're at it, you might also think a little about what they have that you don't. There is a rich sense of community among the outcast."

Everyone wants to be heard. These men wanted to be heard. It's easy enough for us to listen. It's easier and more comfortable for us to descend into judgement ("...the smell, the cell phones..."). These men had no filters, there was just no bull sh#@. It's just emotion and need, right out there in the open. And they respect each other for having it out and living it out loud and not hiding. I'm white and rich. I can hide my stuff and my needs better than anyone.

Where's it being hidden? What can't be seen because I've filled up the hiding places?

20 Alexander Vickers

Sent: Tuesday, January 17, 2006 3:11 PM
To: corrine@wizardacademy.com
Subject: Diner Experience

Begin story...

The moon's completed three quarters of it's sojourn across night's sky and I've just crossed the threshold into a world unseen by these eyes for a long time-- the 24 hour diner. Prompted to retread old ground with new eyes by the Wizard's call to adventure, I autonomously claimed a table and anticipated my waitress' arrival and the unknown lesson I came to learn.

Despite being the last member of a lonely trio to occupy the diner, the service came slowly.

Recalling the Wizard's derision of those seeking pampered adventure, I laughed at my temptation to complain. Nestled in a booth, I looked upon my silent companions and immediately discovered something.

They had a freedom to come and go as they pleased. A freedom I seemingly had far less of.

Now, I'm not sure these men lacked a woman at home questioning why the hell they were going to a diner during the Hour of the Wolf, but I'd bet a healthy amount of cabbage that it was the case. As they quietly gnawed at their nighthawk fare, I wondered if these people were lonely. Profoundly lonely.

The embossed, brooding circles cradling their eyes made me wonder if this was a ritual for them.

In their countenances, I could locate no trace of a magnificent obsession inexorably pulling them out of bed each dawn. Instead, I saw slumped shoulders and boredom, and, as a human being, it made me sad to see the language of the Defeated.

I would have loved to have the courage and the power to breathe fuel onto these dying embers, but I know no man can give another man his purpose. It made me wonder if there are those living a life more purposeful than mine experiencing the same conflict when observing me.

Perhaps one thing these people could use is companionship. In my hypnagogic state I wondered why it's so hard for some people to be with other people-- Why is crossing the gap from stranger to friend so terrifying? Perhaps, the fear of what could happen is greater than the allure of what could be...

An invention came to mind. A system, if you will, that would facilitate first contact between human beings.

What if people could go to a private clearing house that records their interests, the people they'd like to meet, ensures their not criminals, etc. and then gives them a device that transmits this information within a certain range. If two people are a match and are in proximity the devices alert them and help introduce them minus the usual awkwardness associated with approaching strangers.

I'll take this journey again, hoping to encounter a larger crowd so I may actually eavesdrop. I'm happy I took the Wizard's challenge though and look forward to those yet-to-come.

21 Shane Speal

Sent: Friday, January 13, 2006 9:09 AM
To: Corrine@WizardAcademy.com
Subject: Roy's challenge from this week's MMM

Maple Donuts, Route 30, York, PA.
5am, Friday morning

Stale cigarettes, yeast and grease fills my nose as I sit at the front counter. I'm in it for the full experience, so I open up the pack of smokes I bought from the machine at the front door. Haven't smoked in years and can't believe I paid six bucks for the pack. Pull one cigarette out and tap the filter on the counter to pack the contents. The exposed paper of the packed cigarette fires up with brilliant flame, crackles. I cough at first, but find it a little bit easier with the second and third drags.

Looking around at my new surroundings. Walls originally painted light tan have become sepia tinted from the years of smoke and grime. Overweight Hispanic waitress in a skirt and frumpy shirt covered by coffee-stained apron gets me a large coffee and custard donut. Her name tag says "Angel".

Like the others, I sit and look down at the cup in a too-damn-early meditative stare.

There's four other customers in here besides me, all men. One is an old guy in the corner, slowly rotting in his seat. His whiskered jowls sag low, reaching for the table as he stares down. He's got his ashtray half full already and he keeps his pack right in front of his hand for easy harvest of the next smoke. Two others sit together at a booth, barely talking, looking at some folder or log book, inhaling coffee, possibly truck drivers. One has a full beard, thick glasses and massive beer belly. The other is slimmer and younger, maybe 30 or so. An empty rig sits outside, free of any trailer. Must be theirs.

The last customer is sitting at the counter, five or six seats down from me. He's got an almost-mullet and mustache and he's wearing an Alabama concert shirt and jeans. He's keeping conversation with Angel.

"...I don't know, he says. "I told her the last time we fought that I was done, but she talked me into coming back."

Angel replies, "is everything gonna be alright now?"

"I guess. She just has to learn that I am the way I am," he says.

"Mmm," she agrees half heartedly as she walks over to refill Rotting Man and the two guys in the booth.

As she walks back around the counter to put sugar and Sweet-n-Low packets in the counter trays. They go on for about twenty minutes, discussing his relationship problems that always seem to be everyone else's fault but his. Every now and then, she comes over and puts another inch of fresh coffee in my cup. I thank her each time and smiles back.

It's rather slow and boring in here, yet the place is rather comforting when you're tired and hazy. It's almost like a chapel for smokers and coffee drinkers. Only once did anyone else come in, and it was just a customer buying a dozen doughnuts to take to work. He asks Angel to choose a mixture of flavors from the rack of "Maple Donut's Famous 52 Varieties." After ringing them up, she heads back to the end where Mr. Relationship sits.

They go back to idol chatter for a while until Mr. Relationship changes the subject with a sentence that cut thru my curiosity like a bullet: "Did I ever tell you that I had a World's Record?"

"No," she said as she turned to him with interest.

"Yeah," he says, "it happened when I was divorcing my first wife and marrying my second one." He continues, "Janie an' me were wanting to get married, but we had to wait until my first marriage was done. We had to wait for the divorce papers to go thru. Well, that morning when my divorce was final, I went to the courthouse to sign the papers at 10:30. At two o'clock, me an' Janie went to the Justice of the Peace to get married. Here, it was the world's shortest time between marriages. I didn't even know it."

"You're kidding," Angel says.

"No, really," he tells her. "I used to have a paper signed by Guinness and everything." He adds, "I don't have the World Record anymore. Some guy in California got re-married within an hour a few years ago."

So here I am, early morning in a grimy doughnut shop, drinking coffee and smoking cigarettes, all the while sitting beside a World Record holder.

I stay for about 10 more minutes as Angel and Mr. Relationship and Angel get back to small talk. My lungs feel fuzzy from the smokes and I know that I'd better get back to my normal surroundings. There's enough caffeine and nicotine in my system to jumpstart a Peterbuilt. I pay my tab and Angel tells me to have a nice day.

Walking outside to the brisk and foggy air, I throw the 17 unused cigarettes away in the trashcan outside the door. The clean air feels like good medicine to my lungs.

I smile in satisfaction. Today, I sat near a celebrity.

22 Christian Clapton

Sent: Wednesday, January 18, 2006 11:26 AM
To: Corrine@WizardAcademy.com
Subject: "I'm So Allergic to Cats Man" - Inside the Outside task

With only one 24hr diner in my prosperous Alberta city I was concerned that I wouldn't get the juice that I was hoping for in this intriguing task. I thought that the place would be empty and I would need to resort to eavesdropping on the staff. (which was quite interesting in the end)

I was excited, often I have sat in a mall food court and watched people, yet with reservation due to my not wanting to be spied as I was doing the spying. Perhaps a bit of childhood residue from the not to distant echoes of "don't stare at people...it is not polite" one would hear from a controlling parent.

So hear I sat in cap with pen in hand, sipping on an extra thick chocolate shake made for me by Rebecca my pregnant waitress (several comments were made by her of the impending birth, yet upon a casual glance one would not think this).

I trained my hears on a table of two young men and I dropped my glance to the paper in front of me a heard a tale of theft that was being told with such exuberance I found myself staring at the hand and arm gestures of the storyteller (lets say his name is Jeb). Without skipping a beat, Jeb seg-ways into tales of massive battles, conquests and hoarding of treasures. I then realize he and his associate are speaking about RPVG's (Role Playing Video Games), however it is as though he has walked in these mysterious lands himself.

Even as I am absorbed with Jeb, I hear murmurs of conversations that don't warrant my attention, then from this quiet table of two more young men in front of me where nothing substantial has been heard I am ripped from my travels with Jeb by "I'm so Allergic to Cats Man". I am still pondering this comment less than 6 hours later. It is though my mind hits a brick wall when trying to decipher this statement. What did happen was a short conversation with regards to relatives cat. The two then finished their coffees and left. Interesting.

Rebecca was very attentive to the people in the diner, even though she and the cook were playing monopoly. Random conversations arose here as I moved closer to listen, "...the government is giving me $2100 this month because I am a single mother and I made no money last year". What was this, a hook for deeper, heart felt conversation, perhaps, but no takers.

As the time wore on I started to see a pattern arising amongst the patrons - "Surface Dwellers". Those not willing or capable of going deeper, stepping outside their comfort zone, willing not to have the "how is the weather" conversation. These are the folks that will never get the "big drink" from life. Yet in the same breath, they are happy, I can say they are content to just be. And whether or not they have an inner voice calling to them go deeper is now a mystery to me. "I'm So Allergic to Cats Man"

Can one have the "Big Drink" and be content to just be? The answer is a gem to behold I imagine.

Thanks for this.

23 Nancy Smith

Sent: Tuesday, January 17, 2006 6:46 AM
To: Corrine@WizardAcademy.com
Subject: "Inside the Outside Excursion"

Good morning,

Well, I took the challenge and now I'm back in my office – my comfort zone.

First, a few details. I'm single, female and 49 years old, so I took a female with me. I live in Columbia, SC (in the middle of the state). We were seated in the Waffle House at 4:50AM outside of town a bit in an area where I rarely travel. Maybe it's the demographics, but it was not as busy as I had hoped. However, this gave us time to concentrate on the conversations heard.

What impressed me most was the waiter. He obviously had worked at this location for a while and definitely knew "his customers". As it happened (through being attentive and maybe a bit nosy) I gathered that the "regular" waitress in this location was ill (in the hospital) and a new girl had filled in just for this shift. Even before his customers got into the restaurant, he told the waitress what they would be ordering and how they liked it. He greeted them with a warm smile and made sure they got what they needed in a timely manner.

His pride and joy was his "chopper", which he discussed in detail with two other gentlemen. Obviously, he was "remaking this baby" and was very excited about it.

Two other gentlemen were seated in a booth and carried on a little banter with the waiter. It seemed the topic of this morning was illness, as this customer's wife was ill and also hospitalized.

Upon reflection, these folks are not so different after all. What they possessed that impressed me most was kindness. Even though they were "outside my comfort zone", I saw that they tried to make each person feel good. My friend and I were not regulars; however, we were treated with the same kindness as the others.

I've made this saying my motto for some time now – "Only kindness matters in the end". This motto really came to life for me during my experience.

While thinking on this, I do remember being in a Waffle House (about 6 years ago) outside of town at 2:30AM. The conversation there was much more lively. It centered around a "big fight" between a couple that included hair pulling, scratching, and cursing. The "storyteller" for this event was quite comical. Obviously, that made an impression, as I still remember it 6 years later!

It was a unique experience. In fact, I'd like to try it again in a different location. It sure gives a "kick" for your day.

Thank you for giving the challenge. I sure enjoy those Monday Morning Memos and I've also purchased some books. Keep up the good work!

24 Andrew Francis

Sent: Wednesday, January 11, 2006 8:10 PM
To: Corrine@WizardAcademy.com
Subject: Re: Monday Morning Memo from the Wizard of Ads

You can tell a lot about a man, by the way he spits. The way he carries himself. His choice of targets. Funny how such inane habits begin. Funnier yet, how other men feel compelled to follow suit. Perhaps it is a right of passage, a way to open the communication door. Because being 'men' we can't just open up conversation with other men all that easily. Well unless it is about the damn ice and snow we just drove through or can agree about how cute the ass is on our waitress.

It's warm in here. Nice to have a break somewhere familiar. This diner looked good. But then they all look good this time of day. Warm, the smell of food and voices. I get to join in, if I want, but I run the risk of being cast an outsider.

"Would you pass the salt?", the burly guy next to me rumbles. "Sure, here ya go." You just passing through?

The vocal tones seem to relax in him, as he decides that I am probably ok. First he looks me over and makes sure I am not a 'slicker'. Them kind don't fare well here. I knew that. Looks like I passed. "You riggin'?", he asked. "Nah" I replied, in the casual yet gruff tones I heard the others using. "Just traveling through".

I saw the gold band on his finger and asked if he had any kids. "Yup, he replied." Pret-tin-near, growed up. My youngest keeps telling me that one of these days he's coming on the rig with me. Gonna drive, just like his old man." We both chuckle. A sense of community has developed between us. Partly because we can tell that the other person is not 'full of shit'. Slickers are often full of it. They can sweet talk the tail off'n a donkey and we ain't got much time for talkin' tails off'n donkeys.

I could sense that we were both quiet men, only bold and brash when we needed to send the message that our territory is sacred to us.

The conversation quieted down. Soup was too hot. Took a lot of blowin' on it.

Time came to throw my coat back on, pull my cap down tight to my ears, and head back out.

"Be, seeing ya" I said to my new friend. "Take er' easy" he replied. I knew we would probably never see each other again, but that connection would remain. It runs through the lot of us. We've shared the same toils, worried about how we were going to feed our families. Worried about the mills closing and the jobs dwindling. We've tried hard to understand our women, even if we have a funny way of showing it. And those very women know a secret...

Deep down inside every one of us boys is a teddy bear heart.
And they use it against us sometimes.
Oh yeah, and don't be spittin' in the same place another man does. Ain't how it's done.

Andrew Francis

ps: I didn't exactly follow your rules, Roy. I didn't have to go to the diner to experience those folks. I come from them.

Your weekly emails somehow always seem to be 'just at the right time for me'. I have traveled my life's path, striving for many a thing, only to come full circle, to the 'diner'. I have started reshaping my business. I opened the first contract with a company to work much like you did with your first twelve. But at a modest sum until I have my 'stuff' together. I see the same circles that exist in our diner, in many walks of life. I intend to settle into this one. And dang it, just as I came to that conclusion, your email arrived but a few weeks later about that very thing.

Interesting, as Spock would say.
I shoulda charged more.

25   Tim Kirk

Sent: Monday, January 16, 2006 11:14 PM
To: Corrine@WizardAcademy.com
Subject: Inside the Outside Experience

Dear Mr. Williams,

We have met before. I was one of four businesses that came a couple of years ago to the Academy to review our businesses while your associates watched from another room. I was the last business analyzed and thankfully it was after opening a few bottles of very nice Cabernet!

I was helping develop a piece of packaging equipment for the industry and the long and short of it is, the person I was working with, although he was a creative genius as an engineer, couldn't seem to find time to answer the phone to the many people I had interested. He still calls once in while to see if anything is happening, but alas, it's hard to sell equipment when you simply don't return calls. He hasn't figured that out!

I want to thank you for your time that day and for the autographed set of books you gave to me. I had a wonderful experience; I especially remember my conversation afterwards with Michelle discussing the day's events.

Now regarding the Inside the Outside Experience, I have to fudge a little bit on the rules, but this one experience I had simply stands out and was so much fun, I just have to tell it. It is a story I have told many times.

I am a manufacturer's rep for a bar code labeling company to industrial accounts for the past 20 years. I had a demonstration setup for two of our pieces of equipment at a meat packing plant to apply labels to cartons as they came down the production line. This location specifically made the pizza toppings for Pizza Hut and it smelled just like pizza in there, however the story I am about to tell took place the night before.

I picked up my technician who flew in from Chicago about midnight at the Wichita, Kansas airport to go to Hutchinson, Kansas. As we are leaving, I took a route I wasn't familiar with and all of a sudden we are in a maze of road construction detours. I mentioned this to him and he starts humming the theme music from the Twilight Zone. Do-do-do, do-do-do, do-do-do. He says "I can tell its going to be one of those trips".

He's a young, stringy, gangly kid, about 25 with no love life that I had never met before and as he starts to tell what he thinks about women and life I have the same Do-do-do, do-do-do, do-do-do going through my head, "Yes" I think, "It is going to one of those nights", because I am a happily married man unfamiliar with his experiences.

We finally get into Hutchinson about an hour later after wandering through several county roads that make you wonder if you're lost. We find his hotel which is way on the outskirts of town. As he checks in, he says he's hungry and needs to eat.

The clerk looks like a deer in the headlights and says there really isn't anything in Hutchinson, Kansas that time of night except maybe a convenience store, but then she remembers that downtown is a place named Crystals that the locals go to and it might be open.

We meet up with another sales rep who is a gregarious and funny Swede and we start cutting jokes about the locality on our way into town.

Now Hutchinson is a typical Midwestern, agricultural town and the dust is constantly being kicked up into your face no matter where you go. The town is composed of old brick buildings and brick streets and the traffic lights are simple composures hanging from a wire strung between two poles. We have to stop and wait forever at all four of them even though there isn't a sole elsewhere to be found which we thought was funny.

But we finally turned a corner and saw Crystals which basically looked like a Denny's on the outside. What blew our minds though at 2:00 in the morning was the parking lot was jammed.

What really blew our minds though, there weren't any cars! They were all pickup trucks and not just any pickup trucks—they were all custom duellies! All had flaming paint jobs with dingle balls decorating the perimeter of the windows. They had little toy dogs on the dash with lit up eyes and heads bobbing around. Easily half of them had a set of Longhorns mounted on the front hoods. (Congratulations by-the-way National Champs!)

You would have thought we were at a hot rod custom show. Each truck had to easily cost tens of thousands of dollars judging by the way they all had so much chrome and the undersides were lit up with neon lights even though no one was in them!

We walked inside and it was like walking into another world. Do-do-do, do-do-do, do-do-do! We each knew this was no ordinary night. One thing struck me quickly though, and that was this was an old

Sambo's breakfast house. It had the old decorations and the funny, molded seats and they were all full.

Everyone was wearing hats. Most had fancy, intricate feathers in them. Everyone had on cowboy type clothing, but not modern style, but the old, old stuff you would see Clint Eastwood wear—the long, oil coated leather down to mid-calf, boots with spurs, some had lariats hanging from their side. What in the world is going on?

We also started to notice that they were all very big and we were very small physically compared to them. However, they were all laughing and cutting up and having a good time.

Just then a big, and I mean BIG waitress came by with a cart of food. It wasn't the little Denny's Grand Slam, it was a buffet and she proceeded to load it onto a table with two huge people sitting opposite each other.

And then it happened, the hostess came up to us and flashing her gold tooth at us, smiling as big as Baltimore said "Welcome to Crystals, what can I do for you sugar babes!"

She was perhaps once of the largest women I have ever seen. I looked at my tech from Chicago and he was like Wile E. Coyote—his jaw had dropped to the floor and his eyes were bulging. I could tell he was scared to death and was wondering if he was going to make it out of there alive! Do-do-do, do-do-do, do-do-do

We asked for a table and she said she had to clean one up if we would wait a minute. In retrospect, I think she was amused that we had shown up at her place because we were ducks out of water.

It's when she turned her back to us and went over to the table to clean it, we could hardly contain ourselves because I mean she was huge! The Waffle House has tables just like this place. They are molded booths where two people can sit on each side--at least normally that is.

But as she leaned over the table from the end to clean it, we realized that her behind was so big, it completely obstructed the table and both sides of the chairs. What got us most was that she was wearing spandex—lime green spandex and she had a beehive hairdo!

I looked down the row and realized that she was one of the smaller people in the place besides us! All the booths had two people in them, one on each side and they each took up the whole side that normally seated two! Do-do-do, do-do-do, do-do-do.

Of course the Swede is now doing a caricature analysis, (as quietly as possible of course) and we just couldn't stop laughing. It was like being inside a cartoon factory.

There were beards and mustaches of every sort. ZZ Top would

have blended right in! I will never forget, one guy was all in black, with some sort of a black top hat, long black trench coat and wearing sunglasses with a beard that was about two feet long. One of my friends said—"Hey, I was wondering what had ever happened to Cousin It from the Addams Family, he's living here in Hutchinson!"

Our hostess came back to take our order and I mentioned that the tech had said he loved bacon and could eat a lot of it. She winked at him, reached over and pinched his cheek and said "I'll take care of you sugar!" Do-do-do, do-do-do, do-do-do

I think we asked for bacon, scrambled eggs, juice and toast, each breakfast on the menu was around $5.00. They brought the juice—in one liter cups.

About 15 minutes later they brought the cart. The bacon literally was on a platter the size you put a Thanksgiving turkey on. There easily had to be about 5 pounds of bacon piled about 6 inches high and I am not kidding. For toast, there were about two loaves of it, and for eggs there were about two dozen of them scrambled.

She kept coming by and asking if we needed anything more? What was wrong with our appetites? It looked like we hadn't eaten anything! Duhhh! What was most funny was she seemed to have taken a shining to our skinny tech and she kept imploring him to eat up, he was too skinny. She then said he needed to keep coming back every night so she could fatten him up! It what hilarious!

We were the only people under 350 pounds that night in the place and probably the first ones like us who had been in there in a long time. We tried to guess what is going on? "The Huge Night People of Hutchinson Kansas" that only come out at night?

The neatest thing about the whole deal was we didn't fit in but they welcomed us in. They thought it was funny. We thought it was funny. They were happy and laughing and carrying on and having a good time and so were we. We were out of place but we were accepted and I have never forgotten that and I remember that as one of the most fun times I ever had—even though I could never have imagined it.

So that's my story, I hope you enjoyed it, I enjoyed writing it for the first time ever, although I have told it many times.

And I know you mentioned a gift of initiation, but I didn't go alone, and it didn't just happen and besides you have already given me an autographed set of books which are special to me.

And also in this memo you gave me inspiration to continue with the book I am writing when you said "People tell me they want to write. I respond, "You can't find a pencil?" In truth, few want to write. Most want only to have written".

That hit me right between the eyes because I have been working on a book I call The Checklist Health Scoring Journal for a couple of years and it is a struggle to keep on writing. My main problem is actually to pare things down. But essentially I was inspired by my 14 ? year old son who took aviation ground school and on his first lesson then asked the instructor "Where's the checklist?"

Since I am interested in health issues, nutrition, aerobics, sports, etc., I thought to myself "If a youngster can go to ground school and then fly a plane (which he did very nicely his first time up), then why can't we as adults have a ground school on the fundamentals of diet and exercise and then use a daily checklist to go by?"

So I developed a 100 point daily checklist to go by and it's tough to hit 100 points. I developed the "ground school" and its subjects regarding bad vs. good habits, etc. But the main thing is, you get instant feedback that day on your progress. You know if you are on the right flight path or whether you are crashing and burning! Basically it uses the philosophy that in order to manage something you need to establish a baseline of what makes you—you today by measuring your inputs and outputs. Then using incremental improvement, you make small changes and track it to see if it works.

The target audience I think is what Michelle Miller's expertise is all about. It is baby boomer women over 40 who are most interested in their health and the ones who control the purse strings in the U.S.

A checklist system works well with women because I have certainly trained perhaps hundreds of them on complex machinery in many industrial factories here in the Midwest. I know just exactly how they want to learn. They become extremely analytical and to the point. I can guarantee when I go to do an install, the women will show up with a pad of paper and pencil in hand and they write down in detail the sequence of how to run the machine. (It is gratifying for me to step back and then watch them teach the others exactly as I taught them. Women are great learners and great teachers. When they become task-oriented, they focus and get it done!)

So that's how I teach them—with a checklist and they do a beautiful job of learning and then operating the machine. Why can't we do that with our own minds and bodies health and fitness wise? I think we can, I like to encourage people. I don't know why, but I can meet someone and almost instantaneously tell if they have big sign on their forehead that says "Encourage Me—PLEASE!" So I do!

I will finish my book, start a website and get onto Amazon and a host of other locations I have scouted out. Then I want to take Michelle's class on Wonder Branding to Women to really get the message right and promote the book. I see this as a second career because I like sales and marketing. (I have a measure of success with my current career having made our honor council numerous times including the past four years straight. They give me a nice plaque and I store it with the others in my closet!) But right now, my son mentioned earlier is well into a four year Bachelors Degree of Aviation at Southeastern University of Oklahoma in Durant and the fees and tuition are spectacular so that is eating up income but it will all be worth it!

Mr. Williams, I sincerely appreciate your time. I appreciate the wonderful Monday Morning Memo's and I have saved every one of them for the past two years and read them often for inspiration and guidance. I like the ones about people who started on a shoe string and made it. I like the ones that inspire me to write and complete my book. I liked this last one about the 0.05% holding everything together.

I especially appreciate you speaking boldly and unashamedly about Jesus Christ. When I read the 0.05% it reminded me of Colossians 1: 15-17: 15: He is the image of the invisible God, the firstborn over all creation. 16: For by Him all things were created that are in heaven and that are on earth, visible and invisible, whether thrones or dominions or principalities or powers. All things were created through Him and for Him. 17: And He is before all things, and in Him all things consist".

I take that to mean that He is the one that holds everything together. I remember a college professor saying he and science didn't know why electrons and protons and neutrons didn't just whirl off into space—they didn't know what held an atom together, but the Bible says it's Jesus who holds it all together! Wow! Just five simple words: In Him all things consist. What's so hard to understand about that?

Oh well, it's late and I am up in Kansas again with a group of women to teach in the morning on how to run the new piece of equipment I am putting in. They'll have their notebooks in hand and the guys will have their hands in their pockets waiting for me to leave so they can then try to figure it out for themselves! HA! Who needs a road map?

Thanks again and God Bless.
Tim Kirk

p.s. My wife of 30 years and I love Austin. I was an air traffic controller at Bergstrom AFB and she was a student at UT when we married in the Base Chapel in 1976 which is now under the terminal! We were just there in November 2005 to see a country western performer, Dale Watson at the Broken Spoke (that was an Inside the Outside Experience!) who recorded my Dad's song, Bright Lights and Blond Haired Women that Ernie Ford recorded way back in 1950. We had a good time. Have you tried the Catfish Parlor on Ben White just east of I35 that I told you about yet? Still the best hush puppies and tartar sauce and catfish in the world! How about La Fonda San Miguel's?

Catherine Astalos

26

Sent: Wednesday, January 18, 2006 11:58 AM
To: Corrine@WizardAcademy.com
Subject: 24-hour diner/ Travis Grill

"It costs 25 cents," answered Charlie, the homeless man, as he walked in and toward the counter, to the question of how much a bus transfer costs asked by one of the five middle-aged men sitting at the counter of the Travis Grill in St. Clair Shores, Michigan this morning.

After the brief exchange about how a guy on the bus gives him money every Friday that he uses for "beer money", Charlie went to the other end of the counter and ordered a warm cup of java to escape the snow storm that was coming down outside.

It was 4:45am and the roads were extremely slippery. My first stop at National Coney wasn't open so on to the 24 hour Tim Horton's just outside of Detroit. With only one customer at the counter I moved on to another 24 hour Coney. Not much luck there other than a police officer, two guys just getting off work and talking about electrical work that needed to be done at the house, and a man chain smoking in the booth next to me reading the paper.

I moved on attempting one more location in another section of town. Bingo! This is what I was looking for. Beverly behind the counter, one older man at the very end of the counter, an obese man a few seats down, a couple hiding in the early morning hours from their indiscretions, in the booth behind me, and the five sixty-ish men in hunting fatigue jackets.

I sat down at the counter (minimum of two to be seated at a booth), and began my journey out of "my box". I came in on the end of a conversation with the five men, all of which new each other and Beverly the waitress by name. I heard something about someone being let out of the mental hospital and jokes of who was going in next. That conversation moved into one of the men saying that he was going to do a favor for someone (couldn't hear the details), but wasn't going to do it until after midnight because he has angels that help him later in the night. Next topic: the Lotto, reminding the others that the next one wasn't until Saturday so make sure they got their tickets. It bounced from topic to topic: weather men only say "showers" not rain or snow showers so that they won't be wrong. This started a debate about a local TV meteorologist and how he does tell us which we are going to get snow or rain showers. Next, how the Jeep started as a military vehicle and the first consumer Jeep was called a CJ for "Civilian Jeep." (Being in Detroit, the topic always comes around to cars at some point). I loved the line about when I was looking for a new car back in the 90's (the last time he had bought a new car). Next topic: the nerve of the US/Canada tunnel (we live on the border of Canada which is may explain why I am one of the 12 to do this experiment) taking coins and paper bills in a machine to go over the border but not giving change. Like most men the topic moved on to the NFL Playoffs and who was going to make it to the Super Bowl (being held in Detroit next month). This segued into the conversation of how much it costs to take a bus now days.

Beverly chimed in a couple of times to let them know that Mile High Stadium was open now, only to have them look at me and say that if you ever need to know anything just ask Beverly, the hairdresser. She knows everything. This only fueled things as a few minutes later she took it upon herself to let them know it costs $1.50 to ride the bus. (I learned something).

Beverly's attention was taken away by the thin, slightly grey, bearded man (the cook). The older man at the end of the counter found reading glasses that had fallen on the floor a couple of stools from his. The cook suggested they were may be Dennis's glasses. Beverly thought not and suggested Tim's. Either way, they would keep them at the cash register until that night when surly the regular would be back to get them.

The obese man was quiet only to tell Beverly that his eyes were bigger than his belly and he couldn't finish his two eggs and hash browns. It seemed like an oxymoron. He then left for work.

To be honest, it didn't seem like any of the five men needed much. As one got up to leave they talked briefly about going fishing and how what batter they were going to use to fry them up. They have friendship, food, shelter and laughter. They seemed happy.

I left an unusually large tip for Beverly as she thanked me and told me to be careful being that the roads were so bad. I was back in "my box" by 6:15am (I know I was supposed to leave at 5:30am but conversation was too good to leave). What a morning!

Daniel Granger

27

Sent: Friday, January 13, 2006 9:15 PM
To: Corrine@WizardAcademy.com
Subject: Details of my excursion

No need for a clock. April's Hazel eyes signify that it's precisely 4:37am. I'm about 6 miles East of my comfort zone. I hide my family in Valencia, California. Pleasantville, as far as you're concerned.

I'm not in Valencia this morning. I'm exactly two city blocks from an estate riddled with dwellings designed for transit. I'm baffled by the contradiction of a home that moves. Because I live in Valencia, where compassion oozes from every pour.

The name of this town is Canyon Country. Aptly named. It might as well be another country. From Valencia, we can look down into the Canyon and see a people marooned between steep walls and know that they will never climb up to our level.

April slaps my Chicken Fried Steak and eggs down on the counter in front of me. Still doing her best impression of a stone. She follows protocol and offers me Tabasco with my meal. But I never take Tabasco before 4:45. In the far left corner are a group of twenty somethings in sleeveless t-shirts. Their aura invites me to a beating if I stare too long. Their conversation is smuggled just beneath an earshot. A local trade magazine invites me from the vacant seat to my left. Santa Clarita Motor Sports informs me that "It's Play Time." This is to serve as ample cause for purchasing a $6,000 Four-Wheeler. I feign an interest. The only other person to focus on is Earl in the far right corner. Clearly a regular, Earl's passions lie in collecting pins to garnish his fishing cap. He's enthralled with his morning paper and keeps his eyes between it and his ice tea.

If there were a dog around, he'd be eating my breakfast. Apparently, April thought I requested my glass of water in the chicken, not and it. I continue to nibble so as not to blow my cover. 5:00. No new patrons. What the hell kind of assignment is this? I become a student of April. She coasts from station to station. Slow. Miserable. Thick glasses and a hair style as exciting as lettuce. Her features and figure beg that you ignore her existence. Attention starved. Must have never had a father to affirm her femininity. Her womanhood left to wilt and die. Solitary. Stuck in this diner. Stuck in this town. Between Hell and mediocrity. I could teach a class on April.

Enter Peter. Twenty-three. He takes his seat beside me, and immediately rekindles a rapport with April. As it turns out, April has a story. Our solitary heroine has a seven-year old daughter and a husband at home. He was recently laid off and is scraping by as a tutor. She works the late shift in order to continue her daytime education. An undergrad at C-SUN College. She has applied for her graduate degree at Stanford and Berkeley. Her field is "Psychiatry" and she has recently scored a "540 on her SAT." I'm not sure this pencil's out, but I continue to listen. Her desire is to council children. So she proceeds with Peter.

Peter has just arrived from work. His new job in the pharmaceutical industry demands that he work in the refrigerator section of a warehouse, loading boxes of product into a truck until dawn. He works for the second largest supplier between Bakersfield and San Diego. But he's not in it for the prestige. It's the medical benefits he's after. A Pacific Islander, but native of Virginia, he came out to Canyon Country to keep himself out of trouble. Today there are two things that make Peter tick: Medical insurance and the chicks. He shares his woes of being in a new town, wanting to meet new people but is prevented by his job, which requires him from 6pm till sunrise. This significantly reduces his ability to prospect for the chicks. He is condemned to run his game by sunlight. Were it not for his manipulative bosses, he'd be free. They have suckered him into working again on Saturday.

A counseling session ensues. It is here that April emerges in all her splendor. She shares the virtues of using boundaries in relationships, even with your boss. She applies the Narrative Paradigm, telling him the story of a friend who escaped the grip of an oppressive boss. Peter acknowledges her wisdom and his session is nearly over. What can I do for Peter? He's already got the health insurance. Should I consult him on methods for filling his funnel with the chicks and improving his closing ratio? Not sure that would help him long term. It is said that almost everyone who wins the lottery inevitably returns to their original financial state within ten years. Such it is with Peter. I feel no other calling in the matter. Peter pays his bill, peaces out, and exits my world forever.

It is here that I realize what they have that I don't: Simplicity. Best illustrated by Peter, what if my motivation was as simple as health insurance and chicks? Not literally. But there must be a peace in keeping life so simple. I live a strangled life. My ambition is the millstone I wear as a necklace. Perhaps I can excuse my ambition as a means to helping the people of Canyon Country. This inverted cast of

Cheers. Perhaps they could benefit on a more corporate scale. Perhaps the answer lies in my study of advertising. Just keep serving my clients, one at a time, as they grow by multiples. I'm gaining on my goal of becoming the first local sales rep to make a million dollars a year selling radio. If I can make ads work, then I can consult businesses, churches, non-profits on how to advance toward their goals. If I can revolutionize institutions, then people will change and be helped. It's all about the big picture. Or is it? Perhaps it's about loving individuals. One at a time.

Back to April. What does she need most and how could I get it? Is it Jesus, money, a kind word? I don't know April. And I don't know exactly what she needs. I know she's working all night to support her family and her ambitions. I'll leave April a $250 tip and before my trip back to Valencia, where I belong.

My wife and I scheduled a mission trip to Africa four years ago. The man co-coordinating the trip told me plainly, "You don't go to save Africa. You go for Africa to save you." I never made it to Africa. But I did make it to Canyon Country. I lingered a moment to ensure that April accepted her tip. April offered a mild thank you, but didn't act like I saved her soul when she saw the $250. It didn't change her life. I don't know how much it even helped her. Perhaps she thought me a 26-year-old creep who's trying to find a date at 4am. But I learned that I can't really help April. All I can do is listen. And when asked, perhaps give an answer for any hope I have in me. Any other attempt to change a person leaves you with an unimpressed stare from the Hazel eyes of an exhausted waitress named April.

28 Bart O'Shea

Sent: Monday, January 16, 2006 6:06 PM
To: corrine@wizardacademy.com
Subject: Assignment/A response.

I did not do the assignment as specified because I have done it hundreds if not thousands of times. My fulltime employment is as a police officer in Madison, WI, population 205,000. I have been an officer for 15 and ? years. I read your site and receive your memo due to my part-time job as a massage therapist. My wife and I had tried to start an on-site chair massage company but that failed. During that time I had read your books and then was invited to attend a Wizards presentation by a radio station salesperson and so became very enamored of your work.

The first thing that comes to people's minds when I mention working in Madison is the college kids, Madison being home to the University of Wisconsin, the hardest drinking university in the country. That is actually a very small part of policing Madison. Madison's proximity to Chicago creates a large lower income population that moves to Madison to escape the violence of Chicago, occasionally bringing it with them instead.

I worked midnights for the first 8 years of my career on the southside of Madison, which is home to a large segment of our low income population. I am now back working a swing shift from 8p to 4a. We often went for breakfast in the early morning hours, after the barfights. We exclusively went to small diners, The Curve, in particular. Police officers often go to small diners because you get to know the cooks and you can often see them cooking. Most people don't think of this, but cops do. Large chain restaurants often hire work-release prisoners as cooks and I would not trust those people to prepare food for a cop in uniform.

This assignment that you have asked people to undertake is problematic for the following reasons:

The assignment is extraordinarily elitist and appears to be blithely ignorant of this fact. I initially thought the premise was tongue in cheek but then realized that you were serious. The underlying assumptions that your readers are on the right side of the tracks or had not created their own success and had not "risen" from the wrong side of the tracks. You neglected to post the warning to not tap on the glass or feed the outsiders.

You are apparently an insider. What are you inside of and what is the barrier composed of? One of the more original thinkers currently being published, Eckhart Tolle, spent several years wandering penniless, as an outsider, in what he describes as a continual state of joy.

The timing of the assignment is off. 1:30 am is too early and the observer may well run into the bar crowd, which is not representative of the downtrodden species we are looking to observe.

Instruction #2. A whole other world exists right next to all of us all the time. Your neighbor lives in an entirely different world than you. What is a tragicomedy in the making is the American middle and upper class. Current estimates are that 60% of the US population is two paychecks away from bankruptcy. The people living in suburban upper class bliss, and reading your articles, are part of that group, as they wave happily to each other in their new SUVs and then lie awake at night terrified because they know that at some point the house of cards must tumble down.

Instruction #3. There is no rich sense of community among the outcast. You, as the benevolent, sympathetic observer, perceive in the banter a tie that does not exist, or if it does, is as wispy as the cobwebs you may brush aside. This perception points out how important the viewer's own perspective is to interpreting that which is observable. I would be willing to bet a paycheck that most of the people do not know each other's last name, phone number and have never seen each other outside of the diner other than by happenstance. I was a bartender for 5-6 years prior to police work and I worked in a small shot and a beer place as well as huge nightclubs. The regulars at a bar, regardless of size, are similar to the diner crowd. The banter is usually self-deprecating humor and light jabs at each other. The jabs are light so as not to tear the delicate threads that bind them in that particular space for that particular time. The relationship is both peculiar and particular. I have found, both in the bars and the diners, that the conversation is mainly the voicing of complaints. Both groups mainly look ahead, at their meal or their drink, because they are actually not interested in what another has to say but are simply waiting their turn to voice their complaint. This is not specific to income level as I have observed this in high income bars as well. Prayer, being an oft repeated, persistent statement of belief would point to the fact that the more these people, and all people, complain, the more they have to complain about.

Interesting point about smell. Smell and bad teeth are the quickest way to identify people who are "outsiders". The lower income the apartment building you are going into the worse the smell. Low-income, high density buildings smell like hot grease, dirt and bodies, living but unwashed. Crackhouses smell overwhelmingly of the powerful ammonia smell of urine. On a more pleasant note, one of my favorite things is to go into an older elementary school because it just smells of innocence and children, the old woodwork seems to hold in the smell of youth and cookies.

If eating in a diner, where basically no crime ever occurs, on the "wrong side" of the tracks is actually discomforting, then people should really examine how insulated their lives are.

The assignment reminded me of Gary Sinise's phone call to Mel Gibson in the movie Ransom about the Morlocks.

Cathy Mosier

29

Sent: Monday, January 16, 2006 6:41 PM
To: Corrine@WizardAcademy.com
Subject: a kitchen

    There is a place in Washington DC called Joshua's Kitchen... it is operated by a chef named Paul... yep Paul is a certified chef and yet he chooses not to work in an upscale DC restaurant but rather in the basement of a church with a continual crew of volunteers... he patiently teaches the willing hands how to make a "rue" essential to cheesy grits... on a daily basis he feeds over 200 souls at each of 3 meals the kitchen provides... Paul had recently been to Jamaica with his son and had enjoyed their time together... he said the reason he was working in the kitchen rather than a restaurant was because he had been there and done that and the only thing he had earned besides a wage was a divorce... working in the kitchen he was able to mentor men and women who would not have been given a second glance on the street. Paul said he wants his son to know that he made a difference in the lives of others. He wants him to remember that not the money. These same men and women were sleeping in the alley behind the church because the heating vented there. Emanuel a 20 something youth from England was also working in the kitchen. He said in Europe there are no places like this to help those less fortunate. Emanuel was staying at a youth hostel where he shared the floor with roaches but the lady upstairs was nice enough to let him sleep on the couch. An older women named Alice was working in the kitchen. Alice is 72 years old and worked circles around me. She is a daily volunteer in the kitchen. She can't quite make it on Social Security so she works in the kitchen for food. Social Security takes care of everything else. Alice would like to have a paying job. She has tried to get a job only to be told that she is to old, to frail (NOT), or ... you know the drill. Alice is fiercely independent, and yet others are not. We served on woman named Doris who had recently moved to DC from South Carolina because the social services were so much better. Doris is hoping to get her brother to move here too. He suffers from bipolar disorder as does Doris and she feels he would be able to function better in DC. Doris certainly seems to be doing well. She explained to me her daily routine. She said Joshua's Kitchen was the best place to eat in all of the city. Unfortunately, after signing in for meals for a week she had to find another place to eat. But after a week away she could once again come to the kitchen. Doris said the women's shelter was OK for lunch but breakfast wasn't so good. The church's food pantry was an added bonus, since she couldn't walk far having fallen and sprained her ankle last week. Carl sat and showed me card tricks never once speaking. Another man said Carl hadn't taken his medicine in weeks. Carl had told him he didn't like the way he felt when he took them. So Carl comes to the kitchen for food and silent fellowship.

This is a real experience... unfortunately, it was during the summer when my husband was not traveling in Asia so he could stay with our children. And yet I am still struck by your questions... because I think what people are searching for is someone to listen... just listen... not comment... not try to fix things... not suggest what or where they should go. Just listen... with both ears wide open and mouth firmly shut. Listen while looking on the person. Giving them your undivided attention. Allowing them to own a piece of you through your listening. And it's not just the outcasts who want to be listened to.

I teach all day kindergarten at a day care. I have a masters in early childhood education. I am to expensive for the public schools in my area. They would rather have someone fresh out of college for less money. I have taught kindergarten in the public schools before my children were born. Then we chose to reduce our spending so I could stay home with them. I have been working in this all day setting for 5 years. And I am having the time of my life. But there are outcasts here too. Parents who would rather someone else discipline their children. Care for them when they are ill. Teach them manners, along with math and reading. These parents don't know what to do with little 5 year olds. They surely don't listen to them. Otherwise they would not let them sleep in the same room with their 13 year old step brother. Then the parent wonders why the child won't stay in her bed... What will happen to this little girl? She tells me she is afraid... that her brother talks to her... that she can't sleep.

So I do what I can... I listen when people talk... I listen with not only my ears but my heart as well... I support my church's Adult Survivors of Childhood Abuse classes... I make the trip to DC to work in homeless shelters and kitchens. I teach my children people have worth and should be respected and valued. I teach other people's children the same thing. I hope I am teaching them that they are respected and valued as well.

Joanna Hannigan   30

Sent: Tuesday, January 10, 2006 2:45 PM
To: Corrine@WizardAcademy.com
Subject: 3 AM between cultural doorways

Dear Roy Williams:

There's a busy, bustling truck stop between Charlottesville, VA and my plantation in central NC, which I've blown past many times traveling between my Washington DC studio and the real place I call home in NC. Last weekend, I was in need of food and hot coffee at 3:20 am. The many towns I passed through were locked up tighter than an old maid's hope chest , so I slowed down, went inside this always busy eatery and ordered a scaled down version of a trucker's breakfast. It was enormous, especially compared to what was on the plates of folks seated to my right and left. Though they were bundled in layers of clothing, these didn't seem like plump or well groomed people. The light above the counter was bright and harsh, revealing ragged nails, tiny cigarette burns in clothes, and hair that had perhaps had never been professionally colored or styled. They slurped coffee, crushed between their teeth ice from their water glass, and devoured solitary pieces of toast, donuts or sausage biscuits. Not a crumb was wasted. A few folks paid, not by whipping out credit cards, but by grabbing change from pants pockets or peeling a few dollars from worn wallets. In my slowed down mode, I watched them come and go while I poked at my food, and sipped my surprisingly good coffee. The man seated to my right asked for a coffee refill.

I easedropped on animated conversations between two old women, between a older man and his grandson, between a man dressed in stained overalls and the waitress. They all seemed happy to be awake at 3 am, though a few complained they didn't have enough money for a desired pack of cigarettes or gum, and that filling up their tank left them with just enough money remaining to buy a toothpick. Not a single person whipped out a cell phone or bragged about their car, house or life style. I wished there was a way I could offer them my basket of toast, slab of ham, or triple size portion of home fries. I pushed my food away and asked the waitress if she had a pet who might like the scraps I couldn't eat. She raised her heavily penciled eyebrows. The man to my left introduced himself as "Bowser, a well trained mut" and promptly dug into the leftovers on my plate, which he demolished in a flash. Before swiveling off his stool, he stuck the slice of ham between two pieces of toast, thanked me sincerely and headed out the door to his slightly dented pick up truck. He handed the ham sandwich to someone in the truck. I smiled, paid my bill and left the waitress a generous tip.

My very thought as I left the truck stop was "what do folks like these need most, and even though I'm philosophical, rather than religious, do I really help them via contributions to charities and volunteer activities, or am I just another clueless blind person?" I still haven't answered my question, however, I've promised myself that in 06 I look more and listen, slow down, frequent more down to earth businesses, and remember that one can be happy at 3 am if lucky enough to find a clean, well lit place, and share a meal--or one of life's many bounties.

I have all your books Mr. Williams and hope to attend the Wizard Academy in TX in 2006. My favorite book is Accidental Magic.

Mary Lou Davis

31

Sent: Monday, January 16, 2006 11:12 PM
To: corrine@WizardAcademy.com
Subject: eavesdropping

I must tell you how much I enjoy the Monday morning memo. Sometimes I do not get to read this right away on monday morning but then times like this evening when I feel a bit down, I read the memo and I am re-charged!!

Now with regards to the eaves dropping challenge. I live in a small town of 13,000 people. There are no seedy areas of town or any late night truck stops. There is no part of this town that I am afraid to go so I will tell you what I did do. On New Years day, (I eaves drop whenever I get the chance never knowing the other party) I went to a local coffee bar with the newspaper by myself. Sitting to the side a little I began to sip my latte while perusing the paper. From this vantage point I could clearly hear the conversation of a couple of middle aged male patrons(ok, older than middle age). I was quite amazed to hear them discussing their need for annual medical checkups, encouraging each other to get hearts and prostates checked. They also discussed the demise of one of their son's marriages and how they are so lucky to still be married today as they admitted to not be great husbands in their younger days. One talked about golf games after work, joining buddies at the pub and just not getting home for the dinner hour all the time. It was very interesting for me to hear that men do realize this was not right, that it took a lot of patience for their marriage to survive and that partners in marriage means something very different today than it did 30+ years ago.

Just so you know, I am 46 and divorced. I did not have the patience of these men's wives and for a moment I wondered how things might have been different, for me or for them if each of us had lived through the others time period.

The experience certainly made me think and reflect which is my favourite thing to do on New Years Day. I often go to dinner or a movie alone and always try to steal a few minutes observing and innocently eaves dropping on total strangers. I don't want to know the peoples names, I just want to know about people.

Thanks for sharing that this can add value to ones perspective.

32
Ken Wentz

Sent: Monday, January 23, 2006 12:49 PM
To: Corrine@wizardacademy.com
Subject: A Night at Bingo

Good conversation is not limited to the matronly waitress at the diner on the outskirts of town. Try a night on the floor of your city's largest Bingo hall.

So how does any post baby boomer Art Director get himself into the inner sanctum of Bingo. Have a child who plays in his schools jazz band. Do that and Lord knows you'll be signed up for all sorts of things you would never otherwise entertain in ones lifetime.

If you've ever worked a Bingo as a volunteer you know the drill. Arrive at an otherwise unassuming great hall, decorated like some bad version of Circus Circus, find your floor supervisor and sign in. Your name is already beside some task that has no real definition of what you'll be doing but you know you'll get an explanation later. All the while you keep thinking that your child really is the next Chet Baker and you can do this. Thoughts of Vimey Ridge and securing some beach in some other era seem down right parallel. Of course your guilt over that thought takes over because it is just a Bingo, and you will survive. Survive the dark cloud of smoke from the over 500 patrons, all who have never seen a TRUTH campaign and think Jarrod should eat more, cause "he just doesn't look healthy".

I was Radio 1, cool...I got a walkie talky. My wife, oh yeah she was another unwillingly participant in this social experiment, was a Prize Runner.

Simply put, I got to run over to the Bingo winner and confirm the ticket to the Bingo caller. Who by the way is the unofficial head cheese of any Bingo hall. He has the ability to make any volunteers short life a living hell or prop you up to a senior lieutenant in his temporary army.

Tim; jeans, tee-shirt, dark thick unnaturally black hair coiffed in the Bingo mullet. Chain smoker, but I assumed that was a prerequisite for any Bingo caller, with a dark sultry voice that had enough authority to it to make you stop and listen intently to his every letter. And as a Radio, I listened intently.

But it's the patrons that can make this evening pass more quickly. Let's get the physical descriptions out of the way. 99% of Bingo patrons are overweight, and over half of those are obesely so. Big deal so is my

Mother, actually most of the woman looked like some version of my Mother. Gray hair, sweat suits of some mix or match fashion with a graphic screen print on the chest. A chest that heaved every so often in a loud smokers hack. But boy were they sweet. Gentle to a fault and with a smile that melts every grandsons troubles away. I'm sure that they all have a secret hoard of cookies and candy that is hidden around there home waiting to cure some grandchild's blues. Some even had those grandkids pictures set like shrines next to their troll dolls and Bingo splotchers. Funny little combinations like that adorned every table. I got to talk to hundreds of people who would never cross my pass except hidden as some unseen demographic in my next ad.

My wife says I enjoyed myself too much that night. She was right. I loved talking to that mix of folks. That night I wasn't an Art Director with my Starbuck coffee and Mac. I was Radio 1, first lieutenant of Jim.

33 Michael Jones

Sent: Tuesday, January 17, 2006 3:41 PM
To: Corrine@WizardAcademy.com
Subject: 4:45 this morning at TTT Truck Stop

This comes too late in the day to qualify for the Wizard's offer, but it was important to me to let you know that I took him up on the challenge, and I'm not Canadian.

At quarter to five this morning, I was sitting in a corner booth at the Triple T Truck Stop in Tucson, AZ.

In a room which would seat over 100, there were three people sitting at a U-shaped counter. Their conversation was so comfortable that I knew they must be regulars. In the corner, the cashier nodded off.

Within 15 minutes, the place was bustling with activity as truckers pulled off the road for a morning break. The conversation near me centered on the government conspiracy (we're big on conspiracy theory here near the border) to ban cellphones in vehicles and in the workplace. The main contributor to this line of thought looked like a monk lifted out of the middle ages. Only the clothing was out of character.

Talk moved from cellphones to weather. Then to snakes. "Will cats kill snakes?" "Yep. So will roadrunners. Seen it done." Another participant: "Wish cats would kill damn raccoons. Can't keep 'em out of my barn. The first speaker was insistent on keeping to the subject of snakes: "I'm scared of snakes. I look down before I step. Spiders don't bother me, just snakes. Big ol' hairy spiders hanging on the ceiling--I just get the shop vac out. Sucks 'em right off the ceiling!" The monk opined that hogs will kill snakes. The mention of hogs moved the subject off of snakes and on to home-butchered vs. store-bought meat. Then to vegetarians, and the foolishness of same. While this conversation was going on, individuals in military uniform came, ate and left in silence. They might as well not have been there as far as the monk and his friends were concerned. The conversation migrated to other foolishness--in particular politicians. One man hated the thought that California was legislating against smoking in public. He met his match across the counter: "The thing is, there is no choice. And if that galls you, get up off your ass and get a pro-smoking candidate to run. This is America. It's all about self-interest. Cigarettes are the most heavily taxed item in the country. If you don't like it, find yourself a candidate that thinks like you do."

This was a great exercize. My wife thought I was crazy. Maybe I am.
Thanks for the MMM!

Carlin Comm

34

Sent: Tuesday, January 10, 2006 9:44 PM
To: Corrine@WizardAcademy.com
Subject: A Meal with the outcast

While this may not qualify under the terms of your offer, I can say that I recently did something very similar, and I totally agree with your points in the recent Wizard email.

I spent 40 days away from home, making an independent video documentary, Survivors Stories, featuring the survivors of Hurricane Katrina (and a couple of Rita, for good measure). I literally left home when I had "almost enough gas money to get there". I got to sleep in the back of my van, a pretty small Chevy Astro with no windows in the back. I FELT outcast at times! I froze going across the northern States, then lost a lot of sweat once I turned south. No Air Conditioning! I can honestly say that I fit in pretty well with the survivors. Most of them took me pretty seriously, as opposed to some Media type who flew in for the story and was then going to leave. I stayed a few days at a Catholic Charity shelter in Memphis, and slept on a strangers couch for about a week while waiting for enough money for the return trip. But I did eat plenty of meals with people I may not have otherwise spent time with, and I learned, again, to appreciate things like a good bed and a shower.

I'm not overly social type, I prefer to spend time alone most days, but learned to get outside my self in a lot of ways on the trip. I'd walk up to strangers, like at the Red Cross, and ask if they'd like to share some stories.

I'm now well into editing the footage, and will be soon looking for ways to distribute the final program. If you'd be interested, I could use the help! Publicity is always welcome, as well as contacts in a world I know nothing about (yet!).

Ideally, (gee, I'm writing a book here, go figure) I'm hoping I can get national exposure for the documentary. I'm not so much interested in fame, exactly, but I could put a big jump in income to good use! I learned some lessons from this project, and I'd like to leverage the experience and income into a bigger, longer term project. I'd like to be able to do mobile video production full time, live in a bus, gypsy mode, full time. I'm very excited about doing something along those shows where the guy shows up at a different small town every week, and just finds interesting people to talk to, etc. I even have the fiancé thinking its not so crazy anymore! I would like to be able to do a follow up with the people I talked to, and would really enjoy being able to help them out (proceeds from the video, etc).

Now for some other interesting tidbits, as per your email, yes, as it would turn out, I am Canadian! Ha, just had to laugh when you mentioned that. I served in the US Navy for 9 years, Desert Storm vet, but I'm still a "resident alien", green card, etc. Even before reading your prediction about "those Canadians", I was drawn to the project, and may still go find a diner that fits the description. Its a small town here, so not sure if any exactly fit what you mean. I do know what you were describing. There is a Mexican taco truck parked by a pawn shop that looks like it attracts some outcast types, though. If not, I think between the shelter and the truck stops, I'd be pretty close.

Anyway, thank you for your emails. I look forward to Mondays, and save them all in a folder in my email reader. I'm learning a lot! I've got some of your books / CDs, liked the Beagle series. (Just moved, they're in a box, so I can't remember the exact title, sorry!). Keep up the awesome work, hope to make it down to check out the Campus there. I was tempted to detour on the way home this year, but knew gas money was questionable, so stuck to the shortest route.

Hundley Batts

35

Sent: Monday, January 09, 2006 6:47 AM
To: Corrine@WizardAcademy.com
Subject: Excursion into "another world"

This is a practice of mine. I grew up in a housing project in Huntsville, AL. started in Radio by purchasing an AM station on the trailing edge of FM domination in 1987. Now owning five radio properties 3 Ames and 2 FM's with only one licensed for the metro and using a lot of your philosophy and ideas to compete in this market place. I eat most mornings at an all nighter and not only listen but talk to the patrons as they discuss their desires, emotions, failures and wishes.

It's interesting how they become quickly your friend and advocate because "you" of all people will stop and talk, eat and even wave at them in public and chat with them in other settings where they are working as janitors or waiters or porters or clerks or other so-called menial labor positions. They will tell you that other people of your statue want even look at you let alone SPEAK!!

The other interesting thing is to go back to the project and visit people who are there and hold a front porch discussion with them and their neighbors. Surprising things can come out of these kinds of settings that allows you to have perspective beyond your on imagination. These kinds of experiences will develop in you a healthy "uncommon sense" perspective on life and the pursuit of happiness. it has been proven that wealth nor poverty can keep people from depression, success or failures.

I have been practicing what you preach!!!

36 Brian Schmitt

Sent: Wednesday, January 18, 2006 7:41 AM
To: Corrine@WizardAcademy.com
Subject: Eating at Alli's

    Typical of myself, I arrived at 5:28am. Looking for the most strategic place to sit. Close, but not too close. Not from fear of being too close, but for fear of having to be involved, or even worse- committed. Three Carharts sat at the bar, so I chose the closest booth. The waitress, clearly wishing she had one less new customer, strolled over with water and utensils. "Coffee and water, please." The special was ham and eggs. Making it easy I agreed.

    Funny, the things that get "remodeled" in places like this. The furniture was as old as me, but the lights hanging over the bar looked like they belonged in a wireless, mocha colored café. Local news was on the TV perched above the coffee maker, no Fox or CNN here. This place used be one of my Granddad's favorites. Back then it was the Seven Gables truck stop. Now it's Alli's. And the only reason a truck stops is to park in the huge back parking lot for short rest. Wonder if they eat here or drive on into town for a chain. I drove to the extreme opposite side of town from where I live. Not because of the compass' arrow. It just happened to be the best place to try to get out of my zone.

    What a spread. Half a plate of ham, eggs, toast, and a mountain ridge of hashbrowns. And, a smile. Which grew when it was returned. Most of the conversation was being fed up with politicians, fed up with the weather, fed up with large corporations, and looking forward to 4pm. They never mentioned family, but they spoke of their neighbors with kindness. An elderly woman entered and they greeted and sparked conversation with her like she was an old friend. A mutual friend had cleaned up her yard and they poked a little fun at the absent acquaintance.

    She stopped this time, on her way by and apologized for letting my coffee get low. She was swiftly back with a fresh pot and graceful pouring.

    As I listened and ate I tried to perceive what these people needed. Aside from getting their basic needs met, they were barely making it financially. Which didn't seam to be a problem for them. Perhaps being a part of something that would make difference in the world they were so dissatisfied with would be the answer. Or, maybe they do need help financially, but just haven't talked about it. Or I haven't perceived it. I think the biggest difference I could make would be to keep coming here, probably around 5:15 in the morning, and begin to make friends. Possibly more than anything they would just like genuine friends. Someone not wanting something from them. Of course, this could all be blabbering from a guy who sat in booth for an hour and ate breakfast.

I do hope the waitress has a good day. I hope that whatever binds her will be loosed.

37

Daryl Eldridge
as submitted by Brian Schmitt

Sent: Wednesday, January 18, 2006 2:53 PM
To: Corrine@WizardAcademy.com
Subject: Another Adventurer's story

Ok, so now I'm writing you because my friend, mentor, and boss, also took the challenge. But, he didn't write you about it. I am going to tell you, so you know there are those of us who live differently, with purpose and passion, because we couldn't live otherwise.

Daryl went to a Waffle House in the wee hours of the morning last week. He felt it was very difficult to complete the objective. It wasn't the part about getting out of his comfort zone (Daryl is almost a stranger to comfort zones anyways.) He found it difficult because people are so disconnected when they are face to face with strangers. An all night eatery next to a busy highway is mostly composed of strangers. I don't know much about his adventure beyond this, because the conversation turned.

Daryl took this idea and used it again, only this time in a casual restaurant on this side of town. He observed a family of four who ate the entire meal and only spoke a handful of words to each other. Mostly eating in saddening silence. Again, I can't give much more to this story. I wasn't there and haven't heard most of it myself.

I would like make a deeper challenge. Go to a local youth center. A free one, that lets whomever walk in and only requires that they be a kid. Kids see right through any pretenses, and they yell "BS!" when they see it. Want to be out of your comfort zone? Go by yourself and just play with the kids.

Rhonda Mills   38

Sent: Monday, January 09, 2006 9:46 AM
To: Corrine@WizardAcademy.com
Subject: A response to today's Monday Morning Memo

    I am responding to this week's Monday Morning Memo challenging us to experience "new cultures" across town or within our own society, and write to you about them.
    Just a little over a week ago on New Year's Eve, my husband and I were traveling through Fort Stockton, TX, with our three kids, plus, one son-in-law and one son-in-law-to-be. We had just spent the past week immersing the children in one of our favorites places on the planet, Terlingua and Big Bend, Texas. Our purpose was to expose them to one of America's true last wilderness frontiers, along with the area's outlawish inhabitants: the kind of folks who will never be dragged into modern development---there's still not a stoplight in the region--- without some hefty kicking and screaming along the way.
    During the vacation our kids were successfully exposed to everything we'd hoped and more, but we mistakenly thought the culture experience had ended when, at the end of our vacation, we left Study Butte for the Odessa airport, four hours away.
    It reoccurred at the Cheyenne Springs Truck Stop & Restaurant in the non-descript town of Fort Stockton.
    Upon entering the restaurant, our first clue that we were in uncertain territory came when we asked to be seated in the non-smoking section. "Well, hon, ALL of our tables are smoking," shared the hostess, rather matter-of-factly.
    And, yes, it did seem that she had not understated the situation. The place was busy, and every table seemed to have a curl of gray haze cheerfully hovering over it. But, having been on the road for several hours and faced with the issue of hungry children (not to mention the prospect of a marginally memorable food experience at the Odessa airport), we decided to inhale our share of second-hand smoke and stick it out.
    And, interestingly enough, I'm glad we did.
    In that one-hour at the truck stop, our kids saw a slice of Americana stripped of its pretention or general concern about what others might think. We found ourselves surrounded by real people, the kind who don't find it necessary to clean up to go to town. People who work with

dusty, onery cattle at all hours of the day and night. People who were wearing as much grease and oil as the oilfield equipment they'd been working on that morning. Waitresses. Truck drivers. Native Americans. Hispanics. Old, weathered men with tough-looking hands. All who, I'll venture to say, probably never lost a night's sleep over whether or not they'd ever have a corner office with a view. These were people dressed for who they were and what they did, and their conversations revolved around subjects drawn from everyday honest living, from cattle prices and truck problems to one man's apparently passionate friendship with a dog named Buddy.

Most of these folks seemed to know one another, whereas we might as well have been from Uranus. We glaringly didn't fit in, a feeling which none of us are used to. We all felt uncomfortably conspicuous, over-dressed, and somewhat guilty about jetting around in airplanes, taking nice vacations, and having a rental van with a DVD player. None of these people would have been impressed, that seemed for sure.

So, we rather sheepishly hunkered down around the safety of our table, suddenly finding a profound interest in the water glasses, the salt-and-pepper shakers, or the particular lack of bend in a fork's tines. We just sat there quietly chewing our Brave or Squaw cheeseburgers (seeing as how no one in our party had had the confidence to tackle the magnificent Chief Sitting Bull burger---a gastronomic engagement we figured was better left to professionals). Our ears, however, continued to swivel around, picking up bits and pieces of conversations, while our peripheral vision wondered at the proud displays of velvet cowboy-and-Indian paintings hanging on the walls. We knew we were in the presence of authenticity, and it pretty much clammed up the usually gregarious, hey-look-at-us! Mills' family.

We exited the Cheyenne Springs Truck Stop having been indelibly impressed or disquieted by "something." A "something" so memorable that a week later, it continues to occasionally weave its way in and out of our conversations. Granted, some of the things we experienced at the truck stop were comical. For example, Cheyenne Springs may be the only place in America where you can still walk in and buy the 1993 Sports Illustrated Swimsuit video, and for only three bucks. But, mostly what we experienced at Cheyenne Springs was a good-sized dose of humbleness.

Our family makes an honest living, and we strive to do good unto others. We don't wear Prada shoes or use Waterford crystal. But, we do sometimes get caught up in where to go next, what airplane to buy, what show horse to train, etc., while other people are finding abundant satisfaction in things like a dog named Buddy. So, in answer to the question: what could we have given the people at Cheyenne Springs? I'm not sure much. But, they certainly left us with something---a reminder that life can be good and content and rewarding at a far less complex level.

And, as for the presence of "nearby" cultural experieces, Mr. Williams is right: you don't have to travel to Patagonia or Fiji or the far ends of the earth in order to be amazed. Or influenced. Or humbled. America offers plenty of those opportunities; you just have to make yourself available to them.

By the way, I am a new Monday Morning Memo subscriber. Our friends the Heningtons at Far Flung Outdoor Center in Big Bend told us about you.

39 Marta Rode

Sent: Monday, January 09, 2006 12:54 PM
To: Corrine@WizardAcademy.com
Subject: Monday Morning Memo Inside the Outside Challenge

First time responder but absolutely loyal reader of the Monday Morning Memos.

My name is Marta and I live in a town (of 4,500 people) with no 24 hour eating establishment. It is a unique situation however, because the town is a tourist destination with a couple of other industries (it was established as a railroad town in the early 1900's, and also is within a National Park in Canada, so it has a strong federal employee component) which makes for quite different worlds in a very small confined area. It's a unique and beautiful town located in the heart of the Canadian Rockies – Jasper.

I have a small graphic design company (which I've been neglecting for the last couple of years while on an acting assignment for the feds – doing their electronic media/ graphic design stuff). So all in all, I fall under the 'computer geek' category in the last decade or so of my life.

I have however just in the last week decided to a little of the crawling that you suggest in this weeks Memo. Not in the exact way that you suggest, but I've improvised my own technique. I'm a nearly 40 year old woman and have decided to take a boo into someone else's reality to see where exactly it leads me, so I went and put my first full 10 hour day as a carpenter apprentice/ grunt labourer this last weekend. It's wonderful peering into a completely different world view. These people are different than the ones that you describe in that they do own credit cards, and cell phones, but no email, and a completely different perspective point than the one that I'm used to peering from. When you talk about crawling on your hands and knees, getting on your belly and squirming under the fence, it resonates, because I did that this weekend – literally, and fully enjoyed the experience.

I have been fortunate in my life because I've had this sort of experience – diving into a new world view – thrust upon me several times in my life, and I love the challenge. My folks ran away from Bulgaria when I was 10 years old, and we were caught and thrown in jail at the Yugo/Austrian border, then spent time in an immigrants camp in Austria, followed by an initiation by fire in Canada (where I was the only one in the family who had the privilege of having had English lessons, but much to the chagrin of my parents, my teacher was a narcoleptic, so the first few years were harder than they should have been).

These experiences however have been absolute blessings in disguise. Although hard at the time, they have made me a stronger, more confident person, and I enjoy discovering the way that the human body and mind deal with such challenges. I also know that any challenge can be overcome.

I'm quite stiff in my upper body as I sit and write this (from my 10 hours of drilling concrete, and sledge hammering bolts into my holes), but it's a good soreness. It's self induced, it came with a great learning curve, makes me feel that much more powerful as a human being, and I know that I can hold my own when it comes down to it. I'm doing this self imposed challenge on one of my days off from Parks each week, and hope to learn a great new skill set. It's a bigger time commitment than sitting at a restaurant for an hour, but I know that it will pay for itself tenfold in the future. I'm addicted to the 'learning curve' I've taken up a bunch of sports in the last 9 years, and have totally fallen in love with them (feeling quite confident that I can hold my own with 80% of the population – don't want to mess with that other 20%). The computer geekedness is also a relatively new element in my life (only started noodling with computers in about 1998 – my formal education is in Anthropology – not very marketable in my neck of the woods), so I totally understand where your challenge this week is coming from. A wonderful wonderful place.

I love your Monday Morning Memos, and send them around to friends regularly that I think could benefit from them (my husband is a VP of Marketing at the ski area here, and we talk about your memos regularly - they're golden). I see the bigger picture behind them, and respect you for your efforts.

Kudos and continued success. I would love to attend one of your seminars but the distance makes this a challenge that is not feasible at this time, but you never know what the future holds. I'm just one lottery ticket away from signing up for all of your seminars and hanging out there for a while to really get the wisdom to penetrate.

40 Melanie Scherencel Bockmann

Sent: Wednesday, January 18, 2006 9:16 AM
To: corrine@wizardacademy.com
Subject: Inside the Outside challenge...

Diner

It's early, it's dark, and the all-night diner is practically empty. I push the glass door open and move toward the bar to sit down just as the waitress comes around the corner. Her eyes are tired, but her smile isn't, and she cheerfully informs me that the stool I'm about to sit in is "kind of wobbly."

"You might want to sit on this one instead," she says, pointing to another stool. I tell her thank you, and slide onto the brown vinyl cushion.

"Coffee? Orange juice? Tea? I can even make you a cappuccino if you like," the waitress offers. I wonder if she's had a few coffees herself. Her energy level suggests she has. Her hair is tied in a knot behind her head, and wisps of it float down around her face as she looks at me expectantly.

When I tell her I'll take a peek at the menu first, she nods and whisks away to refill the white, red, blue and yellow sweetener packets on each of the surrounding table tops. I can barely see the cook through the kitchen opening, and I feel a twinge of guilt when I realize I'm relieved to see him wash his hands. While he rinses away the suds, he looks up into the mirror and mouths the words to the rap song that's playing on the radio. His head bobs to the rhythm.

"Have you decided?" the waitress asks, and I order. Her name, according to her name tag, is Michelle. In a few minutes I'll know that she has a boyfriend and a son, and a hamper full of dirty laundry that she plans to take to the all-night laundry mat before she goes to bed, which I'm guessing will probably be about the time the sun rises. She's gotten all of the sweeteners distributed, and the salt and pepper shakers filled, but she couldn't find the window cleaner, and table number 22 desperately needs it.

Another employee makes his way in a few minutes before his shift starts—a young guy in his early twenties whose name I will soon know is Darren. He sits down a stool away and spreads a newspaper out in front of him. Pen poised, he tackles a crossword puzzle. Darren commutes from his apartment 30 minutes away, where he lives with his girlfriend. It's the only place they could afford, and now he's looking for a job closer to his new home; in the meantime, he waits tables here. He used to work at a bar at night also, but he couldn't handle the lack of sleep, so now he's down to one job.

Michelle is getting ready to leave, and Darren takes over. Two men come in and sit down—one on either side of me. Darren walks to the counter and grimaces. "It's way too early to deal with you, dude," he says to the guy on my left. Darren splashes coffee into his cup and then into the other man's cup to my right. The two men laugh and toss a few disparaging remarks back and forth before sipping their morning brew.

I notice an old man with a long gray pony tail and a bandana at a two-person booth not far from the bar, and I wonder if he's asleep. Michelle walks past him on her way out the door. "You doin' okay, Willie? Cuz I'm leavin', so if you need CPR or anything, you'd better tell me now." Willie mumbles something, and Michelle disappears with a laugh through the swinging glass doors.

The man to my right, Patrick, unfolds his newspaper and informs me that the old man in the booth is Willie. "He's a painter. Kind of weird. But nice."

As new people arrive, I realize that I'm sitting in the middle of a crossroads—the meeting point between those who are just beginning the day, and those who are ending it.

John, to my left, is working a temporary night shift at the new Home Depot. He has a six-year-old daughter, a gold wedding ring, and clear blue eyes. He tells me that his dad once bought a house that used to be a Meth lab, and not long after was offered a lot of money to sell it, but he chose not to because he didn't want to pay capital gains tax.

"He could have filed a Section 1031 and reinvested in a higher-value piece of property to avoid capital gains tax," I offer.

John looked at me blankly, and then shook his head. "Yeah. He didn't want to do that."

I realize I should do more listening than talking.

"Hey, can you get my toast?" Patrick, the man to my right, says when Darren walks past.

"Oh, just shut up," Darren says with a grin, reaching over the counter as the toast appears in the window. "Here's your toast."

"That's an awfully big plate for two small pieces of toast," Patrick complains.

"Yeah, well, we know how you eat and we don't want you to make a mess on the table," Darren shoots back.

Patrick informs us that a prior waitress had once tried to touch his toast after she served it. He stabbed her with a fork and drew blood. "I didn't mean to," he says, "but it was fun. She never touched my toast again."

Patrick is retired. He stops in often for breakfast often enough to know everyone by name. He reads us small excerpts from the newspaper, including the story of a half-blind, half-deaf seventy-six-year-old criminal who was executed, and apparently had to be wheeled in a wheelchair to his execution. For a moment I think Patrick is sympathetic. Then he says they should've executed him 25 years ago. Patrick despises President Bush, and wonders how things would have turned out if Gore had been elected instead. Especially since everything Bush touches blows up or gets tainted. Social Security and Medicare have been ruined beyond repair. He says he guesses that's what happens when we bring religion into the White House. I keep my mouth shut and listen.

More people wander in—a tired-looking nurse, an off-duty police officer, a man with a pre-teen son—and new topics float back and forth over coffee and creamer, jelly and toast, eggs and pancakes. They're curious about me; and a couple of them ask me what I'm doing up so early, what I'm doing in this neck of the woods.

"I decided to get up early, and thought I'd drop in here for some breakfast," I say as I sip my hot chocolate. They're satisfied with my answer.

I ask myself what they have that I don't. And I realize that they're here—truly here. They seem to be living in this conversation, this cup of coffee, this moment. I, on the other hand, almost unconsciously rehearse a proposal I plan to give to my boss later in the day, and wonder if the stock market is going to be kind.

What do I have that they don't? I have hope that hasn't been strapped down by resignation. I'm following the horizon. They will probably be back tomorrow morning to talk about how the government, the school system, an ex-boss, or a social disadvantage has put them two steps behind. I have some stories like those; but I won't be here. I'll be navigating my way through, and letting memories of people who didn't believe in me spur me on with greater determination. If I could give my new acquaintances one thing, it would be hope. And yet, I'm not sure right now how exactly that would be accomplished. Can you teach a blind person to see?

It's still dark outside when I push back through the swinging glass doors on my way to leave, and I'm conflicted. This place is a cemetery for dreams. And yet, my mind is full of fun, colorful images of the people who graciously let me into their world, and I'm glad I came. No matter where I go for the remainder of the day, I'm going to have to earn my acceptance. Here, it was free.

As I open my car door, I can barely see my breakfast companions through the window. It's a snapshot of life. And it's beautiful.

41

Al Rider

Sent: Wednesday, January 18, 2006 7:58 AM
To: corrine@WizardAcademy.com
Subject: Encounter at the Counter

The 3 a.m. hour is half-way finished with its work for the day and mine is just beginning. I get dressed and step outside into a few inches of snow resting on a bed of ice. What am I doing? I'm nuts!

I'm on my way up the road to a truck stop at the invitation from a man I have never met. Oh, the power of suggestion. Of three to choose from I've chosen the one with the most trucks parked outside.

"Coffee this morning?" It's a question from a smiling lady stationed near the cash register. "Yes, thank you," as I take a seat at the counter not far from the lady. I position myself in front of the pass through window complete with a wheel that holds the orders for the cook. I am alone.

Country music fills the place courtesy of a song that says "I'll meet you in the middle" from Big Cat Radio. I've noticed that radio stations are "Cool", Big this or that, Giant, 100,000 watt super duper whatever. What do the self proclaimed big names mean?

The message on the phone receiver in front of me says "save time & money, dial double-zero for AT&T." A group of small vinegar bottles rest on a shelf. Their different shapes and sizes are perfect for a chess game.

The coffee arrives along with a menu. My server gives me a moment to look it over as she returns to the register and begins talking with a co-worker who says she isn't going into work today, the weather's too bad. She holds two jobs.

The server approaches and asks for the order. I look into her blue eyes and gaze at her face that I'm sure doesn't reveal its true age.

"I'll have an egg over-easy and a biscuit with jelly, please."

"Is that all?" she asks as she writes it down on her order pad.

"Yes, mam."

I watch the cook through the pass through window as she moves to the grill to fill my order. I can't see her face but it's interesting the way she moves to the familiar cooking surface. She's a professional using the tools of her trade. I see her wedding band and wonder if her husband is asleep or at work too.

"More coffee?"

"Yes, thanks. How's the weather north of here?"

"I don't know, it gets slicker the further south you go. Especially around the Kentucky Tennessee border."

I glance over to an "Accurate Weigh Scales machine" sitting in a corner. I speculate about the sales pitch given by the person who placed it here.

The breakfast arrives complete with the order ticket slipped neatly under the biscuit. Quality control at work.

"Can I get you something else?"

"No, thank you."

"Well, you enjoy," as she smiles and moves away.

I take a good look at her and remember part of my assignment for this secret mission. What does she need most and how can I help her get it. I think about it while eating.

Wonder if anyone ever asked her opinion on anything about education, health care or community or economic development. What she thinks of inflation, the cost of living, budget, where she shops. Why do we keep inviting the same people to answer the same questions about community issues? How about this lady? Would she appear on anyone's "list" of expets, knowledgeable sources, and educated gurus? Very doubtful. Why? Who better to ask about the challenges of everyday living. Who better to give true insights to life's persistent issues? Why not have genuine conversations? An authentic heart to heart.

The Chamber of Commerce crowd could learn a lot from this lady.

A regular arrives. How can I be sure? The way the server greets him. They immediately engage in a free-fall conversation. I can't make out much of the content but the context is unmistakable and clear. There is a desire to connect, to share and a willingness to talk and listen with the same intensity. How refreshing.

They visit and I get more coffee as she apparently has a clock inside that says OK, it's time to pour coffee for the other guy.

Then it dawns on me. I am in the moment. I am present. I am not thinking of what I have to get done today or about yesterday.

Mr. Williams' assignment is the cheapest, yet one of the most helpful, self-improvement workshops I've ever attended. It's 4:56 a.m., I've spent $2.94 and I'm feeling very blessed!

42 Matt Hunt

Sent: Tuesday, January 17, 2006 5:21 AM
To: Corrine@WizardAcademy.com
Subject: meal at 4:26 am

    4:26 am and I'm on Indiantown road on the outskirts of Jupiter, Florida. 7 people total exist in this one and only 24 hour restaurant in the whole city, the pancake haven of America, IHOP. Two Police officers (both male), two waitresses (both female), one cook (chain-smoker male), myself, and a borderline hobo (male) who is speaking with another person (not visible, possibly imaginary) about Bible scripture.

    The Police Officers are engrossed in their conversation while snippets of garbled radio calls eek out from their shoulders. They ignore all of it and carry on their conversation. The two waitresses are calculating their total shift windfalls and comparing in a competing manner as to who did more in revenue, verses who served more actual customers. This carry's on for about 20 minutes. The Cook is vying for the Cops attention with low volume, smart comments, wearing a nervous smile, but they continue to ignore him. He appears to be a mechanical extension of the grill line.

    The most interesting character is the borderline Hobo. I paint him in this manner because I'm really not sure if he's homeless, or the "Howard Hughes" type? His clothes are slightly worn, but have a unique crispness to them, as if he deliberately has them laundered. Sort of a "King-of-the-Hobo's" type guy.

    During the whole 43 minutes I'm there he incessantly convinces the non-apparent person across from him that "Colossians 2:16-17" is what Paul is desperately explaining to the people of Colossae that the Feasts of the Jews are shadows of things to come, but the substance is of Christ! Now as I listen, I find myself tuning everyone else out, because I'm fascinated with Biblical Scripture and this guys just going on and on. I get out my pen and cryptically write everything he keeps saying but he's talking faster and faster and lower and lower. Frustrated, I want to interrupt him and ask him to repeat what he just said but I'm too "chicken" to let him know I've been eavesdropping on his conversation with who knows who. I look at my notes and see "we need to understand the Jewish Feast days to understand the symbolism of Christ for the Church", "The rapture of the Church (Christ's body he explains) is real", "God always warns his people… and his people are the Jews, not the Church (the Church represents his body)".

I find all of this mesmerizing in an eerie sort of way. Was I supposed to be here to listen to this? Is this just some homeless guy ranting on? Why can't these images I'm processing ever be clear-cut so I understand what I'm seeing and hearing? Are they supposed to be vague and ambiguous or is it because I lack faith???

The silent pondering is broken by 3 Guatemalan migrant workers who come in to pick up a take-out-order. I notice that the 3 of them are only getting what looks like 3 orders of food, with tons of coffee. I look out to their truck to see 6 others who intently stare at the 3 as if they are all going to split the food. 2 minutes later my assumption is correct. These Guatemalan's are the folks who live in "real" Indiantown. A town 18 miles west of where the IHOP is located and there are no 24-hour restaurants out there. It's a town filled with Florida's migrant working population who do all the work the privileged in Palm Beach County won't do. These are the guys who cut grass, build buildings, pick up garbage, and do all the manual labor that makes this glamorous County the jewel of Florida. They travel 18 miles back and forth everyday, usually cramped 10 to a vehicle, down the only two lane connector to American paradise. Getting home at 11:00 pm and getting up at 4:00 am, day in, day out!

I'm only up to do this project. What a sloth in comparison to them I think. I start feeling guilty about what I have and realize that my Bible guy has paid his bill and is gone! I frantically look for him, but see nothing. I guess in the diversion of attention and my focus changing hands back to the World, he slipped away. It's then I realize it's like a metaphor for God. Take your eyes off of him I think, and your back in Satan's playground, the "World" as the Bible says!

I laugh at myself, leave a hefty tip and get back in the car to drive home. I start wondering what these folks need most and I ignore everyone except for the Guatemalan's. I wonder how they can seem so happy, while working so hard. I wonder what it's like to share 3 meals between 7 men. What kind of bond they have. Are these rules for them inherent in their society or is it because of their circumstances that they learn to share so well? What can I help them get, or better yet, what did they help me realize in myself?

I think the guilty part crept in because I know I'm wasteful with much of what I have. And here they were with little and not wasting anything, instead sharing all they had! And finally, my Bible guy!! Man, I wanted to ask him so many questions and like smoke in the wind he vanished...poof!

43 Tony Armstrong

Sent: Monday, January 09, 2006 9:01 AM
To: Corrine@WizardAcademy.com
Subject: Inside the Outside: Tribeca Dreams

Last Friday afternoon I was minding my own business in Toronto when my friend Lindsay tricked me into flying down to New York City to see the play Doubt (a parable). In the theatre I had a short conversation with the struggling actor sitting next to me. "David" wanted to see the play with the original cast because it was his ambition to appear in Doubt one day.

After the play Lindsay and I took a taxi to Tribeca for dinner. Lindsay had lived in NYC for almost 14 years attending Julliard and struggling to build his career as an actor. He had no doubt that he would succeed.

At dinner we were seated next to a table of young actors who were discussing Shakespeare. While we were not there to listen to other people talk we couldn't help ourselves - in the crowded restaurant we might as well have been sitting at the same table. A steady supply of Mojitos however helped us retreat into our own space and we focussed instead on the play (Doubt) and our meal.

It wasn't until we left the restaurant that we began to reflect on our flight from reality. Lindsay had left NYC years ago to move back to Canada and to build a successful exercise equipment and training company - far from his original dream of becoming an actor. He had appeared in several plays and on television since leaving NYC but nothing to call a career. It was while we were walking in Tribeca that we started discussing the actor in the theatre, the group next to us in the restaurant and the thousands of other hopefuls that were living in New York City chasing the dream of becoming an actor.

We found ourselves in an after hours bar (more Mojitos) surrounded by the staff of the restaurant we had just left and dozens of other people just like them - actors searching for a role. Our bartender was a tired looking woman in her mid-thirties. She was at the end of her journey as a struggling actor in New York. We sat at the bar and listened to the patrons sharing the results of their week - auditions, rumours of upcoming plays and half financed opportunities that were going to change their lives.

I am a man in transition. Secure with a fantastic family (wife, 5 kids and a dog) I am in the process of reinventing myself and my career. Do I have my doubts? Sure. But I pretend that I have no doubt and focus instead on how I am going to succeed.

Every person in that bar - even our tired bartender - had no doubt that they were going to succeed. We shared our stories and offered some perspective on each others dreams. The bar reminded me of a poster I've seen often (attached). We had found ourselves in that poster - on the boulevard of broken dreams.

The question that I left that bar with was not how many of those people would succeed as actors (probably not many - if any at all) but how many of us would benefit from the experience of chasing our dreams.

44 Jason Foux

Sent: Wednesday, January 11, 2006 5:32 PM
To: Corrine@WizardAcademy.com
Subject: My Diner Experience

HOBO SOUP

Hobo soup is made by mixing half a glass of hot water with almost a whole bottle of Heinz Ketchup and a pinch of salt, creating a free serving of tomato soup.

I'm sitting in P.G.'s Diner, watching a girl play one of those new Gameboys (I can't remember the name of the latest generation of those devices). She sits alone, two tables away from her parents because she's not a little kid anymore and it's not cool to be seen with your parents. She's too old to sit with them, but too young to pay for her own meal. Her pink shirt almost matches the Pepto Bismol upholstry of the God-awful seats. With the exception of myself, she's the only person sitting alone. In five years, she'll realize that her parents are two of the coolest people she knows and she'll be taking them out to dinner instead of avoiding them

"I'm leaving on a jet plane
Don't know when I'll be back again."

That song is playing and it always reminds me of that scene from the movie Armageddon.

The hobo and his friend each have a glass of their signature soup and seem to be enjoying it. I've heard of Hobo Soup before, when I lived in Houston, but this is the first time I've ever seen a person actually consume it.

A couple of tables away, a man in a navy blue shirt with white paint splattered on the sleeves sits with his wife and their two kids. He probably isn't a day older than me. I'm envious of him. My whole family hasn't sat down at the same table together since Christmas of 2004.

Brown-eyed Girl is playing. I love that song.

I just finished the best damned Philly Cheese Steak Po Boy I've ever had. On the other side of the tinted glass divider sits two black fellows. One of whom is working on his own Po Boy. He looks exactly like the old man from Sanford & Son.

They're talking about recent conversations with other members of the church they both go to.

And it looks like I've found the pair of intellectuals that every coffee shop and diner has. Both are dressed clad in black, the way you think of photographers, morticians and Johnny Cash. They're probably twenty-three or so and they have spent the past ten minutes debating our nation's role in Iraq. Give them an hour and they'll solve all the problems of the world. But I'll bet my next two paychecks that neither one knows the meaning of life. I should educate them.

I ask the guys with the hobo soup if it's really that good.

"Tastes better than that Campbell's shit." One of them replies. He pulls his straw from the glass of soup and offers it to me (the glass, not the straw). I suck out the last drops of DrPepper from my own straw and wipe off the end. It tastes just like canned tomato soup.

A girl sits with her boyfriend, talking while they wait for their order. Her phone rings; she doesn't answer. Their food arrives and her phone rings again. She turns it off and they continue visiting, uninterrupted, while they eat.

Riders on the Storm plays through the speakers of the diner. I begin eating my hashbrowns, after I turn off my phone.

The End.

45 K.C. Fleming

Sent: Tuesday, January 17, 2006 1:08 PM
To: Corrine@WizardAcademy.com
Subject: Re: Monday Morning Memo from the Wizard of Ads

    As I prepared for a three day trip to Memphis, TN to visit the St Jude Children's Research Hospital in preperation for our upcoming Radiothon, I came across a Monday Morning Memo I had not yet read. Its Wednesday. I either need a BlackBerry or two more hours in the day. At any rate, I always look forward to Roy's weekly wisdom, sort of like the excitement that brings me back to Boston Legal, or Lost each week. This MMM did not dissapoint. It offered up a challenge I opted to take. Knowing I would be venturing a few hundred miles down the magnificent Mississippi for a memorable trip to Memphis, I would have an excellent opportunity to visit a diner in an area of town, and the country, that I don't usually visit. After pondering this for a moment, I found myself asking how I would find time to visit the diner, write a response and email it back to Roy, when I hardly seem to have enough time to read all of my email in the first place. Thinking back to the amazing days I have spent at the Wizard Academy in Buda, I realized I owed it to myself to write as Roy requested. I needed to take the time to actually do this, and here I am ....doing it.

    Now that I've introduced my situation, attempted to use proper punctuation....I'm going to write....like I usually write. Sometimes it flows, sometimes it jumps around like a squirrel dodging raindrops. You'll notice lots of.....dots. I'm not sure when, how or why I started this habit....but the dots....in my writing....sort of represent a breif thought......or moment or reflection on where the writing is going.....a vehicle to transport me from one thought to another.....that inevitably leads to the leaping story line of whatever yarn I am attempting to spin.

    So...here we go....dots and all....recapping this mornings adventure at a Downtown Denny's in Memphis, TN. With Roy's inquisitive nature planted firmly in my pocket, paired with my inborn Irish Curiosity, I had no problem wandering three blocks south, two blocks east and up seven steps into an all night Denny's. The home of the Grand Slam wasn't bustling with Sunday morning...been to church....need coffee and eggs group....but with the inhabitants of the world that Roy spoke of in his Memo. Those of another world...and it was my job to peek.....remember....and report back. There were three tables that owned patrons......one, a silent father and son....quietly awaiting their food....looking not at each other nor anywhere else in particular. This wasn't an uncomfortable silence I was witnessing, it was simply silence. Neither spoke.....they just waited.....patiently....for their food....before they headed on towards Chatanooga or Branson....or maybe off to wherever Mom might be waiting for the boys monthly visit to end. My waiter stopped by......splashed some coffee in my cup (with a finger ring to small for my average size fingers....was this a tea set from Denny's great Aunt) and smiled. He seemed to be pleased with his position in life.....he was large, overweight, sweating........but happy. I ordered a skillet thing with eggs, cheese, hasbrowns and bacon. Sort of a plaid meal.....all sorts of things crossing each other that seem to work very well together. At this point I observe two adjoining tables and their patrons. One table, seemingly locals, finishing up another late shift down the street, in to either grab a quick bite.....or just get outta the rain....the other table.....two folks in for the same convention I was. I could tell by their lanyards. I was surprised to see others had ventured "Across The Tracks", for there were other available all night eating establishments that would supply similar fare to act as a sponge to their bellies full of Beale Streets Beer. For whatever reason, they were in this dingy Denny's...and were rambling non stop to the locals about all they had seen on Beale. The locals seemed entertained by the ranting madness of the woman from Montana....and the eye rolling disapproval of her apparent co worker. The locals seemed very comfortable in the conversation....the outsiders....were exactly that....outsiders that didn't seem like they had enough time to check their email either.

As I grew tired of listening to Montana Mary ramble on about her evening......up strolled a well dressed, drunk man. I knew he was drunk by the way he was looking at me. I have tended bar....and I know this look. Sort of an annoyed....WHEN ARE YOU GOING TO TALK TO ME look. He asked where he could get food.....and I thought.....uhh....we're in a restaurant......and I was guessing he knew that....so I suggested he take a seat and wait for someone to take his order. He looked at me ...puzzled.....and sat at an empty booth between me and Montana Mary and her local listeners. He went straight to his cell phone and, for whatever reason, I wondered what lies he was congering up as he dialed his wife. While I don't know for sure if it was his wife he was dialing.....he did start out the drunken diatribe with, "Hello Honey.....sorry I didn't call......" I was almost leaning in to listen ....CRASH.....a bus boy dropped a tray....and everything stopped. It was one of those pauses in life where people sort of look at each other and realize we're all on a similar page...but I could only think how DIFFERENT the pages we were all on. It was then I noticed Dave the Dad and his boy Bob had already gotten their food. Mine should soon follow.....   Did I mention that right when the tray fell....the waiter was staring at Cell Phone Phil....attempting to get an order?? I don't think he got one...becuase the guy was too busy lying to his wife...or whomever....so the waiter was off to help his co worker clean up. Two more sips of coffee and I notice him back....trying to get Cell Phone Phil's order after dropping off Montana Mary's table full of food. No luck....they drunk guy is paying NO attention to the waiter.....so he heads back to the kitchen...returns with my food and I am thrilled. Cell Phone Phil isn't. He YELLS at the guy...asking where HIS food is....and the waiter....who we'll now name Nice Nick reminds him he is yet to order.....in a friendly manner. Phil jumps up, waving his arms as if he's just lost his belongings in a hurricane...demanding to see a manager and wanting service. He drops a few racial slurs and is now at MY table pointing at my food. Nice Nick is explaining to hte manager that he TRIED to help the guy but the guy ignored him. It was at this point, Clark Kent took off his glasses and said....."SLOW DOWN HOT SHOT....he tried to take your order TWICE...I saw it. You were too busy......(((I BIT MY TONGUE AT THAT POINT, KNOWING MY LIMIT))" I think the manager understood...and asked the guy to leave....he threw down a plastic menu and grapped a piece of toast off of Montana Mary's table as he stormed out. We all looked at each other.....and I don't konw whose hands hit together first.....but we all started clapping...and then things went back to normal. Mary was too busy with her Denver omelette to talk, the locals were happy to be out of the rain, Dave the Dad and his Boy Bob were settling up with Nice Nick, who offered to pay for my food since I stood up for him.....explaining that folks don't usually do that for people like him. I paid in full....and walked out...wondering what this fella really thinks, "people like him" actually are.

 What an interesting look at the same world we live in, from a totally different angle. I'm glad I did it......and apologize for rambling in an unorthodox manner filled with Dots.......when I returned to my room....I was glad I stood up for Nice Nick....and wish I could show him there are more good people on earth that are more than happy to help, "...people like him." I wish I could tell Montana Mary to let people enjoy a cup of coffee out of the rain...and that the world doesn't rotate around her beauty (yes, she was gorgeous). And lastly, I wish I had more comfortable silences....like Dave the Dad and his boy Bob seemed to enjoy throughout the episode....maybe I'd have enough time to read Monday Morning Memo's on Monday.........and not have to wait to find time on Wednesday.

Thanks for taking time to read this ....uhh....I'm not sure what you'd call this to be honest.

46 Don Saathoff

Sent: Wednesday, January 18, 2006 10:47 AM
To: 'Corrine Taylor'
Subject: Instead, Dying

The assignment is to go to an all night café and observe. It is an attractive activity to me – I like to watch people. Then, I am called to go to Longview – my wife's seventy-nine year old father is in the hospital. Drive 270 miles to his side rather than 10 or 20 miles to an all night café.

I observe, but not as originally intended. I am in a hospital. I see many old people, some families, confusion, crying, language barriers. But they are not top of mind.

My father-in-law, P. J., has Alzheimer's – in the later stages. He has with a large pouch in his esophagus, collecting food and infection. He understands none of this. He knows some pain, but the pain of confusion is foremost. It weighs at family; tears flow; wine flows; prayers stretch; late nights fill with reflection; pain subsides – a little.

P. J. enters hospice, not a place, a service. Hope for recovery distinguishes; hope for little pain grows. A six foot five Nigerian-born gastroDoc soothes with unexpected bedside manner. Pneumonia, a pretty good way to go – who knew? – is the likely result. A few days, a few weeks – my wife wants to be with him when he dies – "a once in a lifetime opportunity" – she really says that.

Who is P. J.? A kind, gentle man. A true Christian – a true servant. A loyal lover of his wife, his family, God, the earth and humanity. He knows little of his past deeds: reading to elderly, teaching Sunday school, passing out meals. He rarely speaks in sentences – maybe some whose meaning is known only to him. Not much food or water is taken in.

Shriveling, dehydrating, sleeping, snoring, coughing – these consume his days. A few good moments – he smiles when he sees our three year old daughter. Mainly, he talks gibberish and points at things that scare him.

Then, P. J. shocks. I tell him "I love you." He responds "I love you too." As his end nears, he loves – with his last few correctly firing neurons – I know he means it. P. J. owns a roadmap to heaven.

We wait – four days turns to six, and probably more to come. I still want to do the café assignment. Instead, I experience something vital.

P. J. inspires and doesn't yet expire. Wanting the best for my wife, her family and P. J. – wanting him to die. Not a shred of malice. Wishing for the death of a very fine man. Hard to say goodbye, impossible not to.

This is not the assignment Roy prescribed. Instead, it is the one God provided.

47 Brent Nightingale

Sent: Wednesday, January 18, 2006 10:16 AM
To: corrine@wizardacademy.com
Subject: Experience #1

When the shriek of my alarm clock woke me from a deep sleep at 1:30 a.m., I wasn't sure this was such a good idea. With a temperature of only 19 F outside, my very warm, pillow-top King-sized bed felt pretty good. But having already made a commitment to myself that I would do this, I quickly dressed and made my way to one of only two 24 hour eateries in our town. Fortunately my garage had kept any snow and ice off my car, and I didn't even have to step into the cold to drive off.

On the edge of town, along the main highway, the eatery is across the street from another truckstop that used to be a 24 hour joint, but now closes between 1 and 5 a.m. The truckstop would have drawn different clientele, but it was closed so I didn't have a lot of choices of where to spend my hour. I've only been in the truckstop a couple of times before – each time to put up a poster, inviting people to attend an event at our church. As far as I can tell, no one ever showed up due to the posters, even though they were created with the most expensive computer program by an experienced graphics designer. Hmmm, perhaps our cleverly thought out strategy isn't working…

My town is small, at only 11,000 people, and I had no doubt that this would be a less exciting hour than some of the others who took you up on your challenge, but I figured I might still learn something. I was away or busy for many of the nights the past week, including the weekend, so I was only able to forge my experience on a rather quiet Tuesday night / Wednesday morning.

There were only a few people in the eatery when I walked in. A twenty something couple sat talking in a corner, while a fifties looking man sat with what looked like business papers scattered on the table. I wondered about his life. What was he doing that brought him out to an all-night eatery past two in the morning to do some work? He had no wedding ring on, so he may have been single, and it struck me as being slightly sad. Then again, he probably wondered what I was doing just sitting there all alone making some kind of notes on a single sheet of paper.

Looking outside for a while, I noticed that traffic was heavier than

I expected. Again the thought ran through my mind, what were all these people doing awake at this time of night? This was obviously a slow night for the eatery. The lone waitress sat down for a while and looked like she was fighting sleep, then got up abruptly and restocked the pastry shelves.

Several people wandered out of the two bars across the street when they closed down shortly after 2 a.m. This time I found myself wondering how long they had been in the bar, and how much they had to drink. All of them got into vehicles and drove off, not a single taxi arrived to transport anyone home.

I noticed that the parking lot of the truckstop next door was completely full. I counted more than forty rigs sitting and waiting for their owners to catch a few hours sleep before continuing down the road. Shortly before 3 a.m. a couple of the rigs pulled out of the parking lot and headed west, while another rig turned southeast toward the U.S. border, only twenty minutes away. Two kitchen workers came out to talk to the waitress, while two young men in their early twenties pulled up in separate vehicles. Both young men were very loud, yet not in a disturbing manner. It was quite obvious that they were regulars, and they knew the waitress well. When the one young man pulled in, he appeared to be weaving and almost drove over the curb, which made me suspect he'd been drinking. The thought crossed my mind that this was now the second time in less than an hour that I'd made some rather judgmental thoughts about people out drinking. Is this why I never mix with this crowd? It seems very easy to sit and judge people when you know nothing about them.

All of the individuals that I saw during my hour in the eatery seemed to be comfortable with themselves and their lives. At the very least they were at ease with each other. I know this is a very tame experience, but even so, it was still not natural for me, and I certainly did not feel at all at ease. Even the FM station that normally plays "light rock from the 90's and today" played a different style of music. I recognized mostly songs from the early 80's including Tom Petty and Blondie – songs that I've never heard on that station during the day.

As I sat there, it reminded me of another experience I had about thirteen years ago. My family headed east on holidays that summer, and my wife and I decided it would be interesting for our family to experience a change in culture. We took our three children, all under the age of ten, and we stayed and worked in an inner-city mission that we'd heard about in the heart of Chicago. Back home we'd never seen a junkie shoot heroin in broad daylight like we did during those three days. Nor had we seen police openly ignore the numerous alcoholics and drug addicts sprawled on the sidewalk. When we asked a cop why they didn't arrest them or do something with them, he snorted and asked what specific things we had in mind that we thought would do any good. We didn't have an answer for him. It dawns on me as I'm writing this, that it's been a long time since that experience, and I'd almost forgotten about what we saw. In fact, it's been far too long since I've had any kind of experience like this.

Though seemingly not much happened last night, I realize that this was an important experience for me. Even in my small town, far removed from inner-city Chicago, I discovered a new, albeit small, segment of society that I simply never cross paths with. For the most part, the people I saw seemed lonely, but then again, that may just be another judgment on my part – I'm beginning to think I'm good at that. I don't understand a lot about their lives to know why their lives revolve around such different hours than mine, and I'm not likely to ever know much about them without deliberate action on my part. But before I can make any decisions about what they need, I need to get to know them. That's the next decision I'll have to make. Am I truly willing to take this a step further and commit time and energy to get to know them and their needs? If Jesus spent enough time with the undesirables that He was called a friend of sinners, I suppose I should as well.

Thank you for the challenge. It was a great experience!

Bertwin Lord

48

Sent: Wednesday, January 11, 2006 7:44 PM
To: Corrine@WizardAcademy.com
Subject: My nite at home!

My night out of my "comfort zone"

Growing up in a farming community surrounded by the real lifeblood of America I was graced with something that others will never know. Back alley cafes and eating on the other side of the proverbial tracks, is daily fare in my neck of the woods. A deep sense of community and belonging is coupled with ones acceptance of ones station in life.

Recently I received a newsletter asking me to go to a 24-hour eating establishment between 0130 and 0530 in a part of town that I rarely go. The only problem with this is that I live where the 24 hour restaurants are. It is nothing for me to go there as I am usually there once I get off work at 0100.

The next task I was given while eating and listening and absorbing this strange new reality was to think of what these people need most and how you might help them get it. While you're at it, you might also think a little about what they have that you don't.

I am sure you can see why I find this comical. I am the individual that is to be studied; I am the strange new environment that needs to be explored. So realizing that this was not really aimed at expanding my horizons I decided to make it so anyways. I tried to look through the eyes of those who have no understanding of who we really are. Here is a brief lesson.

Have you ever heard that there is nothing more dangerous then a man with nothing to loose, well how about a man with nothing to look foreword to? This is a very drab way to look at individuals who live like I do. It is not that we have nothing, or that many of us will never find a way to better our situation that defines us. We take what we have, and the cards that we were dealt and we do the best that we can.

The one part of the newsletter that bothered me was when the writer informed women that they did not have to go to this experience alone. Instead they could take someone for protection. I am not saying that the writer had misgivings about the caliber of people that were going to be at an all-night diner, but instead wanted to address the misconception that are common amongst those who may view this as a hostile environment. I am not sure about all others, but I know that when I am at a dinner at 3 a.m. I am not thinking that anyone else there is going to have anything that will interest me.

Would you like to know what is going through the minds of those who are sitting at that diner? Would you like to know what thoughts permeate their minds? Well mostly the thoughts are not of the bigger picture, or who is going to be elected, or what lobbyist is doing what. Instead thoughts are on worries over family, job, boyfriend, girlfriend, husband, wife, cousin, sister, brother, mother, father, boss, co-workers. Does any of this sound familiar?

Would you like to know what it is that we need the most? What you like to know what burning desires fill out hearts? It is not a better mail system, or saving the environment. Instead our desire is to pay off our car loan, or finally make enough money to buy a house. We desire to be able to make a better life for our children and their children, but only on a local level.

One of the biggest differences that we feel when compared to those who might come in to study us is that we are directly affected by political choices made that we do not understand.

When the war in Iraq is discussed in the diner it is not talked about abstractly, it is personal. We do not refer to the war by its leaders, but by our sons and daughters that are fighting in it. When we discuss the casualties of war it is not abstractly, but by crying out the names of John and Michael, and Tony, and Steve. We hide our sorrow, but bear it more.

When we talk about tax breaks of prices of gasoline this is not in regards to if we can buy that new boat, but if we can afford to fix up the car. We do not talk about the bus only for easing up traffic congestion so our 95 pound wife can drive our 2 ton SUV to get groceries.

It is true, we do all live together. There are those amongst us who are thieves. We do not have the most educated children. We do not have the best of everything. Our priorities are not in the same place as those with the power. There are those amongst us who live with 10 people in a $300/month apartment but drive a $40,000 car. We like things that are shiny. We are loud. We are passionate. When you add all of us together our buying power is phenomenal. Our backs are strong, and our hearts are large.

Andrew Jackson knew that the power was with the people. The ACLU and NAACP are two groups that have thrived off of the passion of the lower class. Even if their ideas are flawed, they are the only ideas we hear.

Marty Murray

49

Sent: Sunday, January 22, 2006 10:44 AM
To: Corrine@WizardAcademy.com
Subject: Scraped by a Fin

January 22, 2006 - 4:25am at Stretch Truck Stop a few miles north of Fond du Lac, WI. I walk in and notice the place is somewhat busy. There's one man at the peninsula shaped breakfast bar, two other men eating alone, a mixed group of 5 taking up 2 booths and 3 rowdy, half-drunk looking guys in the corner. I instinctively do not get eye contact with the 3 rowdies. Sitting down at the breakfast bar two stools to the right of the other man, I acclimate myself to my new environment. The waitress doesn't acknowledge my presence, so I sit patiently for 4-5 minutes before this rather cold (frosty), unhappy looking woman brings me a menu. I smile and greet her "Good morning". She grumbles a "Good morning" back sans smile.

The mixed group of 5 is the liveliest. A sober, local group of friends in there early 20s, they talk aloud amongst themselves as if they were alone. Conversation ranges from cats to the army. The biggest guy in the group with an "Army of One" shirt on begins talking about enlisting. Pulling out the results of his ASVAB test (Army vocational test); he is noticeably excited about the possibilities the army holds for him and proudly shows his friends, "everything right of this line are the occupations I qualify for". Does he know what he's getting himself into? No, but who does at that age. He has enthusiasm for what can be. I wonder if his four friends have that.

In the meantime, frosty the waitress serves me breakfast. No signs of a smile yet. Her conversation with the others has been negative. It's been a long night for her. The man to my left leaves and is soon replaced by an elderly man. The rowdies totter out too. The cook, taking a break, tells a smelly dog story to another waitress who is counting her tip money and telling herself out load, "Remember. Don't spend this money!" Another waitress patiently stacks Heinz ketchup bottles opening to opening in an effort to make one full bottle. You know these bottles. They're the kind you think about breaking open just to get the ketchup out. Anyway, I learn that stacking the bottles is step 1. Once the ketchup stops flowing from the top bottle to the bottom bottle, she takes a ketchup-swabbing tool to collect the small globs toward the opening of the top bottle. During what I would describe as a mind-numbing process, I notice she looks very content in what she is doing although she doesn't appear to be altogether there. Her mind is off in some happy place.

Trying to strike up a conversation with the elderly man next to me, I begin to engage him in small talk. I ask him, "Are you a truck driver." He says, "No. I can't B.S. enough to be a trucker. I can't sleep. That's why I come here. It's my home away from home". "Sure is nice weather for January", I declare (30 degrees in Wisconsin in the middle of winter is nice weather). "You betcha. Every day you don't have to scrape, is a good day!", he proclaims. Scraping is what we northerners have to do to get the frost off our car windows most winter days when our cars are left outside. It was warm enough or the dew point was such that morning that he didn't have to. In a few moments time I learn that this man was 71 years old, retired from the local Mercury boat engine plant for 9 years, was originally from Ohio, his wife died when his 2 daughters were 10 and 11, and the youngest daughter committed suicide last summer after having a baby girl. Post-partum depression it turns out. I wonder if this is why he can't sleep. A lady friend joins him and our conversation ends.

It's time to pay my bill and I reflect on the service I received. It wasn't very good. She wasn't very pleasant. I recall a memo I received once suggesting giving a large tip for bad service. Those are the ones that really need it the most. Not the money necessarily but the gesture. I begin a little small talk with Frosty while she takes my money at the checkout counter for my $10.39 bill. $9.61 is my change. I lay down the five for her. She stops mid sentence. A big smile comes on her face and she thanks me graciously. She's suddenly a different person. I grow to like her in seconds. She's actually bubbly now as she continues our conversation. Her replacement shows up and she gives her a big hug. Giggling, she tells me to have a great day. What a difference! A little patience and one scrape of a fin on the counter is all it took.

Danielle Delgado

Sent: Thursday, January 12, 2006 11:48 AM
To: 'Corrine@WizardAcademy.com'
Subject: Re: Monday Morning Memo

I start my commutes to work in the usual way, not wanting to go but in a hurry. This is where I would usually rant about having a child with no concept of time... but then again he's 4. He won't understand "Time" for at least another 6 months. Let me not digress here, I'm not here to talk about that. I'm here to talk about my favorite hobby - people watching. Some thing about watching people really interests me, what they do in public, how they talk, who they talk to, what they're wearing, what they're doing.

In New York it seems that people usually just mind what they're doing and ignore everyone else, but do they really? I mean on my commute this morning as I was standing against the train door (yes I know you're not supposed to, but it's probably the cleanest spot on the train), listening to my ipod. I really didn't feel like listening to people talking this morning. I'm looking around and seeing what people are doing. I see two ladies talking, one is dressed in business attire (very trendy) sitting in a seat and the other lady is standing wearing scrubs. You assume that she probably works in a doctor's or dentist's office, a clinic of some sort, perhaps, maybe she's a med student, but whatever she is I guarantee you she's going to be on her feet all day and I guarantee you that the woman she was chatting with, sitting in her seat wearing trendy business attire would probably be standing for a very minimal amount of time at work. Did it ever dawn on her to offer this "friend" of hers her seat? Probably not, or maybe she just didn't care. Then again I was listening to my ipod so I didn't exactly hear the conversation (it looked rather gossipy)... perhaps she did... probably not.

I'm scanning around the train watching people reading books, newspapers, and magazines, people standing and sitting drinking coffee. Almost everyone on the train has become a member of the ipod society. I'm telling you those things are going to take over the world. When Armageddon does come it's going to be a battle between Bill Gates and Steve Jobs and whose crap is better. And yes I too am a member of the ipod society so I know I'm being a hypocrite as is human nature so stop judging me. But again I'm going on a tangent; let me get back to the subject at hand, checking out other people.

Anyway mostly everyone is doing their own thing. So I turn my head to the left and I start scanning the other half of the train more intently and my eyes fall on this tall heavyset Asian man. He's dressed pretty nicely, I could guess that he's either a student or he works with computers, and again I am only guessing. But he's sitting there and he's picking his nose. PICKING HIS NOSE! I don't just mean put your finger up there and scratch and stop. I mean this man had his finger jammed up his nose looking for buried treasure-if you know what I mean. I decide I'm going to stare at him the whole time he's doing it. Come on, use a tissue! And every time he finds something he digs it out rolls it between his finders and flicks it. I feel bad for the man sitting next to him.

People there are just some things you do when other people are not around; picking your nose is one of those things. I felt like the whole train was full of buggers. I felt like I was breathing in buggers. I wanted to scream stop and right when I was about to (yes I really was going to say something to him) he stopped. His nose was all red from his fingers stretching it and the irritation from digging around up there.

Now, I am FAR from being the etiquette police. I do my make-up on the train and I eat on the train and talk on my cell phone on the train, but I draw the line at disgusting things like picking your nose, scratching your behind, and all that good stuff (note the sarcasm). Where should we draw the line? Where do you draw the line?

Bob Emmert

51

Sent: Monday, January 16, 2006 3:52 AM
To: corrine@wizardacademy.com
Subject: out of the comfort zone

    I just got back from the only 24-hour eating establishment in the area I live in (Houghton Mi.- the Wizard has been here for an advertising seminar).
    The challenge in the last mon. morning memo was compelling; I couldn't stop thinking about it, so I decided to try it and be one of the 12.
    We live in a very small town, and I didn't expect much. We have a "Perkins" restaurant, which I do go to occasionally. I don't see too many "other side of town" people there, but then I've never been there in the middle of the night either.
    When I got there I thought, "At least I can sit on the 'smoking' side that I never sit on just for a change." But the more interesting looking group was on the 'non-smoking' side (which I found out later they had chosen by accident- they wanted to smoke). I arrived at about 2 am.
    I over heard a lot of swearing and anger, talk about females, and snowmobiles. One of them had a cell phone that kept ringing with a rap music ring tone and the young man kept trying to answer it, but no one was there- then it would ring again a few minutes later. One of the other guys used his phone to call a friend to get him to come to the restaurant for breakfast. There must have been more to it than I know because the person he called came, but stayed outside in his truck. The guy in the restaurant called again, but the truck soon took off.
    There was also a table with two guys I took to be college students, but I couldn't hear a word from them. On the other side of the restaurant, there was group of five people who were meeting there for some reason. They looked "normal" so I didn't choose to sit by them.
    The waiter, in response to my question, said it is often this busy at bar closing time. I also found out that the restaurant is usually empty at 4-5 am.
    My impression of the group I sat near was that they are lost- alcohol was a big part of their evening, anger, foul language- they have no hope. What can I do? Not much if I never see them....
    As a note, I do know a guy that does hang out on "the other side." In fact, I asked him this morning at church if he knew of any places to eat that are open between 1:30 and 5 am. He verified my choice by

replying. "Just Perkins, but if we were in New York there'd be lots of them!" He's a Viet Nam Vet, currently working a few hours a day at his most current job, attends AA meetings, and dresses in salvation army clothes that never match or fit. He's a very friendly person who befriends everyone. I don't think he has a credit card, or internet access. When you talk to him, you have to be ready for anything, like sudden topic changes, or bits of wisdom like the one I heard this morning, "Doing nothing takes a long time."

    Last thought- I didn't make any really stunning discoveries, except perhaps that it felt better that I thought it would to do something this different even when nothing "great" really happened at the restaurant.

    Thanks for the challenge,

Larry Muller

52

Sent: Monday, January 09, 2006 9:52 AM
To: Corrine@WizardAcademy.com
Subject: The Other Side

You guys always seem to touch on my favorite subjects---while not within the past 24 hours - here is a snapshot of my walk on the real side of life. While in Cabo (staying in a luxury resort) venture off the the main streets (sometimes only 1 block) and see life as it really is---diapered children running around the streets with no shoes/shirts and believe it or not, uncombed hair. The mother is barely dressed in rags hanging the days wash (more rags) on a makeshift closeline strung between the failing porch and sun sheltering tree---where is the concrete and drainage on these streets?

Does that old man always sit there? Try your best to speak to someone in broken spanish learned in high school and college and get greated with broad smiles of broken and missing teeth. But they appreciate the effort you made to speak with them.

Take an early morning walk (2:30-3:00 am) out of your magical las vegas hotel?/resort. Go to the back of the hotel, you know, where the turcks are directed-as the valet directs you to the front door- and Strike up a conversation with the guys on the dock unloading the days provisions—You will find they are married/single/divorced/have kids/hate kids/love their job/hate their job----you know what, they are a lot like me!

My favorite dose of reality is right around the corner from virtually everyone in america---Walk into your local 24 hour Walmart at 3:00 or 4:00 in the morning--then sit back and educate yourself with the people who make our world turn--They generally have their name "monogrammed" over their pocket , they wear some type of uniform that identifies them as a "?" when you see them on the street or in store store (or maybe they cooked our hamburger)---they wear funny hats that hide their ears, they walk, some limp, and others in the motorized wheelchairs - all seem to move in slow motion. Most of these people poised to make our life easier while doing their best to provide for their own families....for some time i have tried to gain the courage to take my home movie camera into our local Walmart (at this time of the morning) and interview these characters as they go about the business of life.

53

Jeff Dunn

Sent: Wednesday, January 18, 2006 11:08 AM
To: Corrine@WizardAcademy.com
Subject: Answering the challenge

Roy,

When I read your MMM on Jan 9, it came one day after our pastor had preached on sailing. Or, more specifically, taking our boat out of the safety of the harbor and out into the dangerous open waters where our boats were meant to be. I pondered your challenge all day, then all week. I wanted so much to get out of my safe harbor and plunge into the open waters of an all-nite café to see what you saw. But I had been battling a really nasty virus since before Christmas, and my energy level was very low.

Last night, however, I felt well enough to give it a try. I went to a bar attached to the Cain's Ballroom in downtown Tulsa; there was a concert at the Cain's last night, so the place was full. I sat there for nearly two hours, writing, watching, observing, listening. Amazing. This is not a place I would hang in, and not with this crowd (mostly teens) or for this music (sounded like small animals being tortured). The bands were playing in the ballroom, but kids were coming and going early in the night, then staying in the bar for more extended periods. Here are some of my observations.

1. The girl with tattoos completely covering both arms. She was no more than 18. How will she feel about her artwork when she is 28? 45? 70? How will this steer her life choices from now on?

2. The boy who looked so awkward with his cigarette. Was tonight the first time he had ever smoked? Was he enjoying it? He was puffing so hard and fast as if it would be his last.

3. Most everyone was in pairs or small groups, except for the woman who sat near me. She was alone drinking her beer. What did she think of these teens? Was she observing like I was, or just trying to be alone with her beer? Or did she sit there and wish she could be 18 again? Did I?

4. The kids all look and sound as if they are having a great time--

and I suppose they are. But what are their lives really like? What will they do tomorrow at school or work? Will they have fun then as well? Or is this an oasis in their lives, a short break away from the desert they live in daily?

5. They are enjoying tonight's bands (much more than I was), but I'll bet they know nothing of the bands that had built the Cain's. Do they know of Bob Wills and the Texas Playboys? Tex Ritter? Spade Cooley? Do they know anything about Bob Dylan, who played here a couple of years ago?

6. I love their youthful energy and passion!

7. I did not sense any anger in their conversations. I felt safe among them, even though I was not "of" them.

This was a very fun exercise. I enjoyed the challenge. Where do I go from here--that is the question.

Thanks, Roy, for issuing this challenge. Hope I met your expectations.

54

Eric Peterson

Sent: Sunday, January 15, 2006 3:45 PM
To: Corrine@WizardAcademy.com
Subject: RE: Monday Morning Memo from the Wizard of Ads

Searching for a sit-down restaurant that is open at four in the morning in the city of Oak Harbor was unsuccessful. Asking the seniors from the area for eating suggestions I was greeted with crooked brows and strange looks. "It's for this marketing project" seemed to satisfy their inquisitive looks.

"Nope, gotta head to Mount Vernon", was their reply - a town 45 minutes from where I live.

As a high school teacher, early morning excursions to towns 45 minutes away aren't normally feasible. I planned my visit for Sunday morning, to follow a half-marathon I was going to run Saturday in Mount Vernon. Incidentally, I was born in Mount Vernon and my parents still live there so I had a place to sleep.

Lying in bed, I am restless with anticipation. At 4 a.m. I slip out of my sister's old bed, stretch the tight muscles left from yesterday's run, and drive to Denny's about 3 miles away, the only 24 hour eatery within 40 miles.

Walking in I'm greeted by a young waitress who says, "Mr. Peterson?" At first I don't recognize her, but her name, Erin, quickly comes to mind as I remember that she graduated last year and was friends with a number of my students. "Are you here for breakfast at 4 in the morning?" she asks with a crooked smile. "Yup, just want something to eat", I reply.

Erin seats me at the front counter and we chat about how she works two jobs, started at the local junior college but put those plans on hold, and how she is planning to marry her current boyfriend someday. She also talks passionately of plans to travel to Spain to live and be a bartender for a couple of years.

I order breakfast and look casually around the restaurant.

There are about a dozen people, all couples, one family with a daughter, and an older gentleman quietly drinking a cup of coffee at the counter.

Pulling into the restaurant there were three taxis in the parking lot. I'm assuming the drivers are in here but am unsure who they are since everyone is sitting as couples.

A young, skinny man sits with his girlfriend at a table by the window. He is eating a hamburger, fries and a shake as his girlfriend watches. Only because it is 4:30 in the morning this strikes me as odd. Later I smile listening to the other waitress describe him as "amazing" to Erin. She had just brought him a sandwich and more fries that is following the cheeseburger, fries, and shake he was eating earlier. She jokes that he may wind up in the hospital with some gastric problems or hardened arteries later this morning.

The waitresses talk with the older gentlemen at the counter about the regulars that come in during the morning, calling everyone by name and asking where they are. They know everyone's schedule and menu preferences. A short time later another older gentlemen comes in and sits down next to the guy. I get the impression they know each other but aren't really good friends. They talk about how one of them has a day off and is just up early.

They talk football, what other retired guys are doing, the swans in the fields and how to keep them away, and random topics that include Medicare and the medical profession.

A third gentleman joins these two about 5:00 and sprinkles light commentary to their conversation without ever looking at them. He appears to be a farmer with dirty fingernails, no wedding ring, and a hat from the local seed company. They all sit and sip coffee throughout the morning. Oddly, the third gentlemen keeps turning and looking at me. I assuming he is trying to figure out what I am doing or writing.

After an hour I get up to pay. At the register Erin says she has "too much intelligence to waste on not going to college", which I agree and she smiles in satisfaction. In my truck I watch through the window as she picks up the tip I left her - all of the cash in my pocket - five ones, a five, and a ten. She looks around the restaurant then just stands looking at her hand.

Driving towards home I think about what these people have that I don't. Being the only person alone in the restaurant that morning, it is blatantly obvious that they all have "friends" or someone they are with. Even the old guy has someone to chat with. I think of how my life is lived mainly in solitude. Except for a few friends that live in other towns, my only daily friends are co-workers that I see every day. Time that we spend together is usually prior, during, or following some type of school activity. The race I ran yesterday was even supposed to be run with another teacher from Oak Harbor.

What these people need most and how I might help them get it - this is a little more difficult. This is a question that I will continue to roll in my mind. Maybe I need to spend more time in 24-hour restaurants to gain some clarity?

55 Mark Mackesy

Sent: Wednesday, January 18, 2006 5:29 PM
To: Corrine@WizardAcademy.com
Subject: Experience

I'm cheating here.
My experience came about with the sudden onset of horrible stomach pains one early morning. This went one for 40 minutes before I suggested to the Lovely Doris that we go to the hospital. I struggled into track pants.
"You must be really hurting if you're going to wear those pants in public", she said, taking me seriously.
I believe in public healthcare. I believe in waiting your turn. I have read the storys about long waits for care at Canadian hospitals. And I would like to believe that getting a bed in the emergency ward pretty quickly had nothing to do with Doris working at the hospital for 18 years or that when the nurses at check-in asked me what was wrong, Doris spoke to them in medical tongues.
So there I was in a bed in a downtown hospital at 2 in the morning. To my left was an older sounding man. The nurses asked him by name how he felt. "Better, thank you" he responded. "Could I just rest a little longer?" Of course, responded the nurse.
Across from me was a young man. He had bandages on his head. He did not seem not happy to be there. He was also drunk. "I've got to get back, man!", he cried out. " I'm suppose to be back at midnight!". It became apparent to me that he wasn't aware that the witching hour had come and gone. "I've got to take my medicine!". It also became apparent to me that he was probably an escapee from some sort of halfway house. The nurses talked to him calmly, but whenever they walked away he started up again.
Meanwhile an old woman on my right was not happy.
"I have to call my daughter", she said in an Ukrainian accent, "She's going to go to my house after church and I won't be there". A nurse brought her a phone. She dialled.
"Hello?,,,,is _____ there?....wrong number... I'm sorry..." She hung up. This would play out continuously as long as I was there. The lady would ask for a phone. A nurse would bring it. The lady dialled a number that probably was 30 years out of date. The people on the other end would politely tell her _____ wasn't there. She'd hang up.

Thirty minutes later, repeat.

Two cops walked in. They went over and talked to the young man. When they finished talking the nurses started getting him ready to leave. They turned and regarded the old man to my left.

"What are you doing in here, _____?", asked the male cop. He obviously knew him.

"I fell on some ice", mumbled the old man. The cop grunted something and turned away. Shortly both the cops and the young man were gone. I wondered how long the bed would stay empty. I wondered if the young man would one day take the place of the old man.

More time passed. Doris never left my side. A nurse came and woke up the old man to my left. He got out of bed. He didn't smell too good. He walked out of the room.

"Goodbye ladies", he said with great dignity. He sounded like the mayor, "Thank you very much". "You're welcome, _____", chorused the nurses. I contrasted how he interacted with the nurses compared to the cops.

Eventually the drugs they gave me wore off and the pain was gone and so were we. The doctor said it was probably had some kind of virus.

"What does that mean?", I asked Lovely Doris.

"That's what they always say when they don't know what caused it".

"Great."

"Beats 'We'll find out in the autopsy'", she replied.

56 Jack Ancona

Sent: Monday, January 09, 2006 8:38 AM
To: Corrine@WizardAcademy.com
Subject: I'm In

How interesting it was to read the memo today. I sat in a place just three days ago for the very reason you state in your memo. In fact I was with my wife and we had just come from an emotional meeting about a loved one of ours. I felt as I looked around the room as I often do when I come to this type of establishment; who are these people and where do they com from?

They live in the same city. Some I assumed are employed, have children, bills, worries, and many of the things I have. If they look disheveled they more often than not are smiling. It always occurs to me that if they seem to have problems than how serious are mine? I have always felt that everywhere in the country or world there are places like this and they truly represent the cross section of the culture. The reason I believe all of this is there is because anybody can go there price is no object. Those who go there for price have no choice those who don't go there by choice. That to me is the adventure the exploring if you will.

I often bring my children during the day so they can get out of there sheltered environment.

Good memo

Evan T Williams

Sent: Sunday, January 15, 2006 8:33 AM
To: Corrine@WizardAcademy.com
Subject: Inside the Outside

Expanding My World

It's not unusual for me to visit an after hours eating establishment. My wife has an event decorating business and if she is short handed in the take down process, I will go along to help. We often stop for a bite to eat in the wee hours of the morning however I usually don't pay attention to the other patrons.

Last night I went by myself to a truck stop about 13 miles out of town along Interstate 79 on the Pennsylvania West Virginia border. It was a little after 1:30 AM and I was dressed in a sweatshirt, blue jeans and an old barn coat so as not to draw attention to myself. I looked around as I approached the restaurant and observed there were about 30 to 35 eighteen wheel rigs parked near the gas pumps and 4 pick up trucks and an SUV parked at the restaurant.

Upon entering I looked around for a familiar face, the only one that looked vaguely familiar was one of the cooks who could be seen through the open kitchen door. I positioned myself at a table between the counter and a table of three young men who appeared to be in their mid 30's. Three men sat at the counter separated by two to three stools. The men at the counter appeared to be in their late 40's to early 50's and didn't speak to each other but seemed to make light conversation with the waitresses. Two of them seemed to be regulars since the waitress addressed them by their names.

The three younger men at the table were more animated. The first part of their conversation that I picked up on concerned the mine accident that occurred in West Virginia almost two weeks ago. The truck stop is only about an hours drive from the mine. The men seemed to believe that had the miners attempted to exit the mine through another section rather than wall themselves off, they may have survived. The conversation then shifted to the Steeler play off game with the Colts which was to take place the next day. There was a lot of laughing as they discussed their golf games. It seems as if they played two times in the past week which caused me to wonder why I don't take more time to play. I was thinking that I have all the "toys" that I have ever wanted but I really never spend quality time with myself. I began to think about the

SIG course that I just completed several days earlier, and how Mark had suggested that we schedule and take time to think... My mother's work ethic continues to haunt me.

I finished my chili, cherry pie and was nursing the last of my third cup of coffee when a white pick up truck just barely missed the side of the building as it parked. The reason for the near miss became obvious as the occupants came into the dining room. The driver was so drunk he could hardly stand up. The man who was with him appeared to be relatively sober. They sat at a table adjacent to me and after about five minutes were joined by a female. The female suggested they move to the smoking section and the drunk became agitated and began to verbally abuse the girl. This seemed to set the waitress off and a confrontation ensued. My waitress suggested I move to the counter and poured me another coffee. I could hear the cook calling the police from the kitchen. Things were starting to get interesting and various scenarios were racing through my mind. This is a relatively red neck area and I would expect that several patrons in the restaurant were carrying firearms. I also was aware that a fight may begin soon as the other men in the restaurant were positioning themselves and the testosterone levels were rising.

The drunk got up and said he was leaving and staggered over to the waitress who had confronted him. He appeared like he was trying to give her a hug as she pushed him away towards the door. His sober friend attempted to give the waitress a five dollar bill as they were leaving. About seven people spilled out into the parking lot, the three of them followed by four of the male patrons. The drunk staggered, fell and then proceeded to get up and into his truck along with his friends. They left before the police arrived.

Since I was now seated at the counter I was able to get a better look at the one cook who sort of looked familiar when I had entered. I realized that she had been a patient of mine and   eight to ten years ago I had extracted all of her teeth, I can't remember whether we made her a denture but she didn't have any teeth in at the time... Now I have wives tell me that their husbands have never seen them without teeth, others say their husbands don't even know they wear dentures. This cook didn't at all appear to be self conscious about being edentulous in fact she really seemed to be quite at ease with herself.

My proposed one hour venture continued for almost two hours. By the time I left there appeared to be a real sense of community among those present. We seemed to have had an adventure together.

Glennan Wrinkle

58

Sent: Friday, January 13, 2006 2:30 AM
To: Corrine@WizardAcademy.com
Subject: Re: Monday Morning Memo from the Wizard of Ads

    I drive over to the Flying J Truck Stop on the far western edge of the Oklahoma City metro area. Roy has forgotten to remind his readers how much fun this assignment is when you're intoxicated. I've ditched the polar fleece in favor of a red flannel shirt circa 1993. It's a pleasant reminder of the times when Kurt was king and Britney was just a Mouseketeer. I've also parked my Infiniti G35 in favor of my parents' 1992 Pontiac Bonneville. My cover must not be blown.

    I sit on a stool at the front of the restaurant only 5 feet away from a trucker on his dinner break. If I were to create a stereotype for a trucker, this guy is it. Overalls, 24-inch ponytail, big bushy salt and pepper beard, black polyester jacket proudly proclaiming another truck stop in Iowa...oh yeah, this is going to be fun.

    I waste no time in butting in on his conversation with our waitress. Her name is Crystal, the same name as my younger sister's, although I think they've taken very different paths in life. My Krystal graduated from OSU and is a beautiful, successful Speech Pathologist. This Crystal is a waitress at the Flying J. But both are very good at what they do.

    The trucker is weaving tales of wildfires throughout the midwest. Ahhh yes, this is a hot topic nowadays. And how appropriate!! I'm currently writing a song for my album entitled "Burn Ban." Tonight is the night I will finish the song.

    "A tire flew off a truck off of I-70 in Eastern Kansas and burnt through a farmer's wheat field. Ain't that a bitch!!" I give a hearty laugh and shake my head as if this is the strangest story I've ever heard. Truth is I really don't care, but if this man can feel important and appreciated for the next 45 seconds, it is completely worth it to me.

    Time to order. For a moment I forget that I've been on Weight Watchers since 1 January. I look at the trucker's plate and order the same. Holy cow that's a lot of calories! Chicken Fried Steak, 3 scrambled eggs, 2 pieces of toast, hash browns, and gravy. I wonder if the trucker has ever considered a diet. His waist is at least 46 inches, 10 more than mine but well deserved.

    The trucker reveals to me that he's from Omaha, Nebraska. I'm only 29 years old but I can ALWAYS talk weather and geography with anyone in the U.S. Luckily, I have a dear friend from Blair, Nebraska and I spend the next 7 minutes of my life talking about Blair and Omaha. The trucker reveals his "Cliff Claven fact of the day" that Blair has a higher per capita cop-per-citizen ratio than any other city in America. I dare not call B.S. on his claim. This man is clearly enjoying the spotlight and the gratuitous laughs I'm providing.

The food arrives and it's more than I've eaten in the last 2 days. No chance in hell that I'll get a to-go box though. I dump Tabasco sauce on the eggs like I'm marking my territory.

The trucker is finished and gets up to leave. I inform him that I'll be paying for his meal tonight. Money I have, inspiration...not so much.

He is truly touched and thanks me for my generosity. "Not a problem," I proclaim, as I throw up my hand in a salute of kindred spirits.

The trucker walks away and I'm left with Crystal as my only companion to finish the country fried steak and eggs.

I notice that Crystal's purse is identical to my 4-year old daughter's. I make a comment about it and Crystal shyly brags that it's the "hottest thing going on with purses." I chuckle, secretly thinking that it's a sad world if my toddler is a trendsetter.

Nonetheless, I finish my meal and it's time to head back across town. I hand my ticket to Crystal, along with a $20 bill. Money I have, inspiration...not so much. She doesn't hear me the first time I tell her to keep the change. The second time I make sure to also let her know that she's very good at her job and I appreciated her kindness. Crystal is truly touched. Perhaps my tip will help to pay the high natural gas bill she is sure to receive this week. Perhaps it'll go into a savings account for her to attend cosmetology school. The options are endless, but I truly hope for the best for Crystal. She's honest, hard working, and I wouldn't hesitate to hire her. Nowadays, that's saying a lot.

Robin J. Elliott

Sent: Monday, January 09, 2006 10:52 AM
To: Corrine@WizardAcademy.com
Subject: The Other Side of the Fence

I visited a diner on the east side, the worst drug area in Canada, and enjoyed an interesting experience.

Instead of writing reams, here's the basics for you:

1. Much better community spirit than in my business world, however I had the distinct impression that this would end abruptly if any one of them came into money or got the opportunity to go somewhere else and get money. When I asked about this, I was proven correct from their experiences. Seems they stick together because that is the best for them in terms of self interest, not altruism. What goes around comes around - sort of insurance policy for when harder times hit.

2. Apart from fetal alcohol syndrome and other unavoidable experiences and occurrences, most reluctantly admitted that they were there because of their own bad choices.

3. As is usual on the west coast here, anti-American sentiment runs high, which is pathetic to me. I immigrated to Canada eight years ago from South Africa, and while I never hear Americans bashing Canada, I hear Canadians bashing America on a regular basis. The same goes for my visit to the east side.

4. Overwhelming socialistic/collectivist thinking-it's the government's fault, it's the fault of the rich, they owe us, we're hard done by, etc.

5. They all fiercely avoided any work offers I made.

I guess Ayn Rand was right when she wrote Atlas Shrugged.

Best Wishes and many thanks for your excellent Monday Morning Memo.

60 Jonathon Durbin

Sent: Friday, January 13, 2006 12:15 PM
To: Corrine@WizardAcademy.com
Subject: MMM Initiation Homework

Arriving at the restaurant at 2:15 AM. I ordered my breakfast from Donna. While the workers may not have Internet access, credit cards or cable TV, the workers sure have cell phones. I know these because as I was about to place my order, Donna answered her ringing cell phone and had a brief conversation. Apparently, there is another waitress, one younger and blonde.

Table of guys was asking where she was.

Josh was also working that night, trying to convince some of the other customers to allow him to pour a pot of coffee on them, then, split the lawsuit settlement. He was asking for a 50-50 split, the customers were bargaining for something closer to 70-30. He said he needed to pay for school so he could get out of this job and the money would help. A better job opportunity might present itself he would remove the ring that pierces his eyebrow.

If you were to ask Donna what she needed, I believe she would answer a rich husband. I would way what Donna needs most is a time machine, so that she could return to the point in time when her and her husband separated, and change her mind, and find ways to make it work.

I do believe that if I thought allowing Josh to pour a pot of coffee on me would really solve his problems, I would have done if for 5-95 slice. What Josh really needs is support. More than just "you're a pretty good ol' boy" support, but someone who had a genuine concern. I doubt his teachers in the outlying areas of Alabama thought he would amount to much, and didn't try to push his to be.

Now I don't have a time machine, or wasn't around Josh while he was growing up. I think that if Donna however saw a real, true love relationship, it would give at least a ray of hope that love is real, if not from a man, at least from God, so that she can see how wonderful of a creation she is.

Josh needs a purpose. He needs to see that there is more out the than school and that he should to something great, world changing even, whether or not he has a piece of paper on the wall or not. He needs to realize that he has gifts and that he needs to use them, not just serving platters of food.

I believe that Donna wants to be a lover, loved and giving love. Josh wants to know that he has a reason for being here. It reminds me of the Monday Morning Memo. I need to be a pencil-giver. Show people their purpose, and encourage them to reach for.

Thanks for the push to my belly; I may just try to live my life on the other side of the fence.

61 Josh Withell

Sent: Monday, January 09, 2006 9:57 AM
To: Corrine@WizardAcademy.com
Subject: Inside & Outside

This Monday Morning Memo couldn't have come at a better time as I have just returned from a 5 week trip to Thailand & Cambodia. This trip was not made up of 5 star hotel resorts & lounging on the beach but rather true backpacking & traveling. My goal was not to relax but to experience the culture of the people.

Place & Time:
It's not in a midnight dinner but rather a dirty street corner in Cambodia where no paved roads exist, gasoline is sold from pop bottles, and homes are placed upon four large posts, 8 feet off the ground.

What They Need Most:
Through the eyes of a Canadian I would have to say they need everything but based on the marketing definition of needs... shelter, water, food, clothing & security they only need one thing. Cambodia has more landmines per capita then any other country in the world & it's not uncommon to see people of all ages with missing limbs. In order to feed their families & make a living the people of Cambodia are forced to farm the land that is scattered with mines. Security is the number one need of these people.

Happiness. These people smiled from ear to ear with every word & only expressed their enjoyment with life as they shared their knowledge of Canada. Most of them had few material possessions besides the clothes on their back but I couldn't help but be jealous of their smiling faces & tight community.

I'm not sure if the above even becomes close to what you intended this activity but I felt that I would share my findings with you none the less.

Larry Beaverson

62

Sent: Monday, January 09, 2006 11:42 AM
To: Corrine@WizardAcademy.com
Subject: Restaurant Experience

    This does not meet the qualifications of your challenge, but I just had to tell someone.

    Forty years ago I lived for a short time in a small town in Missouri called Elmer.

    A few weeks ago I was in Missouri and decided to go back to Elmer to see what had happened there in my absence. I smiled as I drove into the outskirts of the village and saw the familiar bean-pole water tower with the town's name on it. The sign at the town limit proudly announced "Elmer, population 98." They hadn't changed that number even after I left forty years ago.

    I stopped smiling as I drove into the downtown area. It was a ghost town. All of the buildings were there as I remembered, but they were either gutted with fire or the roofs had caved in due to lack of repair. Mine was the only car on the street. I saw no sign of life. The little post office was still there and appeared to be open for business. There was a Body Shop with old cars spilling out into the street that I suppose was open for business. That was it.

    Sadly, I drove through Elmer and made a U-turn to leave before depression set in. On the way back through, the boarded-up store fronts seemed to share my sadness. In the middle of town I noticed a little sign on one of them that announced Restaurant. I stopped in front and noticed a light hanging from the ceiling inside. Since the bottom half of the window was boarded-up I could not see anyone inside. There were no cars out front, but there was a small weathered sign on the door that said Open.

    I always feel a bit foolish when I go to the door of a store when it is closed, but in this case there was no one around to observe my foolishness. I parked in front. When I got to the door I still could not see if there was anyone inside. To my surprise, the door opened. It was a deep room with many small tables filling up the front. At the back, near the kitchen, was a large family style kitchen table. Seated at it were three people all looking at me. Two men and a woman.

    I was obviously a stranger to these parts. I felt as if I was interrupting an important conversation as I walked to a small table near the large one. We were all obviously a bit nervous, but when we collected ourselves we exchanged greetings. The woman stood and took a couple of steps toward me and I asked her for a cup of coffee.

Everyone relaxed a bit as she went to get it. One of the men also got up and went to the kitchen. That left one man at the table. After I got my coffee I moved to the large table with him. That helped us all to be more friendly. The man was about 70 years old and began talking about the weather. After we exhausted that subject, I decided to get down to business. I told him that I had lived here for a while 40 years ago and this was my first visit back. The couple in the kitchen stopped whatever they were doing and looked out over the counter. They all looked me up and down, with no sign of recognition.

I told him that I was surprised that little was left of downtown Elmer. That opened up a whole new conversation. He was an expert on his hometown. He told me of a fire years ago that had gutted several of the buildings. The roofs on several others just caved in. Elmer used to be an important Railroad town, he expained to me, but when the Railroad died, so did Elmer.

"That wasn't the real reason the town died," he quickly added. "It was T.V.," he confidently announced. I noticed an approving nod from the two people in the kitchen.

"Before television, everybody used to come to town to socialize. They came to the stores, the restaurants, and the churches. As soon as they got their televisions, they quit coming," he said.

I don't remember much of our conversation after that. I could not think of any reason to dispute his wisdom. "It was T.V.," I thought. I did not have a second cup of coffee. Not that I was not enjoying this experience. I just wanted to get back in my car, get on the road, and think about what he said. As I drove back through town past the ghostly buildings, I think I said it out loud, "Yep, it was T.V."

Jim Rubart   63

Sent: Wednesday, January 18, 2006 5:16 AM
To: Corrine@WizardAcademy.com
Subject: Inside the Outside from Seattle

One of the 12

I wanted to head northeast, to Monroe. A lot closer to home and almost comfortable. But I played fair and went instead to a weary Denny's on 4th avenue; just enough south of downtown to hit Seattle's underbelly.

But, surprise, it wasn't the underbelly. It was just a world I've always stepped over. Wait. Can't say that anymore. The people I eavesdropped on aren't under me. A better analogy is the inside of a greenhouse at night with all the lights on. Really hard to see the people outside my little glass cocoon. But they're there.

I felt awkward. Felt out of place being the only Caucasian in the place other than the guy in the kaki shorts who looked like Kris Kristofferson if I squinted a bit and who kept walking out the front door only to return to his seat at the counter a few minutes later.

What did they offer me?

A glimpse of friendship. The woman and three men at the table next to me sent stories about each other back and forth like dandelion spores. The laughter following each anecdote was contagious. Then some of their dreams and needs started pouring out.

"I want to buy a house."

"You'll do it. Someday baby!"

"I need a cheap mechanic; it's a lot of money to fix my car." Then she sang it, "A lot, a lot, it's a lot of money!" More laughter.

"No, never been ... but someday I'm going. Watch me."

"I first met you years and years ago, a long time ago. We been through it huh?" (Made me consider how many friends I have from "years and years" ago.)

I long for that kind of affection between friends. I long for community. Not the superficial, "How're the kids Bob?" or "Those Hawks are making us proud this year!" type community. I mean rip your guts out, lay them on the table and know I'll still be accepted type of community. The laugh till you can't suck in another breath type community.

Think Rudolph. Who had more connection with each other? The

perfect little elves cranking out the choo choos, or the misfit toys?

What can I offer them?

A smile. A genuine smile. I can pray for them without them ever knowing it. I can hand the waitress my credit card and whisper, "charge me for the table next to mine." (The price of my meal and theirs plus tip? $55.74. The look on the waitresses face when I did it? Beyond priceless.)

And I can be honest enough to admit I didn't think I would fit down there. But I did. My house might be a little nicer and my car needs less repairs. But I'm the same as them; looking for friendship, longing for laughter, resting in hope.

And determined to stop living in the greenhouse.

Lew Hofmann

64

Sent: Tuesday, January 10, 2006 12:10 PM
To: Corrine@WizardAcademy.com
Subject: Bizarre conversations

    I followed your rules to the letter, "before" you had written them. I have always looked forward to the opportunity to experience the out- of-the-way stops in my travels. Culture is not just in the big cities. It is along the back roads, truck stops, rural bars and eateries where locals and transients are most likely to be found.

    One of the most entertaining was a conversation between three "down and almost out" characters at a pre-dawn breakfast stop along old US Rt. 40 in Colorado. I don't believe the three guys were acquainted before this encounter since they were not sitting together, but were sitting on stools along a counter drinking coffee and within conversation distance of one another. I believe at least one of them was hitchhiking through the area.

    The conversation caught my attention when it got to what could only be titled as, "Jails I have been in." It was your typical "I can top that..." conversation which began with one guy telling about a jail in Arizona that was the worst he had been in. Another said, "That was nothing, I was in a jail down in west Texas where..." Anyway, the details are lost, but if they were telling each other the truth, each had many experiences in jails around the country. I expect that, like most of these types of conversations, there was an element of truth and a lot of braggadocio. And the bragger with the most horrible experiences comes out the winner. A tape recorder would have been invaluable. Sorry you were not there.

65 Melvin Laskin

Sent: Monday, January 09, 2006 1:59 PM
To: Corrine@WizardAcademy.com
Subject: early morning club

I'm writing about the past because currently I am unable to make it to an out of the way place. Actually I'm already in a kind of out of the way place. But I have been there. I have sat in bar and eaten barbecued chicken feet with the working girls in a Kowloon bar. I've taken a slow walk on a rainy night in Adelaide and a cold night in Seoul, ridden the subway in Moscow and had to use my inadequate Russian to find the correct passage to the next subway line. I've spent long periods taking about everything in the world from girls and whiskey to politics to people in a Albany, Georgia eatery at 4 in the morning.

I bought your book, The Wizard of Ads, in the Atlanta airport last January while waiting out an ice storm, and have been receiving you newsletters since then. Your points should be obvious but I am continuously amazed at the blank faces I see when presenting them. I guess I'm not a salesman because I don't have the patience to slowly and methodically explain my point (or yours in many cases). But after a long time (years in most cases) I see the first shoots of the seed that I planted break the surface.

Don't send the gift, I left the US at the age of 40 and moved to Israel with my wife and two daughters. We've been her now for 18 years and love it. I accidentally slipped out of the fence a long, long time ago. I just wanted to let you know that you are known in other regions.

Tracy See

Sent: Monday, January 09, 2006 9:33 AM
To: Corrine@WizardAcademy.com
Subject: Outsider in America

My story might not count, because the rules were bent a bit. After a divorce, I (newly single woman) deceided to move cross country alone from my home in Upper Michigan to the Texas Panhandle. I went from a completely white, middle class existance among trees and lakes, to a dusty west Texas cattle town where 65% of the population is exclusively Spanish speaking - where there is a distinct, largely uncrossable, and made-to-be-noticable line between the classes, which is also the same distinct line drawn between races and religions. There are the white Baptists and the Mexican Catholics. Being a white Catholic makes me part of a small group - a village oddity - not trusted by either group. I was actually told by a 20-year old white man that I was the first white Catholic that he had ever met (I met and recently married another village oddity - another white Catholic non-native).

Hereford is a town of extremes - wealth and poverty, summer heat and winter chill, the east side and the west side, but so small a town that you don't have to go to the other side to see the differences. It's a town where you have to be bilingual to be employable (and since I'm not bilingual, work 35 miles away in a college town), where the decent jobs are held by the family members of the movers and shakers, and there's little room for outsiders. I had never seen before the busses of migrant workers living in camps outside the city limits. I'd never lived anywhere where the teen pregnancy rate was 62%. I'd never met anyone who had 5 family members in a one-bedroom house, making $3400 a year and thinking they had the world by the ass because they were living on this side of the border. Although we're a day's drive from the border, this is one of those towns where immigrants somehow get to - their first stop.

Living here has softened some previously held ideas and hardened a few as well. It's been 4 years here, and I'm still 1500 miles from my comfort zone. I hope that Mr. Williams makes an exception in allowing me into his exclusive club because mine wasn't a one-time midnight visit, it's an everyday thing. He is right, though. It is life-changing.

67 Patrick Rice

Sent: Friday, January 13, 2006 5:06 PM
To: Corrine@WizardAcademy.com
Subject: Initiation excursion...

Not being one to usually bite, by my calculations I would be the 13th initiate into the club. So, my choice was to excur during the wee hours of the morning, Friday the 13th.

My challenge? Convincing my honey.

"No, Honey, I'm a guy. I really do have to go alone."

"No, Dear, I wouldn't like it if you were the one doing this, but the rules state ladies can bring company."

"Yes, Sweetie, I probably would follow you, too!"

Anyway, after the resolution busting Pinot Grigio and peanut butter M&M's, she softened.

At 12:57AM my wrist buddy count down timer sounded a muffled reveille. I almost succeeded in stifling the digital nuisance. I'm sure I'll here about that all weekend, too.

Option one closed, I was on scene at location two by 1:35AM.

Thursday night turned Friday morning, the place was surprisingly empty.

Other than the night manager, those present appeared to be barley past the curfew age. It reminded me of that right of passage growing up, where I finally got to stay up later. "Hey, look at us. We're adults now."

Sure.

I picked a booth across from every guys dream: three girls to one guy. I was angling for the best lighting given my secret agent, photo challenged TREO 600.

It was kind of embarassing trying to take their picture, but I'm sure fumbling through handy paperwork and books while omlette hunting maintained my cover.

The background music wasn't. That is, the staff must have boosted up the volume to help keep from falling asleep. Thus, it was difficult to maintain continuity in conversations coming from that booth, or anywhere else in the resturant.

From what I could glean, the peach-fuzzed lad in the sport coat, who didn't order anything, liked to show off with big words. He's probably in training for a professorship somewhere.

Oh, well. I enjoyed my omlette. And, now I have a picture

(attached) to dissect for Power Writing lesson six.

As far as thinking about what those people needed, I'd say, a life. Just kidding.

Actually, they seemed to be enjoying the freedom of youth without obligations. I never once heard any pieces of conversation about jobs, or responsibilities. There was a little bragging about alcohol consumption and hangover bravado, but nothing serious.

And, their seeming freedom to enjoy the present, even if it was two in the morning, was refreshing. We all need that reminder. It's nice to not take life so seriously all of the time.

So, I didn't really see opportunity for contribution this go around.

Mission accomplished, and almost cozy in bed, my Sweety reminded me:

"Pat, do you think you're ever going to lose that weight?"

"Good night, Dear!"

68 Luis Alejandro López

Sent: Tuesday, January 17, 2006 6:16 PM
To: Corrine@WizardAcademy.com
Subject: MMM Assignment

Hi Roy. I'm Luis Alejandro Lopez Galindo. I live in Guatemala, as you may know in your trips, it's not the safest city to go to a 24 hour place and sit down and observe, but I found and alternative: This weekend I had a trip to Flores, Peten to play in a couple of concerts (I'm a musician) and decided to "follow my heart". I found other worlds, one not much different from what I've seen before. The other, a little bit risky one at glance but surprising at the end.

Flores, Petén. Is the urban area of the mayan city Tikal. The bus trip is 8 hours long from Guatemala City, so we traveled by night to keep us away from traffic in our tour bus (not with the commodities used by mayor US musicians, but comfortable enough to travel on our own). My assignment is composed in two parts, taking advantage of my late-travel situation.

Friday, 1:00 a.m.

Before we hit the road we stooped at a gas station, the ones like Seven Eleven. There were about 20 persons traveling with us, including musicians, sound techs and staff.

Most of us stopped for drinks and snacks, so we rushed in and out, but had enough time in the line, the cashiers were so slow. As I entered, I watched a couple sitting down eating hot-dogs and nachos, apparently after a night's out clubbing, I could tell by their red-ish eyes. Two men got in for beers, cigarettes and grabbed a CD from the front display. A family got in for food; a man, his wife and two teenagers boys. All of them started at us in surprise, the large group of "free spirits".

The party couple

The thing I thought they needed the most was some conversation and a different kind of entertainment, just for a variety. They seem like a couple that's been together for so long they pretty much were used to each other's company.

In Guatemala there's not much to do in the nightlife entertainment except from clubs, restaurants and bars, I guess it's pretty much the same all over the world. Once in a while there will be good concerts and the real good cultural acts, but thery are always directed to small audiences and advertised in a boring "cultural" way. The plays are usually satiric comedies; the music is usually cover bands, the restaurants and movie theaters are great, though. I thought of a lot of things but all them were already done and some without any success (magazines, promoting art, sponsors for greater exposure for arttis and other entrepreneur acs). I do think the problem's root is in the education, staring in cultural value in the city's population, artist's development, and the country's high levels of people that can't read and write (I'm not sure but it's more than 85% of the whole population).

The party couple seems peaceful and happy, maybe they didn't want to talk at that time, just refresh and go home...!, so I guess the one thing they had that I don't, was having a good time in silence (I'm a very conversational person), or the mediocre commodity of custom to each other.

The men
They seem like the labor class. Truckers, maybe. They surely were having a party at home, and ran out beer, cigarettes and background music, or maybe just got out of work and decided to spend some hours having a drink, a smoke and new music. Either way, this is another entertainment issue, this time I tought of "Healthy" entertainment.

One thing they had that I don't was a different kind of life-style, another segment of the market if I could called like that. They prefer to spend their money in after-hour pleasures instead of day-lite stuff, because they probably don't hava a day life, because they are driving. I'm not much a party dude, although being a musician automatically relates me to the rock-star life, I'm a lot different than the prototype (Otherwise I wouldn't be doing this right?). (Laughs).

Night traveling family
This guys we so different than the other "subjects". This family seem like they were doing a long trip. You could tell by their faces they hadn't eaten in a while and the kids just woke up. They got in, the teenagers recognized some of the members of the band, and asked for autographs. (I kept myself away to maintain my observer roll). The family chatted for a while. The first thing I thought they needed was a hotel or to whatever their destiny was with bus or plane tickets. Near they are there was a hotel and usually the bus lines are pretty good. So apparently there was nothing I could thing they needed that they could get themselves. But, the experience of riding and meeting people they admire, I think

that was priceless. One thing they have that I don't was the gut of driving by themselves that late, for any reason, but surely was a good one to travel late all together, I don't know if it was for visiting friends, vacations, a family reunion, I don't know and I didn't found out, but surely was a huge need to do it. I could just think about their safety. (It's not the same traveling with your family that to travel with 20 musicians.)

Bottom-line

The party couple, the two men, the family and also us, past thru the gas station for refresh, drinks, food and stretch. So I guess making the gas station experience safe and to have everything one could need it's something I could do. This will be accomplished only If I turned into their customer service manager or marketing consultant. That's not hard to do. The thing's that I could helped them with, regarding entertainment it's to keep playing and to think about other ways to promote art thru music and the radio ads I produce, because the people that can't read and write, surely has a radio with them and can hear. That's a first step. Them hopefully as I grow as an artist, will influence on the government to educate in a better way.

Saturday 3:30 a.m.

We played at a club. The show finished at 12:30 a.m. There were some friends of mine from the college, so I decided to stay a bit longer. It was assignment time!: it was 2:00 a.m. already. First I began observing people in the club, but then everything seem pretty normal, when suddenly some friends of my firnds, that lived in Flores asked us to go to an After-Party, so we accepted to go.

We arrived at a fancy housing facilities. I though they were drug dealers or something because of the place, the vehicles and bodyguards, I was a little bit concerned and calling myself a fool for going. My first impulse was get out of there, but my friends seem comfortable, so I acted comfy too.

I meet the owners and as I chat with them, they told me they owned some farms in the area and feed and sell cattle. They went to college in Guatemala City and spend their weekends helping their parents. So that explained the wealthiest and security, it was a rich family and Guatemala if your rich, you have a great chance to compromise your safety, and also if you are in the public eye. They surely were in the public eye of their employees and people that lived in and near the farms. In the house there were three basic groups, and this is what I observed so far:

The Rich Farm Kids
I thought they didn't really need peace at first, but in the other hand they do every time they are in Peten, because in Guatemala City, they don't have bodyguards it's just when they are in Flores. So pretty much I think what they need is Peace of Mind.

They have tons of money that I don't, but not everything that comes with money it's good, including safety, friends and social life, the good things they have unlimited resources to do lots of stuff that average people can't on regular basis, like travel, invest in their own companies, self-paid studies in other countries, gear and other things money do buy. Peace of Mind can't really be purchased, but it can be anesthesia with good security company, doctors, church and even psychologists maybe.

The friends
They kind of looked that they not really care about their friend's possessions. They treated them pretty well and like everyone else. Most of them grew up together. Since they were also collage students, I guess by keeping their friends, they're being smart. Maybe one day they will have invertors or associates form their companies.

The guests
We pretty much just observe, I'm kidding, I was. We chatted, meet new people. Since most of my friends are still in collage, all night went from conversation to card games and jokes. We really had a nice time.

Bottom-Line
Since I graduated collage I've used that to get my self into places that as a student I can't. I began giving public speeches and seminars for Junior Achievement in Guatemala, so that gives a little bit of exposure and I just started teaching in my University. But this visit gave a closer look to potential in acquaintances and young adults growth. Also a promotion solution, going to seminars isn't enough, neither graduating, Guatemala's youth need to commit to dreams and explore new country expansion in whatever everybody does, if it is arts, business, sciences, sports and anything else.

69 Robert M. Pratt

Sent: Thursday, January 12, 2006 8:26 AM
To: corrine@wizardacademy.com
Subject: inside the outside

Dear Mr. Wizard;
    The sun was not up, yet it wasn't dark. There's a surprising amount of light on the city street at 5:15 in the morning. There was a chill in the air, yet it wasn't cold. I was on a mission. The parking lot was had less vacancy's than one would expect that early in the morning, though it was a 24 hour diner. The vehicle of choice was a pickup truck. Mostly years past their prime and obviously ready for another day of work.
    Inside it was baseball hats and facial hair. From USN Seals to Bills Autobody to those which gave up legibility years ago, caps were the common factor. But a stronger tie was the cigarettes. Name brands on the table top with fancy lighters. Generics on the counter top with matches. In shirt pockets and reaching out from purses. Had there been a No Smoking sign, it had long ago given up hope. But I could not honestly say the Waffle House was full of smoke.
    As customers came and went I realized that they all knew each other. From the senior citizen with the slicked back mullet to the middle aged black man, they had been seeing each other for years. They didn't just stop in for breakfast, they went there on purpose.
    Conversation ranged from a complaint about "him wakin me up a 3:30 and me tellin him I ain't gunna get out of no bed at 3:30", to "those sob's at the shop not bein able to fix the gd airconditioner on the ole lady's car". But the common thread to the overheard conversations was health care. One lady advised another she needed to go to the doctor even if she didn't have insurance. Another related how even at the low cost clinic they asked for one hundred dollars, which she promptly informed them she didn't have. Still another asked what was the use of having insurance anyway cause the gd deductible was so high it didn't matter anyway.
    The irony was overpowering. I was sitting amongst a group of lower income people and listening to complaints about the high cost of health related issues. Yet they were willing to pay to indulge in a very expensive habit which is virtually guaranteed to ensure they need that very same healthcare system. Wow!
    Thinking back to the assignment, what do these people need, my

first thought was they need to stop smoking. But on further reflection, that would probably kill them quicker that the cigarettes. The cigarettes were some sort of social bonding agent. They allowed them to gather and be part of the same group. They appeared to be the glue that held these people together. No, they don't need to give up cigarettes.

What they truly need is affordable health care. Not good insurance, but affordable healthcare. A place where you can get attention and not expect a bill that is at least a weeks worth of pay. A place of caring, not of monetary gain. And you know what? We all need that.

And what can I do to help them get it? Well it just so happens that a charitable health care clinic in town, one where you pay what you can afford, will soon be getting a new radio PSA promotion. It's a small step but who knows.

Kristy Iris

Sent: Wednesday, January 18, 2006 11:53 AM
To: Corrine@WizardAcademy.com
Subject: Your challenge

Dear Wizard,

I took your challenge. As an American citizen and one who loves a challenge in the name of human inquisition and market research, I found the mission calling to my intellect and soul.

I am a New Yorker. That's right, I live in Manhattan. As big as we think, our radius of comfort is small- the island of Manhattan. Brooklyn and Queens are far off lands. The temptation to take a road trip to Canada to see these great adventurers in their habitat was very tempting. The call to step outside of my comfort zone forced me to cross a river into a land which to us New Yorkers is a galaxy far, far away- New Jersey.

The wee dark hours were quiet in the freshly rain washed city that never sleeps. My female status required an escort of a fellow Monday Morning Memo reader- of male status and of imposing stature to join in this journey on the PATH train to Jersey City. The journey is often the joy more than the destination.

I morphed into my childhood hero, Harriet the Spy with my note book, ready to notate my observations at the destination. But, wait, here, all around were the random souls that live and work in the dark hours of the morning. Characters all. If I created them as characters in a play, they might be considered over the top and unbelievable. The two that looked just a step above homeless performed the most stereotypical acts of throwing trash and urinating on the train tracks. What do they need? Well, a garbage can and a bathroom. But would they use them?

Eventually, the train came and there was more to observe. The cops that didn't talk to each other looked miserable. There were men asleep. Was this their bedroom or their way to end the day? The return trip had more people on their way to work. None looked happy. There was no excitement to where or what they were doing. I referred to my notebook, in spirit of Harriet the Spy- a tape running through my mind- who are these people? What do they need the most? How might I help them get it? What do they have that I don't?

We landed in Jersey City, New Jersey intent on finding the "mother ship". We made our way down streets searching for the watering hole- a diner to give us a peek at a world we sleep through and do not imagine.

The strong wind required effort to walk against and the mist moistened my face. The traffic lights and fast food signs reflected off the wet pavement. We took down a street at random and found a man in a brightly lit doorway that directed us to a diner down the street. The way he looked at us confirmed that we were not someplace that we fit in. We fought the wing and flying debris. My partner was accosted by a large piece of garbage that propelled through the air at him like a bat out of hell and smacked into the stomach of his wet nylon ski jacket. I yelped. Then, a snake of plastic as wide as the sidewalk slithered up to us. We jumped over it, only to have it back track and wrap around our legs. Yikes!

    We come upon the VIP diner. Is it open? I decide to take a picture with my cell phone's camera. As I cross the street to go in, my partner is reassuring the manager/owner that I am not taking the picture for any incriminating reasons. He is deeply suspicious as is the other owner/manager that is watching from a window inside. This causes a bit of a stir. Their fears are somewhat assuaged that I am harmless.

    Alas, it is empty. We are the only ones frequenting the "joint". A few people come and go. One waitress gets her tea and sits down at a table to read the paper. I watch our waitress refold the ratty dish rag and rewipe the counters a few times in pure obsessive compulsion. I think that I would want someone like that working for me if I had a diner. Her work is very purposeful in attending to every detail for the next shift. There is a deep sadness about her. What does she need the most?

    I decide to get in the game fully. I go down to the waitress sitting solo with her papers. I notice that she is reading the rags like the National Enquirer. I introduce myself and ask if I might have a couple of moments of her time and her thoughts. She is suspicious but open and lets me join her. I tell her that I am on a mission to find out how I can help others. This, she seems to think is a good idea and will then consent to share with me. I inquire what might she need to make her life better. Her response was a blank look that replied, "I don't think of solutions." The computer readout: does not compute.

    I needed to change my strategy if I was going to keep her engaged. I asked what was most stressful for her. Bingo! In that moment, she lit up and was a torrent of details about her coworker whom she relieved and did not work side by side for the last 8 years being the most stressful aspect of her life. Ah, yes. The problem. She was very comfortable being in the problem. The solution was foreign to her.

My inner Harriet noticed the "literature" she read and that she needed good affordable dental care. My heart saw a woman who has been a victim to her mind's focus on problems and not solutions. How can I help her?

How can I help the sad faces I sat across from on the return trip to my comfort zone? Aromatherapy for trains? I pods with music for baby boomers that don't have or use computers? My inner entrepreneur saw a million ways to go that were possible ways to help others. Where to begin?

Wait! I took a deep breath and came back to myself and saw that what I do will help them as I reach more people with my business, which I know is my purpose. It is so easy to be swayed from one's path by a shiny new idea. I found a new level of purpose in knowing that I have to reach those that exist while I sleep to living better, more fulfilled lives focused on their solutions.

My trek home from the train was steeped in deep contemplation of my life's direction. I visited a land only a few miles from my home and yet a galaxy from where I am. I found a knowing that if I keep on my own path, I will be able to help those on their path across the river and across the world leave the land of problems and settle into a world of solutions.

Thank you for this challenge and your amazing work. I look forward to meeting you at one of your classes and playing in your world. This American is awaiting your next challenge outside of my comfort zone. I always carry my passport with me!

J.D. Cave

Sent: Saturday, January 14, 2006 11:27 AM
To: Corrine@WizardAcademy.com
Subject: Inside the Outside

The Game after The Game

It's Thursday night, Poker Night. Considering the luck I'd been having I'm thinking about not going this week. But it's not really just the cards. It's the fraternizing with the guys, having a few laughs, a beer or two, and that big block of extra sharp cheddar that pulls me in. And there's an additional incentive this week. I've read about a challenge the Wizard of Ads put forth to his 31,000 readers. He said only 12 (and of these only 6 would be Americans) would actually go to an all night eatery and listen to what the "other half" had to say. He likened it to crawling on your belly and getting dirty to have that 'experiential' feeling and discovering what it's like out there at 3:00am. To see, to sense, to feel what happens in our world while we sleep. The Wizard, Mr. Roy Williams, wants readers of his weekly 'Monday Morning Memo' (remember, he's guessing only 12 will actually follow through) to get a glimpse of a whole other world that exists beside the one we know. Wow! That's enough of a carrot for me. I don't care if I get bad cards again this week. Unconsciously, I must have been hoping to get knocked out of the Texas Hold 'Em action early so I could leave. As luck would have it, I win and stay until the end with the payoff, a fistful of cash in my jacket pocket. Now I'm ready for a unique experience for the price of a few cups of coffee. I'm headed to the Southside Diner.

The drive takes about 45 minutes and on the way I'm wondering what and who I'll see. It's just after one o'clock in the morning and the Interstate is packed with big rigs. What must they be hauling and where are they going? Why do they seem to take up the entire road and do they ever get pulled over for going 18 miles per hour over the speed limit? Maybe I'll get to ask them some of these questions at the diner. No. I need to be quiet and just listen. I remind myself of the parameters of the Wizard's challenge as I get out of the car and go inside. There's a quiet eerieness in the darkness and I'm excited about what I will discover inside.

Not many patrons are seated. The best opportunity I have to eavesdrop looks to be a booth adjacent to one where 3 men are busily chatting away. I take the seat. As I unfold the newspaper and settle in, the lone waitress asks the same one word question she has no doubt proffered thousands of times.

"Coffee"?

Yes, please. I make a point to notice her a bit closer and wonder. Why is an elderly, white haired woman of at least 70, working in an all night truck stop? Is it by choice? Reality smacks me for the first time on this mission. Of course it is.

I'd like to just come out and ask, "Ma'am, can you tell me why you're here tonight"?

It's the first example I see tonight of people who are not like the ones I usually associate with.

A little voice inside my head tells me ...'Hey stupid, she's here to make a living....Duhh'.

She's probably been here for over 20 years. She has no retirement plan and can't pay her fuel bills and groceries just on Social Security. She either has no kids or they don't care. I'll bet she lives alone with a cat or two and drives a 15 year old car.

I'm grateful that's not my mother serving coffee on the nightshift. I'm already planning to give her a good tip, regardless of the service I receive.

As she brings the first cup with creamers, the conversation from the next booth centers on women. I can hear the three men talking either about wives or girlfriends or both. It's not Dr. Phil but one of them seems to know how to handle the female sex in just the right manner. As I pretend to be looking at the classified section of the newspaper, I jot down notes.

Did I hear him right? Did he just say '... the best thing that could happen to her is that she gets knocked up by somebody else'? Gosh, he did! Reality smack number two.

Yes, I'm in an all night diner and these are truck drivers. Shhhhh, the conversation continues, pay attention.

"She just loves to get beat up", says the guy in the green shirt.

"And if she aggravates me, she knows what's coming next."

I'm pondering these words and can't help but think about some woman hundreds of miles away is thankful that her husband or boyfriend is on another 7 day run. Do people really live like this? I'm doubting that any woman REALLY likes to get beat up. But what do I know? I live in a somewhat insulated world.

The smoke is thick as I recall doing two packs of Marlboros a day some 30 years ago. Then it dawns on me (another smack), the guy in the plaid shirt could be ME! That could be MY rig outside and I could be headed to Atlanta with a load of generators. Their conversation is being drowned out by a repeat of Hannity & Combs on the wall mounted TV. I wish it wasn't so loud. It's almost like I'm listening to Paul Harvey's 'The Rest of the Story' as the station fades out before I can hear the ending. Come on, come on! They continue to chat for a bit more before getting up. I missed the ending.

The old white haired waitress lady freshens my coffee. I like her. As I look around for another booth, it's pointless. I'm the only customer here. Drat. This was just getting good. But not to worry. Let's try the Waffle House just down the street. Perhaps there's some action there. I leave a ten for the coffee and head for the door, giving mom a smile.

The Waffle House holds promise. It's just after 2:00am and there are a few customers inside as I pull into a parking space with renewed enthusiasm and excitement. Why doesn't everyone do this from time to time? There's a booth with 2 girls and a guy, all about 18 to 24 years old. I stake a claim to the booth next to theirs. Yes, coffee, please. This waitress is much younger here and also looks like she really needs the job. I unfold my paper, slide the notepad underneath, and get my pen out, ready for another adventure.

The threesome is laughing and they seem to be having a good time over an early morning breakfast. Within minutes they are joined by three more girls, also very young, attractive and fairly well proportioned. OK, I admit it, I'm a man. One of the new girls slides into the booth next to the guy and the other two take a smaller, two person booth across from it. They are all 'together' and it's obvious they all know each other.

"Where have you been?" asks one of the girls to the three who just joined.

"I had to stop and pee" was the reply from one. Then she adds, "what happened to your truck?"

"Oh, that. Well, I was like getting ready to turn right, and I thought he was like turning left, and then he like turned right too, and then, shit, he hit me. I did a U-ie"

"Damn."

"Yeah, tell me about it.

The conversation is flowing and my pen is working overtime. The guy says that this was the third time the truck had been hit and he wasn't driving in any of the accidents. He had been silent for about 10 minutes and his voice commanded attention. I wondered what one guy was doing with 5 attractive girls at 2:30 in the morning. They all seemed to be happy. But according to the Wizard, that's not unusual for folks at coffee shops in the middle of the night. I assumed they were college students since it was a college town. But somehow they didn't fit the mold of the typical student I had seen here.

"What did you have to drink tonight?" asks one of the girls to another.

"Two Margaritas, some Gran Marnier, and tequila."

Wow! I wondered why she's not on the floor. I sense that this is not a once-in-awhile outing but a matter of routine with this group. And that doesn't mean the scrambled eggs, bacon and toast. It's the booze.

I begin to ponder what these young people do, if anything, for a living. Then the clue comes.

"How did you do tonight?" one of the girls asks.

Ah-haa. Now we're getting somewhere. They've just been bowling, I think, or maybe they had a chemistry test at the university.

"Oh, I only did about two and a half," was the reply.

Wait a minute. That's a lousy bowling score. And even a dummy should know the periodic table enough to get better than a 2.5.

Then it hits me. They're talking about money. My brain is trying to configure this group with this clue. One guy. Five attractive girls, late at night. Oh no. They're hookers and he's the pimp. Is that possible? I try to stop quizzing myself so much and listen to the group for the next chapter. Their conversation has me riveted and I try not to crane my neck quite so much so as to let them know I want more.

"Yeah, I told him not to touch me. I told him if I want to touch you, I will, but you don't touch me."

"People want to give you cards. I just take them and throw them away later"

"Me too."

"Did you see that new girl. She's got flat titties"

The light bulb finally comes on in my head. I'm not stupid after all. They're exotic dancers at the club across the state line. They've just spent the past four hours stripping and showing off their naked bodies in a dimly lit smoke filled room full of men. Bingo. At last I have it. Now their conversation shifts to babies, ex-boyfriends and husbands, and they make it seem like the things they are describing happened 50 years ago. They're so young.

"I was almost on a milk carton," says the blond. "I called my mom almost everyday and told her I was OK. I told her I wasn't in a ditch or nothing. She died of cancer."

"I ran away when I was 16, got married two weeks after I turned 17, and had Jenna. All I wanted was a baby and a ring," says another.

These young people have had some hard knocks. Maybe that's why they must do what they do. Their bills need to be paid. I make no judgements. I rationalize that dancing is better than the next step. It's 2:42am. According to Mr. William's guidelines for this evening, I'm supposed to seek a way to help these people. I wish I could. I truly wish I could.

I have a knot in my stomach knowing that there are countless other coffee shops with thousands of other well meaning, hard working people in them, each with their own unique story. I hope they are happy. I think they are. And I think that some of them have a happiness and contentment that others envy. I can't explain why. I secretly wish them well.

As this crowd leaves, I prepare to as well. When their car pulls out of the parking lot, I go to the counter to talk with the two waitresses in the restaurant. I ask if these are "regulars". The waitresses snicker a bit and say 'yes'.

"But they don't tip for crap" says the one who served me.

I tell her it's been a special night for me. "Let's fix that, shall we?" I say.

I reach into my jacket pocket for the stash of poker money and leave two twenty dollar bills on the counter. Somehow I sensed when I raked that pot earlier in the evening that it would come in handy. They smile the biggest smiles I've seen in weeks. I wish them well and bid them a good morning.

This has been a good experience. I wonder why more people don't do it. I've been here before, many, many years ago as a young man. I could just as easily be among this crowd as a regular. Maybe that's why I can identify with them and why I came. I say a short prayer and thank God for letting me have a better life. I thank Him for good health, a successful business, a wonderful wife, loving family, and good friends. And I'm ready to go home and be next to my best friend in bed. She'll ask me tomorrow how it went. I'll show her my writing.

Mr. Williams promised a "gift" to those who would take the time to have this experience. It is he who deserves the gift by enriching the lives of so many others. Thank you, Roy. I already have everything I need.

72 Delia McCallister

Sent: Friday, January 13, 2006 12:37 PM
To: Corrine@WizardAcademy.com
Subject: Adventure in Reality

Driving to the restaurant at 4:30am on Weds. I had a pit of anxiety in my stomach. I was instructed as a woman to take a friend along, but I could not think of a friend that would understand my need for this excursion.

The waitress looked at me a bit oddly as she seated me, I guess the number of suit wearing patrons is few at this time in the morning. she was quite pleasant, but looked tired and worn. I asked if she had been on shift all evening to learn that this was her second job and she had been up since 8 am the previous day and was looking forward to the 6 hours of sleep she would get before starting the next 14 hour work marathon. Single mom, only a high school education, stuck in a small town-but for the grace of God go I.

The crowd is quite thin. A man and woman sit at the nearest table talking in low, harsh tones. She seems quite angry and at regular intervals gets up to use the restroom. I think to myself "what would I give her if I could?"--I decide strength to believe that she could stand on her own. Ten minutes later they leave.

The truckers start filing in next, two at a time--strong men ready for the day. What do they need most? Belief that this day will go well. What do they have that I don't? As I watch them greet each new stranger that steps up to the counter I know that it is the ability to genuinely say good morning. In the business of marketing no one really says good morning for any other reason than to be courteous. The truckers say it to each other as a wish of good favor. What a lovely way to start the day.

I get up to go and wish Sammy (my waitress) a genuine good day--just to make sure she will have one I leave a $20 tip for my $2 cup of coffee. I walk away richer.

Wayne Lincourt

sSent: Tuesday, January 17, 2006 10:49 AM
To: Corrine@WizardAcademy.com
Subject: January 17th, 2005 – Wizard Assignment

Dear Roy,

It was 42 degrees Fahrenheit at 4:30 in the morning with the temperature dropping as I left the gated community where I live in North Dallas. I was heading for the underside of downtown to find the kind of eating establishment that would be open at that time of the morning and where I would be most likely to share breakfast with some of the most down-and-out individuals in the city. Well, maybe not the most down-and-out since they wouldn't likely be having breakfast, but at least people I don't ordinarily associate with.

I didn't have any trouble finding the eateries; the only problem was…there weren't any people at them. Not other than the employees, mopping the floors or sitting idly at a booth waiting for traffic. After a half an hour of cruising the dark, nearly deserted streets, I found some activity at a MacDonalds near the Grey Hound bus station and pulled into a parking spot. A half dozen people were waiting for the employees inside to open the door. Fortunately we didn't have to wait long because the wind was picking up, whipping away your steaming breath along with the rest of your body heat.

As we shuffled inside and stood in line to order, it was apparent that there was a mix of travelers; homeless people bundled up in their blankets and too many layers of clothing; and some local regulars who greeted one another with comments about the ball game, the wind, and personal references that I didn't understand because I didn't know their history.

The homeless people were quiet and solitary, keeping their heads down and not making eye contact as they got their cup of coffee - their ticket to escape the chill wind and warm their insides before going wherever it was that they were heading that day. One man wearing a pink parka read the paper while another sat mumbling to himself; not in an annoying or threatening way, but just a word now and then under his breath as if conversing with someone else not completely present.

The regulars were coming through the door now; a line of people joking and talking and looking around to assess who might or might not be present this morning. One man wearing a coat with a big patch on the left sleeve shaped like a shield and who I took for a security person or courier carried a small, tightly wrapped valise, and seemed very much at home. With him, or more likely simply entering at the same time, was a man with wild long hair and a beard. The two were laughing and joking as they passed my table. The man with the wild hair was dressed in many layers, so that he looked overstuffed and the flannel shirt on top appeared too small for the bulk of him. At first glance he looked like a homeless person, but he didn't behave like a homeless person. He wasn't cautious or spare in his movements but walked and talked with a degree of energy I didn't see in those who had been waiting patiently for the doors to open admitting them into the warmth. He looked around, apparently checking out the other patrons although not in an obvious way, and helped himself to the coffee like he had somewhere he needed to be. An undercover policeman? A professional panhandler? I don't know, but I don't think he slept in an alley last night.

As I sat observing and thinking about what these people as individuals and as a group needed, it occurred to me that this MacDonalds was exactly what they needed! Whether it was a place to get warm, to have something affordable to eat, to exchange pleasantries, or just use the bathroom, what government agency could create such a clean, bright, colorful environment to welcome these people? With Frank Sinatra playing on the sound system and a policeman who walked through checking that all was as it should be, I thought what a comforting, safe environment this business provides its patrons.

I'm quite aware of the many charitable activities engaged in by businesses of all sizes in this country, but never considered that MacDonalds provides a social service in the course of it's daily business of serving modestly priced food to the public. I doubt that's what you had in mind with this assignment, but that was my big revelation.

I'm a middle class American. My exposure to the most affluent and privileged in our society is akin to the glimpse a pedestrian has of an opulent store window filled with upscale clothing, jewelry and photos of exotic destinations. But I know poverty up close and personal. Growing up poor in a rural community differs from poverty in the big city only in that it isn't as easy to escape into a community of like individuals, and the opportunities, both good and bad, aren't as abundant. Some people would romanticize bums, thieves and drunks, like Steinbeck did in his writing. They mistake vestiges of altruism borne out of loneliness or the bonding effect of getting high together with nobleness of character. The truth is that there's nothing noble about laziness, drug addiction, or dishonesty. There's nothing honorable about lying, cheating, stealing, or taking advantage of good people's generosity. And there's nothing redeeming about being a "victim" of circumstances.

Certainly there are individuals afflicted with mental illness, disease and disabilities who need our help; people who have taken a wrong turn or been slapped down by fate. And I believe most emphatically that society does have an obligation to care for these people the best it can. But on this morning, I saw different people in different circumstances, brought together by the warmth and light of a commercial establishment serving hot food and beverages, creating…a community. And whether it's the community of a MacDonalds or the community of Man, people have always found solace in the community of others. You asked us to consider what we could do to help these people? My conclusion - buy stock in MacDonalds.

74 Phillip Mahan

Sent: Tuesday, January 17, 2006 9:12 PM
To: Corrine@WizardAcademy.com
Subject: Inside the Outside email

    I hope that this email finds you and everyone at the academy well. I know that Becky must be close to having her baby, and my wife and I are keeping her in our thoughts. Below are the paragraphs that I wrote after taking Roy's assignment from last week's Memo. I have included my address at the end of the email although you will probably recognize me as the one who keeps bugging you about the Muskogee manuscript.

    3:15 am in waffle house, two older lonely men flirting with the waitress. Their conversation was a continual discussion of the fact that they would have to go outside to smoke. Can you believe that they would pass a law to keep us from smoking while we eat? Twice during my waffle and 3 cups of coffee, the older man turned to me to bum a smoke. I had to admit that I didn't have any with me, and that I had never taken up the habit. This sparked a debate as to whether I had voted for the ban on smoking in local restaurants (I had not). I realized that although I had gone to the other side of town, I might not have gone far enough to join the fraternity. Two old white men, a short order cook who remained silent except for the repetition of orders, and a waitress who was counting down the minutes until she could go home were all that I encountered. I will try this again in the coming weeks, and try to see other slices of the lives of others.

    In my job as an Information Security professional, I listen during lunch to hear what I can hear. I have been known to pull people from my company off to the side after they return from lunch and repeat confidential information that I overheard during their meal. I want to thank Roy for this assignment in the Memo, as it has given me a new frame of reference for my dropping of eaves.

    Happy new year to the wonderful people at the academy, and I hope to see you all soon. I'm also hoping that there are more than a dozen responses to last weeks memo and that the Americans step up to the plate and write.

    Arooo, Arooo!!! May your beagles run free and happy.

Michelle Butler Hallett

Sent: Wednesday, January 18, 2006 6:21 AM
To: corrine@wizardacademy.com
Subject: "Inside the Outside" challenge -- "The tip"

There were no sugar bottles on the table – you know, the glass ones with the vertical lines and the domed steel lids. Hell, the only restaurants in St John's with sugar bottles are the dickied-up retro bistros where lunch starts at $20.00 (roughly $22.00 US). Lots of waxed paper wrappers, though, balled up incompletely, now sprung out and dented. Empty cups. Crumbs. And the counter-guy grinning from a three dollar tip given to him by a regional hockey celebrity recuperating from knee surgery.

I'm in a Subway on Water Street, downtown St John's, in the province of Newfoundland and Labrador, up in Canada. Oooh, Subway, jeez Michelle, aren't you outside your comfort zone. It gets better – the store is one of several owned by my parents and sister. A portrait of my Dad used to hang in the doorway, welcoming people to the store. Yep, that upper middle-class upbringing stains you deep.

At least it's 4.30 in the morning. And I'm wondering, watching the hockey player – I don't know yet who he is – why I'm trying to impress some American advertising guru. But I'm not. The whole looking outside yourself to understand humanity – yeah, I get that. Empathy within conflict: that's what moves us in novels, movies, plays, even well-written history. This fucked-up world will not change until we can all develop compassion, and the path to compassion is empathy. Storytellers must first learn empathy and compassion themselves before they can expect their stories to elicit the same. I've been eavesdropping on, and talking to, strangers since I was a teenager. I write fiction and drama, and if all I ever wrote was literally what I knew, or, as many take Hemingway's advice, what's literally happened to me, I'd have one book, as boring as it is thin.

So, like the flawed and occasionally stupid Jacques Cartier in the Tragically Hip song Looking for a Place to Happen, "I got a job. I explore. I follow every little whiff."

And I actually agree with this American advertising guru when he points out that to write, you need to explore. Observe. Experience.

Now, I'm normally up at a disgusting hour – 4.30am most weekdays – so I can work on my fiction before getting the kids out and myself to work at Steele Communications, a division of NewCap Radio Inc. (I'm a copywriter. And I signed up for the Monday Morning Memo after Roy Williams spoke in St John's on my company's invitation.) So for breakfast this morning I got up at 4, after a crumbling night's sleep that ended with a dream of rolling-over my mother's SUV, and drove to downtown St John's.

Anyone who's heard of St John's has probably heard of George Street, which has more bars per square foot than any other street in North America. Yeah. Early mornings, when it's still stickydark, it's stubborn partiers, too happy or too inebriated to go home just because the bars stopped serving at 2am, and people frayed out on alcohol from a plastic bag, pot, Ecstasy, Oxycontin, crystal meth, or even just adrenaline. These people are nearly indistinguishable from the university and college students with their professionally coloured hair, leather jackets and maxed out credit cards, from entertainers and bar owners scouting out a bite before going to bed – indistinguishable until you listen.

Subway on Water Street is a great place to listen.

This particular Subway, in business since 1985, has seen broken windows, vandalized bathrooms, drunks throwing up or passing out, numerous robberies, and once, a mentally ill woman weighted by delusion and so distraught that she ripped the cash register monitor off its thick steel post. Wahoo, beer and skittles and suffering gladiators, the squalid little voyeur in me cheers, bring it on!

A handsome young man is surrounded by admirers, two female, one male, in the line ahead of me. He's an athelete, perfect posture, sharp jawline, but his lips are gently pursed – could be arrogance, could be pain – and his brow is heavy. He doesn't smile. The counter-clerk can barely look him in the eye, and his voice is cracking with happiness, with the good fortune to be talking to this guy. The athlete asks for chips with his order, adding "Surprise me" when the counter clerk asks what kind, and then he declines the soda fountain Coke products – not sure why. His wallet is thick with bills. He leaves, preceded by admirers either reminding him who they are, or just grinning, reflecting back the light they see coming off him.

The counter-clerk wants to say "Holy shit," but stops himself. He tells me the athlete's name and explains that he's not playing because of knee surgery. "And he gave me a three dollar tip. And man, he's, he's worth money, serious money. He's wearing that old sweatshirt, but he's worth money! Now what can I get for you?"

"How old is the coffee?"

"You don't want that."

I get a sandwich and sit down to eat it, the only customer. Jalapenos, lord, I got jalapenos at 4.35 in the morning.

Then a man about my father's age blunders in, spins once, and asks, "What Tums isht?"

The counter-clerk says, friendly and loud: "Sorry, b'y, we don't got Tums."

The man's disgusted. He speaks as though his dentures are gone, but he had all his teeth. He's wearing wrinkle-resistant pants, good lace-up winter boots, a warm Montreal Canadiens jacket and a ballcap. His hair is short and clean; he could be a neighbour in the burbs, the one who comes to snowblow your driveway. He says, "What time is it?"

"Ohhh. Sorry, I thought you wanted Tums. Nearly twenty to five."

The man turns to me and holds up his white plastic bag. In it are two bottles of beer on their sides, clinking once. He says, "I need to know what time it is so I can find a place to sleep. I've been up for two days." He turns back to the counter-clerk to ask him to call a cab, but the clerk darts to the back of the store to talk to a co-worker – hoping this guy will go away.

But the guy leans on the counter by the cash register monitor and talks about how he's been drinking for several days, sleepless for two, got kicked out of the house and now really ought to head to detox – he says this with old and comfortable knowledge – but the crowd at detox will take his last two beer from him. He holds up the bag and asks us: "Do you think they'll really take these from me?"

We agree yes, they likely will.

The counter-clerk adds: "Your cab is here."

The man leaves, holding his white bag – the handles are stretching – and reels round the corner away from the cab. Then he stops, looks at me through the window as though asking for a map, then rolls his eyes, crosses the street and gets in the cab. The counter-clerk rolls his eyes now: "I didn't think I'd get rid of him." He grins at me, again the lone customer at a dirty table. "God, there is nothing to do down here." Theatrical, high-voiced, pimply. "Do you know buddy gave me a three-dollar tip?"

Michael Staires

Sent: Wednesday, January 18, 2006 11:03 AM
To: Corrine@WizardAcademy.com
Subject: re: Waffle House story

The Other Side of Midnight

My eyes open at 1:50am, a full two hours ahead of schedule. The house is quiet and there is no noise at all coming from outside; no dogs, no wind, no nothing. It's the kind of quiet that actually makes noise inside your head—the kind of vacuum your brain has trouble processing.

Quiet is the first thing I notice about my over-night excursion to the other side of my comfort zone. I live on a busy street in West Tulsa. Outside noise has become the constant backdrop to life in this part of town. Passing cars and trucks and emergency vehicles on the street in front of my house or from the near-by intersection of expressways, the banging together of freight cars in the train yard not one mile away, dogs (including my own) doing their best to warn the neighborhood of unseen doom by barking their heads off at all hours. But on this night...it is quiet.

I decide to go ahead and take off. I slip out of bed, put some clothes on, grab my journal and leave the room to a muffled "Good luck" from my wife. I was looking forward to the challenge.

Years ago, when I was dating my wife my father-in-law would always say, "Nothing good happens after midnight." Of course, I knew exactly what he meant. Don't go to the other side. There are things there you do not understand and cannot control. But in this case I was hoping for something good to happen. Something inspiring. I was going to willingly venture into the world that exists on the other side of midnight and I wanted to experience something extraordinary.

Living only about a mile from the Turner Turnpike gate, I had scoped out my plan of attack the previous day. Although there is no traditional 24 hour truck stop diner at the busy east terminus of the turnpike there is a Village Inn and a Waffle House...either one I was sure would make for a great experience. I was wrong.

Arriving at the Village Inn by 2:15 I discovered that they were closed! Unheard of! I headed down the street to the Waffle House. The lights were on...this was the place. When I pulled in the parking lot I saw a Tulsa County sheriff writing a ticket with lights on sitting behind a small sedan. I looked inside the small restaurant...it was empty except for the small staff. I toyed with the idea of just going back to bed but soldiered on to tackle my contingency plan.

Across town on the east side of Tulsa is another glut of truck stops, gas stations, even the new Cherokee Casino. Certainly an interesting place would present itself. I didn't know exactly what I was looking for but I had this romantic idea of walking into a place full of truckers and having this flood of interesting situations hit me in the face. I was now on a quest. As I drove across town I passed a couple of promising Denny's and another Waffle House, but no, I was headed for the real deal on the other edge of town.

I made it to the casino and immediately knew that this wasn't the place I wanted to venture on this night. There were signs for another Waffle House but I never did find it. I saw a great looking truck stop restaurant that was closed and I found another small, very promising looking café…open but empty. What was going on? Where did all these famous long-haul truckers eat when they were hungry at 2:00am? Did Tulsa have this negative reputation within the nationwide trucking community as an overnight dead spot? Did truckers pass the word not to stop here but to push on to some other distant oasis? My contingency plan having failed…I headed back to the west side.

As I drove I remembered passing a different Waffle House just off the highway in a quiet little neighborhood just a couple of miles from my house. Three or four cars in the parking lot…it could be a good place to try. When I pulled into the lot the cars were still there and the place had some activity so I parked the car and went in. It was now 2:50am.

As you probably know, Waffle House restaurants leave little to the imagination. This one was small with booths lining the outside windows and smaller booths along a kitchen counter. There was also a counter with seating for three or four more.

When I first entered I was hit by the stuffy heat. It wasn't that cold outside but the place seemed oppressively hot. I headed toward an empty booth and sat down realizing I had picked a non-smoking booth. It's kind of funny…this small diner was no more than 800-1000 square feet and the Smoking/Non-Smoking line was right down the middle. Smokers go left, non-smokers to the right. I settled in.

My small booth was close enough to the counter that the waitress could take my order without leaving the kitchen. Her name was Jennifer and she appeared to be in her mid-20's and about four months pregnant (although I'm always wrong about that kind of thing). She was pleasant, seemed to be hard-working and as you can probably guess, she called me

"Sweetie." There were two other ladies working; another waitress whose name was Schi (pronounced "Sky") and the cook whose name I didn't get. I could tell these women had developed an easy working relationship. They seemed to enjoy their work and they were good at it.

As I scanned the room and took notice of the other diners...all in the Smoking section. There was a table of three co-workers—two guys and a woman—all identified by their matching ID tags worn around their necks. They were busy talking, laughing and smoking like chimneys; obviously decompressing after their shift. The only other diners were two girls and a guy sitting in the corner booth. They were too far away to hear their conversation and I was blocked by the cash register and unable to see them very well without becoming painfully obvious. As I waited on my scrambled eggs and toast, I took a look around.

To my left, was an enormous (it seemed much too big for the small room) juke box. It was belting out the Patsy Cline single I Fall to Pieces chosen by another patron before I walked in. Perfect.

I noticed a couple of signs on the wall: "NO FIREARMS allowed on the premises." I'm not sure if that made me feel better and more safe about choosing this restaurant or not. Certainly, I was glad that they prohibited firearms in here but I wondered what kind of place had to have such a prominent and bold-faced sign. Was there some bad history? Did the manager decide after the last "incident," I guess I'm going to have to put up a sign!

The other sign I saw was "PROFANITY OF ANY TYPE WILL NOT BE TOLERATED AT ANY TIME." I couldn't remember ever seeing a sign like this in any restaurant that I had been in before and made a mental note to watch my language if things didn't go well with my scrambled eggs.

There were a couple of other, smaller signs. All I could read was their headline, "HOUSE RULES!" I hadn't seen so many signs on the wall of an eating establishment since grade school. I found myself wondering if today would be an "outside day" or if we'd have to stay in gym for recess. The song changed to Tammy Wynette's famous ballad, Stand By Your Man. Oh man, can it get any more perfect than this?

One of the guys with the ID tag got up and walked past me on the way to the bathroom. I could smell the lingering bite of his cigarette smoke as he passed. On his way back to his table, I noticed a nasty scar that ran from over his right ear around the crown of his head to the back. He wore his hair short enough to notice the scar...some sort of badge of honor. Hmm. I sure hope he obeyed that sign about the firearms.

My food arrived ("Here you go, Sweetie") and too late I realized I'm not remotely hungry and this isn't the "dieter's plate." Big food for big people. A young girl walked in and sats at the counter. From the discussion it seemed that she is a waitress here whose shift was over a couple of hours ago and now she's come back in to hang out for a bit before going back home. Like the other three staffers, she seemed to have a comfortable way about her and genuinely enjoyed the company of her co-workers. An old guy walked in and, like the girl, he sat at the counter. He was one of those "I'll take the usual" guys. The waitresses all knew him, even the young girl who wasn't working. He was quiet and the staff left him alone bringing him his coffee "just the way he likes it."

As I ate I thought about this tableau being played out in front of me. These people were all connected in some way. They were all "night people." I had always known that this other world existed but I had never personally entered in. This world is populated with shift-workers, waitresses, emergency workers, and others who ply their trade in the overnight hours.

In a way, I was envious. This seemed like a simpler world, a quieter world. No television here. No one was stressed or seemed too busy or harried and I couldn't remember the last time I sat in a public place and saw no one...NO ONE...use a cell phone. They don't exist here. In some weird way I had entered another reality where these things were unknown. The juke box, the easy conversation, the smoking in a public place, even the heavily fried food seemed to be from some other place, some other time. There are fewer people in this world, less traffic to contend with and fewer distractions. Could it be that I was missing out? Was this the life I should be living instead?

The trio of friends in the corner got up to leave. When they came out into view I noticed that one of the girls was dressed in chef's garb. She was asked where she worked and after a long drag on her cigarette, the words "Ford's Filling Station" and the smoke that she had inhaled tumbled out of her mouth together. Ford's is a trendy upscale restaurant owned by Harrison Ford's son located up the street a couple of miles but in a lot of ways, it's thousands of miles away from here. I just can't understand how after a full night of preparing "cuisine" in a place like that that she would want to come and eat diner food in a place like this. On her way out of the place she raised her arms to the ceiling and semi-shouted, "LA in a couple of weeks!" Who knows what that was all about. Good luck.

The young girl at the counter decided she should take off as well.

She needed to get to bed...her shift starts at noon and she still had some errands to run. For the life of me, I couldn't think of what kind of errands someone like her had to run at 3:30 in the morning. She said good bye and wandered out into the night to a chorus of "see ya laters" from her mates.

I thought about Jennifer and the child she was carrying. Certainly this world was slower and less stressful but what about the overall stress of being up at this time of day...everyday. What kind of environment was the Waffle House to carry a child into? I imagined the conflict in Jennifer's future. She'll be living in this night world but her baby will likely need to be raised in the day world that we all live in. Jennifer would ultimately have figure out how to survive in both.

I took another, closer look around. I could see it on the faces in the diner. There was a heaviness on these people. The compounding heaviness that comes from living out every day at night. That cannot be easy on a body.

It was time to leave. I gathered my things and reluctantly shrugged into my coat. My short venture into this world exhausted me and weariness was starting to take over. I made my way to the register to pay and I saw by Jennifer's name tag that she was not a waitress at all...she was a Waffle House Sales Associate. I hope that got her another dollar an hour. I paid my bill, left a generous tip and walked out. Jennifer thanked me for the tip and said, "See you around, Sweetie" as I left.

Curt Dieckelt

Sent: Thursday, January 12, 2006 2:26 PM
To: Corrine@WizardAcademy.com
Subject: Inside the Outside - Brandon, MB. Canada

My name is Curt, from a small town in Manitoba called Brandon (two hours west of Winnipeg). I'm 26 and have a Wife and 1 young child with another coming. We live in a new area in town that most would say is a "good area". I've always been very responsible growing up.

I struggled to decide if I should take your challenge... even if it is only 20min away. After a lot of thought and consideration and (why the hell would I do this?), I finally set my alarm clock to 4am Thursday morning.

The place I went was a 24hr truck stop restaurant called "24hr Restaurant".

I might have not done this right, The restaurant was empty, except for one guy sitting by himself drinking a coffee, and one young waiter. I ended up ordering a breakfast special, eating it and then leaving.

On the way home I just kept thinking why I went ahead and did this....was it a waste of time? wrong place...wrong time?

Why did I go? Truth is... part of the reason I went is so that I wouldn't be someone who says they are going to do something and never do. Other part...I didn't want to be one of the people who didn't take the challenge.

I have been feeling bored & trapped for the last few months. I hope that this could be the first baby step to break out of my boring life.

I'm going to try again at a different place and a different time.

78 Anne Sallee Miles

Date: Wed, 18 Jan 2006 01:53:50 -0800 (PST)
To: Corrine@WizardAcademy.com
Subject: the challenge

    Doug Adams wrote about a restaurant at the End of the Universe. The Waffle House at the Brooks exit off of I-65 just outside of Louisville is not at the end of the universe...but at 2 am it is a universe unto itself.

    I am at a counter, sipping coffee, purportedly studying a book. The place is divided in two, a smoking section and a tiny non-smoking section. The non-smoking section is completely empty. Across the road is a large truck stop, the lights blare and semis roll in and out of the parking lot despite the first heavy snow of the season. The waitress, Sandy, a slight brunette with crooked teeth behind her friendly, tired smile, tells me that the crowd has thinned. There are only two booths taken now. They were really busy earlier. In spite of this, she hasn't made enough in tips. She sits at the counter in between trips to the coffee pot, adding up receipts and puffing on a Pall Mall.

    To my left, a woman in her mid-thirties orders a cheeseburger platter. She brushes stringy hair from her eyes as she focuses on the paperwork in front of her. Odd that, as she is dressed in sweatpants and a t-shirt. A ballplayer's jacket hangs off the stool. Her imitation leather purse hides the paperwork from view but as she begins to rip sheets from a book and place them in a case I realize that they are the trip logs of a trucker.

    Behind me, two ladies in their 60s sit with a man of equal age. All of them worn by life, they chat gaily with a second waitress. They speak of cats and their medicines, of a local neighborhood. The man is mostly silent, puffing on his cigarette while the women talk. They nearly drown out the noise of the occupants of the last booth: a tow company dispatcher and his co-workers. The booth is their office for the night.

    Glancing to the parking lot, I see "D & H Truck Repair" in plain block letters on the side of several tow trucks. The dispatcher takes calls on a cell phone from the booth, laughing when he hears one caller arguing over who in the family has Triple A.

    One of the drivers goes to the john, leather clad and bearded, he looks as if he would be more comfortable in a pack of motorcycles. One of the grandmas asks if he kept the seat warm for her as he returns. Surprised, he laughs and asks if she plans on visiting the men's room.

The youngest waitress scans want ads in the corner and announces that she can become a CNA if she can come up with $299 and work at Green Meadows with her sister. The third waitress nods knowingly, her round face solemn as she declares that is where SHE will be working soon, as soon as she gets her car back. The younger waitress, a pretty blonde, wonders aloud if perhaps she could try to become a police officer instead. She is 21, and she has heard that she doesn't have to have any college. Then she flips to the car listings and reads the ads, dreaming of a new car.

Later, the shift ends for the waitress with no car, the youngest one leaves to drive her home and then returns.

The tow truck crew is joined by a stranded trucker. Loudly, they talk about insurance companies. "A band-aid will cost you $300 if a doctor gives it to you. But if an RN or LPN gives you one, it doesn't cost as much." The truck driver brags about how much his insurance covers. The tow crew then begins to discuss the pay at other tow companies, their benefits, their time off.

The woman to my left finishes her cheeseburger and fiddles with her phone. Nodding to her paperwork, I inquire, "Are you a truck driver?"

"My husband is," her face lights up her plain features. As she smiles I see that her bottom teeth are missing. But her smile is genuine and she seems grateful to talk. "I do his paperwork for him," she explains.

I learn that this woman has been married for four years to a truck driver and travelled with him the entire time. Once, she got tired of being on the road, picked a city and leased an apartment for two months. Other than that, she just rides with her husband. They met on the internet. He was in Illinois, she was in Florida. They chatted online for 6 months and then she flew to meet him in person and they have been together ever since. "My family thought I was crazy when I did that but they love him now," she confides.

In the truck, they have a DVD player and a VCR and TV, all of which she has won in truck stops. "They don't give you cash for those gambling games in there, they cain't, " she explains. "But they can give you STUFF. I already got most of my Christmas presents for people. It's new stuff, good stuff. Don't matter that I didn't buy it, it's new." She happily shares her memories of her first trip to Vegas and her hopes of stopping soon, being on her own again in Bethlehem, PA. She has never been there but it's close to New York City and she wants to see the Queens and Brooklyn and go to "Atlantis" which is like Vegas. You can gamble there. Proudly she shows me her pictures on her camera phone. They are of giant stations of the cross in TX. "We didn't know what it was until we was almost up on it. Then we saw it, the world's biggest cross. They got a statue of Jesus with the nails in His hands. I could almost feel it."

She hasn't seen Vermont, Maine or New Hampshire yet but she wants to go. She did get to slip into Mexico for a day though, when they went to Arizona. Her eyes sparkle as she talks about the amazing things she has shared with her husband. "He's the one, too. He doesn't drink or do drugs like my other two husbands. The only bad thing he does is smoke and everyone does that." Matter of fact. "He's the right one for me." Still, it is hard to be in the cramped close quarters day in and day out. When they stop, she has to go sit out where people are for a while. "But I text on my phone all the time. And I can IM. And I have games. I got the biggest package I could. And I send postcards wherever I am, to all my friends." She doesn't use the cb radio though. "Those men are all crude. I lived on it when I was little though."

She had a dog for a while, she shows me the picture. He went in the truck with them everywhere. But he was stolen last week, all she has now is the picture of him.

We chat for a bit longer, I pay my bill and tip the waitress more than the meal cost. Her crooked smile is very grateful as she wishes me a good night.

This world is very different from the one that I know. It is more open. People greet each other as if they are old friends, talk across the room, across the tables. Mere acquaintances, they become friends for the duration of their stay in this oasis. They give each other advice and seek connections, share their struggles with money and their frustrations at the limits they battle. There is no posturing, no calculation, no name dropping, no polite pretending. There is cussing and smoke...and laughter.

What do they need? The one thing I saw, the undercurrent ... was a need for hope and goals. Those things comprise the relief from daily struggles. The young waitress dreamed of a new job and car. The other waitress hoped for a different medicine for her diabetes and hoped to drive again. The tow crew looked for opportunities to change companies, get a better salary, better insurance. More time off. The camaraderie they shared was that of folks who find themselves together and ask, "Do you know how I feel?" With a small sigh of relief when the answer is yes. In sharing their anecdotes, they find encouragement.

The trucker's wife was different. She was not just dreaming, she was already realizing dreams. She obviously craved interaction with people, but she had found a way to somewhat meet that need with her mobile phone and its functions. She treated it as if it were the most precious possession one could own. And to her it WAS, because with it, she had found a way to meet with other women, to make friends and have a community, even from within a truck. Her roots were virtual. But this woman was seeing things she'd always wanted to see with someone she loved and respected. She had taken a huge risk and followed a dream. I saw her walk back toward the truck stop as I was leaving, a plodding and plain silhouette against the glow of the neon lights. I wondered if she was going in to play a game and win more prizes. She didn't have the luxury of getting up in the morning and going into her own bathroom, no she had to use a public shower, but she had something else. She had a new adventure ahead of her every day. Sometimes that meant seeing the biggest cross in the world on the horizon, other times it meant seeing a face carved from a mountainside by water. I had the feeling she shared her daily adventures with Someone besides her husband, and saw Him everywhere....her sense of wonder made that evident.

Even toothless, her smile was beautiful.

Anyhow, I took your challenge and had an adventure myself. I'm glad that I did. I wish that I could find more of that openness and wonder in my own little world. But maybe I'll carry some of it with me now. I hope so. Thanks Roy.

 Todd C. Roth

Sent: Tuesday, January 10, 2006 1:34 PM
To: Corrine@WizardAcademy.com
Subject: My excursion

I am writing today in response to your Monday Morning Memo of January 9, 2006. As I read the memo I found it very ironic. For you see, I made that journey on Saturday night, before reading your memo. A few of the details are somewhat different than what you outline but I think you will find it interesting.

After an evening of taking down Christmas decorations from my home's interior, I was feeling a bit, well, blaaah. Christmas is one of my favorite times of the year and when time comes to "undecorate" it leaves me feeling a bit empty until the hum drum routine of post holiday life kicks back in. So about 12:30 A.M. Sunday morning after all the boxes were packed away back in the closet upstairs, pangs of hunger began to become more noticible. My girlfriend, whose help was instrumental in the "undecorating" process, suggested a small, out of the way cafe that she used to frequent when she was growing up.

The Good Luck Cafe, is located in an area of town primarily comprised of low income people of Hispanic origin also known for it's dive bars, street corner drunks, gangs, you get the idea. It is important to note that this is not the first time I have been to this restaurant, but it was the first time in quite a while. The last time was after a night of clubbing and the only thing I was interested in on that visit was getting a steaming bowl of menudo in hopes of staving off what promised to be a monster hang-over.

As we pulled in to the parking lot, I vainly noticed that my Lexus appeared to be the nicest and newest car in a parking lot dotted with beat up pickups, older model cars of various makes and models, a couple of motorcycles, and while emabrrassing to admit, this gave me a since of pride. As we walked into the establishment, we were greeted by a warm, friendly lady, whom in Spanish directed us to a booth on the far wall. At this point it's important to know, I don't speak a great deal of Spanish. The atmosphere was quiet, the late night club crowd had not yet hit. The table next to us was a middle aged couple, the man dressed in western attire, the lady in a shiny outfit that to me appeared a bit gaudy. They were holding hands across the table and speaking to each other in Spanish. Although the context of the conversation was inaudible, it was apparent they had been out for the evening and were enjoying each other's company. Other couples similarly dressed, a few younger people, sharing plates of food, a few biker types sitting at the breakfast bar, again engaged in their own world of conversation. After ordering with my girlfriend's asstance (remember I don't speak a lot of Spanish), I noticed as the waitress walked away her kind smile, her white outfit, and her cheap tennis shoes. I wondered at that point why someone in this business would not wear top of the line Nike's, or Reebok's to make life on her feet easier? Was it because she had kids at home and maybe would rather spend her hard earned money on their Nike's and Reebok's? Or was it because wearing a name brand on her foot simply wasn't important to her? I wondered if the meal at this restaurant, this particular night was a special celebration for some of these people. Maybe they had saved up all week to eat out. Maybe this was a sacrifice for them. They all seemed to be having a great time, whatever the circumstances. They seemed to be happy in the world at this place at this moment in time.

All this, while I sat, considering this just to be another charge on my credit card to be posted in my checkbook sometime Sunday.

Wondering how I was going to pay all my Christmas bills, which credit card had the best interest rate, should I buy a new car to go with the new year? These were things most likely the people whose air I was breathing did not, could not concern themselves with and they seemed all the happier for it. Oh i'm sure they had their problems, probably much deeper than mine but yet they were not consumed with them, or at least didnt appear to be, as was I. The food came, it was delicious. The service during our meal was better than I receive at most of the $30+ entree restaurants I frequent. As we left, I paid the tab, looked around again and saw kind faces. Most I would never see in the restaurants, clubs, businesses that I frequent everyday. It made me think of a time in my life that was more simple. A time when I worried about how I was going to put gas in my old clunker, saving up to go out to eat, making the rent payment on my small apartment. My management position in the automobile business has been good to me. It has afforded me luxuries, a nice home, a new car whenever I want, but with all this I think the people in that restaurant on Saturday were wealthier than I, in many ways. Would I trade places with them, probably not. Is there something I can learn from them, absolutely. At the end of days, how many new cars I drove, what zip code I lived in, whether my credit cards were gold or platinum won't be important. Although I knew this already, I think God just gave me a little reminder that night. Maybe a new message for a new year. Whatever it was, it was valuable, and I left that restaurant that night after a good meal feeling better. The ride home was a quite one, the car radio playing softly but not much conversation. As I drove out of that part of town and out of those people's lives, I wondered, what they did for a living, where they lived. I pulled back into the driveway of my home and waited for the garage door to open. It seemed like an entirely different world. Sunday came, work called, and life is back to normal. But I cant help, especially after the feelings I had Saturday night and reading your memo yesterday morning, to try and keep a more realistic perspective on things. Afterall, money is just a means, a means to either bring misery or joy. This year I think I am going to focus a little more on the joy part. Worry less, give more and become a better person in the process.

  In closing, thank you for your memo, I find it a wonderful thing to brighten every Monday, but this week was more special than usual. Thank you for allowing me the opportunity to share, I find it strange, I would not share this with my girlfriend of 4 years but I will e-mail it to someone I have never met. Human nature sure is strange isn't it?

Jeff Burns

Sent: Wednesday, January 18, 2006 2:46 PM
To: corrine@wizardacademy.com
Subject: Inside the Outside Reducks

About an hour ago I had one of those so called character building moments. I was nearly finished with a humorous tale of why my assignment was late and the adventures I suffered to make it happen, when I found myself pressing an unfortunate combination of keys which vaporized the email in front of my eyes, and I have no idea of whether it was received or just vanished. Regardless it was an original piece to time and place thereby not disposed to recreation, but I need to ask your patience as I try once again to explain the contents within this email.

Due to illness and large quantities of frozen precipitation, I was unable to track from the far reaches of the frozen North in search of a civilization where they might have an eatery open throughout the night until last night. So I let my wife read the actual MMM in order to quell her suspicions I might be doing something unseemly I drove to the far reaches of Spokane 100 miles to my south and west. Upon reaching this bastion of culture I was frustrated to find there really isn't a wrong side of Spokane, just a couple of drug dealers and a street walking icicle or two amongst Inland Northwest urban poverty. After 90 minutes of searching, an amount of time equal to that need to drive every main street in the area and only finding an empty Denny's I decided to try option 2, the truck stop on the outskirts of town.

Better luck here finding live bodies, however their conversations were drowned out by CNN on televisions in front and behind, 80's Musak shushing out of the ceiling speakers and a smoke sucker doing whatever smoke suckers do in a restaurant where no smoking has been allowed for 2 years. So instead of failing miserably, (I have yet to fail miserably when requested by Roy to do something great in my life) I wrote a poem outside of Post Falls Idaho at 4 o'clock in the morning.

black asphalt, moistened by clouds past
rising steam among steel dragons
it seems the die is cast
4 O'clock the dragon tamers steady
shower number 548 appears to now be ready.

blond waitress, dyed to hide the maybe
reminds the cook beyond the grill
be sure to check the gravy
a favorite of the black road slayers
now is not the time for us as players.

gray warriors, hard from white line fever
arrive to stave their hunger
with food laid bare by cleaver
bellies over belt from plate piled high
they need no menus to order by.

friendly banter, honed by year nights serving
steaming liquid from yellow pot
flows into cup deserving
will today bring sun or stormy weather
don't know dear, it's time to hit the leather.

slayers throne, sitting high above the freeway
behind the throne a nations wealth
whose timing has no leeway
and a grateful people notwithstanding
will never appreciate a road demanding.

    P.S. My daughter said I might want to rethink the rhyming for cheese factor. I don't know much about poetry or rhyming, but it made it more challenging, and the company seemed to demand it.

Blaine Parker

Sent: Wednesday, January 18, 2006 9:52 AM
To: corrine@wizardacademy.com
Subject: Open All Night

ALWAYS OPEN

It's dark here.
Which seems to be normal.
It's always dark here.
Even in the middle of a bright, sunny day.

It must be something about the location. Here at the edge of downtown, there's a pervasive sense of always waiting for the other shoe to drop. High rises to the north. Empty parking lots right nearby. The freeway encroaching just a block to the west. Several blocks to the south, the gigantic neon and glass kiddie toy where pro sports teams and rock stars strut their stuff. And a scant dozen blocks to the east, Skid Row. (I recently wrote a radio commercial for one of the missions there. The mission received a phone call because of it. Not a donation, which was the point of the ad. A complaint. Apparently, it is politically incorrect to refer to the area as Skid Row.)

Nevertheless, the place is here. Since 1924. Always open. Or so the sign claims. Even in the face of catastrophic weather events. Though apparently, the riots in the wake of a controversial jury verdict did prompt somebody to go find the door key.

It's different when you come here on a Sunday morning at 10am. Then, it's funky but chic. There's a long line of happy yuppies, artists, and NPR subscribers all waiting on the sidewalk to get griddle cakes and breakfast sandwiches or, in the wake of the Atkins revolution, steak and eggs with bacon and sausage.

After dark, at least tonight, things are different.
But it's always open.

It's always open, and always old. The furniture looks like cast offs from an Edward Hopper painting. It could've come from the set of Bonnie & Clyde or Paper Moon. Depression era chic. Hipsters find it funky.

The place is owned by a politician, an affable, liberal Republican—something the liberal Democrat locals accept begrudgingly. There's also a story that all the employees are ex-cons.

To look at them, it's easy to believe. Their eyes don't look like the eyes of coffee shop waiters. There are no waitresses.

It's dark outside, and it's dark in here. The lights are on, of course, but with the high, high ceilings, it seems as if the light isn't quite prepared to make the journey all the way to the seating area.

What's surprising is the crowd.

There isn't any.

Typically, it's a challenge to find a seat here.

In the wee hours, the staff outnumbers the patrons.

I sit at a table by the wall. Looking around, I can be fairly certain the conversations on which to eavesdrop will be few and far between. Loners in old clothes hunkered down at their little islands do not normally talk much. Unless they're raving. (Note: proximity to the area formerly known as Skid Row.)

I order from my ex con. He doesn't have much to say. He maintains a professional detachment.

Across the aisle and a few tables down is a man who looks like he's in his 50s. The years haven't been easy on him. But he looks like he's weathered them without complaint. He looks like a shorter, fatter, older Barney Miller—which would probably make him Albert Einstein. He's eating…something. I can't tell what it is. He appears to be enjoying it. I guess.

My food arrives. It looks as old and worn as everything else. But it's tasty. Much better than in The Joint. And as I eat, I'm fascinated by the lack of a soundtrack in here. The occasional sizzle and clatter of cooking and dish washing punctuate the quiet. A big diesel bus growls past on Figueroa. Little else.

In the wee hours, here on the edge of downtown on the left coast, nobody has anything to say.

I take back what I said earlier. The furniture is not cast off from an Edward Hopper painting. It is an Edward Hopper painting—along with everybody in the place. These are the nighthawks at the diner—just older, fatter, and not as well dressed.

I hear a quiet retch. I glance over at Barney Einstein just in time to see him discretely regurgitate part of his meal into his plate. He remains nonchalant. Taking a paper napkin, he covers the plate and slides it away from him. As the waiter happens along, Barney says, "Hey, can I have a to-go box?"

Where am I?

Back on the street, I walk around the corner to my car. I stop and look at it. By the light of a nearby street lamp, I can see that it's dripping wet. It hasn't rained. But my car is dripping wet.

"I washed it for ya!"

I turn. A gleeful, skinny black guy with a shopping cart towering with god knows what is coming along the sidewalk.

"It looked like it needed a bath, so I washed it for you. If you don't like it, you don't have to pay me nothin'!"

I look at the car. It is clean. And it did need to be washed.

I find a five dollar bill in my pocket and hand it to him. "I love it. Nice job. You enjoy your evening."

"Thank you, sir. Why, thank you very much!"

As I drive away, I wonder where he got the water.

I suddenly wish I'd given him a ten.

Where else but here?

I love this town.

82 Jeff Lukesh

Sent: Wednesday, January 11, 2006 4:01 PM
To: Corrine@wizardacademy.com; jeffandjill@sktdalton.net
Subject: Man, I'm really missing that hour of sleep.

Three AM
"That's me, I'm a mess."
"Aren't we all"
"Went to that meeting yesterday, but I was in a bad mood. I was running late, got onto the street right behind this guy going fifteen. I'm tailgating this guy really close, older guy, silver Bravada. Wanna pick this guy, I can just see him veering off in the ditch."
"Only happens when you're late."
"I'm stuck behind this guy all the way, and then he turns right into the church, so I just keep going, flip a U down the road and go back, hoping he's went inside."
"Oh man, that's great."
"Sheesh. So I go inside, Tim's sitting there so I go up, figure I'll sit with him. I say 'These seats open.'
Tim's like 'I don't think they want anybody sitting here.' All of a sudden this big guy whose gonna be speaking yells across the room 'You can't sit there, sit over here, I don't want anybody sitting over there.'
So I'm already in a bad mood, I almost turn around and left, but I'm like, you know, just wanna get to know some people, so I walk over, but I'm glaring at him the whole time."
"Should have told them what you do for a living."
"Ha, yeah. They want me to go to Myanmar."
"Really, how long?"
"Month, three weeks minimum. I told 'em no."

Don Morelock

83

Sent: Thursday, January 12, 2006 11:08 AM
To: Corrine@WizardAcademy.com
Subject: excursion

Mr. Williams:

Thank you for your challenge to go to the all night diner. As I walked in at 5 this morning, it was actually pretty slow, a few people sitting alone at their tables. Then it happened, a waitress walked in, you could tell she was very cold, the temp was just above freezing. She left her house at 3:30am and walked to work, it was 5:45 when she came in. As I drew her into conversation to find out what happened, her story came out... We all have a story to tell. By my estimations, she wa in her late 30's. She had arrived in Texas just a few days before, her home in Georgia had burned to the ground in late October. Her boyfried convinced her to come to Texas where his family is. Problem is, once she got here, the boyfriend took a temporary job in Austin. So she was without a ride. This determined lady, not to loose her job, walked 4 miles in the cold & dark and by herself.

My problems shrank quickly as I listened to hers.

Thanks for the challenge, and I will do it again.

84 Anna Huthmaker

Sent: Monday, January 09, 2006 10:52 PM
To: Corrine@WizardAcademy.com
Subject: Experiential Occasions

Mr. Williams,

Let me say up front that I do not qualify for your experiential project because I did not adhere to your rules. At least, not this week........Your essay described, perfectly, one of my philosophies of life, and I just had to take the opportunity to thank you for trying to get others to crack their worlds open a bit!

When I was in college, I came home for the summer, looking for a job. My parents encouraged me to find employment in an office, where I could dress nicely, answer the phone, and earn the next semesters tuition without too much fuss and muss. Instead, I took a job in a 24-hour burger joint that was fully staffed by career waitresses and line cooks. I spent the summer immersed in the world that you described, and I count it among one of the most influential summers of my life.

My parents could not understand why a classical musician like myself would want not only work to a job like that, but to also become friends with the people that I worked with. All I can say is that I knew that quality in a person could be found in the unlikeliest of places. You call these people a 'community of outcast' while I call them the "minimum wage army". They run our country from their burger joints and gas stations, and if we live our lives insulated from them, then we lose out on such riches!.

I live and work in a world of symphonies, universities, and art museums. However, I find my adventures far from those venues. Yes, I have spent afternoons in Masai villages and evenings in Chaga huts. My heart races at the thought of those amazing times. But no less are the adventures that I have found here at home. The seedy gay bar in the industrial district, the postage stamp-sized bowling alley on an Indian reservation, the peaceful dairy farm of an Amish family, and the two-day long bluegrass picking party complete with moonshine............these are also my adventures. They take me far, far away from my normal life, and I come away from each one having gained a further understanding of myself and the lives of the people around me.

Like I said, I do not qualify for your contest this week, but I am sure that it wont be long before I find myself once again in the corners of our society, meeting people and making friends. Thank you for encouraging others to do the same! And as for your 'gift of initiation'........may I suggest a gift basket complete with a paper place mat from Waffle House, a coffee mug from the Huddle House and a syrup bottle from I-Hop. If only we could include a bottle of that smell.........you know the one.......the mixture of burnt coffee, deisel fuel and stale cigarettes. Now that is what I call a gift of initiation! :)

It makes me smile to think about it!

All my best,
Anna Huthmaker

PS- That small group of minimum wage earners that worked I worked with that summer?

The week I left, they brought in a total of seven cakes, three bouquets of flowers and three stuffed animals. The love and warmth they showed me is with me to this day.

85 Mike Kenyon

Sent: Friday, January 13, 2006 3:09 AM
To: Corrine@WizardAcademy.com
Subject: Visiting a diner - late night

11:10 p.m. - tonight is the night for the Wizard's assignment. I'm keeping track of the time so that I don't leave too early, or get distracted and forget my planned adventure entirely. The location is set - Denny's. Unfortunately, I live in one of those small cities strung like mottled pearls along the I-270 cord that reaches to D.C. Between here and D.C. there is quite possibly no place except a Denny's open. To the East is Baltimore, and there I could find a diner with some risk. Yet that is an hour away, and in the arms of the city where Poe died - of rabies, no less. Baltimore has a respectable murder rate, which makes the town edgier than my suburban environment.

My town will do. Recently, renovations took place in key, poor areas, and the people who once haunted front steps with hungry, haunted eyes were pushed - where? The public housing facility was leveled last year, and surely all night diners like Denny's offer a temporary release from the pressures of night. I suppose that the mere fact of my visit at this hour reveals a kinship between us at the diner. Will I see ghosts of my future, or a former past along the counter in the early morning hours?

It gets colder, and only 10 minutes have passed. There is still time to fill before I head out, linked with the small band of adventurers the Wizard has set to the task of getting outside ourselves. Tonight, Denny's. Later this weekend, I will be in Baltimore, so if my time on the road is fruitless, there is a second chance. Will I meet Emily Dickinson tonight, or the nameless characters of Hopper's Night Owls? And what did the Wizard mean when he asked:

While you're eating and listening and absorbing this strange new reality, think of what these people need most and how you might help them get it. While you're at it, you might also think a little about what they have that you don't. There is a rich sense of community among the outcast.

2:45 p.m. - I take the dog with me, and leave him in the car. He's moral support, and while I don't expect trouble, it's nice to have a friend outside for the ride home. I go inside to eat, while he curls up to take a nap. I've let my imagination run away me a little - though I choose non-smoking and take my seat. A quick scan reveals almost no one present. Great, I think, taking a seat, I choose the worst night in history to come to my late night diner; adventure for one, sir?

Yet it isn't entirely empty. Caroline is one waitress, and Trina is the other. In the next booth sit two guys just off work - Dave and Buster's is where one of them bar tends. The bar tender is effusive tonight, full of compliments for Caroline. He sees her differently tonight, with a young, inebriated passion. His friend is just supportive. The bar tender calls out for Caroline, and praises her recommendation for his breakfast order. As I hear his banter in a too loud voice, I think this is a genuinely friendly guy, and while he doesn't actually love Caroline, he is sweet enough that he actually likes her. Hmmmmm - I make some notes.

What do these people have? Time - sociability - alcohol - and the friendly, open courtesy of late nighters. It does not appear that anyone is planning or scheming. In fact, the atmosphere is almost festive, light hearted. There is no profanity, and the laughter from Caroline and Trina is sweet in the air, which is tinged with the smell of hot oils and tobacco.

I gradually slip away from myself, detach from my esoteric concerns, and fall into the rhythm of the early morning crowd. Someone asks if the take traveler's checks, and my heart leaps when suddenly someone appears at my window, arms and legs stretched as though clinging for dear life. This makes no sense, as the diner is at ground level. Then the figure wipes clouds on the glass, obscuring the night. It is a window washer, as incongruous as King Kong on the Empire State building. I notice that no one is talking on a cell phone, and I forgot mine at home. I finish my breakfast, and let my mind wander to a different project. I don't know anyone here, yet I am relaxed. They seem accepting of one another, and their time of day. The bartender is talking with Caroline, who doesn't seem that interested, and Trina, who does. I actually like the bartender, and begin to cheer for his side. Caroline drops the bill on my table as 2 Hispanic couples slide into the booth behind me.

At last, I think to myself, a little conversation. I notice at this moment that I am the only one in here who is alone; everyone else has company. The Hispanics, talking in varying shades with their beautiful, accented English are two couples, with two men and two women. They begin discussing women. First they reference a woman who is 'rich'. Next they talk about various women who have big butts, and then on to women they asked 'when are you due' when the lady wasn't pregnant at all. They laugh easily at their mistakes, and they laugh without any trace of vicious attitude or callous indifference. Like the others here tonight, they flirt.

Their conversation shifts to who has light skin, and then I lose track of their conversation. The bartender is getting ready to leave, and he has his friend take a picture of him sitting in the chair while Caroline and Trina stand behind him. The friend uses a cell phone for the photo - the first cell phone I've seen all night. Trina is laughing - pure music in her laugh, a light, fairy footstep trilling. I make a note 'these people are all so damn cheerful'. The window washer comes inside to do his work. I see that he is not smiling. I try to remember the assignment as I summarize my experience so far.

There are no dramas present tonight. It is a light, comic atmosphere all around. These people have love, they have laughter, and they have a light hearted quality I'd forgotten. Not once did I hear anyone reference news events; mainstream talk radio is background static in these conversations. I doubt that many of these people ever discuss politics, or possibly even vote. They are not cynical, they just have a different focus. It is as if they are absorbed by life when I and others are absorbed by 'issues', 'considerations', or some other label applied to an aspect of life. They give off the sense they are engaged with one another, involved in their lives, living unselfconsciously. My fellow diners are direct, straight forward, and they could live in any time with this same approach. I am with the main bulk of a people, the ones who do not get accounted in history texts and yet do most of the living, the laughing, the loving, and the dying.

The bartender leaves, and a new couple comes in. She goes off to the bathroom and he takes a seat at a nearby booth. Eventually his partner comes to the booth, and I hear laughter. Still no one is talking on a cell phone. Somehow, one of the women from the group behind me starts talking to the guy from the recently arrived couple, and she says something about Shontay. Shontay stands up, and says "Cheryl!" The two are reunited, and begin talking about hair. Cheryl is introduced to Nate, who is there with Shontay. It is all wonderfully free of posturing. Greetings are warm and genuine, and there is a lot of laughter. These folks send Christmas cards, and they mean what they write on the card.

The Wizard asked 'what do they need'? In truth, they do not seem to need anything. They seem well adjusted, like people who marry for love, and stay with each other through thick and thin. Here, at least, most of them appear to have work that doesn't sap their vitality, though I notice that only the bar tender ever talked much about his work. These folks possess the gift of sociability. I sense that even when they aren't talking, they are still approachable and generally optimistic. What do they have that I don't? Each other - actual relationships, actual friendships and people to go out for breakfast at these early hours. They have a connection with this place and this time that I lack, and I suspect that they have a social connection I can barely conceive. They appear to fit in where they are, and they exude a confidence that comes from belonging. They are not the outsiders - I am.

Soon the sun will come to shoo the damp dew from the ground. I pay and leave. The dog is asleep in my seat in the car; I wake him, give him a pat, and we drive home to bed. I'm tired, yet I feel rested, calmer than when I started my evening. I'm going to Baltimore on Saturday, and perhaps I'll find a place there for a different visit to a different diner. I will be sure to write if I find a place with a cheap breakfast. At this time, I can report that I've met the elusive 'main street' people, and they are far, far from main street. That, perhaps, is the key to their success. Avoid the many distractions of daylight hours, and simply live.

86 Gregg Stutts

Sent: Wednesday, January 18, 2006 8:21 AM
To: corrine@wizardacademy.com
Subject: Denny's field trip

I left home a little after 4:00 a.m. I had debated whether or not to go. My wife is out of town for two weeks of training with YoungLife. My oldest daughter went back to college earlier in the week, so my three other children--15, 13, 10-- would be home alone.

I dressed quietly, left a note that I'd be back at 5:30 and slipped outside. I stopped at the ATM to get $20, got some gas, then headed toward Denny's at the intersection of University and Asher in Little Rock.

All of my kids have attended public schools in Little Rock, which are probably 75% African-American. I have attended numerous sporting events where I've been among the very small handful of white parents in the audience. That never bothers me. Still, I knew that the Denny's at this location would have me out of my element.

There were about a half dozen cars parked outside when I arrived around 4:15. I parked next to a car that was running. The guy in the passenger seat was trying to sleep.

I went inside and saw five or six young African-American men and two women hanging around in the waiting area near the counter. Some were seated on the bench trying to sleep. I assumed they were inside just trying to stay warm. Mostly, they smoked cigarettes and milled around.

The hostess/waitress was white, overweight, rather plain looking and friendly. She seated me in the non-smoking section near an older African-American couple. I sat facing the crowd of people near the front of the restaurant. I watched and tried to listen.

The couple near me barely said a thing. The man mostly sat with his face in his hands with his eyes shut. The woman didn't say much either. She was drinking hot tea. He may have had coffee. She had a ring. Not sure if he did. There was little conversation and even less intimacy. He was either tired or hopeless. I wonder what she was feeling.

Stephani, the waitress, put on a fresh pot of coffee for me and I sat waiting, listening to light jazz type music coming from the bad sounding speaker overhead.

Stephani returned several minutes later with a hot mug. After wiping off the smudge of ketchup, I added some half & half, and took a sip. I ordered the Original Grand Slam and she said, "Not a problem." I heard her say that more than once. Considering it was the night shift and she was the only one on duty, besides the cook, she had a great attitude.

As it turned out, the crowd at the front was waiting for take-out orders. With only one cook on duty--it wasn't a short wait. Their food finally arrived and they left.

The remaining guy sitting at the counter was a young white guy with a black cap and black hair with blue highlights. He seemed annoyed that his food was taking so long.

A few minutes later, another African-American guy came in wearing a FedEx uniform. He was seated at the table next to me. He ordered chicken fried steak, eggs and toast, then read the newspaper.

I was surprised to see two young, attractive white women enter the restaurant. They sat down at the counter near the guy with the blue hair, who had since received his meal. His demeanor changed. Could have been due to the food, but I suspect it had more to do with the women.

I wondered if the women were prostitutes or if they were coming in after last call at a local club. I tend to think they were just out partying. On a Tuesday night though? One of them said a friend had broken up with her boyfriend who had apparently taken her clothes and car keys.

Within minutes, several of the guys who had left earlier came back in and sat down with the girls who had just entered. The African-American women they'd left with weren't with them.

One of the white girls sat at a table with three of the African-American guys. I think she ordered a salad and a glass of milk. Odd choice, I thought. No one seemed uncomfortable. I assume they all knew each other although they didn't seem to fit together. They talked or flirted or both.

The girl at the counter removed her jacket--revealing a tattoo between her shoulder blades. I liked it. She and the blue-hair guy talked and smoked. Sometimes she put her head down on the counter. I was too far away to hear what they talked about.

Stephani used to be an intake officer at a jail down in Louisiana. She got bored with that work and now attends the University of Arkansas at Little Rock or UALR (pronounced "Yuler"). She's got her bachelor's and is working on her master's in criminal justice--headed toward a doctorate. Her goal is to work in a private crime lab where she'll make big bucks. I never would have guessed.

Two more white girls came in. They looked like teenagers, but I'd guess they also attended UALR, which is close by. They sat down with the others in the smoking section. Of everyone in the place, except maybe me, they seemed most out of place, but they weren't. They fit right in with the group already there. They had community.

The FedEx guy's name is Victor. He had just finished the Little Rock-Memphis run. He drives for the freight division. His shift starts in the evening with a run to Memphis and ends the next morning back in Little Rock after stops in places like Forest City, Conway and Hot Springs. He finished early tonight. I guess he stopped in for breakfast so he wouldn't wake his wife and his two sons just yet. The boys are 2 and 9.

He's been with FedEx for four years, driving the night shift for the last two. He spoke highly of the company and said that the starting salary for a driver is $65,000. The toughest time to drive is between 3:00 and 5:00 a.m. when 70% of truck accidents happen. That's when guys are pushing it and trying to stay awake. Victor sleeps about six hours a night. It's tough to keep the room dark.

He asked what I did, so I told him I work in publishing with an organization, a ministry that helps marriages and families. He agreed that it was tough to stay married today and that men have not lived up to their responsibilities. Men want out when things get tough.

We talked briefly about the passivity of men handed down to us from Adam. Victor shared the observation that when Adam blamed Eve for his sin, he was really blaming God, because it was "the woman you gave me" who was at fault according to Adam.

The older couple nearby had left by this point. Stephani was genuinely happy to get some quarters in her tip from them. They come in handy when doing laundry.

It was time to get back home, so I said good-bye to Victor and paid Stephani at the register. I gave her the one quarter I had along with a five for her tip. She was grateful.

I took a different route home--along I-30. A FedEx Freight double-trailer, like Victor drives, passed me going east. I prayed the driver would stay awake.

I was back home within fifteen minutes. Only the dog knows I was even gone. Well, Stephani and Victor know, too. And maybe so do some of the others--maybe wondering what the story was with the forty-something white guy who didn't seem to fit.

Jesse Zellmer

Sent: Monday, January 16, 2006 10:15 PM
To: corrine@wizardacademy.com
Subject: Roy's Challenge

THE VALUE OF PIE

"Pizza" is lit in neon. A decent part of town, the early hour of the morning doesn't bring any weirdo's or the great-anticipated drama. Nice idea, Roy. Nothing interesting here, but hunger exists, so I will order. I will make something up while I sit here to satisfy my disrupted sleepless night for a stranger with a dull challenge. My fictitious mind starts at the beginning. Of course the experience will be of my mind's conveyance of how I have it figured out and should share my wealth of opinions with those who dine at a place like this, at a time like this, without the resources I posses.

Descriptions on the menu don't describe anything. I chose what I want, then glance at the price. I suspect this order is backwards for this place.

I guess it makes sense that the good-looking, clean-cut, styled dude that just walked in has just finished slinging drinks at a classy, downtown bar. Again, this was a great idea Roy. Interesting. I wonder what it would be like to bartend until this hour. Is it his second job, or a living?

Back to my gifted, creative storytelling mind. Perhaps my do-gooder nature goes to the ghetto, picks up the tab for every patron, and leaves before a thank-you is given. Yeah, that is a good answer to Roy's challenge. Plus, I can us that story for the next year to make me feel like I am a regular Joe amongst everyone else.

Surely, that is far more exciting than a bartender sitting alone who ordered two cokes.

"Sue...she likes two cherries in her coke", he says with the familiar-you-should-know-that-by-now smile. It's a girlfriend he is waiting for. How cute.

He unbuttons his shirt, slouches a bit to relax and waits. Visibly tired, I sympathize – should be sleeping right now. My time is valuable and I may not maximize it tomorrow.

Now I have stopped thinking about making up a story, as I am irritated. Is this what is supposed to be exciting? Nice challenge, Roy!!!

A pretty girl walks in and heads right to the bartender. Well, he certainly woke up, not a visible sign of fatigue when he jumps up to hug her. Her attire signals she is a waitress, but different colors from him, so different place of employment. Perceptive I am.

"I will have pepperoni on my side and she would love sausage and mushroom on hers. Thank you Sue."

Ahhhh, it has clicked. It took him calling the waitress by name twice for me to conclude they come here often. Wow, Roy you should be a little proud that I am picking up little details. Not too bad a challenge…I am getting good.

My steak sandwich arrives. Or course, I required no mayo and the simple task has been avoided. Since this is a do-gooder event, I'll keep quiet. Plus, I am not even paying much for the meal.

Back to the couple.

"I had a good night baby." She says.

I wonder if they played good music, then I realize she is talking about the tips she has in front of her on the table. He also has tips on the table.

She eats one of her cherries, looks at him with a thank-you-for-being-thoughtful-smile. How cute. The money is in various piles, they figure the total. Now it is separated into two piles - one much larger than the other. He puts the big one in his pocket. Why does he get most of it?

There is a little pile of money left over and it sits next to the pizza that has just arrived. They dive into it making small talk. Yes, Roy you were correct, they seem very happy. In fact, they seem like they are in love.

Ahhh, I bet they are taking a majority of the money to pay bills, rent, and other responsibilities first. I am observant and good at this.

In all seriousness, I am slightly jealous of what seems like a love not based upon materials behind it. Certainly, one can ever say they fell in love when they were on top of the world. Two young people loving each other for which they are now instead of who they haven't become yet is a pleasant sight. Think of famous people who find love after fame? I digress.

Okay Roy, the challenge was worth MY experience, but hasn't turned into insightful glimpses of the miracle on the horizon.

My bill comes. I leave a generous tip considering the mayo. I figure it only polite to not leave until the couple does since I dined along side of them this morning.

Sues goes to their table: "You guys want me to wrap up the rest?"

"Yes, the best pizza I ever had." She says to Sue, but smiles at the bartender.

I should've had pizza. Darn, probably won't be a next time either.

Sue comes back with the best-boxed pizza and the check. He takes money from their pile that was left and leaves it on top of the paper slip.

Time to go.

You win Roy. The pizza wouldn't have been good to me tonight. I wish I could have had the same pizza they had, but instead I got the following:

Pizza isn't as good when you have money!!!

88 Jack McAdory

Sent: Tuesday, January 17, 2006 8:42 PM
To: Corrine@WizardAcademy.com
Subject: It's 5am at the diner...

It's 5am at the 24 hour diner in Annapolis MD. The place is brightly lit and only has a few patrons. I walk in and sit at the bar on a swivel stool. I am greeted and offered coffee. I order my meat lovers omlette and begin to check out my fellow patrons. Two cops are sitting in a booth in the corner. Quietly chatting. I receive very little attention from our constables on patrol. I guess I'm not their typical client that would cause them to have to perform their official functions. Actually I look like a large middle aged ex-pro ball player except my knees still work and I'm still in shape. I also smile and look people in the eyes. It is a technique that allows me to go places most would avoid without having any trouble at all. I use the skill so often, I haven't had to think about it for decades. My companion at the end of the bar is an older gentleman, overweight with a widely spaced comb-over, you know only 15 hairs a quarter inch apart and glued in place. He is wearing a SPCA sweatshirt. He is reading the paper. In attendance at his side is the manager and the waiter. They know him well. They chat and verbally jab at each other good naturedly. The manager and the waiter flow smoothly between chatting with each other in Greek, and with their customer in English. I ask the old man if he works with the SPCA, because of the sweatshirt. "No" he says, "some girl gave it to me." He says it as though women line up to give him gifts. His voice is a great mimic of Marlon Brando's pertrayal of the godfather.

I find out that the waiter goes by the monicker of "Spike". Except for his short hair cut, there is nothing "spikish" or "dangerous" about him. When I ask if that is really what he goes by, he just shrugs and smiles and confirms with a "yep!" The cops, done with their chat, slip silently out. If they paid, I didn't notice. The other patrons are a couple that could have, and probably should have, been named "Spike". They sit in the segregated smoking area. I know that I should probably have picked a rougher side of town, however, around here, it goes from colorful to homicidal in about 6 blocks. I finish my omlette and chat for a few minutes with the manager as he processes my VISA. He tells me that the real characters show up a little earlier. I plan to come back and see how the other half lives!

Dave Baxter

Sent: Thursday, January 12, 2006 5:46 PM
To: corrine@wizardacademy.com
Subject: squirmed under the fence

I visited Mark's Texas Hots on Monroe Avenue in Rochester NY at 3 am this morning. Seats about 70.

Things I noticed:

2 pretty girls in their 20's laughing as the left an adult book / video store across the street with a male friend about the same age.

5 homeless people standing in a two block span. All separate. No interaction that I could see. One in a storefront doorway. The others simply on the sidewalk. At least one was a woman. It's also possible that some of some of these people could have been selling drugs.

2 boys who might have been 12-14 years old sharing a ride on a stingray bike. May not have had coats on (cold here). Looked like they were on a mission.

A couple in their 20's were in the restaurant when I entered, but were asking for a doggy bag and then left. They hit me as after bar types. Bars close at 2 am in my home town.

3 drunk 20 something guys were settling up at the register and trying to navigate their way to the door, and then terrifyingly, probably to their car.

I've been in real estate as an landlord and as a realtor since 1982. I've sold $5,000 properties and $500,000 properties, and regularly eat in all kinds of restaurants, with customers, and between appointments. The most interesting to me about this morning was this small restaurant had 6 employees on at 3 am. I would guess all in their 20's, 3 men and 3 women. Two might have been children of the owner, as I heard one of them say "remind me to tell Dad we're low on ketchup." 6 workers at 3 am? Wow. One of the guys was a tall burly guy with a wandering eye and a large colorful tattoo (probably $500+) on the side of his neck. He was pontificating on how comfortable his $100 boots were. He could have been the bouncer when needed. The cook was a skinny guy and hit me as someone who took pride in his work as he put my plate together. I didn't get a good read on the others.

I had a $2.53 plate of scrambled eggs and wheat toast. Both were done perfectly.

On the way home I saw a skunk cross the street near the street that I live on. Neat.

Thanks for the fun exercise.

90 Terri Pauser Wolf

Sent: Sunday, January 15, 2006 5:52 PM
To: Corrine@WizardAcademy.com
Subject: An entry--sort of...

I stumbled on your website and your "Get-Out-Of-Your-Comfort-Zone" call to action from a link on a friend's blog. Hearing from my friend and his invitation to read his new blog took me back to another life: magazine editor, association communication director, advertising account executive, and copywriter. After 20 years of meeting deadlines, writing about topics from pig feed additives to health insurance policies, I decided to get out of my comfort zone and go to nursing school.

I didn't sit in a café for an hour like you suggested, but I decided to consume a whole banquet with this career path. For years I craved the adrenalin of meeting deadlines, coming up with the perfect tagline, and problem solving a brand issue for a client, but a piece was always missing. Through my studies and licensure as a registered nurse in 2003 at age 41, I found an incredible richness beyond the doors of my office and my computer. I've traded my corporate suits, manicures, and business cards for experiences that have paid more than any communication job. I crawl on my belly on a regular basis now. Nursing has given me the opportunity to go places that I never would have imagined. Intimate, gritty spots where I am shown that life is never what I think it is. Here's a glimpse of a patient experience—my regular café experiences--from last week.

I steered a wobbly-wheeled, hand-me-down stroller, gray-green from usage away from the clinic conference room. A co-worker asked me to watch Alberto and his sister while the doctor met with his parents. His 8-year-old sister chatted as she walked beside the stroller containing her brother, restless and upset at being separated from his mother.

Alberto (name changed), in pajamas and a grayed pair of white socks, threw his head back and became hidden by the stroller canopy. His four-year old body racked with sobs and pleas to see "mommy." I suggested we go to the clinic playroom and looked to his sister for ideas on what might calm him down. The screaming continued. Other patients looked to see what was going on. Nintendo? No. A movie? No. A book? No. Screams and kicking continued to come from the stroller.

On the other side of the clinic in the conference room with its one large imitation walnut laminate table and several swiveling office chairs, the screams would come, too. I watched the group: mom, dad, interpreter, doctor, nurse, social worker, get situated as I pulled the stroller out of the room knowing what they were about to hear. I felt awkward with this intimate information about their son. Didn't want to look into their eyes in case they could figure out the secret I held. Alberto's mother and father would hear the news they feared and break into sobs. Through a Spanish interpreter, they would be told that Alberto would need to be referred to hospice care. The tumors that had claimed both of their son's kidneys had returned to now claim lobes of his lungs. There were no more drugs to pump or radiation to burn into the rogue cells to stem this battle with cancer. The scans don't lie. We had evidence for what we said that seemed other-worldly, impossible. Bright spots on a blue piece of film told the story.

Meanwhile, I felt helpless. I was the mother of two teenager daughters and a pediatric nurse. I knew a little about calming children, but nothing seemed to work with Alberto. Resigned, I just sat quietly in front of the stroller trying to think of what to offer a dying child who was in the throes of a tantrum. It didn't seem possible, that this young life so full of vigor at this moment was being squeezed cell by cell. This child, who had endured months of hospitalization including two surgeries to remove kidneys, regular dialysis, and multiple chemotherapies, had done everything possible and this was the outcome.

Soon the voice in the stroller quieted and his sister offered a new toy, a package left from the holiday gifts that arrived at the clinic from charities each Christmas. Intrigued by the glittery plastic, he forgot for a moment where he was. Another patient required my attention so I left Alberto to play with his sister and the newfound toys. I returned a few minutes later to find him surrounded by his parents and the interpreter. I looked into red-rimmed eyes and saw hands pulling at tissues. They knew what I knew. Now my helplessness returned. What do you do to calm the parents? I put my arms around Alberto's mom and held on. This silent communication was mother to mother.

As I drove home that day with tired legs and sweaty scrubs, I wondered why I had traded in my communication career for this type of punishment. Being in the presence of a child and his family as they contemplate an imminent death is like crawling through a sewer. But I realized I would crawl through it again and again. Having that moment with Alberto's mother, a time of telling someone how much you care without saying a word, stays with you forever.

91 Mark Fox

Sent: Wednesday, January 18, 2006 9:24 AM
To: corrine@wizardofads.com
Subject: middle of the night homework

Breakfast

The 1st noticeable thing was this; I live on what arguably is the busy street in Utah. However at 4:00 am, I could actually back out of my driveway without having to wait. Driving away from home I notice it seems a lot quieter than normal. Maybe that's why I could hear a faint pinging sound in my Jeep's engine. It has 124,000 miles on it and has been a great car so far. I hope it's not getting sick.

One thing unique about Utah is the combination of snow and moonlight. When there is a full moon (or close) the reflection of the moonlight off the snow covered mountains and fields glows bright enough to read a book; especially at this time in the morning. Usually my 1st reaction when driving is to start channel surfing the radio. But for some reason I like the quiet and don't feel much like listening to music this morning.

I pass two cop cars in a row. Maybe it's just me, but you can almost feel them peering suspiciously at my Jeep. I don't have any hard data, but based on years of observation, I am certain Utah has the highest Cop ratio per capita in the United States. There are cops everywhere. When you witness a 16 year old girl pulled over for a major felony, such as "turning right at a red light while the wheels still have a slight rotation to them" it takes no less than 3 separate squad cars and a SWAT team to bring her down.

I notice that the Comfort Suites, which is always hard to see from the road, has the brightest sign this morning. I then notice that many of the smaller mom and pop type shops have their signs lighted as well. And they stand out in contrast to the majority which are as dark as the inside of a moose.

Actually there are quite a few cars on the road. I expected to see trucks, but not this many cars. I wonder how well the advertising works; leaving your sign on all night I mean.

Driving early in the morning is not foreign to me. I fly hot air balloons for fun. But this morning seems a little different. I don't really have a goal, like getting to the launch field at a certain time, double checking the weather, etc. I am supposed to be on a mission to.....well I am not sure. To see if I can learn something new about life at this time in the morning. I am not sure what I am looking for really, but my antennas are up. As up as they can be at 4:00 am.

So I find the only place that is open, a truck stop. I walk in and I am rudely tackled by the "please wait to be seated" sign. So I wait....and wait. It is not crowded by any means, only 4 or 5 booths occupied. The man vacuuming the carpets reluctantly shuts down his machine to address me. "booth or table?" I take the table.

He hands me a pile of menus and tells my either Rena or Charlene will be with me shortly. The menus are full of everything you can think of....but breakfast. They seem to be pushing something called "Downtown Bayou". For some reason neither 17 shrimp Jambalaya, 17 shrimp etoufee, grilled chicken gumbo, or blackened flat iron steak sound appetizing right now. Maybe I'll try this place again for dinner some day.

Finally I find the breakfast section. Not really being a breakfast person, the "standard issue" eggs, toast, and hash browns sounds good. It may sound typical, but not for me. My usual breakfast is a granola bar and a glass of milk.

"Coffee?" ...."No thank you mam."

I am used to the shock and sudden jerk back of the waitress's arm which is already committed to a pouring motion. Breakfast servers are always appalled that a red blooded American man does not want coffee in the morning. 25 years of inquisitive facial expressions. I wonder what would bring this county to a standstill quicker, the Columbians cutting off the beans or the Arabs cutting off the oil?

I look around the diner in some more detail. Three of the booths have men... solo. The other booth has two men who obviously know each other and seem to be regulars. The last booth strikes me has sad. It is a man and 3 small girls. No mother. I assume that he is divorced and has the kids today. Although it does seem strange that he is up at 4:20 am, especially with one of the girls who is no more than 4 years old. I can imagine the man's "fun meter" must have been pegged getting her up that early. They are almost through eating, so they have been here a while.

I continue to look around the diner. Oh good...more cops. There are 6 of them in a large booth together. All of us are seated in the same corner/section except the cops who are seated at the furthest point away from the rest of us. I wonder why.

I notice my both, and all the booths for that matter have phones on the wall. I wonder how much they get used in this cell phone age? I also notice that the table has Redmond Sea Salt. The fact that there is Sea Salt at all is a surprise to me. Having sold health products before, I know Redmond is one of the higher quality brands. I didn't know truckers were in to magnesium and manganese. The guy in the booth next to me is in deep thought and is intentionally not making eye contact with anyone. I wonder what is bothering him?

The two regulars both have notepads and are exchanging notes and data of some sorts. I was surprised to seem them writing so much instead of just chatting. I now notice that all of the patrons have note pads and are taking notes or jotting ideas, less the divorcee. He has enough to keep him busy. It looks like everyone is preparing for the day.

I suddenly realize I have pulled a fashion fopah by not wearing a camouflage baseball cap. I am the only one without one, even including two of the girls. I can't do a lot of eavesdropping; there really is not a lot of conversation..just note taking. Noticeable absent is anyone reading a newspaper.

One of the regulars gets up appearing to get ready to leave and forgets his coat. His waitress jumps in and saves him. He obviously sees this as an invitation to flirt. It is not the 1st time these two have met or engaged in this kind of conversation. The waitress says "how much money did you leave in it" holding the coat in her hand. The man says "you know I don't have any money". The waitress says "oh yah that's right, your wife has it all" Somehow the last comment goes over like a turd in a punch bowl..

The divorcee and the girls get up to leave. As one of the small girls turns to face me, I am relieved. It's obviously his wife, she is just 4' 10". I was mistaken. Suddenly he doesn't seem sad to me anymore.

My food has not arrived yet, but I am in no hurry. I am not sure my innards are awake yet anyway for food. Somehow my plumbing is not on the same schedule this morning as the rest of me. I notice all of the tables are very clean and the accessories are all in order. Those that are not, Rena is promptly attending to. Tabasco, salt, pepper, sweet and low, jam rack, ketchup on its head, (chest facing forward), and the dessert flip chart are all smartly in their place.

I notice many details that I wouldn't normally, maybe because my antennas are up. The pictures on the wall, the wall paper, trinkets everywhere, and the ice cream roll cart, and

...Whoa!......I just caught Rena looking at me. Not the "who the hell are you" stare I got from Charlene, but you know...that look. Now it has been a long time, but I have experienced that eye contact before. It usually is in a bar after some girl has had few drinks. Their snap back, look reflexes are much slower then and once in a while you can catch 'em.

I was convinced a girl hasn't looked at me like that in 20 years. But wait ! maybe they have, but I haven't been paying close enough attention. It seems like a stretch but it makes me feel better anyway. Especially since Rena is not too bad looking....you know... for a 40 something country girl.

My breakfast is served uneventful and by the time I get it I think my innards are finally ready. More and more males, 1 and 2 at a time, start to stroll in. Each one strengthens the theory of my fashion fopah. Again they all seem to be quite the quiet bunch. Not a lot of conversation to eavesdrop on.

I finish my breakfast, get my check from Charlene, and head for the counter. As I stood there waiting for some time, I tried to figure out if I learned anything on this mission. Nothing earth shattering comes to mind.

I know the importance of "situational awareness" and paying attention to your surroundings. Looking for opportunities. But maybe with nothing in particular to do on this mission but "observe" my antennas were tuned a little finer. You can see a lot of things if you try looking.

Suspicion confirmed. Rena sees me from across the floor and promptly drops her accessories like a hot potato to come to my attention. There is that look again. Maybe I still got something left after all !

Again, I am not sure if I really learned much but I will try it again. Besides diners, there are a lot other things I don't normally do that I could try. I am hoping this report doesn't really get graded, because I am not sure I would pass.

As I head for my car, in strolls another wave of law enforcement. Great...more cops.

92 Antonio Guerrero

Sent: Wednesday, January 18, 2006 11:51 AM
To: Corrine@WizardAcademy.com
Subject: comfort zone challenge submission

My name is Antonio Guerrero and this morning I accepted your challenge to push my comfort zone and see a world I am not accustomed to. My Journey began at about 4:15 am with a close friend who is a female subscriber of the newsletter and wanted to take the challenge as well, however due to safety issues we decided to go together, however we did not speak to each other as per your instructions. We are located in New York City and after a discussion on possible places to go visit for our journey included a drive to Canada to really make it a mission. We decided on something far more uncomfortable, different and unknown, a train ride to Jersey City, NJ

Our Journey into the unknown began on the dark, cold and wet New York City streets as we made our way to a PATH train station. The PATH is something few New Yorkers if ever ride and most may not even know about it as it is not part of the famed New York City subway system. As we made our way into the leaky cold station we quickly came to realize we were entering into a different realm. The platform was empty as we arrived with not so much as a clerk to great us as we entered the turn style. After about 5-10 minutes a pair of young men who just finished partying for the night arrived on the platform and upon their arrival one of the men quickly proceeded to use the rails as his personal restroom. After this occurrence I began to think about honor and respect and how it can not be obtained with out 1st achieving it for oneself and began to think about how the rest of the Journey will play out and what lesson await me on the other side of the river.

At about a quarter to 5am the train arrives. As we enter we are greeted by the tiered frustrated faces of two port authority polices officers patrolling the train and 3 other passengers. As I sat down and began to observe my fellow passengers I noticed they all had something in common something far more then the need for sleep, They too looked frustrated and sad however not quite aware of it. As the ride went on I continued to observe everyone on the train to see if any expression will change and whether awake or asleep they all had this frustrated unfulfilled look and energy about them. Even the police officers who had the company of each other didn't say so much as a word to one and other or exchange looks they both were away from each other one sitting one standing starting out into nothing. I came to realize and feel the reason for the looks on my fellow passenger was that none of them were living in their purpose they were living in the daily grind knowing they where not in their purpose yet not seeking their purpose and perhaps that is what frustrated them the most.

Just after 5 am we arrive at our location. As we leave the large bright train station we immediately hit the streets of Jersey City in an area which feels and looks as if it has been forgetting by time. The streets are wet and empty with strong winds seemly coming from every direction. We began heading toward the direction with the most lights hoping to find a diner or some sought of 24 hr establishment in which locals may visit. While on our search we find a worker possibly enjoying a break outside and ask him the location of the nearest diner of which he happily gave us. Of the people we have run into tonight this seemed to be the only person who was content if not happy. After receiving our directions we proceeded to head to the local diner while being attacked and hit by flying debris and trash from the city streets. We arrived at out destination about 15 minutes shy of the 5:30am cut off time. My friend wanted to capture this moment and while I walked across the street to verify the diner was open she remained on the opposite side of the street and took out her trusty camera phone to attempt a picture of the establishment and it's signage. As I am waiting by the door of the diner keeping an eye on my friend a panicked man comes out and in a hurried voice asks me "what are you doing?" "You taking picture of my car?" to which I quickly replied no and stated what we were in fact taking a picture. My immediate feeling was of sadness for this man who for some reason has chosen to live his life in fear, mistrust and paranoia. I began to wonder what caused him to live with this (in my opinion selfish) need for everything to be about him. I also wondered how I might be able to serve this person and others like him in the work I do and the person I am.

At last we enter the diner and take seats at the counter. The diner is empty but for one waitress and two men sitting near the back one being my fearful friend. The waitress comes to bring us our menus. I am surprised to see the same look on her as I saw on the faces of the passengers on the ride over. The same look of being out of purpose and a great lack of passion. She too is not quite in the mood for small talk or conversation. We proceed make breakfast orders and await other patrons and hopefully a morning rush. As our food arrives we hear the door open and immediately a smile comes to my face and an inner voice saying "YES!" I turn to find another waitress coming into work to begin her shift. As we begin to eat my fearful friend departs leaving just the two waitresses, one gentleman, and my adventurous partner and I. The waitress waiting to start her shift sits down with the morning newspaper and begins to share with the remaining gentlemen some of the more terrible and tragic news the paper has to offer. I begin to start thinking that is no way to start a day. A new day to find or live in your purpose, a new day live and experience joy and happiness, a new day at a chance for a new beginning. I take notes of my thoughts and finish my meal and proceed to sit in silence until it's time to leave.

    As I sit and type this submission to you I am left with the feeling of having a spiritual journey and some what thinking I've missed the point and true intent of your challenge. However as for your question of what and how I might be able to give to the people we encountered on our journey, and on what they need I am left with the conclusion that I can best serve these people by being a model in living my purpose and sharing my knowledge and experience to all who I might come across. And to do my best to leave a gift with everyone I may come in mild contact with. Be it the gift of a smile or to radiate positive energy their way or perhaps a small blessing of happiness and good will as I come across them.

    Thank you very much for this eye opening challenge and I am honored to be probably among the half dozen or so American to have participated. And thanks to your challenge and the warrior spirit of my friend and me, we will make this challenge a regular somewhat at random part of our lives in order to expand our minds, comfort zones, and over all world. For now it's onward to 24 hour diner at 3am in Montreal, Canada over the next couple of weeks to truly open our eyes and expand our world and truly see how others live and how we might be able to serve them

Ken Wieczorek

Sent: Tuesday, January 17, 2006 7:17 AM
To: Corrine@WizardAcademy.com
Subject: Inside the Outside

I enjoy reading your Monday Morning thoughts each week. In many cases, it sets the tone for my week. I was particularly interested in your January 9th, "Inside the outside."

I am a 3:30am early riser and usually get into work by 6:00am. My routine is to park at a public lot and walk the 5 to 6 blocks to work. Occasionally, I will stop for breakfast along the way at some all night location before I get to the downtown area. I also walk pass a central city bus depot. Just across the street there is a doughnut shop that stays open all night. The breakfast places are usually on the outskirts of downtown and not in the best of the cities neighborhoods. I have been doing this for over 20 years.

So your article in January 9, 2006 Monday Morning was of great interest. However I would like to add to the "challenge" to include a walk through the downtown area to observe and if the occasion arises a hello to one the "night people"

In most cities law enforcement and the city council do not want "street people" around during the day. So a routine is established consist of an exodus of these individual to places outside of the city and a return during the late night. Over the years, I watched the ebb and flow of these individuals like the tides along the shore.

One of the rewards of my routine is that you occasionally get to know a few of these "people" and they will recognize you and will say hello, although some can look downright scary they are for the most part individuals that have found it difficult to come into the "Inside." Most are people that seem to have that "one door closes" close and have never found that "another opens" door. Most are looking for the handout, which I will occasionally accommodate them.

Overall, our safety/security is taken for granted by many of us. I am not talking about the type we all see in daily headlines. I am referring to safety that of sleeping with all of our belongings tied to parts of our body for fear some one may snatch it away. The next time you get a trash bag, use a grocery cart, read a newspaper or unpack a cardboard box, think about what these objects mean to a whole class of people. For many they carry all their possessions, keep there feet warm and provide shelter from the cold.

That trip to the diner, the shift from 2-5, is a carnival of people and experiences. These people keep the gears of our civilization greased. Servers from clubs, bartenders, bakers, bouncers, truck drivers, musicians, delivery men, call girls and some you could only guess at their profession. What they all have in common is the night. Put them in the day setting and they will standout like a surfer in Kansas. If the diner is rich enough to have a TV playing, it becomes the catalyst for understanding a different view of the world, which you will never get from sound bite interviews. Listen to them joke about a commercial that tells them they "need" that brand new 2006 Jag or how they need to surprise their girlfriend on the steps of Note Dame with a diamond. These commercials have about as much relevance to them as that getaway cruise in the Bahamas or deciding which financial company should manage their retirement nest egg. What matters to most of them is getting to the next day and paycheck. When you consider the commercials of today, how much is relevant to the real workers of today, who is the "Outsider"? Go by the central city transit bus stop and watch the 4:00 am rush hour of workers that are going home, many to their second jobs, after spending all night cleaning up the "day people" mess, stocking the shelves, polishing the floor, and picking up the trash that some are too lazy to put in trash cans.

How many of these are concerned with the plastic surgery problems shown on Entertainment tonight. After you have breakfast with the real people, go home, watch TV, and see how many commercials relate to their world. Their world is nothing like the sitcoms, soaps, and shows that come across the screen. They have their own brother hood that will come to the aid of each other with their last dime. Take some troubled person in, even if they do not have enough room. You will also find them extremely patriotic about their country and anyone that "messes with it." To them the world is black and white, and not muddled with the politically correct phrases, or special interests. Ask them about goals or dreams and you will not hear a new Lexis, or adding swimming pool to the back yard. Theirs dreams are simple; better job, a new coat, moving to a neighborhood, where "my kid came walk safely to school." Their worries are not about the stock market, but about saving and not having social security around, or what will become of my family or me if I get sick and can not work. These people are paid by the hour; no work no pay, no benefits. They do not get on a computer to check their bank account. Saving $10.00 a week is considered an accomplishment.

The next time you have that $70 dinner with your friends, just listen to their conversations and compare it to your diner experience and conversation. Just who is in the "Inside" and who is on the "Outside." If you really want to feel good, try to do something good without anyone knowing it. Or the next time you have breakfast, bring along some tickets to some event in town and give it to one of regulars, tell then you will not be able to go. Do not be tempted to give it as an ego thing, they will know. In fact you may want to put the tickets in an envelop without anything more than a simple note, "if you found this, enjoy it". There are gift certificates for just about any place. Buy one and give it to someone in need or make it anonymous.

94   Mirta Calderon

Sent: Saturday, January 14, 2006 1:23 AM
To: Corrine@WizardAcademy.com
Subject: Get on your belly and crawl under the fence

    I'm not Canadian and as a citizen of a Latin American developing country I will not follow the rules. But I think I can make a point by writing about my personal experience getting on my belly and crawling under the fence.
    I left my 8-year safe and well paying job because I was just about to turn 40 and I thought that if I reached that age in the same job I was never going to leave. Since I'm not a long-term relationship person I decided to leave before I turned into one.
    I started my own business, which did not go well, so I looked for another job. I sent my resume to a famous human resources company, which call me shortly after I sent it. The company interested in me could not afford to pay the salary I was asking for but wanted to make me an offer (this is when I got on my belly and crawl under the fence).
    The company's headquarters were about 40 miles away from my house. On the other side of the city, or at least on the other side of "my side" of the city. I drove for an hour and did no find the place. I called my friend on the phone and told her that I would continue driving for little while just because I did not have anything to do, but that if I didn't see anything similar to the description given to me, I was turning back. Thirty seconds later I saw the place.
    I went in, two guards opened the gates and showed me the way to the General Manager's Office. I asked where I could park my car, they told me that I should drive and not walk, and that I would find a parking space there -500 mts away from the entrance of the complex-. I drove around the block and found the manager's office. I waited for an hour or so to be interviewed. Even though the pay was 30% less than what I was making on my former job, the place impressed me, not just because of its 90,000 square mts (not feet) but also because I felt an interesting energy. So, I stayed. I was hired by one of the companies in the corporation to boost sales through Latin America. My company has 30 employees, the complete corporations goes up to 2000 during high season.
    I had never worked in the manufacturing industry before, I had never had 2000 co-workers, and I had never worked with people with no education, some even illiterate, I had never eaten a $1.00 lunch. I have never had close friends that had started sweeping floors in the warehouse

and had gone up to managerial positions. I had never worked with married men with two kids making $300.00 a month. My "crawling under the fence experience" did not last an hour, it has last a year (Next Tuesday it will be a year since I started working here as a Sales and Marketing Manager for Latin America), and this experience has taught me that my life was my selfish reality, that the world outside is not the life I live, that the way I managed my money was a shame, that the things that are important in life do not come with money. That our developing countries will never come out of that category unless we educate an empower people. I learned that even though I cannot offer to raise all my employees salaries I can teach them to have a vision of the future, to go back to school and get a degree, to learn English, to learn how to use a computer, and to get out of the vicious circle of the low class society that there is no hope. We have created ongoing training for everybody in the company, mostly to exercise the mind, but also to learn about things that are important in our business.

I have been blessed and feel lucky to have found another world. I do not go around suggesting people to change their way of life, to leave a safe and well paying job, to leave friends, nice offices, private health insurance, boring sales meetings in expensive hotels and look for the other world outside theirs, but I'm sorry for the ones who will never find it on their own, too bad. I´m not sharing the secret. I do not feel more than the ones that have not gone through my experience but sadly I do not see them with the same eyes.

When I decided to quite my former safe and well paying job in the largest publishing company worldwide, I was looking to do something different, to have a little adventure and to learn (I had stopped learning). I found what I expected and more. I found this other world and its people; this world is full of interesting, thankful, warm, intelligent, funny, humble, people. I lost touch with the sharks, and the vultures…there are some here, but they get lost in between the 2000 others. I still have some nice friends in the other world, some say: Oh, how I would like to do what you did…. But I do not think they will ever crawl under their fences. It is not comfortable and they still need the money.

The learning experience has been infinite. Imagine how much I have learned sitting in a strange part of town where I would had never gone, listening to all people there, during almost a year. I came alone. I have listened and absorbed this new reality, I have thought about what these people need most and have found ways to help them. I have also thought about what they have that I don't. My experience has not ended and I hope to be here at least a couple of years more. Funny how this other world was waiting for me on the other side of town.

95 Bryan Nielsen

Sent: Wednesday, January 18, 2006 10:10 AM
To: Corrine@WizardAcademy.com
Subject: Inside the Outside

The weather lady on the news last nigh said we were under a "winter storm advisory." My wife, a certified snow lover, ever hopeful to be able to build a monster snowman in our front yard this winter, smiled at me and said, "blah, blah, blah." Our little code phrase for no new snow.

As I drove away from my home in the hills on the east side, it was certainly cold outside, but there was no new snow. No signs of any on the way as far as I could see, at O-dark thirty in the morning. Nevertheless, I was bright eyed, bushy tailed and on a mission.

I drove under the freeway and was now on the west side of town. The heated leather seats had me cradled in comfort as I complimented myself on being in what was predicted to be one of the very few to take this challenge I'd accepted from an article I'd read online.

I arrived at the all-day day all-night restaurant at 4:27 AM this morning and was seated at a booth around the corner from the bar. I was now one of four customers.

The guy in the booth next to me was half way through his morning paper. The two older gentlemen at the bar were deep in some conversation that I couldn't hear. From their body language and seeming familiarity with each other, I had to assume they were long time friends. Maybe they served in a war together.

I was entertaining other relationship scenarios for these two when I found myself tuning into the music being piped in to this eating establishment. I put my former DJ skills to work and concluded that it had to be Stevie Wonder. The lyrics were being belted out, "This is your day." It was a bouncy tune and I liked it. Note to self. Find this one on iTunes.

But wait, I'm on a mission. I'm supposed to observe what's happening here. I only had the guy in front of me left to figure out his deal. He was still reading the paper. I stole a few glances at the headlines but reached no further glimpses into his life story.

My waiter was nice enough. Took my order. Brought me what I asked for. Seemed like a decent guy. His name tag displayed a very Utah-ish name. Ammon. I never used his name in conversation with him but remembered that my wife had called the waiter we had at the steakhouse last week by name and told him he was doing an excellent job of taking care of us. In my earlier impatience and amidst my hunger pangs, I think he may of overheard some snide remark I'd made to my wife to the effect of, "Our waiter dude better get here soon and take dang good care of us."

We all have names and stories. We all have dreams. I have dreams of making a difference for good in the world. My wife shares these dreams with me. I know we make a diiference for good with each other.

Last week my Mom went to a Kenny Rogers concert. She said that Kenny took a break from singing and (I'm paraphrasing) said, "if we were to put the name of ever person here at this concert on a piece of paper and put it in a hat with your story and your problems, more than likely you wouldn't want to trade your problems with anybody else in this room." Sobering.

Wait we're up to six people. These two have got to be father and son. They're seated at the far side against the wall. Can't hear what they're talking about either. Their mannerisms are the same. They appear to be happy. They even have the same sideburns. Classic.

I don't observe any visible signs of neglect on any of these people here. But I do see the homeless people on my way into my office. Every morning at 8:00 AM the van is there at the park. A somewhat orderly line forms and I notice them getting food and anything else they can gather together to make it to another day. At least it didn't snow on them today.

That's it isn't it? Everybody has a story. Some more engaging than others. There's all kinds of noble stories of people doing wonderful things on this planet that'll never be in the news, or blogged on a website, but I know they're out there. Knowing this gives me hope and inspiration.

Without being privy to the content of the conversations of the people I simply observed this morning, this is all I've got to go on. Now if I were to be more aggressive and put on my journalist hat, I'm sure there'd be interesting enough stuff to know about these folks.

But what can I do that'll make a difference from my presence at the restaurant this morning? Small things. I thank Ammon, give him a generous tip. Ammon says, "Hey, thanks a lot man."

Last night I had 2255 songs in my iTunes. I'm now up to 2256 songs. Stevie Wonders' "Fun Day" is now in my library and an appropriate enough theme song for me today.

96 Bill Reilly

Sent: Monday, January 09, 2006 9:57 AM
To: Corrine@WizardAcademy.com
Subject: " The Gift of Initiation"

My response will disqualify me for the free gift. It really doesn't matter. The people who you describe are not unlike our congregation at New Song Church. Formerly a biker bar, called "The Temple Tavern", and more recently "Mungo Murphs", it has been transformed into safe place to meet God for the people of Drouillard Street, and the surrounding community of Ford City, in the "hood" of Windsor Ontario.

I was honored to share Holy Communion yesterday, with a former inmate, a drug addict, and a mentally challenged adult who gathers shopping carts for a living. I don't show up at New Song for a " warm fuzzy, I'm ok, You're ok" cardboard cut-out sermon. I show up a little early to chat with the folks having a smoke on the front landing, or to tie Ricky's tie. (Ricky is our 52 year old Downs Syndrome worshiper, who sings in a completely different key and cadence, and has been know to pull off a little Riverdance or "one foot shuffle " action during Praise and Worship time.)

The people who come to our Sunday Service, the Friday night free dinner, Thursday youth programme (called X-it), or the ones who drop in because they are hungry or need someone to talk to, come because they can feel real love, and a sense that they truly fit in somewhere. God has changed my heart, to love the unlovely, feed the hungry, pray with someone that hasn't had a bath in maybe a week, and be a friend to anyone who graces our door. It is a Beggar's Banquet , near to God's heart, because He shows up all the time, in ways that astound all of us. I am humbled to be able to serve.

Pastor Kevin Rogers (RevKev as we like to call him), truly has the "Smell of God" on him. A musician and songwriter , he wrote these words in a song entitled " House of Love"

Home for the Homeless
Life for the Lifeless
Church of the broken
Come with your eyes open
Come into this House
Come into this House of Love. *God Bless.*

Bill Oehler

Sent: Wednesday, January 18, 2006 5:15 PM
To: Corrine@WizardAcademy.com
Subject: Re: Inside the Outside column of Roy's

2:45 AM in all night doughnut shop, on the fringe of the poorest side of town where the winners and losers of the midnight bingo congregate after pinning their hopes on a $20 and 5 numbers. This is neither Starbucks® coffee nor the delights of Dunkin' Donuts®.

"Is that big guy they throwed out that old lady's son?"

"Which old lady?"

"You know, the one youz always catches a ride with."

"Which old lady!?"

"You know! Oh, what's her name?"

"If I knew I would't be asking would I?"

"You know, the one youz always catches a ride with."

"You mean Leona?"

"Yeah, yeah that's her name. Is that her son? What is his name?"

"Leona' son's name is, is .....Oh hell, what is his name?"

"That guy they threw out, his name is Leon. They said he was selling drugs in those boxes that he said had cookies in them his mother made."

"Well, Leona makes cookies but her son is not named Leon, I know that for sure though I can't think of his name right off the tip of my tongue and he sure doesn't sell drugs. He does something with computers till late at night, I know that cuz Leona told me so. He comes to bingo with Leona sometimes but he wasn't there tonight. Why did you think that was him?"

"When I was out havin' a smoke somebody said that was his son."

"Well some people have very little to do if that's what there saying about her."

"They weren't saying nothing about her. It was him."

"Still the same if you ask me, saying that about him being her son."

"I don't like that caller tonight."

"Well he's a little fast but he's got to do that if we're going to finish on time. Those slow ones make everybody miss their bus or taxi. I don't like that. I'd rather he go fast."

"I don't like him."

"Why?"

"I just don't."

"More coffee?"

"I don't think of Leona as old. That's why I couldn't think of who you were talking about. She's only 66. That's 10 years younger than I am. She's not old!"

"More coffee?"

"Sure. I can't remember his name."

Et cetera into the night before they pick themselves up an hour after entering and slip out the doors into the night themselves. Small worlds, small dreams, little hope, and no big plans. Waiting for luck to smile upon their world and no plans what to do with it if it ever happens. Stifled contentment consoling lost energies and thwarted dreams. Not wanting to die but seemingly no plans between now and then. Not poor, always another $20 and another hope. Clean clothes, no body odor, a little makeup, hair brushed, though the shoes don't shine. Waiting and watching, not wanting to go home – no one there. At bingo you're not lonely, you're among friends.

Aaron Atkinson

98

Sent: Tuesday, January 10, 2006 12:06 AM
To: Corrine@WizardAcademy.com
Subject: Inside the Outside challenge

Roy, the following happened to me on two separate occassions recently, obviously before you issued the challenge. I have combined them into one narrative since it made a better story. Another of my occassional practices is to hang out with the cabbies at the airport of the city described below. Thier's also is a completely different world.

I may have dropped enough hints to be able to identify the major city in the story. Let me know if you can pin it! Also let me know if you have any comments about style, flow, and delivery. I am working on improving my copywriting.

Finally, whether you send the initiation gift is up to you. I am aware I didn't follow the rules of engagement exactly and the experience you described is something I have done many times. I want to help you get more than a dozen entries!

Now on to this true-life encounter!

HOW my PDA calander/planner got so messed up, I'll never know. All I do know is that I was two hours early for the bus.

I thought I was late, so I ran out of the house without eating breakfast. Now here I am: 4:30am, hungry, and with two hours to kill.

Not too far away is a little diner, Joe's Filling Station, as I later found out. The signage is confusing and difficult to read. Apparently, the owner did his best to make the place look like a Conoco station from the 50's. Trouble is, it looked too much like gas station until you took the time to examine it carefully. Time is what I had plenty of.

The door was open, the lights were on, the tables were clean, and the place was empty. I wandered around for I-don't-know-how-long admiring the nostalgia on the walls when a voice cought me off guard.

"I didn't even hear you come in. Would you like a table?" said a middle-aged looking gal.

"I would, thank you"

Without even looking at the menu, I ordered biscuits and gravy along with juice. That's how I rate a restaurant's breakfast, by their biscuits and gravy.

The waitress disappeared, reappeared with the place settings and water, and vanished again.

She was gone for what seemed like a long time. I actually got up and wandered around the diner some more. In the back of the dining area the TV was on, but for the most part I stayed focused on the memoribilia.

Eventually, the conversation from the kitchen caught my attention. It was difficult to capture the exact words or even the gist but it more and more sounded like an argueemnt. At now five in the morning, I couldn't help but wonder if they were the struggling owners. Perhaps it was the stress of a small shop and few customers (the signage certainly wasn't helping them), high overhead and low cash-flow, "Overworked, underfed, Anatevka..."

I went back to the table and sat down, still trying to catch snatches of the conversation that might give me a clue to thier world. I'm glad I did because less than 60 seconds later the waitress burst out of the kitchen with my order.

"Here ya go. Let me know if you need anything."

She vanished again just as quickly, but this time towards the back of the diner and through another door. I never saw her again. I'm glad I didn't need anything.

I ate my breakfast in the company of my thoughts. I could relate somewhat with them. I had just moved to the area to start a business. I too was going it on my own, without a lot of money, working another job to pay the bills. In fact, that's why I was out here for the bus.

"It sucks," I said to myself, "working two jobs and barely getting paid for one." I wondered if they were in the same situation. Maybe she had gotten things set up and was on her way home to get the kids off to school and then on to another job.

The biscuits and gravy were pretty good. Once again, I stood at the cash register for what seemed an eternity. If I'd had any idea how the thing worked I could have possibly made off with the till. Finally, a man with the diner's logo on his shirt came out of the kitchen. He didn't look like he'd been cooking. My bill was less than five dollars, but I pulled out a ten and told him to give the rest to the waitress.

"She'll be excited to see that." he said. I knew she would because I also know what it's like to "live" off tips.

I would have liked to stay and chat but I had to go meet a bus. You see, I'm the driver. While I'm starting my business, this is, sort of, paying the bills.

Five hours later, I find myself in the heart of downtown of a major American city. Again, I have two hours to kill before the return trip. Because I got confused about the time this morning, I didn't pack a lunch like I normally do. So I park the bus and set off to find an eatery.

"I've got two hours, so no need to rush this," I thought. It turns out I didn't get to eat at all.

As I was walking, I saw a begger sitting outside a house of worship. A woman in a wheelchair sat beside him. A couple of empty prescription bottles on the ground in front gave emphasis to the hand-lettered cardboard sign pleading for help.

"How's business?" I said as I sat down on the sidewalk beside him. (It's not the first time I've hob-nobbed with panhandlers. Some of them really do treat it as a business.)

"It's been terrible slow." said Joe. According to his story, he and Louise got married four years ago. Two years later, a back injury forced Joe off a construction job.

"I can still drive fork. But nobody'll hire ya' if ya' don't have a phone." He said. "I can't keep an apartment since I don't make any money, so I can't keep a phone."

I commented on the huge religious facility next to us, Joe mentioned that he was a member of that group although Louise was not.

"Surely they could do something for you. They're quite well known for helping thier own." I suggested.

"Yeah, I've tried. I have a friend who's pretty high up in there and he got me an apartment earlier this year. He had talked the owner into setting aside some units fer people like us. But a couple of months ago the owner decided ta remodel so we all got moved to some temporary quarters. After that, though, he rasied the rent just enough so we couldn't afford it anymore and we was all back on the street again." He said. "They don't help ya' if'n ya' don't have an address."

Well, that certainly didn't make any sense and I said as much. He insisted that was the way it worked.

Interestingly enough, he also mentioned that the hurricanes in the Gulf states had affected the homeless population of this city - thousands of miles away from the area of impact. This past fall, a flood of refugees were brought in. I remember the papers saying how generous the population of the city and the state were in accepting these unfortunates. It would seem they were still unfortunate.

"They picked clean all the thrift shops where we usually get our winter clothes." said Joe, "Most of 'em didn't even spend the winter. Alot of 'em have left already."

I gave him what was left in my wallet and said I would be praying for them. Then I turned to go since, once again, I had to get to the bus.

99 Mike Lawson

Sent: Wednesday, January 18, 2006 8:15 AM
To: Corrine@WizardAcademy.com
Subject: Inside the Outside

Considering this was my last opportunity to take part in The Wizard's Monday Morning Memo challenge of January 9th, it couldn't have been a better opportunity. Almost 2 inches of snow fell thru the night, something that we had not seen since late December. With the new beauty on the ground, I knew that this morning was "thee" day that I'd witness life in its fullest at an eating establishment...or at least I had different expectations.

I chose a 24- hour convenience store with sit-in area for food called Village Pantry, which are all owned by the giant grocer conglomerate, MARSH Superstores. This particular location was only a mile or more from where I live [Noblesville, IN] , but in a part of town that I rarely go or travel along State Road 32. I'd thought of other bigger 24- hour eating-only establishments such as Perkin's or Denny's which are only about 7 miles away, but due to time constraints as well as what I perceived would be interesting characters [or classification of people], Village Pantry was the place that I needed to be.

I was surprised to pull in the parking lot and see only one other vehicle that pulled in moments before I did. I noticed from my vehicle an elderly gentleman get out of his car and shuffle into the store and around several aisles before shuffling his way out to the front door, his head looking down to the left, to the right, and repeatedly doing so as if he had either lost something or was looking for some treasured keepsake. I walked past him as I enter the establishment and he heads out.

I was immediately greeted by a young gentleman on the front floor that had a few more days of facial growth than I did, although I think that I may have him beaten with a longer receded hairline than he, but I wouldn't wage a bet on it. Perception of ones self, you know. He immediately made a one-sentence comment on the weather and the snow, something that I knew I just knew I would hear at one point during my stop. And one thing that didn't come to me as a surprise in the least. I smiled, without saying anything and made my way back to the fresh donuts section, with a variety to choose from, and appearing to have just been restocked within a short time earlier. Who knows how fresh they actually are; that's not the point. I make my way to the coffee station and stare at the army of coffee pots mind you, not the usual placement of thermos that you find at most convenience stores. As I fill my Styrofoam cup and stir in the man-made sweetener, its where I begin to get hear a long, drawn out conversation from an employee from behind the counter, whom I will call Bill, for all purposes of this story.

After relinquishing a few dollars from my pocket to the cashier for the goods purchased, I make my way to the where the few tables sit and where the tall stools are pressed up against the front windows, just west of the entrance of the building. Bill is most likely a mid-20's man with dark brown hair and an apparent speech impediment. It seems a routine that after every few sentences, he's laughing loudly at his canter, and maybe during it as well. As best my notes say, Bill goes on talking to a late 40's-looking lady, a fellow employee who looks weathered from years of smoke, alcohol or sun tan beds. Perhaps all. She really never responds much to Bill, and if she does, its quiet rhetoric as she constantly moves about her business behind the counter preparing different food for the morning. Bill's very happy, or at least you'd think so from his babbling on about "if I owned this place, I'd give you a raise [he speaks to the fellow male worker; the one who I first encountered about the weather small-talk]," to which the gentleman replies, "no you wouldn't...you couldn't afford to do it." Bill spills on to the female co-worker about "and I would make you assistant manager," to which there's no reply from her accept for a half-forced effort of a smile and she continues about her business behind the counter. Bill's speech is hard to understand, and the replies that he seems to get from his fellow co-workers, you can tell that everyone has been together in that same environment for quite some time. Nothing seems to phase them. Business as usual.

A rather large middle-aged man walks in and bee-lines right over to the coffee as he starts talking about the weather and the snow to the young balding man that greeted me. They exchange small talk as another customer walks in, that I would have guessed would have been mid 50's, but from his conversation with the rather large man, he exclaims that he wasn't born in the 50's but that he's a product of the 60's. The two make small conversation but in the way that you know that the two must meet in here everyday, at about the same time, doing the same thing. Coffee. He too talks about the weather and snow, but doesn't let it rest. He blames the weather man for this recent winter outbreak; "you know they says that we could gets anywhere from 1 to

3 inches of snow, and they couldn't get that right. We were on the high end and got that 3 inches of snow right here. I tell you..." The rather large man has already made his purchase and left midway thru the other man's conversation, but the man doesn't seem to notice, or mind, as he continues on with the younger balding man behind the counter.

A middle-aged lady swings open the door and makes her way to the counter where the younger balding man than I waits on her from behind the cash register. "Is it too early to buy Powerball [lottery tickets] yet?" "Nope, you sure can," he replies as the lady pulls out her loose bills and hands them to the man behind the counter. She doesn't collect any change in return as if she knew the price up front from what I gather is a normal routine for her, and she heads out the door.

A mid-30's-looking guy walks in wearing a winter coat, green sweat pants and construction worker-type boots, all pulled tight, and heads over to the coffee. Fixes himself the liquid drug, pays the younger balding man than I behind the counter, then leaves.

What do these people need?

I suppose that the elderly gentleman himself is looking for something. Sounds stupid, but aren't most Americans doing so? Look at all of the "Get Rich Quick" books and infomercials on television. We all want that, right? Maybe the elderly gentleman is facing a more real means of getting his riches. Looking for what people lose on the ground.

The younger balding man than I that works the establishment. He needs this job, and doesn't seem to have any care that where he's at in life is any intrusion of his dreams. He's content.

Bill. Bill is a happy-go-lucky guy whom even though he's probably as nice as they come, he probably gets on your nerves very easily. People ignore him for the most part. They're used to him. Bill's looking for approval of some sort, or maybe someone to talk to. To just be with. Although the management and ownership role would probably not be in his best interest, he has a big heart for wanting to give his co-workers a raise. After all, he mentioned putting them first and never mentioned himself in a raise.

The two coffee drinkers. The rather large man needs his morning fix and to go about his day. The other gentleman, needs people to listen to him. He's content talking and talking and talking no matter of you're listening, present or not.

The middle-aged lady needs to invest money wisely. I prejudge her on the amount of money that she's most likely spent on Powerball, and she's looking for her "Get Rich Quick," as was the elderly gentleman, but she obviously professes to spend money to make money, even if it's in a business sense.

The young coffee drinker. What do you suppose his need is? Is he caught up in life and maybe work and he's trying to "just do it" day by day?

I don't have the answers I suppose on how I might help these people get what they need.

What about me? What do they have that I do not? Maybe most of them know more about their purpose of life better than I [yes, I read the most recent Monday Morning Memo]. No, I don't suppose that I need a good slapping from The Wizard, but maybe a fresh approach to looking at life and reviving a routine-life to which Leo Fish [played by actor Dylan McDermott in 1995's "Home For The Holidays," a brilliant film] states "par, par, bogey, bogey, par, par."

That's my story in a nutshell, although I'm not certain that I'm sticking to it.

Be GOD's!

100   Jay Larkin

Sent: Wednesday, January 18, 2006 4:55 AM
To: Corrine@WizardAcademy.com
Subject: Pancakes and gratitude

"Pancakes and gratitude for under $7"

Arriving at 'Fred's Place' at 3:05am, I grimaced at the decor that greeted my eyes--What am I doing here? I'm tired, a little scared--but hungry now, so in I go for some pancakes!

As I sit at the counter, I'm greeted by Karen as 'honey'. Middle aged, overweight, in need of dental work and a shower--yet, friendly and attentive to the 'regulars'.

They all seem to know each other beyond names. Some young, intoxicated men, as well as a cabby, trucker, and some others rounded out the customer base.

This group took joy in complaining: "Cheap bosses", "Expensive gas", "too many kids comin' in here since the Denny's on North Ave closed..."

You're almost right about "an all-night café on the wrong side of town eating a three-dollar breakfast, listening to the smelly, funny stories of downtrodden people who know each other well. Their sparkling banter gives me a glimpse into problems I'll never touch, victories I'll never celebrate, a life I'll never have. These are they who will never have internet access, a credit card or cable TV."

Mine was $6.47 (3 pancakes, bacon, and a decaf). Also, I have a feeling these people have access to cable.

What do these people need most? Hmmm, it's too hard for me to judge. A friend? To be respected and liked somewhere (Cheers)? A sense of belonging...

I can give this to them with a smile and eye contact. An east-Indian word 'Namaste' means roughly: "the light (consciousness) in me, recognizes and salutes the light in you".

I don't know if I can 'market' this attitude, but I feel good doing it, and I think Karen did by waiting on me.

I think some of them have a sense of 'not clinging'--they are in the here and now--and deal with it. Me, I spend too much time in the future... (Then again, a few seemed bitter.)

By the time I was done, only 2 patrons were left. And I felt very grateful for my life and 'perceived advantages'. To feel such gratitude-- what a bargain for just $6.47...

Susan MacLean   101

Sent: Sunday, January 15, 2006 4:10 PM
To: Corrine@WizardAcademy.com
Subject: late night lunch

Ok, just in case I doubted the Laws of the Universe, I received this email. Some Monday mornings I, quite honestly, delete it without even reading it. This morning, however, I did check in to see what The Wizard had to say - writing. Writing - after having spent three months reading the how - to of writing a first novel, and spending this past weekend actually sitting down and starting this covetted and cursed venture. I thought it could not be put more clearly in front of me, so here is my account of Friday night at a truck stop style restaurant near my town.

I convinced my friend, Shannon, to spend Friday night at a truck stop restaurant on the highway near our small town. After explanations of a seminar I took on advertising by The Wizard received confused frowns, I'm not in advertising, I tell her simply that I need company and this works - simple sometimes best!

We arrive at 230 a.m. and are greeted warmly by the only waitress present. She instructs us to 'sit wherever girls'. We do. That waitress, Tracey, arrives carrying a pot of coffee that I'm sure is actually attached to her uniform. She is the only one in the restaurant who seems fully awake. We discuss the usual chatter with her and order tea and omelettes.

Keeping in mind the rules, we had chosen a table close to others to eavesdrop more effectively. My first observation is that noone seems to care we are there. I had visions of dead silence and obvious stares on our arrival, but we haven't warranted this treatment. Conversations have continued with the eight men in the reataurant. They are not all seated together, but they all look alike - jeans, boots, long sleaved T-shirts, ball hats with jackets over the back of their chairs. Some are eating, most are drinking the never ending coffee.

Over the next hour my judgements are washed away. The men speak of kids, of wives (the current and the ex), of fatigue, of money problems and of bosses (the good and the bad). They are all truckers, the eighteen wheeler variety. The ones that blow past you on the highway so fast your car shakes. I hadn't given much thought to the men and women who drive them, assumed they were loners who lived on the road. But these men are speaking of the everyday highs and lows that we all discuss over coffe with friends. There is an easy comaraderie among them. Some haven't seen one another in months, but they slip into relaxed conversations of family and catching up on those not present tonight. There is very little negativiity, save for concern over rising fuel costs. These are everyday men with the same concerns of money, family and friends as any you would hear at a downtown bistro.

We leave the restaurant, tipping more than ususal, it seems we are grateful for the opportunity to visit this world. There exhits an underground community, not much differnt than my own. If anything, more accepting of strangers, and perhaps more genuine. I do not feel I need to do anything to help these men, they are strong, hardworking, and proud. But since my visit, I have changed other preconceived judgments and as I'm sure most will note, received more than anticipated.

Christopher Jaquess 102

Sent: Wednesday, January 18, 2006 11:42 AM
To: Corrine@WizardAcademy.com
Subject: "I've become an eavesdropper."

When I told my wife I was going to a truck stop in the middle of the night on a writing assignment, she was troubled. She had visions of me sleeping at the wheel and crashing off the highway. Or, somehow there'd be a brawl and I'd get stabbed, shot, robbed, or worse. It was a blow to my manly pride that she didn't think I could protect myself. But, I chalked her fears up as signifying that she loved me and just wanted to make sure I'd thought this little adventure through. So, with reassurance to her that I'd return hale and whole, I set off to find an open eatery frequented by the blue-collar crowd. I had fears of my own, namely, that I wouldn't find a place with sufficient patronage to eavesdrop upon.

It was difficult to drag my carcass out of bed at 3:15 A.M. I was motivated by two things. The first being that this would indeed add to my stock of experiences and experience is the yeast that ferments into stories that can be written. Experience is the foundation for 'writing what you know.' This would be a good one to add to my stock. Secondly, I was motivated by the challenge of being a zebra among thoroughbreds. When this task was assigned, it was suggested that few that read it would follow it through to completion. This was bait I couldn't refuse to take. The gauntlet had been thrown and I would rise to the challenge.

My fear seemed groundless as I pulled into the Waffle House parking lot just off of US 65. The lot was full of semi-trucks and trailers, a few cars, and a pickup truck with cattle trailer attached. I counted heads through the restaurant window as I parked. There were seven diners, a cook, and a waitress. Not exactly the fertile ground I'd hoped for, but maybe it would do.

As I walked in all nine heads swiveled to me, and I had a queasy moment. I started to follow habit and sit at a booth away from everyone and then I caught myself remembering that I was here to observe, listen and possibly solve a problem. So I sat at the bar close to two other gentlemen sitting side-by-side and chatting idly. I sat at the end closest to a booth that contained a single gentleman with the name "Nightmare" sewed above the right pocket of his uniform shirt. I was so amused by this that even though I looked three times at the name of the company sewn over the left pocket I can't recall it. The farm boys belonging to the pickup truck and cattle trailer were packed four in a booth at the far left end of the restaurant. I would've known them for farm boys anywhere because they were wearing the Missouri country boy's uniform. This uniform consists of Roper boots, Wrangler jeans, Carhart coats, and ball caps with farm machinery logos. I guessed (correctly) that the two guys at the bar with me were truck drivers.

"Nightmare" and the farm boys left before I even got my food and my fear returned. The two guys at the bar talked quietly among themselves and I could only catch snatches of their conversation. They seemed to be comparing experiences when they had served in the military. I ate my waffle, eggs and bacon as slowly as I could. The eggs were quite cold, coagulated, and less than tasty by the time I finished. Prolonging the meal as long as I could still only consumed half an hour. It was 4:20 A.M. and it was beginning to look as if this project wouldn't be very fruitful.

As I sat nursing my coffee hoping for a miraculous rush of early morning diners, in walked a man that to me looked like a TV version of a Marine Corp drill instructor. He had the flat-top, the chiseled features, the grizzled mustache and the big tattoo on his forearm. Apparently the two drivers at the bar were thinking the same thing.

Suddenly the waitress comments aloud, "That's a funny way to park a truck." All eyes turn to look. In walks the driver looking for directions. He stands between the two drivers at the bar and the ex-Marine in the booth as they try to tell where to go. The driver thanks them and leaves. This is the opening the two guys at the bar have been wanting. They've something in common. They're all truck drivers. And, the two at the bar have apparently been discussing aloud what I'd been thinking, that the ex-Marine looked like a guy they'd seen on TV. One guy says to him, "You look like X from that show, (I couldn't hear)." The guy smiles as if he gets that a lot. Then the conversation turns to military service. It seems all three served at one time. The chatty driver at the bar joked that his buddy served in War II. The red-headed driver at the bar shot back, "No War I." "Did you catch any Kaisers?" Then, the conversation turned serious as they began to relate information regarding branch of service and swap stories. The stories moved to children in the service. It seemed that the ex-Marine had one son in the Air Force and all three of the chatty driver's children were in the military, in various branches. As he began to relate, it turned out that his dad and granddad had also served. So, the military was a long-standing tradition in his family. He softened for a moment as he spoke of his fears for his children serving during war time and the worries that never ceased. Then quickly, back to telling stories.

Somehow, the stories moved from one subject to another, smoothly segueing into each other. A story of being in San Diego for basic training, led to a story of in L.A. during a snow storm and talked turned to driving. This led to road stories as the truck drivers swapped stories of crashes and brake burnouts. The ex-Marine story of his brakes burning out coming down a mountain, led to an observation that trucks didn't have a certain kind of brakes back then. The chatty driver interjected a joke about the red-headed driver starting to drive back when it was mules and oxen pulling wagons. Then he cracked about getting out of the way of the Mormons though. (I didn't understand the joke either.) So, the ex-Marine told a story about hitchhiking and being stranded in Salt Lake City. Somehow he ended up in jail and was bailed out by a farmer that put him to work. Chatty driver talked about riding the rails coast to coast.

And, there I left them; drinking coffee, swapping stories, unhurried, grateful to talk to someone before they headed out on the road for another day's drive. I can't imagine spending days without end entombed in the white-noise of the truck cab as the miles rolled beneath. I'd be grateful too! I could understand the desire to talk to living, breathing human in the flesh after spending so many hours alone.

I'm not sure that I observed any tangible needs. Maybe I didn't listen closely enough. The three seemed happy. They all had children serving their country and they were proud of this choice. They all seemed to have lived eventful lives that allowed them to recap the high moments in story and jokes.

The concept of being grateful for the little things was reinforced for me. I walked away from this encounter with a renewed appreciation for God's blessings in my life. I've a reinvigorated sense of gratefulness for the little things that I take for granted. On the whole this may not be an experience I can talk to the grandkids about, but I am grateful for the moment. I am most grateful for the pause to reflect on my own life and feel grateful for all that it contains. I was reminded, as I listened to their stories and jokes, that life is good. I am grateful for its goodness.

103 Andrea Blachly

Sent: Friday, January 20, 2006 10:22 PM
To: corrine@wizardacademy.com
Subject: "Inside the Outside" Response

Hello. When I read your recent memo "Inside the Outside," I decided to take part in your assignment. I tried it mostly because it was an interesting challenge and partly because I was offended that you assumed I wouldn't…either way, it got me out of my apartment.

This morning at 4:30 my girlfriend and I from work went to a Waffle House on the southern edge of town. It's right on a highway across from a truck stop…not a location I frequent. There were two customers seated when we got there, a man and a woman, both eating alone. The two waitresses, Betty and Princess, greeted us as we took our seats at the counter.

Betty was all business as she asked what we wanted, but Princess wanted to chat. She asked me about the college sweatshirt I was wearing and inquired about where we worked.

As we ate our breakfast Betty sat down to rest her feet as she neared the end of a 14-hour shift. Princess asked what I wanted to hear on the jukebox. I told her that I liked county music, but doubted it would be a crowd pleaser. She replied with "Hmm, you better let me pick one out."

I found it surprising through the course of our time there how open both the women were about their lives. Betty is behind on rent and can't pay her car payment. She is on food stamps and swears that without them she would be on the "streets." Princess was in much the same position, but was visibly more upbeat. She joked about her son's baggy pants and tried to talk Betty into letting her do her taxes because it would save her money.

I thought about what these women needed most. This was difficult for me because they seemed to have so many problems…the lack of money, the demands of their children's needs, poor housing, and "dead end jobs." These were problems too overwhelming for me to fix. I planned on leaving a sizable tip, but twenty bucks was going to buy them lunch, not cure their financial burdens.

As Betty and Princess continued talking I became aware that though they were complaining about their lives, they were also playful and obviously proud of their kids as they spoke of them. I concluded that what I could do at the moment for the women was enjoy their company and give them my respect. I plan on visiting them again soon.

Thank you for sharing your thoughts in your memos, I look forward to them each week.

Chris Ramey

104

Sent: Monday, January 09, 2006 7:30 AM
To: Corrine@WizardAcademy.com
Subject: Weak manipulating the weaker

    Ironic you ask. This morning's breakfast at the Red Arrow Diner in Manchester NH provided me that experience. The big red-haired waitress with the tattoo on her back told the 60 year old plumber sitting at the bar next to me about her first experience stripping during amateur night. She said "I was really nervous, but guys like my tits." She grabbed her breasts in such a way that it was clear to a bystander that her morning tips just increased. The plumber, who had seen it all, wanted it all & tried to act as if it were a normal morning conversation. My guess is that he, if he isn't already, will become a regular customer. It was the weak manipulating the weaker.

105 Cory Crawford

Sent: Tuesday, January 10, 2006 2:14 PM
To: Corrine@WizardAcademy.com
Subject:

    I took part in your experiment and it was cool. I went to a Restaurant in my city on the main drag on the other side of town. It was 3:00 am and the place was busy. It had truck drivers, late night coffee drinkers and some very drunk bar hounds. I sat and listened. I heard the truck drivers talk about the troubled times and lack of work. They wanted to change careers and get out of this city. They were very upset with the group of bar hounds as they were loud and obnoctious. The late night coffee drinkers were just out visiting . They claimed they could not sleep, were out cause there spouses were out of town. They wanted to be part of the bar seen but did not participate. They to were complaining about the lack of good jobs and they wanted more money. They were both upset with the bar hounds yet interested that they were paying extra attention to them. Now, the bar hounds were in a league of there own. They were very drunk, loud and noisy. They didn't mean any harm just out having a good time. They were bugging the truckers while trying to hit on the coffee drinkers. They were planning to go out again the next day, might have to borrow some money but who cares. They spoke about the headache they would have the next day and possible remedies to get rid of it. They were not worried about anyone or anything. This went on for about an hour and then I left. This was interesting to do, let me know what you think.....

    Thanks...

Daniel Fryar

Sent: Saturday, January 14, 2006 12:10 PM
To: Corrine@WizardAcademy.com
Subject: Wee hours in a strange land

Yesterday morning I awoke to my alarm clock at 4 am to go do my homework assignment. Then I awoke again at 4:40 and got out of bed.

San Antonio, in my mind, is made up of concentric rings: there's Downtown, inside the loop (410), outside the loop (between 410 and 1604), and the hill country (outside 1604). Oh, and then there's the northside/southside division. I live on the northside, outside the loop, and sometimes in the hill-country.

So I got in the car and headed south, aiming at Downtown or the southside. But I really had no clue where I was going.

I may have been interpreting some deep, mild fear as the intuitive direction of my trusty Rocinante, but I turned off the highway a little before I got to Downtown. I drove around in sort-of the warehouse district for a little while. But I am just getting old enough to be able to recognize a warehouse district; I didn't really think about the low probability of finding a restaurant open there at this hour. After cruising for fifteen minutes, my waning hope lifted a little when I got to the city bus station where the VIA busses were just heading out for their daily orbits. Maybe I could find a place that catered to the drivers and could catch the stragglers in my stranger-net and salvage this excursion. I could almost taste my Gift of Initiation.

No dice. Bill Miller's turned me away because they weren't open for business yet, and McDonald's (which would have been dissappointing anyway) was only open for Drive-Thru.

So I got some pancakes and went home, defeated.

I'm reading Don Quixote, due to the Wizard's praise. I read a couple of chapters when I got home. Don Quixote stood in the road and demanded that some travellers agree that Dulcinea is the most beautiful princess in the world, lest he attack them. He was doing his best impression of the knights in the tales he so loved. Their response is less-than-satisfactory, so he charges, but his horse stumbles and he lays helpless in the road while one of the party's mule-tenders kicks the crap out of him. That's how I felt; I was doing something that I didn't understand and wasn't prepared to accomplish because it was done by someone I respected and admired. And it didn't go nearly as I had envisioned it.

But that was yesterday, and just a lengthy introduction to a relatively short story about today. This time, when I turned off the alarm at 4am, I was lucky to hear an inner voice say "if I lay down again I won't get up," and equally lucky that I made the decision to get out of bed.

I struck out again, a dart headed for the heart of the city. This time I made it to the southern end of downtown to roads I didn't remember ever having driven. Then things started looking like yesterday, as I drove around for forty minutes looking for the place painted in my brain by the wizard; a little diner where all of the homeless people just happened to be eating breakfast well before the sun came up. I sort of feared that the language used to tell their tales would be spanish, but I couldn't find much of anything. I did finally find the Pig Stand. I thought this might be cheating, since it is sort-of a part of my childhood. My dad used to be their warehouse manager, and this happened to be the one that the warehouse was at. But I haven't been to this place it probably fifteen years, so after looking a little longer, I gave up and backtracked to this, which was actually the perfect greasy-spoon setting from the dream I was chasing.

But the new problem was that it was nearly empty. I got there at the same time as the bread-delivery guy. I helped him open the door, but I think I sort-of got in his way. He talked a little business with the cook, got the numbers straight on both sides, then left. There was a guy reading a newspaper at one of the booths, the waitress, and the cook. I went in and sat at the bar. No one was really talking, and the oldies music was a little too loud for 5:10 AM.

I got coffee (top priority) and a couple of pancakes and eggs, sunny-side-up. I heard the waitress and the cook once in a while, but nothing I could follow.

I talked a bit with the waitress. Pig Stands is celebrating its 84th year of business. She has worked there for forty of those. I asked her if they threw her a 40-th anniversary party, but they didn't. She said when she used to work at the Pig Stands on Broadway they would do things like celebrate birthdays or give the day off, but the manager at this one didn't do that sort of thing. She has been working at this particular restaurant for twenty years, but she still seemed to regard it as her new assignment.

She thought she remembered my dad, but wasn't sure. "He's bald and fairly short," I said. "Yeah, and overweight?" "Well, sortof," I admitted. Not a complimentary picture of my dad. He's much better than that in person.

Then a couple of sixty-something hispanic men came in for breakfast a little after 5:30. They were dressed classily in the styles of twenty years ago.

They sat with me at the bar, which felt nice, and talked very openly together and with the waitress. In spanish.

The waitress would slip into english for a few words here or there. They were talking about some marriages that were ending, I couldn't tell if it was celebrities or friends.

I was looking at a newspaper, trying to look like I was reading it and trying not to read it. She kept my coffee topped off, and the food tasted good and I ate slowly.

But I just don't know much spanish.

Language is so important. I live in a wonderful, ancient (by this country's standard) city in which 58% of the population are hispanic, although hardly all of these are spanish or spanish-only speakers. So I cannot talk to or understand at least many of the people I come in contact with, especially with my love of Mexican food.

Anyway, so step three of my assignment brings me to say that if I want to give anything to the people I ate breakfast with this morning, I need to learn how to speak and understand spanish. I cannot give them anything if I cannot give them part of myself. What do these people need most? I can hardly start to guess, since I couldn't decipher their stories. They seemed like they were doing pretty well, relative to the people in my daily world, at getting for themselves what they need.

Divorce really sucks. My best friend and his wife are right now in the throes of it and I hope to bless the world and this sick culture by loving them as they fall apart, to pray that they will not become one more sad statistic. Maybe this is something I can give to them.

And most people could use green and gratitude, so I took the wizards advice from a Monday Memo and tipped her almost 100% of my bill, and gave her a smile and a thank you as I left to find my way back to my comfort zone. Which wasn't easy, since I was a little lost. But I made it.

107 Duane Marcy

Sent: Monday, January 16, 2006 12:15 PM
To: corrine@wizardacademy.com
Subject: Early morning breakfast

This had to be the coldest day of the year, it figures I picked today.

The alarm clock was set for 4:30 AM. It's 4:17 and I wake up to the challenge, not bad 13 minutes before the clock. Why? Why did I get up, is it to get adoration from the master Himself or to be one of the few? I didn't take him up on the free book. I did buy a book during that time. I never wake up this early. Looking out into the darkness I know it's cold out there. I look over to my wife she's sound asleep. What am I thinking ... green eggs and ham, should I, could I, If I could. I can. I will. Sam I am.

Not many places are open this time of morning. I know I'll go to White Castle There's always a lot of characters there. As I drive by and look in. Not a soul. I'll just head west toward the big apple. As I approach a 24 hour diner the lot is full it's a little past five. Things are looking up.

I can see in the window. Groups of people are at tables some have not been to bed yet. A late night snack. I'm still in the parking lot two cars pull up a young man, early twenty's gets out of one car and young girl around the same age gets out of the second car. They greet each other and proceed inside. I'm right behind them. I take a seat at the counter they go to a booth, neither one look as if the were just out all night, they aren't dressed up he takes his jacket off to reveal a tee shirt? In this weather? I think they must be Romeo and Juliet.

The only subculture I find is sitting next to me.

He is an older Greek man sitting here engaging another man to his right in native tongue. The host joins in. They almost seem to be yelling at each other. When the conversation slows down all three men turn to the TV that's on. It's the Greek news with Greek subtitles so I can't even grasp what their talking about. As I sit here I try to put the pictures to the words they use. It doesn't help. The two men at the counter are in no rush, they aren't ordering anything, they aren't eating. This is their living room. The men get really excited and seem to be all in disagreement when the soccer highlights are on.

Now three people are leaving one stops to view the TV, He joins the conversation, NOW's the one chance I have to possibly understand what's being said oh no he speaks fluent Greek He stands there leading the conversation even after his friends leave.

What drives a person to leave their house in the middle of the night to discuss politics? Strange, or is it?

Thank You for allowing me to challenge myself and stretch.

108 Robert Wickman

Sent: Tuesday, January 17, 2006 6:00 PM
To: corrine@wizardacademy.com
Subject: Eavesdropper Homework Assignment

1/17/06

Wizard of Ads Eavesdropper Exercise: I've Become an Eavesdropper, listening to the conversations of strangers International House of Pancakes (IHoP) - IH-35 & Cesar Chavez, Austin, Texas

Here's a neighborhood I rarely visit – downtown Austin next to the highway. I rarely drive IH-35 through downtown. Never is closer to reality, though less precise. Every day is like a scene from Death Race 2000. No sane person drives this stretch of road during rush-hour without a desire for danger. It was designed but the Automotive Repair Business Association and financed by the Contingency Fee Lawyer Alliance. The lower deck is just plain dangerous with its twenty foot long entrance ramps. It's a great location for two of Austin's medical emergency trauma centers – they're always busy. Like the MoPac Expressway is any safer. Hah.

I've seen this IHoP many times in my twenty years as an Austin-ite but never stopped in for a meal, let alone eavesdropping on conversations. When I attended the University of Texas (UT) in the eighties this place was rumored to be a drug depot, gang hang-out, prostitution, i.e., just plain trouble. Bar Flys "in the know" knew Katz's Deli was the safer place to find late night food after clubbing 'til 2:00am and before driving home intoxicated.

I picked this spot because it was the first location that came to mind when the assignment arrived. "Go to IHoP and see if the rumors were true" I thought. In the words of Vernon Howard, "Learn to see things as they really are, not as we imagine they are". And if this doesn't work out, there's a truck stop on IH-35 near Buda that has an even worse reputation! You know the one, Roy.

At 4:45am the place is dead; three cars in the parking lot. I cautiously walk in through the first set of glass doors, navigate the yellow "Wet Floor" cones, turn right, then into the restaurant past the second set of glass doors, looking anxiously for where customers, if any, are seated. The waiter, Adam, attempts to seat me away from the other guests. I assume his name is Adam – that's what the plastic United Nations blue IHoP name tag says. I ask "How about this booth?" "No", he says. Maybe this is not a good idea. "This one?" it's next to a booth with two young women. "Yeah, that's OK". What the hell, you're already here, let's get some coffee and see what happens.

Neil Diamond's Sweet Caroline drowns out what little conversation there is. The cheap, flush-mounted speaker in the smoke-stained acoustic ceiling is crackling directly above my booth. Not a great location to eavesdrop. Who needs stereo when you can have mono with a loose wire?

The two women are laughing. Through the music I pick up "That's disgusting". Why are girls this age out this late? Perhaps they work at a 6th Street club or were patronizing one last night (this morning, I mean). Whatever. They don't stay long, leaving promptly at 5:00am. That's OK by me. I couldn't hear what they were talking about, anyway.

Adam places a light blue plastic coffee carafe on the table with the menu and I quickly order IHoP's finest, the International Passport : two eggs, two bacon, and two buttermilk pancakes. It's a true sampling of Americana cooking, minus the grits. I'm not a big fan of grits – wet sand with butter on top is not my idea of good food.

There's a young Latino male, a large guy, sitting on the booth across the aisle from me. He could be a high school senior, I surmise, because his blue jacket has "06" on the right sleeve. The type jocks wore in high school with their athletic accomplishments all over the front and the school mascot on the back. Blue leather torso with blue fuzzy sleeves. He's spinning a silver cell phone on the pale Formica tabletop. The phone looks like a big, shiny, round-ish suppository pill. You know, the kind that doctors prescribe for hemorrhoids and such. Not that I would know. It spins around and around, slows, and then he gives it another spin. And another. He's bored and the phone is cheap entertainment. Cell Phone Guy's chicken strips with fries meal arrives and he suspends play long enough to inhale his food. Back to spinning the phone. He produces another phone from inside the blue jacket – this one is silver and black, dials a number, waits, and then hangs up, and goes back to spinning the silver phone. No conversation.

Another, older, Latino male come in and sits at the booth in front of the younger male. They face each other. This guy looks dejected and tired. End of a long shift or starting a new one soon? No conversation here, either and this assignment is headed south for the winter. Fly away, little birdie.

My waiter, Adam, is back to check up on things. He sounds like a young Barry White – very deep voice. "Quit this place and go sing",

I think. Perhaps he's already doing that and this gig pays the bills until he cuts his first CD. Kids these days don't listen to Barry White, though. Barry White Raps. That might sell.

Two phones? Why two phones? He tries to make another call on the two-toned suppository with no results. I know a guy who carries three phones but he's a big shot business executive. Who really needs three cell phones and how could anyone keep it all straight?

Adam's primary responsibility at this time of day appears to be pushing a grey plastic service cart to each table and top off every container on the table: salt & pepper shakers, the big, glass sugar container with the silver lid and the little flappy thingy on top that sticks closed when you don't want it to and does not stick when you least expect it. My coffee will be sweet this go-around. Three flavors of cold pancake syrup in blue plastic jars. None are marked with the contents. Pancake Syrup Roulette.

Cell Phone Guy leaves at 5:10am but forgets his little white bottle of prescription pills, forcing Adam to run out to the parking lot, delivering the package just in time. Great service. I guess Madonna's You're an Angel was more than Cell Phone Guy could take. Now it's just me, Adam, and the older guy in shorts and Adam's still filling condiments two aisles over.

Two phones? Cell Phone Man never did get "the call" he was waiting for; neither phone rang. Who's he waiting for at 5:00am and which phone was supposed to ring? Is one for incoming calls and the other for making calls? And what's in the pill bottle? Cyanide, perhaps? No more Madonna songs, please! I want one. Maybe Morpheus gave him a red pill and a blue pill and he has to choose soon or get sucked back into the Matrix – Mr. Smith is coming. Run!

This place is dead.

Who was supposed to call? What makes a man get up that early to sit in a coffee shop on the edge of the wrong side of town and wait for a phone call on one of two cell phones? A job, a deal, a lover? And, how long did he wait, given that he was there when I arrived. And where did he go from here? Maybe Cell Phone Guy went to find the phone booth.

The older guy in shorts leaves and I'm the sole IHoP customer at 5:25am, Central Standard Time. Cómo agujerea! (How boring).

Journey's Foolish Heart. Remember that song from the '80s? Did you know that January is Grammy Month on XM radio? Me neither. Perhaps Paul McCartney knew and that's why he's playing We Can Do It, With A Little Love. More eighties music. I can't wait for

February.

Another waiter arrives, as well as a young man in a tie and they each begin to wipe down tables. Perhaps a manager or the host? Note that the wait staff are Persons of African Descent and the cooking and cleaning staff are Latino (Persons of Central American or South American Descent). Then there's me – the lone white guy in the place. Sorry, Caucasian. Person of Austrian/Scottish/Irish/Cherokee and possibly French Descent. Labels are a funny thing.

Tracy Chapman's Gimmee One Reason to Stay Here. How fascinating!

I know this big, Italian guy in Northern California who, when he attends a party, will pick out the one person he feels is the least like him, the one who would be the last person he would want to talk to, the one he would be least comfortable, and goes to that person first and strikes up a conversation. He says he does this every time; gets him "out of his box".

My question is: how does he know that specific person would be THE last person he would want to talk with? And why would he put himself in the box, only later to have to get out of it?

We have a waitress in the iHouse now. Lots of staff and one customer. Service should be Outstanding!

What does someone say to THE last person they would want to talk to? Elton John knows: Get Back, Honkey Cat! Change is Gonna Do Me Good.

"Hi, my name is Robert and you are THE last person here I would ever want to talk to. Tell me about yourself". That would land well.

A young Latino couple walks in and sits catty-corner from my booth, across the aisle and behind me. They laugh with the waiter as they scan the laminated, full color, photo-enhanced menus. Pictures sure help with the selection process. Are they regulars? And if so, at this same time of day? They seem to know the waiter well enough. Not Adam, the other guy. The Skinny Waiter. Is a skinny waiter the same as a skinny cook – never to be trusted? The guy (not the waiter but the customer that came in with the girl) laughs again and offers to buy her anything on the menu she wants. True love shines through as she takes serious consideration to his offer. Chicken fingers is the magic menu item for this couple. And ice water with lemon.

Quiet down, Elton, I'm missing all the good stuff.

Still giggling, hey proudly inform Skinny Waiter they will eat in. IHoP does take-out? I never knew that! Where's the Drive-Thru? Now there's a marketable idea – IHoP with a Drive-Thru! Look out,

McDonalds, competition is coming to town.

John Cougar Melloncamp's Small Town. Not here, not in this town any more. A-town lost its small town feel years ago after the Dot-Com era came in driving a blood red leased BMW 5-Series and left soon after in a used Chevy Tahoe Z-71. Black, of course. Like a hearse.

Another young couple comes in and sits in the booth to my left, across the aisle from me. In Cell Phone Guy's booth. Caucasians, they are. This place really attracts the twenty-something crowd. Not dressed like they just left the nightclubs five blocks away on 6th Street, these two are quite unique. She's in pajamas, slippers and a jacket and he's in dirty jeans, dirty t-shirt, and dirty ball cap. UT dress code for him, I imagine. OK, not that unique for Austin. The conversation is around getting drunk and playing poker at a friend's apartment. "I cheat", she says. "That's how I manage to keep my clothes on so long". "The glasses make you look smart", he responds tactically. She wants cheese fries. He's a bartender making three bucks an hour in pay and another ten in tips. She says "So we'll be poor when the baby comes". Oddly, they laugh. Adam returns and hash browns with coffee is the couple's breakfast decision.

There's a country song playing about breaking up, something like ". . . take your cat and leave my sweater, you'll thank me . . ." I've heard it before but I don't know the title or author. Let me know if you know.

"How's Houston?" he asks.

"We have a Starbucks, we have a school, and that's about it." Interesting response. Houston's bigger than that. I know. I've been there.

"Have we decided how old you are?" she says, sarcastically and with a sly grin.

After a pregnant pause and a long cat-that-ate-the-canary look, he says "We are twenty-one. If you want to pretend I'm older, you can." These two need a private room, preferably one with clean table cloths (or sheets). "I've done my share of older men" is her response. The country music is too loud to pick up all of the dialogue but it's something along the lines of "When you say you've 'done your share of older men' do you mean you had sex with them?" and a yes-and-no answer from the young lady in pajamas volleys back. The conversation cross-courts to age gaps and what's acceptable and not acceptable. It seems that four years older is OK, six is too much, and four years younger is too many but two is OK. The high school girls want alcohol and then pass out before any gritty stuff happens and the older guys just drop their pants as soon as they walk into the apartment – no alcohol needed. Then again, it depends on what they look like and how you feel in the moment.

Simon and Garfunkel's Kodachrome/Maybelline – great song. " If you brought all the girls I knew in High school and put them together for just one night, it wouldn't match my sweet imagination. . ." Perfect!

Did the pajama couple just meet at the party? Is she from out of town? Are they "hooking up"? They're certainly not old friends. Now they're talking about the different shapes of penises: short and stubby, really skinny (like a French fry); thirty year-old guys trying to pick up Pajama Girl in clubs.

From what I collected through the music, Pajama Girl and Dirty Ball-Cap Guy were at an apartment party nearby (Austin's College Ghetto is nearby) just east of here off of Riverside Drive, and Evan and Emma were having sex in the bathroom with the water running to mask their noises. Pajama Girl and her new suitor left the all-nighter moments ago to breakfast at IHoP. Too much drama, I suppose. A strip poker party at someone's apartment; "who is Emma and why is she ready to move in?". "Do you like to fuck your girlfriend's boyfriends?" he asks. "That's so messed up" she responds.

Billy Ocean's Love on the Run. Hmmm. What's the message here? Am I the only one who hears this parallel?

Pajama Girl spent New Year's with the family, at her Dad's insistence, though he left twenty minutes after midnight with his girlfriend. Evidently, the "family needed to gather for their last New Year together". She has "cancer or something". Not sure if "she" is Dad's girlfriend or Pajama Girl.

Pajama girl serves up a new topic with "For ten bucks an hour, what do you get?"

Unlimited sex" is the response from Dirty Ball-Cap Guy. No topic changes here.

Dido's I will Go Down with the Ship. Interesting.

Adam needs me to close out my tab. His shift is over and he wants to leave. $8.48 says the white slip of paper in pale, purple ink and a fat, pink stripe. Time to change out the register receipt paper roll. Adam tactfully phrases the request as "My manager is making me . . ." but I know he wants to take his tip home so I pay now with a full pot of coffee on the table, tip him 30%, and dive back into the conversation across the aisle. Whaddeyemiss?

"Less bullshit than the (UT) business school". Dirty Ball-Cap Guy is evidently going for an economics degree.

"Where you from?" she asks. We're fishing in deep waters, now.
"Dallas", is the answer.

"A friend of mine confessed his love to a girl with this song (Dido) in the background", Pajama Girl notes. "Everyone thought he was gay. Where did my driver's license go?" digging through her trendy little designer purse. "Ah, there it is."   Evidently, minors are required to renew their license every year. His expires in 2011.

Dirty Ball-Cap Guy lives "just five minutes south of Stubbs in South Austin, off IH-35". Does he tend bar at Stubbs?   She lives in Houston and comes to town often "soon enough", keeps a bottle of booze in the car to do shots (six to ten shots!) before going to the club and listen to music. Recently she "stood next to two guys smoking a joint. The band was sooo good!"

"Hash browns are good!" he says in a sing-song voice - like when John Travolta's character chimes "Bacon is good" in Pulp Fiction. I really get that Dirty Ball-Cap Guy likes hash browns. They have plenty left in the white Styrofoam doggy box to take home and eat after whatever it I that they intend to do next. Judging by the looks and comments, it's obvious.

Pajama Girl offers to pay "I can cover our meal, completely. I have a credit card, no cash."

They leave, probably back to the all-nighter apartment strip-poker party where they first met . . . just a few hours before breakfast.

"What becomes of the Broken-Hearted" is squeaking out of the ceiling speakers now.

"Where are her clothes?" I wonder.

What do these people need most? Someone in their lives who cares enough about them and will let them know they matter, they are worthy, that God loves them, and they have what it takes to be the person they dream they about.   To settle for nothing less. Not just Pajama Girl and Dirty Ball-Cap Guy, but all of them. Adam, Skinny Waiter, Cell Phone Guy, and the others at IHoP before sunrise.   "I wish I could show you, when you are lonely or in darkness, the astonishing Light of your own Being." - Hafiz

What's scarier than rush hour traffic on IH-35? Me on five cups of coffee! It's 6:30am and I'm outta here.

Danna Vitt Rooks

109

Sent: Wednesday, January 18, 2006 10:30 AM
To: Corrine@WizardAcademy.com
Subject: Under The Fence

I'm responding to the 1/9/06 "Monday Morning Memo" challenge to crawl under the fence and outside of my insulated life.

First off, I want to thank Roy Williams for his Monday Morning Memos ... they're a bright spot in my Monday mornings and I look forward to getting a new one each week.

The 1/9/06 Memo really spoke to me. In Julia Cameron's book Walking In This World: The Practical Art of Creativity, she encourages weekly "artists dates" where you go somewhere (alone), and do something different that gets you out of your normal routine/ comfort zone and create some different experiences for yourself, broaden your life view, see things from another perspective.

Since starting this practice of "artists dates" I've included solo meals in a lot of restaurants in parts of town (or other towns) that are well outside of my normal stomping grounds. Roy's right ... I have found interesting people, strange cultures and high adventure on the other side of town.

I'm as intrigued by the waitresses and cooks as by the other diners. One 30-something waitress in a smokey diner with torn plastic booth seats and tattered, coffee- and gravy-stained menus comes to mind ... beautiful, friendly, smart, engaging --how'd she get there and why does she stay when from all appearances she could be a successful white-color professional?

Some of the best conversations I've ever had (or have eaves dropped on) have taken place over a meal... it's where people with a connection bring their real selves to the table. Guards are down and real, meaningful discussions take place.

I especially love going to diners, it's the relationship between the salty staff and the regulars that creates the unique atmosphere -- a comfortable, welcoming atmosphere I want to consider myself a part of, even just briefly for breakfast.

Thanks the invitation to share my experience.

110 Debbie Platt

Sent: Monday, January 09, 2006 5:14 PM
To: Corrine@WizardAcademy.com
Subject: Outsider

We keep adding to our circle. I guess I'm really blessed because I do not need to get up at 5:00 a.m. or go to a rarely visited part of town and eavesdrop on conversation of those who will never have internet access, a credit card or cable TV. Family is an excellent reality check for me. For my family Christmas party this year I had 46 of my realities over. There is a huge mixture of socioeconomic status in this bunch. But, clearly, the relatives from the "rarely visited parts of Detroit" stood out the most. The middle aged children were very quizzical regarding what the cloth with a ring on it was meant to be. They had never seen napkin rings before. The most exciting activity these children had were drinking a can a pop whenever they wanted one. The biggest concern for the Adults was the tardiness of the bus that takes them to their needed places. These people do not have computers, internet service, phones, cars, credit cards or Cable TV. Nor do they even picture themselves with these items. What they do have is forgiveness for whatever you may have done in the past or will do in the future. They have the inherent need to make you feel good. They don't seem to expect or want any type of gifts. They only want your time and attention.

From 1980 through 1990 I never had internet access, a credit card, or cable TV. I was the ol' cliché "single Mom" trying to just make it day to day with my two children. The gas and lights were always being turned off and post-dated checks being written to turn them back on. Coats and winter wear (living in the Mid-West) were in very short supply. Vacations were spent mowing the grass and trying to plant a few flowers. Salvation Army was our Department Store. I never dreamt I would some day make a six digit figure income, own a car, a home, go on cruises, travel to resorts throughout, and even have a built in swimming pool! But I also never dreamed my children would be grown and live responsibly away from me. I never dreamed I would have wonderfully healthy Grandchildren. When I lived on the "rarely visited" area, my circle of family and friends was very small. When we got through the "lean" years and progressed to an easier living pattern, it was easier to reach out to others and add them to our circle of family and friends. There was some comfort with the familiarity of my small circle, but I realize it's important to open the circle and share my blessings with others around me.

A real reality check for me this Christmas season was when I delivered the meals to the seniors in my community. One day a week I deliver meals on wheels for the seniors who cannot get out and they need to be checked on. This is a fairly new thing for me. I volunteered a couple months ago, so I'm still learning as I go. I was very concerned about making sure everyone received a small gift from me. You see, in my own materialistic and blessed world, I viewed it important that they have a gift at Christmas time. I have 26 seniors on my route and some are diabetic so I thought I would hand out notepads and candy canes. For the diabetic I picked up some sugarless candy. I made my deliveries the Thursday before Christmas and made sure everyone got a gift and a card. I was puzzled, though, because no one even said have a Merry Christmas. It was snowing real good that day (got stuck twice) so they would say things about the snow or have a good day but nothing about Christmas. Well, I couldn't believe that many of them didn't at least believe in the birth of Jesus, but what do I know. All I knew was no one seemed to even realize it was Christmas. The following week I made my deliveries and almost half of my seniors expressed sadness at missing a loved one. Finally it hit me. Here I was all excited about Christmas coming and having my children and Grandson home for the holidays. It never occurred to me that none of them had such a thing to look forward to. Even I, as dimwitted as I can be, know it's not about gifts; but, it sure is about family. So, next year I think I will just wish them a good day and not make a big deal out of a holiday that makes them so sad.

Thank you for letting me share this. Most people do not know I have family who others will go to eavesdrop on. I'm proud of my family, but the reason they don't know is because people just really don't care.

111 Stephen Hernandez

Sent: Monday, January 09, 2006 11:52 AM
To: Corrine@WizardAcademy.com
Subject: haha... excursion.

I actually did this about 4 months ago. It was very late and I just came off a grueling job (I'm a computer consultant) and I was hungry. I saw a Denny's open 24 hours not far from my home and I went in and sat at the counter and ordered eggs and home fries and such. (Not good for my cholesterol but oh well.) I felt very strange going in there but my hunger overcame my sense of sensibility at that point and I was to revved up to go home. I saw a bunch of people pretending to be who they weren't. College freshman wearing Movado's but didn't have one dollar for coffee, young guys trying to pick fights to be cool. No fights broke out because of the officers there having coffee. But in the corner I noticed a group of guys playing chess. There were 3 games going on and all were very intent on what was happening. I forget how I went over but I went over and was watching the games. I was asked if I wanted in, but told them I was no good and hadn't played in years. They said I was lucky because the only one open at that point was the best one and I had no chance. I was also told that the best anyone had done against him was to capture 7 pieces from him. Of course I said it was poppycock and I could do better than that. I made a $5 bet and proceeded to capture 9 pieces in a game that I was profoundly beat. It only lasted about 2 minutes and was put in the worst check mate I was ever put in, but I did what I set out to do. Everyone wanted to play me then of course. I played one more game and lost before I left. I went back a week later about 2am to see the same gents and played a few games and lost every one but had one stalemate with the second to worst player there. I stopped going after that because my friends and family told me how much of a loser I was playing chess at 3am at Denny's with a bunch of losers. These guys were all stock clerks at a supermarket, gas station attendants, or similar jobs. No degrees and no real hope of getting out of their rut but they were happy playing chess at 3am. I went back about 3 months later and they were all gone but I don't think I'll forget those weird people playing chess at 3am at Denny's.

Helen Harb

Sent: Wednesday, January 18, 2006 9:19 AM
To: Corrine@WizardAcademy.com
Subject: 24 hour Eatery

Last week when I read your memo and the challenge you put forth I thought "now you're talkin'." Going out into the world in a different way than usual had an appeal to me. I thought Roy is on to something, he is open minded willing to become more and I wanted to be a part of that-for an hour or so. During that hour I really enjoyed the thoughts of who I would take with me and where I would go and how open I would be to this experience.

What happened? I went out to walk my expensive pure bread dog in my upper middle class condo development and as I was walking the startling reality hit me- I chose this life and I like it and worse I really did not want to venture out. Then along came the justifications for why I should not entertain this exercise. The excuses were slim, George my cousin who I wanted to go with me, had to work late and early and it was too much to ask. Secondly my elderly Mother was going in for tests and may need heart surgery so I surly need to focus my energy on that.

So what happened that I did venture out? The following Monday I read your memo and was reminded of the deadline for submission and began to think again of the possibilities of what could happen if I were to do such a thing. But more than that I remembered the feeling of enjoyment I had as I was planning my new mission! Also on that Monday my Mother did have valve replacement surgery and I spent the day in the waiting room of ICU. In hospital waiting rooms there is a cross section of society and part of the society represented were the exact individuals that I might find at a truck stop or an out of the way 24 hour eatery. But none of the differences mattered. We were all there for the same reason-the hope of hearing good news about our loved one. The playing field was level.

That evening I called my cousin George and asked if he would go with me to complete this "experiment." The ensuing conversation about were and when to go was really fun and off we went.

As we set out my thoughts were this: I agree with Benjamin Franklin's statement "God helps those who help themselves." And I had a memory of an encounter of 20 or more years. The encounter was with a woman of the Primitive Baptist sect. She told me the Primitive Baptists believe God saves souls not man. I agree with this as well.

Upon arriving at our destination I found low income, poorly educated individuals. All of which were willing to open their lives to me through conversation.

As a result of our evening I do have thoughts on what I can do to help-them and me.

First, during prayer I can pray for them and during mediation I can send them positive energy while holding the thought of perfect balance and trust. Remember only God saves souls.

Second, when some one comes to me with a request for employment or education use my resources of time and connections to help them accomplish their goals. Again, "God helps those who help themselves.

Third, when being welcomed be welcoming in return.

Cynthia Williamson 113

Sent: Wednesday, January 18, 2006 11:57 AM
To: Corrine@WizardAcademy.com
Subject: Monday Morning Memo Challenge

Tex and Shirley's, a new location for an old local restaurant customered by the same, is situated on my commute between school and office. A "Now Open" banner enticed me to test the inexpensive 'Early Riser' breakfast offer. My Sudoku book in hand, I sat in a booth with no intention of having any interaction past ordering cinnamon French toast and stating the need to refill my unsweetened ice tea without the need to ask.

My concentration was interrupted when two gentlemen reminiscent of the elderly hard-of-hearing commentators in the balcony on the Muppet Show were seated directly across the room from me. Their private discussion forced the rest of the restaurant patrons to unwillingly eavesdrop. Covered topics in detail included Bill O'Reilly on politics, Medicare changes creating havoc in getting prescriptions filled, aerobic exercise in water versus on land, the slow sugar release of sweet potato pancakes over buttermilk ones for diabetics, favorite waitresses based on their abilities to memorize individual customer habits, and that the changing weather patterns are not due to global warming but rather to shifts within the earth's tectonic plates. Annoyed, I finished my meal, and lifted my book on-end to shield the noise. My practice is to not leave a puzzle until I solve it; unfortunately, I was working on one in the 'fiendish' category and under time constraints.

"Hey, is that one of those sew-due-coos? I've looked at them and I can't figure out how to figure it out." Knowing at whom the question was launched, I lowered the book. "Yes," I replied, matching their decibel level, and went back to scrutinizing the number patterns. "You must be really smart to being doing those," he publicly announced.

Now I had two choices: get up and leave or ignore the comment. With a half hour to spare and no hopes of finishing unencumbered, I took the third option of if you can't beat 'em, join 'em so that at least others can eat without any additional shouting. MMM challenge in mind of moving out of comfortable discussion patterns, I picked up my book and tea glass, walked across the room with all eyes following like those weird Disney Haunted Mansion images, and scootched over into the booth next to one of the gentlemen. They were Oscar and Felix in appearance, attitude, and alliance. Sitting next to Felix, I patiently opened my book to an easy puzzle and stepped him through the solving process. He immediately caught on. We moved on to other subjects, of which I learned:

Oscar guessed I was born around 1960 (only off by two years) because Cindy was a popular name then. He continued with the top names of several different generations.

Felix went on to say that disease really started progressing about the 1960s due to the lack of health concerns in that generation.

Oscar countered with that was due to illegal drug use. He went on to ask if I knew that government regulations required stripping the vitamins out of sugar. He heard that from a guy in Vegas and believed it to be true.

Felix stated that Splenda was helping replace sugar in our diets.

Oscar interrupted that oranges could cure almost everything, except they contained too much sugar for a diabetic to eat too many of them.

Felix informed me that Splenda lemonade mixed with orange juice was a great energy boost in the morning and stretched the cost of orange juice.

Oscar's new subject was regarding the re-naming of countries and how many countries the US might divide Iraq into for easier watch-dogging.

Felix spieled a litany of old and new country names, along with the approximate year of change.

Oscar announced he wasn't a Communist or a Socialist but felt something had to be done to protect the health of the elderly.

Felix rattled off several politically incorrect jokes.

Although I was enjoying the banter, I had a conference call to lead and with just enough time to reach my office, had to bid my good-byes. I asked their ages. Oscar was 83; Felix a younger 81. I ascribe to the power of purposely keeping an active mind as a way of living; but until this encounter, my impression of 80-somethings were more in line with my memories of visiting rest homes as a Brownie. Far from that, the brain synapses of each member of this dynamic duo fired sharper than several of the business people half their ages who would be on my call. They were inspirational as well as informative.

Bill Alford

114

Sent: Tuesday, January 17, 2006 11:02 AM
To: Corrine@WizardAcademy.com
Subject: MMM challenge

Seizing a divine moment in the efficient life

Thanks for the rouse.

At 3:30 am, the lens sees, but nothing records. Lack of movement, that's the security program to efficiently save hard drive space. Trouble is, my brain is more adaptive, quickly dulling more and more of daily life, the routine still seeing, yet rarely recording.

Early this morning, rising to the challenge of a new perspective, I've experienced the gift of a hard reset. The needs, hurts and joys of my new neighbors come into focus.

At least for a time, the texture of life is restored.

Chanelle works 8p to 7a at this Denny's before switching gears to begin her 8 to 4 shift at the new mega c-store out west. Her mate is taking classes and not working, leaving her to provide with little room to recharge. Yet, surprisingly, she is the one radiating energy and warmth at the end and the beginning of the day. The "hi babes" and "hons" are flowing as she pours. From my vantage point, deep in the bowels of the smoking section (the logical place for this assignment), her ability to accept the strange and stranger alike make her the foil I was intended to see. She dished out acceptance and kindness for pay, but I suspect also out of her heart. The hugs to her regulars betrayed a genuine care that went beyond mere self-preservation.

It's now 4:30, my blackberry would be alerting me to rise for this challenge if an uncharacteristic lucid wave of energy hadn't already done so.

I find it odd to just watch and observe.

The loners, couples, the assortment of lives packaged together in groups for unseen reasons, all playing out a paragraph of their lives with me in the corner, watching. Some come to share, some to read, study, reflect, or escape. Chanelle pours herself accordingly. Each a unique story, the pages I'll probably never get to read. I wonder if they are even recording.

If my life is like a book, how many pages are doomed to end up blank, wiped from memory by dullness? Wonder what someone would write from a corner in my life.

I have pages of notes that need reflection, but as its approaching 11am, I'm content to send and ponder. What the best of my new neighbors have plenty of, that I need more of, is an open embrace of acceptance, a genuine love of people, in all their uniqueness. We all need acceptance and love and to practice it in return. What I have to offer, is a spark of the divine and a willingness to lay down my net, my efficient life, to pursue and seize truth. Please pass the salt.

Always, at your service

Mark Clark

Sent: Wednesday, January 18, 2006 11:28 AM
To: Corrine@WizardAcademy.com
Subject: "the Challenge"

First of all I must tell you I feel like I'm cheating. You see on a regular basis I force myself to spend time in a world I no longer live in. When I read Roy's challenge I thought to myself…what an advantage I have over most. Roy illustrates that by predicting that "only 12" would take him up on the challenge.

Let me set it up for you….I live with my wife and three children in a very nice area about 15 miles south of Indianapolis, home prices in the area are well above 300,000 million dollar homes punctuate our landscape. Swimming pools are as common as the three car garage. We all talk about private pitching lessons, competitive cheerleading, and whatever other indulgences our children desire. It's not the real world. I am the general manager of a successful start up fm radio station in Indianapolis, are station plays "meat and potatoes" music. John Mellancamp, Led Zeppelin, The Beatles, and Bruce Springsteen you get the feel. I believe it is critical for our continued success to keep in touch with my customer. Where do my customer live, work, eat, go to church, what do they do when they are not at work. I want to know everything about my customer so that I can serve them better than my competition.

So here it begins…Peppy's grill a 24 hour greasy spoon located in a working class neighborhood near downtown Indianapolis. (The smokes as thick as the black coffee.) I threw on a pair of jeans and a sweatshirt (the ones from the Goodwill), I wore a pair of tennis shoes, the ones I cut the grass in, and made my way there about 1 am, it's a good 30 minute drive. Peppy's is not a big place, maybe it seats 40. Although the crowd was thin, I sat myself in an area where I could glean as much conversation as possible. I heard about work, repair parts that didn't come in, all of the accidents from the tow truck driver, a relatively quiet night from the Indianapolis Police Officer, I heard a conversation in Spanish. I left Peppy's grill a little smarter. I took all thirty minutes of that drive home and reflected on where I had come from, where I am now and with more commitment than every to continue keeping myself and my family very well grounded.

116 Shawn Smith

Sent: Wednesday, January 18, 2006 9:43 AM
To: corrine@wizardacademy.com
Subject: Inside the Outside - Report

    First off, I freely admit there is no way I would have done this if Williams hadn't issued the prediction (or was it challenge?) that fewer than 12 of us would. At that, I was determined to be one of the few.

    Monday night I had been planning to go to Pharo's, a truck stop about 10 miles down the interstate. I got there about 2:15 only to discover they now closed at 11. I live in a small town that is not exactly booming with all night restaurants, so I was momentarily stymied. When I got home I looked up truck stops in the yellow pages and, since I was very tired and it was about 3 AM, went to bed.

    Yesterday I called one of the places listed in the yellow pages to make sure that yes, they were open all night. Let's try this again.

    Before I went in I was thinking a good bit about this. To be honest, this isn't so far outside of my usual experience. Despite a B.A. and more brains than are probably good for me, I'm currently working as a waiter (and proofread part-time). Just a year and a half ago, I was doing day labor. I had some idea at least who and what to expect.

    I got to the Buck Horn Family Restaurant at about 1:30 (after driving ten miles in the *other* direction on the interstate). The place was open, but I was horribly disappointed to find it almost empty. When I got there, there was one other group of four people. In the forty-five minutes of my stay, a total of seven customers came through, plus Rosalie, my waitress.

    So I decided to take this as an opportunity to just sit and think. We don't do that often enough today. I realized that although I was sitting at Labor Ready every morning a year or so ago, I still walled myself away as much as possible. I couldn't stand having the TV playing at me all the time, so I pulled my chair away from the others to a corner of the room. I always have at least one book with me, so I spent most of my time there reading. (I deliberately left my books at home last night, by the way.) I pretty effectively insulated myself from everyone else. Destructive as I know pride is, a large part of me still considers myself better than those people.

    What do I have that the others there didn't? In purely material terms, not much. I don't have a lot of money or fancy toys. I guess in terms of opportunity I'm a step ahead of most of them though. I'm planning to go to graduate school this fall (although it's not definite yet) and I know there are all kinds of doors open for me as soon as I can figure out which direction I want to go. Most of the others who worked there didn't have anything like that.

    I would like to try this experiment at least once more as soon as I can figure out where I could go nearby. I consider it mostly a failure so far, but I hope I pass for putting forth the effort.

117 Bobby McGee

Sent: Monday, January 16, 2006 12:25 AM
To: Corrine@WizardAcademy.com
Subject: early morning experience

No problem finding an open seat, the choices were many. Sitting right next to the only other customer in the whole joint might look a bit obvious let alone weird.

My adventure started at 4:30 Sunday morning. The players; the cook, two servers, the guy reading the funnies and myself. Five people headed for this page. If they only knew.

"Good morning!" Did she say that because it was in the employee manual or did she really mean it?

I replied, "It is and I wouldn't have it any other way."

"What'll be? Speak now or forever hold your peace." With dead-eye aim she poured my coffee as the pot hovered from a good foot above the cup. She never missed a drop. She was a pro. I ordered, no menu for me, as this was all about them. If she only knew what I was up to.

The other server and the cook were only visible for a few moments. Their needs were easy to assess. They needed help. Management could have scheduled extra staff to help with their cleanup. The cook said "only two hours and 12 minutes till we go home." Their precise departure already planned.

Meanwhile back to the task at hand. My thoughts turned back to Wilma the waitress. How am I so uniquely qualified to assess what she might need? I just met the woman. Oh I'm sure with my vast resources I'll have an abundance of whatever ever it is she needs. I ask myself, who is she outside of this restaurant box? Family? Friends? What's her purpose?

"What do ya do?" Inquiring minds want to know. I was still attempting to fill the mental Wilma checklist. He was there the whole time, invisible behind his 10 ounce coffee cup, the lingering cigarette smoke and the Sunday funnies.

So here was a moment of truth. I intended to sit, order, watch, listen, take in the show, pay and leave. Now I was a part of the unscripted dialog. What I needed was more information about him?

"I take care of horses."

I started to ask him what he did for a living, but I never got the chance. Somewhere between my horses and my " I hope you have a great Sunday" I learned a lot.

He leaned back in his chair, and smoke appeared with several words." I had a horse one time Steve was his name a good horse I grew up in New York go back once a year. Been gone from there since the early 70's I frame houses and do remodeling work live uptown here with my wife and kids."

I've heard you can tell a lot about a man from his hands and his shoes. Looking at my own hands, precision surgery would be out of the question and as far as my boots; well I was in the barn earlier. I'm not sure of his name, but it appears as if his soft pale skinned hands haven't seen a hammer for quite some time. Maybe in his early fifty's, he has held a few of those cigarettes. Maybe he's got a callous from holding coffee mug handle.

If everything came to a screeching halt, a sudden life's time out right then, what would I know? Where's Wilma? She was drinking her own cup of coffee. She's probably one the 31,000 MMM subscribers who read about this challenge and one of the chosen twelve who will sit down and actually chronicle what happened. And here I am with funnies man Frank and Wilma. Same story, just my page. Upon closer inspection of Frank and his space, he doesn't even have a plate but he does have an ashtray. Franks been here a while.

"Heard of the King ranch?" Here we go again. I never said it but I thought who hasn't. "Had a brother-in-law who was a foreman down there. Used to take my older boys down there. They would ride ponies and chase cows all day. Some of their greatest memories as little boys." Without a spoken word I thought, over the last 25 years I've read pages about the King Ranch. I guess I never really grew up leaving Gen and Roy to Saturday mornings. I could however, with a slight degree of accuracy, speak of the King's great horses, red cattle, and a Texas size ranch still run by family with a legacy.

Here's where I met up with the fine line. You know the one separating good from evil. Black from white. The one where motive is the gas pedal and conscience is the brake. I guess it's not what you could do or what you could say, but what you did and what you said.

My reply was simply "what a privilege to experience the King ranch first hand, most people only get the chance to read about it."

Having just met him two eggs, bacon and fifty minutes ago, his list was filling fast. Incurable insomniac, check. On a chain smoking, coffee drinking diet, Check. Never cracked a smile as he read the Sunday morning funnies (the rest of the paper was undisturbed) check.

"Can I take your plate." More coffee" She never missed a beat.

It's now 7:30; some 3 hours have elapsed since I met Wilma and Frank. The early morning sun breaks the January clouds as I look outside at the horses. I'm no social worker or psychologist, but Wilma; I think she needs to be called be her name, some individual recognition. Not, hey I need some more coffee or could you get me this or that... Frank on the other hand needs someone who is all ears and no ego. Someone who could just agree with him that he really matters. As for the lingering question of what Wilma and Frank have that I don't. The pure luxury of knowing nothing of my four thirty am breakfast jaunt.

I got up from my chair, looked frank in the eye and said, " Thanks, I hope you have a great Sunday"

"I will." I walked over to the cash register to settle my bill. The ticket could have 100 times the cost of the breakfast but it didn't matter. I learned a lot about myself. A Hollywood casting director couldn't find three more suited people for this page. If they only knew.

I looked up and smiled, " Wilma" With a sense of humor, she replied, " that's what my name tag says."

"Wilma, Thanks, I hope you have a great Sunday,"

"Thank you, nobody ever calls me by my name."

Steve Rae

118

Sent: Wednesday, January 18, 2006 5:58 AM
To: corrine@wizardofads.com
Subject: Homeless in Toronto

A January rain in Toronto is never welcomed by the general populace, but for the homeless it's even more unwelcome. The rain finds every crack in a meagre shelter and creeps down the back in what must feel like a cascade.

I've just finished a couple of hours in the heart of night walking the streets in downtown Toronto. Because of urban regeneration, it is becoming a place of monolithic apartment buildings with steel and chrome gentrifying the grit of the streets. But always, a block or two from this new faceless architecture you will find the reality of the homeless.

Harriett, from Cape Breton with the Celtic twang in her voice offered me a date. She promised the best date of my life. I'd be surprised if she weighed more than 80 pounds and she had no teeth, an addict trying to make a few bucks for her next score. I asked her how she lived.

She said, "I try to make a few bucks doing whatever I can."

"And what is that?"

"Anything you want, Speed, Blow, you name it. Or we can go on a date." She smiles.

In all I'm propositioned for sex, no less than six times in two hours.

Rufus from Trinidad, was riding his bike under an umbrella. He cut across four lanes of a deserted Dundas Street to approach me for money.

"Rufus, where do you live?"

"Here an' dere," with his strong Caribbean accent.

"How do you stay dry on a night like this?"

"I don't."

"Is there anywhere you can go?"

"Oh yes man, the Salvation Army has some beds an' a warm meal in the morning, or there's a mission over on Gerrard that I go to some times. They give out fruit and have chairs. I was dere tonight." He shows me the plastic bag, which held the fruit.

I expected to feel a sense of desperation from the people on the streets, but that is anything but the truth. It seems to be more a sense of purpose that drives them. It is a simpler, less complex sense of purpose than the people I encounter on a daily basis probably because the homeless are operating on a lower level of Maslow's hierarchy, but they do have purpose.

"So man, it looks like the Liberals, dey going down." It's Rufus again.

There is a Federal election in Canada next week and it looks as if the governing party, the Liberals, may be toppled.

"How will that affect you, Rufus?" I ask.

"Conservatives say, dey may cut off some of the social assistance, but it probably won't affect me much."

"How do you know this?"

"I read de papers man……before I sleep under them. Ha, ha, ha." He wheels his bike away, but not before I can stop him to give him some money.

"Tank you man, God Bless." He rides away through the puddles.

I walk past a job centre. Inside there are about ten men, more have spilled out onto the sidewalk.

"What kind of jobs are you guys hoping to get?" I ask.

Stan, from somewhere in Eastern Europe says "Whatever they geeve me, I take."

"Do you work everyday? "

"No, some days, no jobs."

"What kind of jobs have you done?"

"Paint, clean, rip up beeldings."

"Where do you live?"

"In room." He points.

"How long have you been doing this?"

"Ten years."

"Why are you here at 4:30 in the morning?"

"Early bird gets job." He smiles.

"Good luck."

I am not sure that I'm qualified to assess what the outcast of society need. I do know they don't need our pity. Canada supposedly has a social safety net that protects these people, but obviously the mesh isn't tight enough to help all. My personal charge that comes from this discovery is that I will find ways to use my radio stations to champion the assistance organizations that exist to help these outcasts.

I felt a great sense of discomfort and a bit of fear as I walked the streets, maybe in time that would dispel, but it clouded my vision somewhat and I was incredibly relieved to see the entrance to my hotel.

A January rain may not be welcomed by the homeless of Toronto, but as I shake the rain from my hat, I can't help but think, it's better than temperatures many degrees below freezing. When the wind bites and it's minus 20 degrees, there can be no escape for Harriet, Rufus and Stan. How do they do it?

119 Lane Dixon

Sent: Wednesday, January 11, 2006 12:56 PM
To: Corrine@WizardAcademy.com
Subject: challenge from Monday's Memo

Early this morning, around 2:00am, I visited a Waffle House Restaurant which is located near some random exit on Interstate 24 just outside of Nashville, TN. I have lived near Nashville for most of my life, but have stayed within certain areas of the city that are considered safer and more "upscale." This particular Waffle House is located on the east side of town, which is considered a less desirable area. Although I did receive some strange glances upon arrival, the people who were seated along the bar next to me turned out to be very interesting. They were a husband/wife truck-driving team who stop at this particular Waffle House whenever they pass through Nashville. The waitress seemed to know them well; and the cook knew what they would have without an order. What struck me as most interesting was how important and appreciated the truckers obviously felt when the cook called their order out to them as they were seating themselves. The experience re-enforced to me how important it is to learn about and listen to my valued clients. Any feedback that either you or Mr. Williams wish to send back is welcome. Thank you for the idea about visiting the restaurant. Have a great week!

Charles Moger

Sent: Wednesday, January 18, 2006 7:55 AM
To: Corrine@WizardAcademy.com
Subject: Nocturnal Exploration

ONE NIGHT IN SEALY

Equal parts maternity waiting room and aircraft carrier flight deck, Sealy's truck stop idles impatiently in suspended animation. And that's exactly what this is, explained Vince, a short-haul driver out of Onalaska.

"The over-the-road guys are dying away; costs companies too much," he says over the rim of his half-liter tankard of coffee. Truckers' hours are increasingly limited and time-off enforced thus driving down earning potential. "They put more trucks on the road and let us drive less. Hop. Hop. Hop. No more long-hauls."

Outside, trucks pregnant with heavy loads are bedded down, a snoring rumble of diesel engines scenting the air with a cologne of burning fuel. Marker lights sparkle, interrupting the darkness of the dirt parking lot surrounding the simple brick building.

Bathed in cold florescent white inside, empty booths keep company with a blaring big screen television. In dysfunctional juxtaposition, a well-worn, once-white linoleum floor seems to share an uncommitted relationship with a mop while the walls are newly clad in hand-paneled blond-stained wood; remodeling ceases abruptly at the toe moulding. Shuffling behind the granite-tiled counter, a lonely waitress meanders along her own route between kitchen, coffee pot and my cup.

This is not what I expected.

Where was the truck-stop mom and her family of gypsy truckers crowding the counter filling up and shooting the breeze? "Some days it's like that," Vickie tells me. "Most days, it's like this. It come and goes, I guess."

There's not much moving here at 3:45 in the morning--except Vince's non-stop dialogue. He's holding court with an unwitting captive; a fellow trucker who blindly veered into Vince's conversational web. Their exchange reveals a sort of trucker's code of decency.

While thirty-something Vince struggles at keeping the conversation alive with the tenacity of an emergency room doctor performing CPR, the other trucker--many years Vince's senior--gifts him audience. Escape is plainly on the man's mind, but his feet remain planted because the road's a lonely ride. Lending a brother trucker an ear is precious currency.

Two worlds collide as the truckers' talk of dispatchers and loads of steel and gypsum unravel, competing for my attention with Lou Dobbs's analysis of interest rates, foreign exchange and high finance. From where I sit, Dobbs seems like a dispatch from a foreign land in a language unrecognized by the natives. "Money ain't everything," Vince tells anyone who can hear him. "I'm done with the road... I can make more money as a prison guard and retire after ten years. Ten years of baby sitting for retirement. That sounds good to me."

Adjusting his Harley-Davidson cap to contain his straggly hair and hoisting his freshly topped-off travel mug, Vince bids farewell. He's a decent guy who won't marry his "old lady" of fifteen years. "Love is grand," he opines. "But divorce is thirty-grand."

"You meet some real characters in here," Vickie tells me as Vince motors out. "They're mostly all good people, though. Not like the guys who came into the I-Hop. They come in to fight. Why? Why come into a restaurant to have a fight. It's nice here. People come. People go. Nice guys for the most part."

Coming and going is Sealy Truck Stop's stock and trade. Shelly came from Ohio, Vince from Onalaska, his talking buddy from Joplin. Charles the cashier is from Bolivia. Their roads and conversations intersect, for the moment, in Sealy. It's quarter to five and the business of going kicks in as headlights stab the night and engines roar, taxiing for take off, prepared for delivery.

Jurie Pieterse   121

Sent: Wednesday, January 18, 2006 7:32 AM
To: Corrine@WizardAcademy.com
Subject: Inside the outside experience submission

Can you truly find the fabled "most refreshing Coke® in the world" in a diner?

A 24-hour diner in a bad part of town at 4am? I was thinking this challenge over but just couldn't really muster up the enthusiasm to repeat something that I'm all too often exposed to anyway. Only two weeks ago I was at an eatery that would pass for a diner, only not quite as upscale. In Florida, Old Florida. A, uh, "town" called Rosalie. But compared to the trailer homes next to it with faded pink insulation flapping in the wind, fat pigs roaming around and flat tire rusted formerly-glorious pick up trucks this place was quite a gem!

It wasn't 4am, but the occupants suspiciously eying out the foreigner were just as other side of the fence, only more alert and suspicious at 11am than the end of shift, start of shift or down and out crowds at 4am in some other diners. You see, my fishing adventures often intersect my path with before sunrise visits to diners in less desirable areas.

So I chickened out of this challenge since I couldn't piece together a diner scenario in America that would stretch my world that much larger. Instead I mentally revisited experiences from my life in South Africa that was way way beyond my comfort zone.

The experience I can share is the day I sipped "the most refreshing Coke® in the world".

Before you read further, this is a first hand experience during the last convulsive years of the apartheid era. I will tell you this story as I would to another close friend, using the terminology of that day with no concern to being politically correct.

I was not alone, but in a group of six people curious to learn more about life in our country. We planned to visit a squatter camp in violence torn Kwazulu-Natal. Trust me, for a white boy from Johannesburg that is more than crawling a little under the fence.

That morning, as we gathered with our 'tour guide' I had that realization that if anyone was going to get killed today, I was the first in the line. There was the Indian girl, young black woman from a rich family just as far removed from this life, the colored guy from the Cape, a white girl and one other white guy. However, he was as English, I'd actually say almost British, as they come in South Africa. So that leaves me as the only white Afrikaans speaking "Boer" in the group. The person with the physical appearance and language most associated with the Apartheid regime.

If anything went wrong today, I'm the one most likely to end up as the man necklaced by the frenetic toy-toying mad crowd. If you're not familiar with a necklace, it was a horrific method of death often used in townships where the terrified victim is pinned down with a tire around their body which is filled with petrol (gasoline) before being set alight alive in a burning blaze of black rubber smoke.

And just before you think our 'tour guide' provided any sense of safety...think again. He had never done this before, but had the delusional confidence of a navy admiral who feels he could lead a ground based desert war campaign without ever knowing the thirst of the sands.

With a taxi organized. Pause. Not anything like a taxi you picture. The South African version of a taxi is a mini-bus 15 years and 700,000 miles beyond its end of useful life, smashed up, retread tires, no working wipers, doors, windows and despite being rated 20 years earlier to have a maximum occupancy of 14 passengers will easily carry 24 passengers, with luggage and chickens on the roof.

Fortunately our mini-bus taxi was privately hired to drop off this apprehensive group at 11am in the squatter camp and then pick us up at 3pm in the afternoon, which was meant to get us out before the tsotsis left the local shebeens and in a state of agitated drunkenness go roaming around and stumble across the white boys who don't belong there.

What an experience! Roaming around a neighborhood you may only occasionally get a glimpse of on TV. And here is the first part of a fascinating experience. People were inviting us into their homes!

Now imagine, you see a strange group of people culturally diverse but distinctly different from your neighbors walking around. Curious or concerned you may approach them to ask what they're doing. After a quick, somewhat awkward attempt at explaining we're taking a look around to see, well, how you live these people most friendly invite us into their homes!

The first home is a typical square shack built out of corrugated iron and the same flat corrugated roof with a few rocks to keep the lid on. The floor, freshly swept with a hand grass broom is cracked, compacted ground. Outside is a fire ring with a few blackened pots and pans, smoke still lazily drifting out of the ashes of last night's cooking. Inside in one corner lies a few blankets stacked on top of a cardboard box with battery operated radio tuned to a station with music and language I'm not familiar with. A single spring metal frame bed sits in the other corner with a grey haired ancient granny sit-sleeping on cardboard sheets where otherwise you'd expect a mattress.

Our shack owner proudly displays her home the way a CEO's wife welcomes foreign executives and explains how, wait for this, twenty-three people live in the shack! I couldn't follow all the family relations that allowed these people to share this home in the spirit of ubuntu but my mathematical mind had difficulty how so many people could sleep in the shack. She soon answered my non-verbalized thought by explaining which people had to sleep in a seated position.

Someone else was proudly showing off the maize he was growing in his garden to feed his family. His wife twice a day would walk a couple of miles to the river to fill a bucket of water carrying it balanced on her head to provide water for the garden, in addition to the trips she makes to get water to bathe, cook and clean.

The final friendly female inviting us inside her home had the fortune to live in a home built with bricks. Actually a few rooms, roof that probably didn't leak and a view of the rolling hills with neighborhood homes far less civilized than this. Our discussions also revealed that technically this was not a squatter camp which is an illegal settlement of land. This, and informal settlement, was legal but not necessarily in the way we think of property ownership and land deeds.

Seven adults called this their home, with only one employed family member, her husband who was currently not there. He gets up at 3am in the morning to walk the 4 kilometers or so to the taxi rank to get a ride into town where he works as a bagger in one of the large grocery chains. Six days of the week to feed a family that included distant family members that would certainly not have been welcomed in western homes.

Before we left her home the black woman in our group being thirsty naturally asked if she could get a glass of water. The most simplest of requests you could probably make of a hostess in almost any other home. Except here there was no running water. She opened the generator run fridge apologizing for leaving us thirsty, explaining the water situation. In the fridge were two items on a middle rack: a block of butter and a can of Coke. Despite our objections the homeowner proudly shared with us this luxury item, a group of complete strange strangers. ared with me was the most refreshing sip of Coke in the world.

122 Daniel Joehnk

Sent: Wednesday, January 18, 2006 8:20 AM
To: Corrine@WizardAcademy.com
Subject: Anywhere's A Better Place To Be

I hope I am one of the many to take you up on your offer. Not to prove anybody wrong, but to allow one to just reflect at a time they are either rushing off or just off to sleep.

I chose Jimmy D's in Gorst Washington. Named after a pioneer in Aviation, Vernon Gorst. In Gorst there is no wrong side of the tracks, the tracks run right through the middle. Keep an eye out for that single white light. It is most likely not a motorcycle.

As instructed I arrived at 1:30 AM, I preferred later but a meeting was called for 7:30 AM and I needed to make it. I am a Lone Ranger and when a client needs me, well Hi Ho Silver...

I expected to be the detached observer. I sat down and was immediately asked what I wanted. Whatchya want honey? French Toast looks right. Anything else? Yes, Hot Chocolate please. That would be with the whipping cream? Uhm sure, OK. I do not think the establishment is PC.

Simon and Garfunkel streaming in from the kitchen. Dining music for the customers, so vanilla that I couldn't name any tunes. The pull tabs were called "Hot Momma" "Chicks" "Game Hunter" and "American Patriot". Nicotine stained walls, not a cigarette in sight. Washington State has a new intrusion on property rights, no smoking in any public building, or within 25 feet of the entrance. 25 feet has just been redefined.

In the corner booth a family, Mom in her scrubs. Looked like she just got off second shift. They all were having a good time. The kids about 3 and 5 were having a great time with their meal.

Across the room two men and a woman. The men were working the stuffed animal machine, the woman was clutching one of them, and there were six more on the table. All three were joking and cheering the efforts to get a grapple to snag a 50 cent stuffed animal, each try was a dollar. The younger man summed it up with "hey look at all we got for just under fifty dollars!" He left a five dollar tip for a fifteen dollar tab.

The middle booth is occupied by two elderly gentlemen, both reading well worn paperbacks. They were like decorations in a movie set, sitting and reading. Extras in the lives that surrounded them. Maybe they were the leading characters. I do not know, give the corpus callosum some time I figure it out in a few days.

The greatest part of the event was the waitress. She never stopped; Emeril's should have such a dedicated employee. As soon as a table emptied she reset it. Cleaned, stopped at every table to help and give a cheer to her clients, always with a sweetie or a honey. She was all of 60, works two jobs and loves her husband even though if he is with Bill he won't be home that night. You see he spent 20 years on the Submarines, a couple of diesel boats, and fast attack the rest boomers. They are both retiring next year to travel the country. They will be back. Jimmy D's is home.

So much for the detached observer. I became part of the exercise.

The attached bar closed at two, the bar maid came in for her sandwich. More talk about the rain. The last customer left about 2:45 AM he immediately composed this letter.

I do not live the privileged life. I work hard, read, think a lot and dream of being a member of the cognoscenti. I have yearnings desires, love challenges and overcoming obstacles. Tell me I can't do something.... Well I am maturing, some. Some might say these people have no hope; maybe they are the content ones. I have been given a large dose of humility this morning. As I rush around these next few days I will faced with a new awareness of what is important. Being gentile, having a ready smile, and calling someone I do not know sweetie or honey and being full of innocence. I will tell you this, relationships are far more important than sleep.

I do not know if I am an alpha, beta or a gamma. Gammas seem happier.

Thank you for the experience.

PS On the way out the door the younger man with the stuffed animals said "Let's swing by the children's ward and drop off these things."

What can I possibly give these people with one notable exception, assuming they do not have Him already.

123 Wendy McNally

Sent: Tuesday, January 17, 2006 9:14 PM
To: Corrine@WizardAcademy.com
Subject: dining with strangers

Waffle House on Rt 17. Never been there before. Driven past it at least five times a week for eight years. My first thought would have been that this place would be disgustingly greasy, based solely upon my last visit to a Waffle House that was in Georgia over thirteen years ago. This place has been invisible to me that long.

Loud rap music was blaring from the juke box. Hmm, I kinda expected the voice of Gretchen Wilson singing Redneck Woman. Two young black men were in the kitchen. One was cooking, while the other was serving. He was wearing baggy jeans and a black visor with WH embroidered on it. Only four others were seated. Two were correctional officers. One was a very large concrete worker, and a grandpa-type in a flannel plaid shirt. Conversation was sparse and hard to hear over the thumping of the juke box, jarring to me before my first cup of coffee. I have to admit, I was not confident that the service would be anything to write home about. As I scooted up to the bar, both employees greeted me with a good-mornin'.

Upon my first inspection of my surroundings, I was amazed at how the salt shaker shined... unlike my buried experience from the past. The grout in between the tiles was actually a lighter color than the tile. Service was not from the beehived hairdo "Flo" that would have served me in my imagination. But from a young gentleman who likes rap music. A gentleman he was too. Polite and conscientious to each customer he served. After the two rap songs played out, the room was fairly quiet, til the country music that I originally expected began to fill the air. The other men paid for their meals and were gone. The large white and scary-looking concrete worker, said "see ya tomorrow" Though I did not interact with other clientele that did turn over while I was there, I was keenly aware that they were not merely passing through since this was the only 24 hour place to eat just off the interstate. These were customers that dine there frequently, if not daily because of the polite service, clean atmosphere and good food.

Prior to my adventure, I imagined eavesdropping conversations of other patrons and having a glimpse into the Fredericksburg redneck lifestyle that is abundant in this part of town. But instead, I tapped into the perception of my own racism. The service that I expected to be poor and inattentive, turned out to be far beyond last months' visit to an upscale Italian restaurant with a reputation for wonderful food and service, where the twenty-something white waiter made many mistakes, forgot items that were asked for and was way-over-the-top shmoozing for a tip. Why would I have a preconceived notion that this man at the Waffle House was not able to serve with a smile, and get the order right? Have I really become that racist and judgmental? I thought I always took people for who they were, not their skin color, religious background or music preference.

I was wrong.

I realized that I live in suburbia and would have to seek further into the city and across the tracks to find what I expected to experience this morning. I also see that I did not have to dig too deep into my heart to find the poison of racism, I did not know was there.

124 Steve Bleile

Sent: Saturday, January 14, 2006 6:51 PM
To: Corrine@WizardAcademy.com
Subject: Homework: squirming under the fence...

Pride, Eggs, and Ham at Gerry's

3:45 is an unnatural time for anyone to eat anything -much less- the ham, eggs, toast, and hash browns that I found before me at Gerry's 24 hour diner. My stomach tensed preparing for the greasy assault. Truth be told... I only ordered something to eat because I almost felt guilty for invading someone else's world. I was not here for a hot meal or to see friends. I was here to eavesdrop. I looked at the ham and eggs as serving the dual role of admission fee and maybe even more realistically –apology.

The place is pretty near packed. Gerry's is about as deep downtown as you can get in Calgary and evidently people like to come here in the wee hours of the morning. To my left there's an older man that I swear I've seen before. Was he the guy who collects the Safeway carts for the quarters locked inside? Or maybe I'd just seen him downtown. In my notes I call him, "Safeway." In front of me is a guy wearing a hoodie. He looks pretty sickly to me. On my right is a group of four. The most distinctive of the bunch is a black woman who is quite loud and seems to be dancing in her seat to the music.

Any hopes of listening to conversations have been pretty much ruled out by the juke box. I will spend my time here surrounded by an interesting cast of near mimes moving to the sounds of "Paperback Writer," "Trenchtown," and if they could hear... my rapidly moving thoughts.

Now, what do these people need? What do I need?

One idea comes to mind, "These people need a bigger purpose for their lives." I volunteer for a local NGO, what do these people do? Then it hits me. I have no idea. This is a disturbing thought. I mean, I'm here to think of how to help these people and I really don't know if they need my help. They've chosen to be here. No one made them come. But surely their family life can't be that great. Surely they can't be truly happy. I don't know that either. No wonder I've felt guilty coming here. I had it in my mind I was going to the zoo for the poor and down cast who didn't have anything go their way in life. Truly, I'm not sure that is the case.

Safeway is gesturing. Ah yes, he wants a cigarette. I smile and wave him off. Truth is I couldn't smoke if I wanted to. Did he always do that? In the fifteen seconds we've spent in our silent exchange he's crossed and uncrossed his legs twenty times. Another man has just come in. His name? Well, I've decided to call him "headphones" because of the somewhat awkward arrangement his headphones have made with his toque.

Gerry's is the only restaurant I've been in since the latest revision of the bi-laws that still allows for smoking.

Ok, so I have no idea if they're happy and I have no idea why they're here. Why am I here? I'm here to learn to write. I'm here because the men's leadership group I'm a part of has been asking "what can we do to make a difference in our city?" I'm here because I'm terribly curious to see what Roy will send me.

The group of four to the right is talking over the juke box now. It sounds like they know the owner of the Cecil –THE most notorious bar in our city. From what I can gather it sounds like they hang out there.

I may not know what they are thinking, but I do know what I'm thinking. I'm thinking that they do need help and somehow it hits me YOU ARE SO PROUD AS TO THINK YOU CAN FIX THEM! Quickly, to protect myself from the darkness I had just unearthed deep in my heart, the pendulum of my mind swings to compensate. I'm sure they're really great people. I bet they really care for each other. I bet they have a deeper sense of community then I do. But, I can't make these bold claims either –not even to try to hide my pride. I truly have no idea what they're like. I have no idea if their laughter is sincere.

Another thought comes to mind. These people aren't poor. They're in a restaurant where they have to pay to stay. They have money. The two guys who came in with the three really pretty girls were decked out in designer clothes that I could not / would not spend so much money on. Really, in the big picture I would have to say I would be pretty hard pressed to find a poor person in Calgary. Past trips overseas come to mind... maybe in China or Africa they have poor people. These people are not poor. The poorest among us has a lot. Really, in all of Calgary, I think the vast majority are worrying about getting more and better stuff then they are about "survival."

Safeway has been looking at me pretty intently for quite a while. I guess it doesn't matter. When I look up he looks away so I've determined to not look directly at him. I'm in his world. He can look at me if he wants. My remaining egg is looking at me too. I've eaten the ham and one egg... I can't bring myself to eat anything else. The time has come for me to depart. I collect my stuff, pay, and leave a good tip. I received more from being here than the meal cost me and I want to make sure my admission is properly paid.

Reflections:

The biggest thought that hits me from this little adventure is that everyone makes their own choices and everyone lives with the consequences of their choices. The people in that diner were there by choice as much as I was. Maybe they had no else to go leaving them "no choice" but to go to Gerry's, but they have made decisions in the past that put them in a position where they had "no choice." I don't know what choices they have made. I don't know what I could do to help them. I don't know if they would want help.

I suppose the best help I can give these people is the same I can give myself. I feel guilty saying I know what's best for them (but I'm sure this is universal) so I'll dish out the medicine in the first person- to myself. I need to take responsibility for all of my decisions. I must live with the repercussions. I can't blame other people because that eliminates my ability to change. I can't become a victim because then I will need to be rescued. I need to admit when I'm wrong. I need to say I'm sorry. I need to say I need help to fix what I've wrecked. I need to admit that I'm scared. I can't wait for someone to guess how I'm doing or swoop into my life to rescue me.

R.J. Laino

Sent: Tuesday, January 17, 2006 7:17 PM
To: Corrine@WizardAcademy.com
Subject: Outcast Assignment from The Wizard

A truck stop in the North Valley of Albuquerque, New Mexico, around the Big I. It's 2:15 am on Friday Night/Saturday Morning - January 14th, 2006.

The graveyard shift waitress is crying. She's in the kitchen, clutching the short-order cook for dear life. She pulls away, starts to say something, but falls back against his chest. Her shoulders lurch up and down in staccato bursts. It looks like she's sobbing. The young cook, all of 21 or 22, seems hapless, awkward and extremely uncomfortable with this woman clinging to his body.

From my vantage point in the cafe, the scene plays like a widescreen movie. It's framed by a rectangular opening that connects counter to kitchen. If you've ever been to a truck stop or diner, you know the spot. This is center stage, where waiters and waitresses stop, pirouette, and slide ticket after ticket onto that shiny chrome spinner. On the other side of the opening, short-order cooks, acting as dutiful dance partners, push plate after plate back into the waiting arms of their cohorts. It's a classic blue collar ballet, repeated a million times a day, all over the world.

Brief moments pass. The woman appears to regain her composure. A furtive glance through the window and she realizes instantly she's in plain sight. She curls her hands under her eyes, wipes away the residue of runny make-up and disappears into the kitchen. A minute later, the double doors between the kitchen and cafe swing open and she strides into the cafe and toward my table.

At first glance, I would have guessed she was about 30 years old, brunette, trim and attractive. As she narrows the gap between us, I realize I was right, yet wrong. She may be 30, but her exhaustion is palpable and she is old before her time. Standing just two feet away at the head of the booth, Claudia (I can now see her name tag) is a beaten soul. An undefined pang grabbed me just looking at her.

She puts on the "everything-is-ok" face and perky voice, and asks: "you want coffee hun?"

"Sure." I reply.

"You take cream?"

"Black is fine."

She leaves momentarily, goes behind the counter and grabs the coffee pot. On her way back, she stops twice to offer refills to folks seated at two other tables in the cafe.

At the first table, a man with a farmers mesh cap is sitting alone, reading a truck magazine. Seems like a trucker, but I don't know for sure. He doesn't look up as Claudia re-fills his cup. He's 50 to 60 years old. He's right out of central casting if you ask for a "stereotypical redneck trucker." He's wearing a flannel shirt, jeans and work boots. He's overweight, smokes and looks pissed at the world. No wedding ring. Somehow, this does not surprise me. He looks incredibly lonely, yet completely unapproachable. The irony is painful.

At a nearby booth, about 3 booths away from where I'm sitting, there are four young Hispanic males in their mid-20's. They're loud and animated, perhaps the result of drugs or alcohol. They're dressed like gang bangers - ball caps perched sideways, baggy jeans, the obligatory chains and assorted bling, gang colors, gang markings and jail tattoos. As Claudia gets close to their booth, they start cat-calling and teasing her. The man on the end of the booth reaches out and grabs her around the waist – albeit without intense aggression.

He says: "What time you off sweet thing?" Second man adds: "Can I get something that's not on the menu?"

They laugh too loudly. Insecurity I imagine. Claudia smoothly backs away. Smartly, she smiles and laughs with them. I wonder how many times she's repeated this scene. How many years has she been marginalized, insulted or mistreated by customers?

I avoided staring, but studied these four young men while they were focused on her. I was grateful things had not gotten out of hand. Truth be told, I was neither willing nor able to confront these men had things gone differently. I had no doubt they had weapons and no doubt they had used them before today. Street knows street, and these guys had the unmistakable swagger that says: "bring it."

The Wizard's assignment questions popped into my head. What does the trucker, and these cholo's, need most and how can I help them get it?

Hmmmm. Is the question what THEY think they need most, or what I think they need most?

From my perspective, what these men need is vision, hope and purpose. They need to believe that their lives have meaning. That they are destined for more than the highway, the gang – the hood – or the county jail. They need education and real-world skills. They need a place in this new, flattened world where they can matter- where they can feel valued. They need love.

How can I help them get those things? I'm not really sure. I know I can't change anyone but me. Two years ago, I stopped creating advertising for watches, cars, energy companies and video games – and joined a joint venture with a stated mission to "help kids connect to their greatness."

We took an active role in community affairs, helping foundations and non-profits craft early reading and nutrition programs for low-income families. Working with the nation's foremost health experts, we developed wellness models for parents, students, teachers and coaches. In addition, we crafted and delivered relationship building processes for teachers that foster high-performing and self-managing classrooms. Early pilot programs in Albuquerque, New Mexico and Bridgeport, Ct. (the two worst school districts in the nation) are underway with trainings, leadership seminars, live student presentations, school assemblies and internet based learning modules.

Thanks to the Wizard Academy, our messaging was designed to speak to the heart of the dog, in the language of the dog. We also conduct "surprise 'Broca" tests on all presentations, trainings and materials on a regular basis.

Will these efforts at early intervention help these 4 young men? I don't know. Perhaps when they are new parents - they'll want more for their children. Perhaps they will see success stories in their neighborhoods and crave a slice for themselves. Perhaps our messaging will get past Broca and touch them in a way that propels action and change. All we can do is keep walking the walk- and reaching out with a clear message: there is hope, you are valuable and you can accomplish amazing things if you are willing to change your view.

What do these 4 have that I don't? Not much. That's not an arrogant statement. I don't think I'm any "better," just that I've been there, done that, and don't miss a thing. I was an outcast. I now spend lot's of time around today's "outcasts." I simply can't romanticize the outcast lifestyle because there's too much destruction in the ripples.

By outcasts, I'm not talking about blue collar folks who drink bud, go bowling and head down to the café for a chicken fried steak on a Friday night. I'm not talking about eclectic artist types who smoke cigarettes and lament the state of thee world over a $5 latte at Starbucks.

I'm talking about real outcasts: the urban poor, gang members, and street people suffering from drug abuse, disease, alcoholism, violence, hatred, crime destruction and death. Today's outcasts are not loveable Damon Runyan characters like Apple Annie and Dave the Deuce. They are violent, uneducated and dangerous - like the 4 in the booth just 3 yards away.

Claudia reaches my table again. I decide to inquire about the kitchen scene.

"I'm sorry for asking, but you seem upset. Is everything ok?"

She was frozen in time for a moment. Her eyes checked mine, searching for my intention - looking for my heart. Just as I was about to let her off the hook with a quip and light humor, she literally sat down opposite me in the booth and broke loose.

"My idiotic boyfriend (who I found out later is the father of 2 of her 3 children) is going back to jail for violation of his probation. He got caught for DWI - his third in two years - and has to do 180 days at county."

She welled up. She sobbed intermittently but she kept going.

"Without his pay, I can't make the bills. I'd be lucky to pull enough doubles just to make rent. But then there's food, utilities and clothes for the kids." She looked absolutely defeated.

I stayed still and leaned in to listen. Her sadness briefly turned to anger.

"What really pisses me off, is that the f***ing asshole will lose this job. We just started to save and got medical benefits. I'll have to go stay with my mother. And she's a freaking wacko. Smokes, drinks and lay's around all day. I'm a hell of a mom, huh?"

I tried to interrupt and offer an affirmation- but she stood up and kept talking.

"Shut up Claudia," she said to herself, "it's your fault for taking that asshole back anyway. Now, enough about my stupid problems, what can I get you to eat?"

To give her a chance to regroup, I asked what the chef's specials might be. She managed a light chuckle - and said- "hun, if I was you, I'd stick with eggs. He doesn't mess those up too bad."

"Three over easy, with whole wheat toast, no butter." I replied in camaraderie with her advice.

As she walked away, I thought about the wizard's question again. What does Claudia need most, and how can I help her get it?

Besides the obvious material needs - money, clothes for the kids and health care - the answer is the same as it was for the cholo's and the trucker. Claudia needs a vision for her life that extends beyond her current view. She's stuck in negative self-talk and self-defeating, self-destructive behaviors that severely limit her possibilities and only contract her world. She needs hope. She need help developing practical skills that will expand her life. Without this transformation, her three children leave the starting gate with a 82% chance to end up in poverty as well. Claudia's inability to see and act upon a better future will adversely impact generations.

I wish the sky would open and the voice of God would provide a better answer than the one I have now. Perhaps I'll pass a burning bush.

Working with young school kids, one thing became clear. You can actually love and inspire them to greatness once you prove you're authentic - and you'll won't leave them hanging. I pray the same goes for adults, but with a lifetime of baggage, it's a much tougher road to hoe.

We need to speak positively into Claudia's life. We need to love on the trucker and the cholo's. We have to be indefatigable in helping them see their best and highest outcomes and build bridges to connect them with those outcomes.

I left the café at 4. Half-dozen others had come in and out, but they were mostly variations on the trucker, Claudia and the cholo's. I witnessed an eclectic group of people all looking for love, hope, purpose and a sense of connection to something bigger than themselves. I pray I can help them find it.

126 Donna Snapp

Sent: Wednesday, January 18, 2006 9:29 AM
To: Corrine@WizardAcademy.com
Subject: Saturday Night in a Lakefront Bar & Club

The ceiling in the main room is painted black and large white feathers hang down every two feet. In the next room, holly and lights are glowing at the ceiling edge and the walls are painted in rainbow colored stripes. As a conservative Christian woman, a homebody, this is an unusual venue for me. Behind me is the stage and dance floor and to my right the long bar runs the length of the room. Melissa, my son's date, is across from me, giving her the best view of the stage and my son, Tim, sits between us with the best view of the stage since this is their first time here.

Tables are filling up quickly all around us; the show is starting soon. I feel safe here. The men in the club either have dates or will not be interested in me. I will not encourage any female interest, so I can sit here, drink, people watch and enjoy the show. I watch nearly nude male dancers on the large screen TV mounted on the rainbow wall. Colored lights are flashing on the stage curtains and dance floor and music is playing but no one is dancing yet. My nephew joins us, squeezing another chair in between his cousin and me.

The announcer welcomes us to the first anniversary show and Daphne and Chi Chi come running onto the stage. Their black costumes are similar, sort of Broadway/ Biker, sexy and slinky. Daphne is 6' 6" and dramatic in black mini shorts and high heeled boots. Chi Chi is shorter and wears an even smaller black bottom with fishnet stockings with patent leather tops mid thigh that show off her curvy legs. All male accoutrements are skillfully tucked away. Their song and dance is over in just a few minutes.

"I didn't even have time to tip them," I told my nephew. But he told me they weren't expecting tips for that number and they would be on again. He would know; he and Chi Chi are life partners and good friends with Daphne and her S.O.

Star is up next, a large black woman I've never seen before. Her hair and make up are impeccable but her dress isn't as flashy as some. But her voice is beautiful and her stage presence grand so I lined up with others at the side of the stage and tipped her a dollar and enjoyed her performance very much.

Next is a club favorite, Nicolette, a large bosomy blonde, who comes out from the curtains in a full-length pink robe. She goes right into her song and, in a few minutes, the robe comes off revealing a low cut top, wide belt and shiny shorts and stockings costume. During her number, many of the audience line up here and there around the stage, holding bills out, including me. By the end of her number, Nicolette has bills in her cleavage, bills in her belt and in both hands. By the time she goes up the steps, some bills have fallen to the ground and the audience yells out.

Nicolette, sweaty and tired from her number, says, "I'm a 300 pound drag queen in a tight costume. I can't be picking up bills from the floor."

A woman in the audience runs across the dance floor to the stage. To reach the dollars she goes down on her hands and knees and between Nicolette's legs. Nicolette lowers herself onto the woman's back and the audience roars. The woman scrambles out backward.

"My knees gave out. An old college football injury," Nicolette shrugs, by way of explanation, not apology. Then, money in hand, head held high, she proudly struts off the stage.

I know Nicolette some and have seen her more outlandish. Often she uses her great size and huge bazoomers as part of her act. Tonight she is more demure. Could it be that new rock twinkling on the third finger of her left hand and Tony sitting proudly at a front row table? Nicolette once told me the last time she had seen her dad he had kicked her out of his house, yelling, "You're no son of mine!" I'm glad if she's found happiness.

Next we have Liza in a red jacket over black shorts, stockings and boots. The jacket has only one button so we can see her bra, covered with multi-colored bells. As she sings and dances, she shimmies to make the bells ring. I have a tip for her too.

Cher comes out in a trademark outlandish robe that is discarded to show an amazing costume for her number. Then we have a male singer in a leather jacket and jeans with a thin moustache and thin jaw line beard that look penciled in. He will come back on later to sing and play Sonny with Cher. Nicolette, Star, Chi Chi and Daphne all have more songs and dances for us and I am continually going up to the stage with my dollars.

After the show the audience finally takes advantage of the music and the dance floor. The performers come out and mingle with the crowd. I am known as Aunt Donna to several of them.

Looking around at the crowd, I can't tell who is male and who is female but it doesn't really matter. And what do they need? The same things as anyone else: love, acceptance, recognition, respect. I think many of them could use the knowledge of the unconditional love of God. Unfortunately, many have turned away from God because some Christians in our society have scorned gay people, pronouncing their sins as "more" sinful than any sins these Christians have. And in their hurt, many gays have believed this and denied themselves belief in and acceptance from their Creator. But I think they need Him as much as anyone else. I have to tell them of His love for them.

Jay White

127

Sent: Monday, January 09, 2006 10:04 AM
To: Corrine@WizardAcademy.com
Subject: Merry Christmas, sir. Smoking or non?

Okay, I have a story somewhat like you're looking for, but with a few small discrepancies. First of all, this happened about 10 years ago, not in the last 24 hours. And it was midday, not in the wee hours of the morn. But it wasn't just any day--it was Christmas day.

I had driven the 5 hour and 40 minute trip from my shoebox apartment in Grand Rapids, MI to my folk's house in Abingdon, IL. for the annual family Christmas. Always a fun time with the Whites...lots of presents, lots of hugs, lots of scalloped corn. But this year would be different.

Mom's sick.

Not just sniffles sick, but put-me-in-the-hospital sick. And that's exactly what we did on Christmas eve.

See, my mom is a workhorse. But during the holidays, she turns into a virtual team of workhorses. Everything has to be just so...the meal, the house, the tree, the decorations. If it wasn't, well, it just wouldn't be Christmas, now would it?

So when Mom went down, for all intensive purposes, so did Christmas. And she would be the first to tell you.

Anyway, it's Christmas morning at the White house and things are not as they usually would be. Normally, there's a breakfast casserole in the oven, mounds of paper in the corner, assorted fathers trying to insert batteries into assorted electronics, etc. But today, it's sadly quiet. No casserole. No paper. No batteries.

Fortunately, we had been able to foresee Mom's inevitable hospital stay and had had a mild Christmas celebration 2 days before. So with all my jing-jing-jingling finished, I decided to head back to Grand Rapids.

After a brief, yet guilt-ridden visit with Mom at the hospital ("It's all my fault...I ruined Christmas for everybody.") I set out for Michigan via I-88 West. If you've never driven through Northern Illinois in late December, consider yourself heavily blessed. Long, flat, gray, and lonesome. Enough to put you into a coma.

As I approached noon, my stomach started telling me I had better tend to it, so I pulled off at a no-name truckstop, the only thing open on Christmas day. I expected an empty room save for the hardcore trucker with his cigarettes and coffee, but I was surprised.

Taking a booth, I surveyed the room. Several families having their Christmas dinner (pot roast platter, $3.99), the occasional loner, face filled with holiday sadness, and of course, the ever-present truckers. My waitress was considerate, but noncommittal. Something told me she worked virtually every Christmas, since staying at home was probably too painful.

And it hit me--there's a whole different world out there of which I am not familiar with. One that doesn't know the precious feeling that comes with a close family gathering or a house filled with love and holiday cheer. As I watched these people come and go, I thought back on Christmas' past. Warm, toasty living rooms. The smell of yams cooking. Comparing presents with cousins. Eating on TV trays in the living room, the game-of-the-day blaring. Post-gluttony naps on the floor.

And I thanked God for every minute of it.

I ate my platter, tipped my waitress generously and left in a hurry. Somehow, that long lonely road didn't seem so desolate anymore.

I think of that dinner every Christmas day, and how that same scenario is happening in scores of little truck stops all over the country. Then I say a prayer of thanks for the Lord's blessings on my life.

Note to Roy--I now live in Marshfield, MO, just outside of Springfield in Woody Justice territory. In fact, when it came time to buy our rings, we went to Woody first. Because there were 2 things I learned very quickly about Springfield when I got into town--Brad Pitt grew up there and Woody Justice wanted to be my jeweler.

From one radio writer to another, nice work. ;)

Kim Dunn

Sent: Wednesday, January 18, 2006 9:39 AM
To: Corrine@WizardAcademy.com
Subject: Diner Challenge

Irving Big Stop
Highway 102
Enfield, Nova Scotia, about 30 miles (and thirty years) away from Halifax.

It's 2:13 a.m. and I arrive at the truck after playing blues piano with my hobby band in a local pub. Outside metro Halifax, Nova Scotia is a very rural place, and it's "ruralness" starts almost at the city limit.

I'm a creative director/writer in my own small firm (I worked for the big multi-nationals and large Canadian agencies and happily walked away from them). I don't like rural. I'm not a big fan of country music – especially the so-called "new" country which is really just bad pop music with a twang. I have always been drawn to cities and I've lived in London, Toronto and Montreal before moving back to the province of my birth (Nova Scotians are notorious for "coming home").

Canada has two national pastimes: hockey and politics. As you're probably aware, Canada is in the middle of a federal election, so most of the coffee talk alternated between how great/lousy/over-rated/over-hyped/underappreciated Prime Minister Paul Martin, would-be P.M. Steven Harper, perennial 3rd-placer Jack Layton, and young hockey phenom Sydney Crosby are.

You may also be aware that the current party in power has been linked to a sponsorship scandal. Millions and millions of dollars were paid to Quebec-based advertising agencies for work of dubious quality or relevance, or no work at all. As you can imagine, it is a key issue in the election.

I heard a lot of "Throw the bums out" countered by "What's the difference, they're all the same." There was some mention of the other issues, but what really struck me was that these were all esoteric to the diners. They may rail about them, but when it came down to choosing who they might vote for, the talk was all about how they and their families might be directly affected by their choice.

It's fine for us with cushy, well-paid jobs to contemplate the social and cultural ramifications of how the government procures its services or dispenses its largess. Most people are just trying to stay one step ahead of the incoming tide.

It dawned on me that too often, we in advertising forget who is actually watching/hearing/reading our advertising and buying our clients' products. Clients forget it, too. We spend far too much time and effort creating advertising that appeals to US. What an eye-opener. The folks out there don't care so much about how "deeply strategic and focused the current iteration of the revised brand stance which allows it to transcend advertising into the realm of, can we say it? – yes. Art."

Like their politics, they want to know what the product or service will do for them.

I also learned that there is no demographic or psychographic. There are only people. With real needs and desires and fears and aspirations. It reminded me to write to people, not at them.

Thank you for this challenge. I almost didn't do it – I thought, I came from there; I remember it But I didn't remember it.

Thanks, too, for the Monday Memo. It's good to see the pretension being taken out of this fun, fascinating business.

David Cahn

Sent: Wednesday, January 11, 2006 9:15 AM
To: Corrine@WizardAcademy.com
Subject: thoughts of 2:45 AM

nothing good happens between 1 and 4 am. drunks are drunker, the lonely are at their nadir, and homelessness becomes critical.

most business's are closed, no one wants the tired, the hungry and the hopeless. wait I'm wrong again.

this diner caters to this crowd- give me your hungry and huddled masses and I'll give you a garbage plate and a home for as long as you can drink coffee.

here everybody has a story that's been told too many times.

you don't dare look into peoples faces, cause if you see their eyes something reaches out and grabs you. not pity, not sorrow, but a sense of lunacy and independence and a certain fuck you to the rules of polite society. at 2:45 in the morning, a wildness comes out that can't be confined and controlled.

that's why they want us in bed by midnight.

it's a dangerous time-to late to be normal-to early to be sane.

130 Michael Urkoski

Sent: Monday, January 16, 2006 8:40 AM
To: Corrine@WizardAcademy.com
Subject: Outsiders

January 15th 2006
2am Sapp Bros. Cafe

As I arrived at the cafe and sat down, I instantly felt a bit out of place.

Not because I was in a strange place, but because I quickly realized, that in this world I was the outsider. I took a seat at a booth, that was located towards the center of the room, giving me the best vantage point for the entire place.

After listening for a while, I noticed that these people all had a light heartedness about them all. Yes, they complained about problems, this and that, but they continue to laugh, and enjoyed each others company. Something I think everyone can learn from them though, is that they may joke and complain about problems, but they seem to have the attitude that, that's just life, and you take it as it comes.

This experience was also a bit different for me because, I used to be these people. I used hang out in these groups. As I thought of one thing that these people need, I quickly realized that they all seem to feel stuck in where they are, with no hope for escape.

Some of them seem fine with that, others want to break through the ceiling. So If I could give them anything, it would be me as proof that you can break out, you just have to want to first.

Michael Lofranco

131

Sent: Tuesday, January 10, 2006 4:48 PM
To: corrine@wizardacademy.com
Subject: Night Crawlers

    I hate winter. It's highly un-Canadian to say so, but I do. Not the snow or the cold, but the darkness. That's what winters are mostly, long dark days, especially in Canada. It's always dark out. I mean lets face it. We wake up and it's dark. We work all day, in a dark office, with no windows, and when we're done at 5, it's already dark. Winter, no, it's not my favourite season. Can't be his either, that guy sitting over there by the window, sure it's dark, its' 4.35 am right now, and I'm sitting in one of Canada's largest coffee chains, a franchises, Tim Horton's coffee shop, pretending to have a coffee, getting out of the cold, running from the darkness. I am pretending that I'm thinking, scribbling notes on a pad. Did you know that Tim Horton was one of the greatest defensemen in the old National Hockey League? Played for the Maple Leafs in 67 when they won their last Stanley Cup, played for Buffalo too in the seventies. He probably loved winter. Now his name is more famous, after over 30 years since he died in a car crash, because it is plastered all over Canada in blazing red letters on these money making coffee shops. He is more famous for coffee then for what he did in hockey. Now that is one of lives stranger realities. I wonder if he even drank coffee? Wish I had their advertising account, or part of it, hell wish I had the money to buy one of these franchises. Maybe I should get out of the advertising business. I guess I'll have to think about that, perhaps in my troubled mind I should just settle for hot coffee, a donut and a place to think for now. Why am I here? Oh yeah. I'm trying to get out of my element so I can get down on my belly and crawl under the fence.

    As I sit hear, thinking, and looking around the room, I noticed that there are only four people in here right now. How do you make money on four people? That guy sitting over there in the corner, by the window, he looks like a maintenance man of some sort, wearing a bright orange vest and yellow coveralls. His hands are dirty, and they are strong looking hands too. Probably has a handshake like a steel vise. He ordered a coffee and a chocolate glazed donut. And as he sits there, staring out over the parking lot I can see he is tired. Lost in thought. I wonder what he is thinking about? Is he done for the night or is he going back out there working on some sewer or electrical problem? I wonder if he is the type of guy who loves the night. Chooses the night shift over days. It certainly is quieter then the day. Maybe he doesn't have a choice. Maybe he hates the dark, or maybe he loves the quiet, one thing for sure he has both tonight. I wonder if he's happy. Can't tell. I'm not as good as I use to be at reading people that way.

From here, you can see the street lights glow a yellow colour and on the rest of the block there are only a few lights on, out of hundreds of homes and apartments. I wonder if this guy in the safety vest is responsible for keeping the lights burning when the rest of us are home and asleep in our beds. What would happen if all of a sudden we had a massive explosion and all the lights went out. Would he move? Right now, as he sits sipping on Tim's finest brew he's probably thinking, just a few more hours to go until his shift ends barring an explosion or something else catastrophic. Simplicity, I wish my life were that simple. Leave my work and no explosions I go home. Seems my shifts never end. I got to learn to take life easier, get a job with an orange vest and yellow coveralls.

The other two bodies in here are both younger men. They look quite awake. Not a place you'd normally see two guys that age, especially at this time of night, or is it morning. I'm guessing they are university students, maybe early 20's; it's not that far from the U of T's north campus. Are they coming or are they going somewhere? Interesting question. As much as I'd like to listen in to their conversation, I can't. It's just too weird. So I'll watch them for a while and see if I can guess what they are saying or where they might be going. One guy is drinking one of those specialty coffee's, looks like a latte of some sort with lots of whipped cream, the other is definitely drinking an espresso. Both are high-test caffeine shots, so I am guessing that they are going somewhere. Between the two of them they probably spent $5 dollars. Good margin, but nobody gets rich on three people drinking a couple of coffees and a donut. Maybe a franchise isn't that interesting after all. Oh I forgot to count my $4 dollars. A jackpot!

I don't want to give you the wrong impression. I am no longer an early riser, not like I use to be in my younger days. When I worked for my family in construction we were always up early, every day. Six days a week. We use to laugh at those who slept in, use to say they are missing the day. Even in the dark. But tonight I couldn't sleep, had this nagging feeling, like I had to do something and I finally decided to challenge myself. So I got up, got dressed, got into my car and stopped at the first 24-hour shop I spotted. I want to take a look at the underbelly, just like Roy said in his mmemo. And I want to observe from a distance things outside my comfort zone and write it down. But apparently the underbelly forgot to come out to this spot. Wait let me think a bit. The idea is for me to see things I haven't seen for a long time, and write about it. Go out and see the night crawlers. That is what I've always called those people who are out there in the dark being a community, being the other strange reality. You know what I mean, we all have seen them at some point, some of us have actually lived it, others have seen it from a distance but they are in every city. Truth be known some are scary monsters, and some are like that guy in the orange vest, working stiffs stuck in the dark. Me, I'm looking for the people we don't want to look at, I want to see what 10 years of hard Canadian weather on the streets does to a man, but tonight they forgot to show up. Maybe I should wait and see what happens. Night crawlers don't keep a schedule.

Almost 5 am, not much has changed. The guy in the orange vest left about 5 minutes ago, the two college guys are about to leave. I figured it out. They are definitely on their way to work. As I looked closer both are clean-shaven and ready for a day. The only question is, what do they do when they're not in a coffee shop at 5 am? I'm going to say, they are about to travel to another city for a meeting or sales call. Good for them, early bird catches the worm. Drive safe boys. Good selling. I use to love to get up early. I love selling, doesn't matter what time it is either.

Ok, you know how they say it's darkest before the dawn? Well, it's darker now then when I got here. The sky looks black, certainly no stars tonight. Must be full cloud cover. I heard earlier that we might get some morning snow flurries. That should be fun for rush hour. Oh wait. Here comes the first new customer. Is this someone interesting? This guy is on a mission, one medium to go, and out the door. Pretty good service from the gal who has had virtually nothing to do except wipe the counter and count the donuts.

Maybe if I sat here all day, and all night I'd finally find something interesting to write about. Or if I get lucky that girl behind the counter would come over to me and start up some kind of conversation. She could tell me that she only works nights cause it's the best she could do for now, and she has been waiting for something better to come around. Maybe we could go back to her place for a coffee .We could make small talk for a while, but I am not very good at that these days. I had better stop now; this isn't supposed to be a fantasy. Makes the time go faster though, reminds me of how I got through college.

Just as I thought this was going to be a total bust, about three cars all pulled into the parking lot. Business is picking up. Suddenly the guy who has been in the back all this time baking donuts and muffins comes out with this giant tray of freshly baked sugar products. I can feel my veins pulsing with anticipation. Got to show some restraint. Our counter lady finds some energy to muster a smile and quickly gets busy. First guy orders, two double double and a couple of twisters and a bagel toasted with butter, to go. The next guy orders a breakfast special, looks like he's going to read the paper and stay awhile. Next guy is a large coffee and a strawberry muffin. Mmm smells pretty good. Wonders what their day holds for them? Everyone looks like they are ready to go. Anybody out there need a good writer?

It's just about 5:45 am and well now I am getting discouraged. I might actually have to do this again so I can see the other side in a different light. Starting to feel tired. My eyes are heavy but the brain is going 100 miles an hour. Everywhere I look I can see the world starting to wake up. There are dozens more lights on all around the block. People already starting their day. It's not that much lighter now then it was 20 minutes ago, but the sun will come up, the day will begin. Yeah I think I'll do this again. Maybe tomorrow. I want to write. I want to learn how to be better at everything I do. I want to do more things that are creative, and I'm tired of feeling like I'm wining when in fact I'm losing. Damn I love and hate the business I am in, is it possible for people to love and hate something? Oh sure I want to do all the right things. I want to do something good for me, for my family and friends, even total strangers. But for now I want to do what it takes to make a living. Then I can do something good for others. I don't know, it's so confusing when you're tired. And as I look out at the darkness, I can see some snow flurries starting to fall. Should be a crazy rush hour. The snow is falling faster. Damn I hate winter, especially the darkness.

Kay Larrick

Sent: Monday, January 09, 2006 7:26 AM
To: Corrine@WizardAcademy.com
Subject: Responding to the challenge

The challenge Roy H. Williams presented to readers to go outside their comfort zone and have an early morning breakfast among strangers on the wrong side of town caught my attention.

About two years ago, I decided to move my career to an area outside my comfort zone. I ended a 12-year position as executive director of a crisis help line where I was safe behind the walls of a secure office and connected to strangers only via telephone to take a position with a daytime shelter for the homeless. I wanted to see Christ in the eyes of the poor and indeed I have.

Previously, I would divert my glance to avoid eye contact with a homeless person on the streets. Today, I look at them directly and in their eyes see a lifetime of experiences I've never known. In conversation I also learn of our similarities. Sometimes, the only difference between us is a checkbook.

As I've built relationships with individuals who are homeless, they have become my friends. Recently, I laughed and thought to myself, "God certainly sends Guardian Angels in all types of disguises." That was after three experiences in one day.

1) One of the homeless men approached me in the office and said, "The rear tire on the passenger's side of your car looks low. You better have that looked at. It could cause a problem for you and we don't want anything to happen to you."

2) That same day, as I approached the staircase to leave the office, another gentleman called out to me, "Be careful on those steps, they're a little wet and slippery. Don't want you to get hurt."

3) And as I left the building carrying my purse, briefcase and a box, one woman held the door open and another said, "Be careful, it's a little icy."

And, the most humbling experience I've had, and it happens on a regular basis, is when one of these "Guardian Angels" says to me,

"Thanks for your smile." I have to believe that they appreciate that simple of act of a warm facial expression because it's a gift they receive less than most of us.

Perhaps a future challenge could be for readers to simply "smile at a stranger." And, the bonus would be if that unfamiliar person was someone from outside their comfort zone.

Please pass on to Roy my applause and appreciation for your creative thinking and inspired challenge!

Chris Hoffman

Sent: Monday, January 16, 2006 6:09 PM
To: Corrine@WizardAcademy.com
Subject: "Hi, Honey!"

    Smoke lingers in the air like a dirty sheer valance and the smell of burnt coffee makes me want to run and hide. But alas, I'm greeted with an enthusiast "Hi, Honey" from a skinny, older-than-she-looks, waitress with a heavy southern drawl. She's surprisingly cheerful for the late (or early) hour. It's not my first time in this Waffle House, but it is my first trip at 3am. I confess - I've been to other "greasy spoons" after a night on the town but not this one! I take a seat in a booth near a window and unfold the paper to the crossword puzzle. I'm guessing that if I bury my head in the paper everyone will leave me alone and I can soak in the atmosphere at my own leisure. I glance for a second at the food stained menu and wait for the skinny waitress identified by her tag as Susan to come over and ask, "What can I get for you, Honey?" (I've been in the south most of my life, but still haven't gotten used to all of the southern terms of endearment people still use. It always gives me a chuckle.) I decide on eggs over-easy, toast and hash browns - smothered and covered! I know I'm going to pay for it later today, but there's got to be some nutrients in there somewhere.

    It's a light crowd at this odd hour. In the booth next to me is a group of four men who are obviously trying to regain a sense of sobriety after one too many at the bar. They laugh loudly and use a lot of four-letter words that I don't know if I should repeat here. Their conversation is basically a recap of their Saturday night escapades. It doesn't take me long to figure out why they are four men at the Waffle House at 3am rather than being somewhere else!

    At the counter are 3 lone men. One is obviously a regular as he beckons to Susan regularly with a strange familiarity. The other two sit quietly drinking their coffee and reading various newspapers and fliers from the free racks outside. Far off in the corner is a couple that looks to be prolonging a date night on the town. The man is seated with his back against the wall and his feet up on the booth and she is leaned forward listening intently to a story I can't hear.

    Interestingly, the most colorful conversation (sans the four letter commentary from my neighbors) comes from the Huddle House staff. Susan, Donna and Steve are happy to air their opinions, grievances and personal trials.

From what I can gather, Susan is married to a fellow that works for the hospital cleaning staff. They work similar hours, but she wants him to change because the day shift gets more overtime. She looks to be about 35-40 years old and has a dog that keeps digging out of his kennel to harass the neighbor's cat.

Donna is probably in her mid fifties and looks and sounds like she's smoked way too many cigarettes. She's offering up advice to help Susan because her ex-husband seemed to never make enough money to suffice. He would never take any initiative according to Donna and always just "skated by". She's the least friendly of the wait-staff so I'm pleased to have Susan at my table.

Steve is the happy go lucky short order cook that likes to whistle while he works. He banters with the regular at the counter and responds cheerfully when the waitresses yell their orders to them. He's got a crooked smile but it doesn't stop him from smiling widely. He seems to be good on the griddle as he performs his egg flips. There's pep in his step that shows he at least takes pride in his work for the moment. He doesn't offer a lot about himself in the conversation preferring instead to chime in with a funny line or anecdote to for the girls. He seems to get a kick out of making people laugh.

As I ask myself, "What do these people need and how can I help them get it?" I keep coming back to questions I have for myself. What made me do this exercise? What is it that I need and why am I at The Huddle House at 3am trying to find it? The last question is the one that I felt I needed to focus on. What do they have that I don't?

The gentlemen seated next to me – camaraderie. For the moment I am seated alone while they put the final touches on a night of indulgence with friends. They seem to be enjoying themselves. Tomorrow may be a different story.

The young couple in the corner is playing the game of courtship. I can't tell if they're on a date or if they're married, but it seems they find comfort in knowing someone is interested in them. There's a flirtatious nature to her movements in particular. The girl is obviously entranced with this man. He may be playing it cool. But how cool should you play it when The Waffle House is the nightcap?

Susan my waitress seems to have the burden of a marriage that hasn't lived up to her expectations. I don't have nor do I want that. She seems to be searching for advice from the wrong person. While she puts on a cheerful face, I seem to detect a bit of despair in her eyes.

Donna appears to have a chip on her shoulder. She seems to feel that life owes her something. I wonder what she's done to feel so overlooked and bitter. I wonder if she's ever made an effort to change where she's going or if she is like so many others that feel something is going to come to her.

Steve our cook this evening is the most puzzling. He's happy. For this short snapshot of time he seems to be content and proud. I hope that he's like this all of the time. I have to struggle not to judge and wonder how anyone could be happy and content as a cook at this place and then something hits me.

Maybe the Steve I'm seeing this early morning represents some of what I want to be. I want to be content and outwardly happy with my life. I want to be proud of the things I do from day to day. I think I am almost there. Most people who know me would say that I have a positive energy and a zest for life. But I know there is more I could do to make certain that I am like that every day. I just wonder how many more 3 a.m. smoke laden Waffle House experiences it's going to take to get me all the way there. The "Hi Honey"'s may grow old quickly!

134 Erin O'Hare

Sent: Tuesday, January 10, 2006 1:39 PM
To: Corrine@WizardAcademy.com
Subject: Belly Crawl

I will start by telling you how very much I savor reading your Monday Morning Wizard of Ads, they always 'touch' me. I have never fancied myself a writer, but have always devoured a myriad of reading material.

I would take your challenge of eating with strangers in the wee hours of the night in a heartbeat, but I don't believe it would be the accurate insight of someone who's venturing out of their normal 'realm's that you are looking for. Not that I don't think I would have anything to learn, I try to learn everything I can from every walk of life I can expose my being to everyday.

I'll try to get to the point. I have been happy as a little child with nothing that the masses of society feel compelled to collect in their big baskets of must have's. I have been happy as an adult with nothing that society tells me I must have to make my existence complete in this society of overwhelming wants. I could easily sit down in a cafe and be accepted into the conversations of downtrodden people, simply because I have been one. I have been a child growing up with the embarrassment and shame of being dirt floor poor. I have been a single mom struggling to feed my kids while working two jobs and dealing with the unbelievable stresses of that position. And ALL the while, throughout circumstances that would drive some people to become drug-addicted night walkers, I have remained happy and upbeat and ever-so grateful of the beautiful life I have and the opportunities I have been presented with. Although I always felt like I couldn't 'catch at break' , I always knew it could be much, much worse.

I am thrilled to tell you that while I haven't walked the yellow brick road, I have been in the right place at the right time. I am now employed by a wonderful company that compensates me very well for my efforts at work. I am no longer paying my bills late and trying to figure out how on earth I'll get by on $5.00 until payday. I am no longer telling my children 'no' every time they ask me for something (nor am I making the mistake of always telling them 'yes'!) I can buy them school clothes and books and take them out to eat. Life is grand.

I think the biggest lesson that I take away from all I've been through so far is that you truly cannot ever judge a book by it's cover. A lesson we all should remember every single day. I am an attractive thirty six year old woman, pretty enough to have done a modeling stint for a couple of years, smart enough to read the classics and always excel at work. No one I work with today would ever guess the horrors I have seen. I am so thrilled to not have to 'rob' change from the bottom of every crevice in my home to put fuel in my vehicle and am also so thrilled that I have no desire to have the latest and greatest, to live simply and treasure every sunset and every note of music. So, I probably will go eat with the downtrodden and then I'll go dine with the pampered!

I am really looking forward to hearing how many people are willing to take that belly crawl under the fence, for some that could be the furthest out of their comfort zone they'll ever go. If they go, they will be different people for the experience, of that I'm sure. Thank you for all of your words of wisdom.

135   Zeke Cox

Sent: Wednesday, January 18, 2006 11:55 AM
To: Corrine@WizardAcademy.com
Subject: MMMemo challenge

    This morning (Wednesday, January 18, 2006) I took Roy up on his challenge (I am glad he included this in this weeks MMMemo, because I somehow missed last week's and didn't read about it until this Monday). I arrived at a Waffle House on the other side of town at 4:55 a.m. I go to bed late (between 2 and 3 a.m. but had decided to wait to go close to 5 a.m. in hopes that there would be more people there). It turns out that there were only two single customers there when I arrived (no one eating with someone else). Music was playing relatively loudly so there was not a lot of conversation between employees (that I could hear). So I decided to take in what I could, by way of paying attention to my waitress (an obviously less than wealthy woman, as were the other employees). When she came to my table she was very kind. She offered free refills on chocolate milk (which I don't think they normally do). As I ordered a waffle and texas toast, she again offered that she would not charge me for the toast. It was an interesting feeling having a woman who is working nights at a waffle house offering me free things almost as if this is how she would like to be treated, when I would gladly have paid the $1.65 for the texas toast. Even though she appeared to have little money, she was a very happy woman and really treated me as well or better than I have been treated at $75 a plate dinners. It brought on the thought that kindness can bring a smile from anyone in any walk of life. If you treat others like you would like to be treated, it is easy to get along no matter what race or economic status. It also makes you respond in kind, when you receive great treatment. In respect to my thoughts of what I could do for her, I felt I could offer a smile and I knew that when I left, I would leave this woman larger tip for her service and in hopes that it would in turn raise her spirits (and I did, $10 on a $4.50 breakfast). It was worth the time to stop and think about what people go through every day just to make ends meet (or at least try to make ends meet). Here I was, by choice, showing up at a Waffle House, as she works probably 8 hour night shifts and who knows how many other jobs to make ends meet. I left around 5:30 and went to the Waffle House on my side of town, to see if there would be more conversation there (it was a raining nasty morning here), but not a lot there, so I had a little more breakfast and observed mostly disgruntled employees there. I hope that a big tip, a smile and a little conversation raised their spirits. Thanks for the idea Roy, and I plan on paying more attention everywhere I go to the little things in life. A lot can be learned.

136 Gair Maxwell

Sent: Wednesday, January 18, 2006 4:43 AM
To: Corrine@WizardAcademy.com
Subject: Ordinary Canadians

It's ten below at 5:15 a.m. at the 24 hour Tim Hortons on Mountain Road in Moncton. An ordinary day in every way except one. Instead of rushing through the drive-thru, I have actually stopped to take time to listen to people who wouldn't ordinarily attract my interest or attention.

I wind up sitting next to a couple of veteran gentlemen. Late fifties, early sixties. No spring chickens but you can't call them elderly either. Two ordinary guys sharing a coffee and ruminating about ordinary things.

"My son has a new 55 inch flat screen"

"Really enjoyed watching the westerns"

"Wife is still home in bed, doesn't like it that I come here at 4:30 in the morning but hey I'm not hurtin' anyone"

"Started comin' here about 9 years ago after I had heart trouble" Been comin' in every day since"

One of their coffee buddies walks in. An experienced woman named Terri who starts jabbing at Willie's chest and asking "Do you know what I am? ...A dope pusher!"

Laughs all around. Two e-mail jokes are produced and more laughter.

More ordinary talk.

Wipers that don't work. Washing machines that don't drain properly.

"Did you try Liquid Plumber?" Cracked chimneys that need replacing .

"Thank goodness it's covered."

"The guy who built that house should be shot"

As I reflect on my experience on the other side of the socio-economic spectrum, I can't help but think these folks are just looking for a few laughs and fewer headaches. And the comfort of friends at 5 a.m. at the neighborhood Tim Hortons.

Lynn Burkholder

Sent: Wednesday, January 18, 2006 9:26 AM
To: Corrine@WizardAcademy.com
Subject: Inside the Outside challenge/ Early Morning Diner

I did it!

I am getting tired of my typical response to a challenge like this. Many times I would read it, think it's a great idea, but never follow through. This time I did. Thanks for the nudge.

The bacon looks like strips of charred leather. Clearly it had been fried many hours ago.

This morning I chose a booth next to the corner with the early crowd and ordered breakfast. What the waitress brought was not what I had ordered. She said the third shift cook wasn't too bright and I said it was ok. The coffee was average or below.

I am getting a few curious glances. It seems that everyone here is on a first name basis and has been for a long time and I'm clearly the outsider. After a while Tony shuffles in and makes his way to a stool. He is old and stooped and his hands are shaking. It takes him some time to get situated.

"How's your wife?" a regular from the other end of the counter asks loudly. Tony doesn't hear him the first time so he asks again. Then he turns and explains to a nearby couple that she has been sick for a few years.

There are multiple streams of conversation going on, but not about much of any consequence, from my perspective. It's just the filling of space with words. They cover the weather and where the drivers among them are going today. There are good natured insults and more talk about the weather.

As I continue to sit and listen, the early corner crowd is long gone, along with several shifts of counter customers. The fading overnight waitresses went home, replaced by chatty morning types, full of clichés.

More customers come and go. Coffee cups are filled, and filled again. More comments about the wind and the rain. More coffee and cigarette smoke and talk about what somebody paid for something or where Joe was this morning or whatever. Somebody sat down beside Tony and he is talking loudly.

There is no talk about computers or email or the internet. No talk of news or current events. No talk of terrorism, the war, oil prices or politics. No retirement plans are discussed or IPO plans or IT issues. The stock market isn't on the radar here either.

For this crowd, there is comfort in familiarity and camaraderie. And all they talked about doesn't really matter, or does it?

Steve Wunderink

138

Sent: Wednesday, January 18, 2006 2:30 PM
To: Corrine@WizardAcademy.com
Subject: Excursion outside comfort zone

The Alien

It was about 2:30 am and I was tired and hungry. I had just last week read the Wizard's commission to seek out an exotic place on the other end of what I am used to so it seemed appropriate to stop now and not wait until I got back to my upper-middle class house to eat.

The Denny's I stopped at was shorter than I am used to. The ceiling seemed to press down on me as I walked in like the drop ceiling had, well, dropped. Around the corners of the tiles I found cigarette stains seeming to get darker and browner as they got closer to the vent. It was like some upside-down drain.

No one helped me to my seat so I found a booth not too close but not too far from the few patrons at the place. I noticed the floor tiles had the same kind of scrunge around them like the mop only touched the surface and never made it to the grout. Or maybe there was no mop, just the bottoms of countless shoes shining the parts that stick up most. The menu was new but the waitress was not. She had a cigarette magically taped to the left side of her mouth that stayed in place when she asked, "What can I get for you, honey?"

"Honey." That was a word that always softened my heart even though my mom never called me that, nor does my wife. Honey, is just a nice, soft, word. I liked it and I liked her. I ordered a glass of water with lemon and some scrambled eggs with ham. She seemed happy and turned away. No caffeine for me even if Roy himself was here. While she was away I focused on my assignment. I had brought in my day-planner and opened it ostensibly doing some planning for tomorrow while I focused my ears on the conversation. I wrote down their names as I picked them up and found they were in an intense discussion.

"When did you get back, Rob?"

"Just a week ago, still haven't found a f...g job!"

"You at the mission?"

"Yea, but they let me stay for a month, so I only got a few weeks left."

"How was back there?" asked a third voice whose name was

Raelynn.

"It sucked man, that place is a dust bowl. Always following orders and never able to just sit and chill."

"That bad, huh? Anybody you know knocked off?"

"Yea, one guy, but we weren't too close…"

I still thought they were talking about jail, until Rob concluded with this: "F…g Iraq!"

Rob, Raelynn, Justine, and an unnamed girl went on talking about his last tour in Iraq. I guess my assumptions went up that upside-down drain pretty quickly. After Iraq the conversation went to where to find a job that was hiring without too detailed of a background check. Raelynn was a photographer for a lounge at a next door Vegas casino who got off work at 2:00 am. Justine was a topless dancer at the club less than a block away and was upset that her boyfriend pinched her breast hard enough to leave a mark, "How am I gonna work with that!" she exclaimed. The unnamed girl was "between jobs" right now and Rob was looking. They talked with ease between shared cigarettes and two breakfasts for the four of them. Their community was close and they talked about at least another seven people who they all knew going through a rough patch, just got a good job, took a Greyhound back to Phoenix, and broke a leg trying to cross Las Vegas Boulevard.

My eggs were gone and my time was starting to get uncomfortable. My waitress came back for a third time asking if I needed anything. She still had the cigarette stuck to her bottom lip and I think it was a different one this time. I left a $20 for a $7 tab and walked into the night. I noticed the waitress pocketed the $20 and pulled up a chair to be with her "family" when I left. The alien in their world was gone.

Steve Lindt

139

Sent: Tuesday, January 17, 2006 8:55 AM
To: Corrine@WizardAcademy.com
Subject: late night excursion

I'll make this quick, because, despite my best effort this morning, I was unable to find an all-night restaurant in which to challenge my comfortable assumptions. The city of Waterloo, where I live, has a population of 100,000 and no all-night restaurants. Right next door is the city of Kitchener, population 200,000, and it's there I went at 3:30 a.m. Like all cliches, there's a bit of truth to the cliche that Waterloo is white collar (two Universities and the home of the Blackberry) and Kitchener is blue collar (auto parts and many social services for the poor), so I assumed there would be all-nighters in Kitchener to appeal to shift workers. Wrong! I cruised all the likely areas and there was nothing open. I even cruised the 'tenderloin' area of the city where I thought there might be a cafe catering to sex trade workers.

This is where things went slightly off the rails. I was pulled over by the police who wanted to know what I was doing, driving slowly through a disreputable part of Kitchener. After checking my ID and running my plate, I explained to the pleasant young officer that I was looking for a restaurant. "Where do you eat?" I asked, and he said "I bring my lunch. There's nothing open (all night) except doughnut drive throughs."

I went home, disappointed, but wiser about the sleeping and dining habits of my neighbours and the vigilant eye of our police force.

140 Lori LaShawn Brown

Sent: Monday, January 30, 2006 5:23 PM
To: Corrine@WizardAcademy.com
Subject: January 28, 2006

First, let me begin by saying that I own a 1977 Seville for which it is seemingly impossible to find parts when she, named Hannah, breaks down. Obviously being without transportation and a lacking another willing participant, it was not feasible for me to find an all night restaurant to visit between the hours prescribed.

I did, however, find the idea intriguing enough to do what I was able to do which was to volunteer yesterday with the local Homeless Coalition, who sponsored a day that numerous non-profit agencies collaborated to offer services in a one-stop shop sort of situation.

When I first got there, I didn't know what to expect as I, and the young lady who picked me up, arrived at the Salvation Army to see a line of people extending out of the door and down the sidewalk.

Politely we asked to be excused to get in and find the place where we might be most helpful. To my surprise, before we got all the way in, I was caught by the shoulder by a lady that I did not recognize who asked me, "Hey, what's your name?"

"LaShawn Brown," I replied. "Aw!!! That's what I thought! This is my classmate, y'all!" she said with obvious excitement to the people in line with her.

I felt horrible because I didn't recognize her until she said, "It's me, Dorothy Collins!" Instantly remembering her name, I reached out with both arms and embraced her. Then she said, "Calvin is here, too. See? There he is," pointing to the front of the line.

When I saw him, he seemed to be embarrassed to be seen in this situation. Ignoring this, I reached out for him in the same fashion, hugged him tightly and told him that it was nice to see him again.

Once Bonnie and I were inside, she immediately began doing intake surveys for the incoming flux of people. Since I had not yet been briefed on what to do, one of my former Social Work Professors took me aside to review the protocol we were to follow when interviewing each person.

On this survey we were to identify ourselves as part of the Homeless Coalition and let them know that the purposes of the survey were: a) to find out which services are being used, b) identify which ones are still needed and c) to document an accurate count of the homeless population in order to request an adequate amount of funding to provide these services.

The first questions we asked, after we asked for their consent to do the survey, were for the last four digits of their social security number and their first and last initial. This was how each respondent would be tracked and not counted more than once.

We also asked questions like the last year of school completed, how many were in their family unit, if they were displaced by Hurricane Katrina and where they slept the night before.

The last question really got to me, especially because a cold front had just come in. Many said that they slept in a shelter, but some said under 'this' or 'that bridge' and one told me that he slept in someone's yard - but didn't really get much sleep.

There were all races, ages and ethnicities represented. There was a couple where the husband was African American and the wife was Anglo. I could really feel the love and camaraderie between all of the people and this was extremely evident with this one couple.

They had been homeless for about two weeks due to unemployment, he told me. He was so loving in his speech and demeanor towards his wife that it was in complete awe. He said of her, on more than one occasion, "What do you think, Honey?" to her and then he said to me, "She's the brains of the operation." (How cute is THAT?)

She gave me the most helpful feedback of the day when I asked them what services would be helpful. She said, "It would be nice if they would stop sending you to all of these agencies that don't really help you. They have you running in circles, not helping you and that is why people end up homeless." (Wow, I had to write that down verbatim and follow up with emails and phone calls to be sure that her words were taken to heart.)

After the intakes were pretty much caught up, there was a back up in the Giveaway Room, so I changed stations and went to help in there. That was the most gratifying experience ever to me.

I got to help people one on one, talk to them and help them as they were allowed to pick one of each item and put into their donated Target bags. I commented to another volunteer that it probably really felt good for them to have a brand new Target bag to carry because it gave them a sense of having been shopping.

Another thing that was awesome about the Giveaway Room was that most of the goods were new and not used. It went like this: I greeted the person with a smile and a heartfelt welcome. I then explained that they were able to get one of each item that we had to offer. They then gave me a preprinted checklist of what was in the room that I checked off as we moved through it together.

I asked, while the supply lasted, if they were interested in some new rubber boots. Many said yes and many declined or found out that we didn't have their size. I then asked if they wanted a new blanket and most were so grateful to get to choose the one that they wanted.

From there we went to the table that had hygiene packs of soap, toothbrush/toothpaste, razors etc. A lady sat at this table and handed out one gift card for McDonald's, Taco Bell, or Subway. Next to her was a table of toboggans, men's new t-shirts, underwear and ladies and men's socks. Toward the end of the day, I found myself suggesting that they take more than one pair of underwear or socks, as there was no threat of running out of them.

The next table held gloves, some miscellaneous clothing in a box, new women's underwear and a box of assorted children's clothing. The last item available was an array of winter coats and jackets.

Nothing in a long time had been so fulfilling to me as it was to help these folks find warm coats that fit and kept them warm. There was this one red women's coat that had a heavy lining and was also a rain slicker. All day long I had been pointing it out to women who came through, but no one wanted it.

At the end of the day, I realized why. God knew that there would be this one woman who barely made it in before the cut off time. I don't recall her name, but I definitely remember her spirit of gratefulness that I wouldn't turn her away. And never shall I forget the pure delight that sparkled from her eyes as she tried on and loved that red coat!

The last voice I heard from that day was her saying, "Oh thank you SO MUCH. Y'all have been so nice to us today. God Bless You."

I told her, "Oh, Sweetheart, you are so very welcome. And God Bless You, Too!"

SOME ADDITIONAL OBSERVATIONS

In addition to the surveys and giveaways other agencies were present to assist in meeting varied needs. They included Veteran's Services, a Teen Homeless and Runaway Shelter, health screenings by volunteer doctors and nurses, mental health services, free haircuts, and a hot lunch when they finished going to all of the stations.

I noticed that there definitely is a close-knit family type of love that exists between this population. I observed them 'lighting up' as they saw someone that they hadn't seen in a while.

I also couldn't help but notice how humble, grateful and polite most of them were when receiving what we had to offer. They were patient with us when things moved slowly. And they were patient with each other courteously allowing as much time as was needed for everyone else to be served. They were also obviously happy and moved to know that people cared enough to do these things for them.

I feel honored to have been a part of this experience. I believe everyone should do something like this at least once. Doing so would not only help us to really appreciate and not take for granted what we have, but it would also personalize the struggle of homelessness and hopefully move us to help 'the least of these' as Jesus commanded us.

The only regret that I have was that we ran out of blankets and I know that at least one man, who needed one, didn't get one. This will cause me to speak with my Pastor tomorrow about doing a church wide blanket and coat drive. I won't be satisfied until this is done.

This was my first time doing anything like this and while I may have been inclined to participate, I most likely wouldn't have written about it so soon afterward - which has greatly preserved the experience. For the suggestion to do so, I thank you.

I realize that this isn't exactly what The Wizard asked for and I didn't do it for a gift, however, the impact of the experience was far too wonderful not to share.

141

John Davis

Sent: Monday, January 30, 2006 6:52 AM
To: Corrine@WizardAcademy.com
Subject: Inside Out

    Escaping small town innocence is hopeless - even on a Friday night. Nothing nearby offered danger or discomfort, so I stopped for my experiment at a Waffle House located near one of Oklahoma's Indian nation casinos.

    Inside I found a sluggish staff of four. The manager cooked. A young waitress shared duties with mine who had seen at least fifty difficult years. Another young woman's broom battled the floor for possession of an empty sugar packet.

    The patrons consisted of six couples who all seemed to be in the thirty-forty something age group. They all wore the guise of red-neck cowpokes lacking wisdom to avoid Indian nation casinos. These couples were in transition from gambling in public to gambling in the privacy of a double bed. The odds were better in the casino. Being alone, perhaps I was jealous, but when one couple played "Your Cheatin Heart" on the jukebox, my opinion firmed.

    My mind returned to the experiment's focus: What did these people need and how could I give it to them? As I pondered, one of the couples stepped up to pay their bill. Mutual back rubs accompanied the look of love in their eyes. My thinking stopped when I saw her smile for him. His hair hung to the length of a hippie wan-a-be, his face was rough, and his outfit genuine. Before me was undeniable proof that love is as blind as a hibernating bat. Her smile was everything he needed tonight and maybe, just maybe for the rest of eternity. I could offer these people nothing.

    After collecting the cash, the young woman who was cleaning up went to the manager and gave a well rehearsed excuse to leave early. The manager consulted with my waitress about the status of responsibilities. My waitress said she was leaving early as well. The manager searched in my direction for sympathy. He was surrounded by employees who could begin the majority of their sentences with "Frankly Scarlet…". I offered the manager a shrug of helpless understanding and stood to pay.

    Hanging outside was a huge sign: "Now Hiring People Who Care!" My eggs had come with a side order of greasy understanding. People who care had already paid their due and were off to bed.

Michael K. Schmidt

Date: Fri, 30 Jan 2006 02:35:20
To: Corrine@WizardAcademy.com
Subject: my story

My desire to slink out of bed at six in the morning is rarely greater than negligible. By contrast, the desire to get up at 2am is virtually nonexistent. Early to bed, early to rise, makes for a work day of yawns and red eyes. My alarm went off at two in the morning and my usual wake up to classical music was replaced by late night programming of someone playing a saw with an electronic back beat. This sound, ostensibly passing as music prompted me to quickly rise from my bed.

Layer by layer I began to dress, preparing for the Manitoba winter air that I knew would encourage me to turn right back around before taking two steps outside. As my garage door slowly creaked up, the rush of cold air poured in, in an ever growing tide, until my cheeks and nose, the only exposed skin on my body, felt its nip and bite. I slipped into my car and sliding the key into the ignition turned gently. With a click and two turns the engine awoke with the same reluctance I had minutes earlier.

I had pre-selected my target; Papa George's Restaurant, located in a part of Winnipeg known as Osborne Village. Determinants for selection were as follows:

o   Open later than any other restaurant in the city, 4am.
o   Osborne Village is home to an eclectic, unique culture; the haven for squeegee kids, Mohawk hairdos and studded leather.
o   I live outside the city in suburban/rural settings; Osborne village is out of my comfort zone.
o   It was to Osborne Village that, ten years ago at the age of seventeen, my best friend ran away from home. She took up residence with a group of outcasts, squatting in rundown overcrowded apartments, doing whatever it took to get the money required for their next hit. It was here that I would visit her on occasion but a place I rarely came to since she left.

At quarter to three in the morning the streets are bare and had it been light I would have assumed the rapture had happened in a highly evangelized city and I had been left behind. Thirty minutes from my home my car passed over the frozen Assiniboine River and into Osborne Village. I parked my car on a snow covered side street, took a deep breath and opened the door. I stood quickly and walked briskly to get out of the cold.

Inside, the lights were dim and it was eerily quiet. After half a minute a set of western style swinging doors creaked open in the back and I was greeted with a warm but forced smile by a woman who appeared to have had a long night. The first section of the restaurant had no one in it and I asked to be shifted to the next room over. There sat six people whose voices shattered the silence present in the other rooms. As I sat down and looked over the menu I was able to make my first cursory observations of the group. They were young, all young and far too young to be out this late. There were two guys, one sporting a five inch Mohawk and both facing away from me. Seated on the other side were four girls, two brunettes and two pretending not to be brunettes.

Their voices carried clearly so that it took little effort to listen in to their conversation, even across the room. It is a well known fact that under mass inebriation one tends to lose control of the modulation of their voice. This was confirmed as the reason for the volume of conversation when one girl asked, "Where is Sarah?" The first reply, "She went to the bathroom a long time ago. She better not be passed out or puking." I was happy to see a few minutes later that Sarah had not passed out and was not praying to the ceramic god. She worked her way as delicately as she could muster between the rows of tables and seated herself next to her friends. As they prepared to place their orders I received the occasional stare, the type that contained the same innate curiosity that mine contained as well, "Who are you and what are you doing here at three in the morning?" Their orders were placed, as was mine and I leaned back in my stiff wooden chair ready to catch a glimpse into seven lives.

It's amazing the details that can be put together in a very short time even from conversations that seem to be superficial. I found myself wondering if this can be gained at any time of the day or just in the deep recess of the night. These were my two thoughts:

- "Man is least himself when he talks in his own person. Give him a mask, and he will tell you the truth." - Oscar Wilde (1854-1900) Night time and alcohol provide two of the greatest mask of all. Did that lead to the depth of information shared?
- Maybe I don't listen enough. Maybe this depth of information

into people's lives is readily available but so often overlooked. In University I often rode the transit bus. Almost every trip, I would climb aboard and place a small headphone into each of my ears. I missed out on hundreds of conversations over the years; glimpses into new worlds, new lives. We read books and get caught up in the lives of fictional characters. Why don't I pay any attention to the fascinating lives of real characters surrounding me at all times?

Their conversation darted back and forth with frequent use of language that could make a sailor blush with shame. Overall the conversation was cursory and stuck to the surface. There was talk of American Idol, Pakistani Idol, road rage, shopping, breast size (which finally encouraged the men to speak) and people they did not like. I have noticed a marked tendency for people to stay on the superficial in most interactions. Unfortunately this was apparent and true in my own life. It is a rare occasion that I ever go deep and it is only with a select few that I know I can trust.

I found myself wondering what these people did that allowed them to be out like this at night. Below is what was surmised by the information shared:

- o The guys were twenty years old and all of the girls were nineteen.
- o Two were enrolled in University but both rarely attended.
- o The other girls were all waitresses at several trendy restaurants and all worked the evening shifts and partied after that.
- o Most rarely crawled out of bed until 5:30 in the afternoon.
- o One girl did not like the size of her bottom.
- o Another complained that hers was going to get too big and then started eating her friends' fries.
- o They all suffered from road rage and believed that every other driver out there is terrible. (Far too few people actually take the time for introspection. Were they to do that, statistically speaking, they would have to look at their driving and conclude that not everyone else in the world is a terrible driver and perhaps, just perhaps there may be a problem with their own driving. It is similar to the girl I heard complain about not being able to find a husband. She tried traditional dating, online dating, speed dating, personal ads and her conclusion was that all guys in the world have something wrong with them because none of them want to be with her. It may be time for some introspection.)

After hearing all of these things there were three things that shocked me. The first was that the ketchup stain on the stucco wall beside me looked like a frowning face. The second was that this group of people eight years younger than me seemed so markedly different than me. The third was when I heard them start to talk about the neighborhoods that they lived in, all of which surrounded the high school that I had attended in suburbia. Had young people changed so much in the neighborhood where I grew up or was I virtually the same at that age? These are thoughts that I haven't yet figured out.

So what did I learn sitting across from seven young people?

o   If I listen and observe I can catch glimpses into lives unfolding. I can learn and grow from the lives and experiences of others.

o   We were all designed for relationship. It was part of our purpose from the time of creation. Seeded deep within all of us lies this desire. Did this group of people share much beyond the superficial? No, but they were together. They laughed, they talked, they shared an evening and all of the experiences that went along with it. Had they been seven people each seated alone my observations would have been strikingly different.

I didn't have any life changing interaction and I don't think my presence there will garner a second thought by anyone unless I was the first polite person my waitress had all day. What I did gain was this: I believe that God started writing an amazing story when the earth was created and it is a story that is yet to be finished. The beauty of life is that we get to write our own part in that story. Our character, who we are and what we become is built from every choice we make. The privilege of life is being able to watch and participate in the stories of other people. I made a choice last night to go to Papa George's and it opened my eyes. You never know how your choices and interactions will affect people and the world. I don't think the world will change because of my presence last night, but last night did change me and there will be more opportunities to come. After all this was my first time. Aroo!

Greg De Rue

Date: Wed, 18 Jan 2006 01:53:50 -0800 (PST)
To: Corrine@WizardAcademy.com
Subject: the challenge

Roy

This letter is concerning your late night challenge. I took up your challenge but have been on a trip in China. So now, on the plane, I can take out my outline and fill in the points. I don't know if it all qualifies as I couldn't write it down until later, however I am still turning it in since it is your doing.

At first after reading the initial challenge I discarded it like most will. I can't do that it... it is too late and anyways I have to be in China soon! After last minute packing two nights before the trip and knowing I needed to stock the house with groceries (yes I do the grocery shopping), I set out to a buy the items on the list a few special treats for my daughter and a gift I would hide for her and one for my wife to find sometime while I was gone.

I took the long way to the mega 24 hour grocery store not sure exactly why. Driving around I suddenly found myself on the road to St Joe Michigan why? Well there is that second home we are looking at I should see if it is still for sale and prepare an offer before I go. Ten minutes later, yes it still is for sale and it's a clear night the stars are spectacular gleaming in the sky and glistening and shimmering on Lake Michigan this is a great view I know we would enjoy it. Instead of heading home I drive around some more. Yes we looked at all of these other houses and that is the one we agreed on. I'll look over here just in case....oh. it is "the bridge". The bridge is the one over the harbor and the mouth of the St Joe river between the city of St Joe and Benton Harbor. "The Bridge" separates the city of prosperity with the one that is spiraling into deeper and deeper poverty.

Why am I at the bridge? You don't just go over it you have a reason. God turn around you have to get ready to go to China. My foot depresses the accelerator and the silver BMW 750iL illuminated to an iridescent glow by the starry night pushed OVER "the bridge'. Heart pounding in my ears nearly drowns out all the noise. Am I crazy this car screams hey mug this dude! I pull on a side street to turn around with the same feeling I used to get as a kid ringing doorbells and then running. There it is, the greasy spoon. The yellowish light pouring from the windows looked inviting enough. Damn that Williams messing with my brain

Well I am here I might as well park right up front and keep and eye on the car. I go in and feel like the scene in Animal House when the college boys go to the black bar.

There are 8 men there and all stopped in mid sentence, I heard the door close behind me and I am sure it locked too.

There is a booth by the front window that I can see my car so I squeeze in. The lady behind the counter doesn't even come around. From behind the counter she belts out "wha'ch you want?" "two eggs scrambled and hash browns well done." I replied. The men had all huddled and were trying to figure out what this white boy was doing here. I was reaching for the cell phone and punching in 911 so all I had to do was hit send.

The food seemed to take forever and I really was hungry now. A shot rings out and I freeze, oh that is my cell phone. Hello yes honey I am fine, I decided to take a drive before I have to go. Yes I am looking at that house I was thinking of putting an offer in on it tomorrow and decided to grab something to eat before I get the groceries. Yes I will pick that up too. I I I love you too" I shoot a look over to the committee still figuring me out as the last six words came out of my mouth.

One booming laugh echoes as I hang up the phone, "No matta how big a hot shot you is momma still runs the roost" I laugh too.

Finally I see counter lady and counter lady barked 'come get it I ain't walken' over to you."

I get up and pull the food across the counter, pick up utensils and a glass of water and squeeze back in the booth. I start eating; the eggs have too much cooking oil in them but the potatoes are good. .

The committee no longer thinks I am an alien so the hushed tones turn to normal, well for me abnormally loud, banter. The huddle melts into men in chairs and in booths. I hear about kids and grandkids playing ball. There was lots of laughing and spirited BS. Also, each was trying to outdo the other on their wife or girlfriend is getting on their nerves for this and that. There were the latest maladies of the body some more graphically than I really wanted to know when I am eating. The oldest guy's mom is real sick and they were glad she made it to 2006 and another whom had a hacking cough thinks he will be evicted soon.

After a while I slide out of the booth and take my plate to the counter, eggs barely touched. Wha'cha wont now?" Just to pay my bill. Why yous bring the plate up her? Well, I guess I thought I had to clear my table as well, being a smart ass than anything else. Why you not eat the eggs? Well they had too much oil for me.

(now speaking better) I know I put too much on purpose I am sorry, it's no charge.

I took a 10 and laid it on the counter;

"Really it is no charge I was mean to you."

"I liked the potatoes and I have been here over an hour I am sure that this is fair for taking a booth for that long."

The door swings open easily. I get a "Catch you later bossman" from the guy who laughed at my wife calling. I wave and say goodnight. I hear several chuckles as the door closes behind me.

I look up man I do love the stars on a clear night.

Greg

PS life is stranger than fiction, I may actually go back there again if we get that house

What is Wizard Academy?

Composed of a fascinating series of workshops led by some of the most accomplished instructors in America, Wizard Academy is a progressive new kind of business and communications school whose stated objective is to improve the creative thinking and communication skills of sales professionals, internet professionals, business owners, educators, ad writers, ministers, authors, inventors, journalists and CEOs.

Founded in 1999, the Academy has exploded into a worldwide phenomenon with an impressive fraternity of alumni who are rapidly forming an important worldwide network of business relationships.

"Alice in Wonderland on steroids! I wish Roy Williams had been my very first college professor. If he had been, everything I learned after that would have made a lot more sense and been a lot more useful... Astounding stuff."
— **Dr. Larry McCleary,**
Neurologist and Theoretical Physicist

"...Valuable, helpful, insightful, and thought provoking. We're recommending it to everyone we see."
— **Jan Nations and Sterling Tarrant**
senior managers, Focus on the Family

"*Be prepared to take a wild, three-ring-circus journey into the creative recesses of the brain...[that] will change your approach to managing and marketing your business forever. For anyone who must think critically or write creatively on the job, the Wizard Academy is a must.*"

—**Dr. Kevin Ryan**
Pres., The Executive Writer

"*Even with all I knew, I was not fully prepared for the experience I had at the Academy… Who else but a wizard can make sense of so many divergent ideas? I highly recommend it.*"

—**Mark Huffman,**
Advertising Production Manager, Procter & Gamble

"*A life-altering 72 hours.*"

—**Jim Rubart**

To learn more about Wizard Academy, visit www.WizardAcademy.com or call the academy at (800) 425-4769